THE OFFICE OF
SHADOW

ALSO BY MATTHEW STURGES

MIDWINTER

THE OFFICE OF
SHADOW

Matthew Sturges

an imprint of **Prometheus Books**
Amherst, NY

Published 2010 by Pyr®, an imprint of Prometheus Books

Inquiries should be addressed to
Pyr
59 John Glenn Drive
Amherst, New York 14228–2119
VOICE: 716–691–0133
FAX: 716–691–0137
WWW.PYRSF.COM

14 13 12 11 10   5 4 3 2 1

Library of Congress Cataloging-in-Publication Data

Sturges, Matthew.
    The office of shadow / by Matthew Sturges.
        p. cm.
    Sequel to: Midwinter, 2009.
    ISBN 978–1–61614–202–5 (pbk.)
    1. Prisoners—Fiction. 2. Traitors—Fiction. I. Title.

PS3569.T876O44 2010
813'.54—dc22

2010006202

Printed in the United States of America

This book is dedicated to
MY PARENTS

acknowledgments

reat thanks are due, as always, to the boys of Clockwork Storybook: Bill Willingham, Chris Roberson, Mark Finn, and Bill Williams, for providing encouragement and feedback during the writing of this book.

As with *Midwinter*, a special debt of gratitude is owed to Bill Willingham, who again graciously allowed me to borrow a couple of concepts that he included in his (as yet!) unfinished novel *Just Another Ranker*, back in the days when we all wrote stories set in the same worlds. If he ever asks for them back, I'll be in dire straits.

Thanks to Dave Justus, who worked tirelessly to comment upon and proof the original manuscript, and to my editor at Pyr, Lou Anders, who is basically awesome.

Thanks to Margaret and Kevin for watching the girls that time.

Thanks to Samantha, Amy, Jenn, Terrie, Lynn, Emma, Jacob, Abby, Patti, Nate, Jeremy, James, Alison, and Yvonne for keeping me fueled up throughout.

And especially, thanks to my wife, Stacy, and my daughters, Millie and Mercy, for allowing me to essentially abandon them for two months while I finished.

Pibil.

Part One

Uvenra slept among the ash at Belekh; the daughter of Uvenchaud was dead by the hand of Uvenchaud and slept among the ash. For a week and a day the king wept. Then Uvenchaud took his chariot and drove it to Prythme, where the gods dwelled. To confront the gods he went there. He shook his sword at the gate; he shook his shield at the gate. Uvenchaud struck the earth with his sword and the earth trembled. The gate opened. At Uvenchaud's threat did it move upon its mighty hinge.

Uvenchaud went into the courtyard at Prythme. In the courtyard Uvenchaud called out. "I am Uvenchaud, whose fist is iron, who united the wild Fae clans; the Fae clans have submitted to my will. As the ruler of them I demand parley."

Uvenchaud stood in the courtyard for a week and a day. For another week and for another day he stood and there was no answer. Uvenchaud struck the earth again with his sword and called out. One of the gods came. The bearded god Althoin, god of Wisdom, whose Gift is Insight, came to match his wits against Uvenchaud.

"Why do you come here?" said wise Althoin. "Why does Uvenchaud come here to disturb the thoughts of the gods?"

"Uvenra my daughter sleeps among the ash. She is

dead by my hand, for she betrayed me to my enemy Achera, the dragon who has slain many."

"You have come here to be judged by the gods."

"I do not come to be judged by the gods. I come to defy the judgment of the gods."

Althoin spoke. He said, "You cannot escape the judgment of the gods. We are seated above you to judge you and to command you."

"Who seated you there?"

"We seated ourselves."

"Then I will unseat you." Uvenchaud struck the earth with his sword, and the god laughed at the sword.

"You cannot kill a god," said Althoin.

Uvenchaud struck at Althoin for a week and a day. After a week and a day he stopped and Althoin was unharmed. "You cannot kill a god," said Althoin.

Ein, god of War, whose Gift is Leadership, came to match his strength against Uvenchaud. For a week and a day Uvenchaud struck Ein with his sword. For a week and a day they struggled, but Ein was not slain.

"You cannot kill a god," said Ein.

"What I cannot kill I can bind," said Uvenchaud. Uvenchaud had a rope, made of fibers from the tuluk plant. The rope was dipped in dragon blood. Uvenchaud bound Ein with the rope. Ein strained at the rope, but he was bound.

One by one the other gods came to answer the challenge, and Uvenchaud bound them. He bound Senek. He bound Urul. He bound Penithe and Althoin. He bound Tur and Loket. Obore and Reinul he bound. Ehreg and Purek he bound. Tenul he bound.

In this way did Uvenchaud bind each of the twelve gods at Prythme.

In Prythme the gods lie. In Prythme they are bound.

In Prythme they are held by tuluk fibers and dragon's blood.

No god judged Uvenchaud for the slaying of Uvenra.

—from *The Chthonic Book of Mysteries*, translated by Feven IV of the City Emerald

chapter one

The sun in Annwn perches eternally on the horizon, swimming in lazy circles that allow it to fully rise for only three hours each day. Never lighter than morning nor darker than dusk, Annwn exists in perpetual transition—always arriving, never arrived.

Annwn was discovered by the Fae long ago and was, for many centuries, a bastion of the pure Elvish folk. But it was later discovered by men from the Nymaen world, those called human, and conquered by them. Over time the two races mingled, and have now become one. Neither Fae nor Nymaen, they are simply Annwni, with some of the qualities of each.

There are many villages in Annwn, but only one city, named Blood of Arawn. The city is built upon seven great ramparts of earth and stone dug out of the otherwise flat grasslands of that world. The oldest buildings of that city—the coliseum, the Penn's villa, the temples—are built of marble, but many of these structures have since crumbled and have been replaced with more modest structures of brick. Only the obelisk at the center of the great market, called Romwll's Needle, remains unblemished after fifteen centuries. Conventional wisdom holds that a pair of thaumaturges sit in a stone room beneath the obelisk, whispering bindings without cease, for it is believed that if the needle were ever to fall, then Blood

of Arawn would fall soon after, and all of Annwn crumble
into dust.

—Stil-Eret, "Light in Annwn,"
from *Travels at Home and Abroad*

Five Years Ago

The flashes of witchlight began to streak the horizon shortly after midnight and continued through the night, growing closer by the hour. Paet
ran through the dappled darkness, ignoring the sky.

The attack had come as no surprise to anyone, but Mab's Army had
beaten even the most alarmist estimates in its timing. Back at the Seelie
Embassy, the packing and burning of documents, which had begun in an
orderly fashion three days earlier, had become a frenzy of activity. Bags were
hurriedly packed; valuables were sewn into the linings of garments; empty
kerosene barrels were stuffed with dossiers and set aflame.

None of this was of any concern to Paet.

Blood of Arawn was an ancient city. Not as old, perhaps, as one of its
Seelie counterparts, but it appeared much older as a result of governmental
indifference down the ages. The cobbles in the streets were uneven, some
missing, and Paet could hear carts and carriages jouncing across them in the
street beyond his darkened alley. He could also hear shouts and occasional
shrieks, as certain of the populace considered the reputation of the
encroaching conquerors and decided not to take their chances. Paet could
hardly blame them; life under the Unseelie was certain to be a disappointment for those who decided to stay.

A group of a dozen Chthonic coenobites clattered past Paet, their faces
calm, their legendary indifference suiting them well this night. Their saf-
fron-dyed robes brushed the cobblestones, the bells sewn into their fabric
quietly jingling. As the state religion in all but name, the Chthonics would
be allowed to continue so long as they acknowledged Mab as a goddess, and
superior to their own. This the Chthonics would happily agree to do, praising

Mab publicly and ignoring her in private. Their own deities had been subdued eons earlier and could scarcely take offense. Or so the stories went; Paet had no use for religion.

There was a scintillating flash in the sky. A moment later the ground shook and Paet stumbled. He stopped and listened as the low rumble of reitic concussions echoed down the alley. Waves of heat from the battle outside had begun to roll over the walls before Paet had left the embassy, and now the city both felt and smelled like a tavern kitchen: stifling, stinking of sweat and overripe food. Paet felt the prickling of perspiration beneath his heavy linen shirt. He continued running.

The district of Kollws Vymynal covered the smallest of Blood of Arawn's seven hills. The East Gate was set into the wall at the foot of Kollws Vymynal, which put it closest to the fighting outside. Here Paet could just hear the clash of blades and the shrieks of horses and men mixed in with thundering hooves and reitic blasts.

How long had it been since he'd left the embassy? His internal time sense told him it was only about twenty minutes. That gave him just enough time to retrieve Jenien and make it to the Port-Herion Lock before the Masters shut the thing down, stranding them in Annwn. Not the end of the world, but close enough.

The streets of Kollws Vymynal twisted and doubled back upon themselves, and what signs existed were printed in tiny ancient script that beggared deciphering. The district's inhabitants had either bolted themselves inside their homes, drawing the curtains and shutters tight, or had joined the frantic knots of refugees. Most were headed toward the Southwest Gate, which meant that Paet was fighting against their current. From the city they would beg passage to a different world or strike out southward, hoping to disappear into the plains villages.

The clock in a nearby Chthonic temple struck three and Paet whispered a curse. This was taking too long.

Paet finally found the address he was looking for at the end of a small cul-de-sac, a four-story tenement that smelled heavily of burnt cooking oil and pepper and rot. This was the address Jenien had written down in her logbook when she'd left the embassy that morning, long before word of Mab's invasion had reached the city. Just the address and a name: Prae Benesile. All she'd told Paet was that she was going to visit a "person of interest," which could mean just about anything. By nightfall, while Blood of Arawn convulsed in preparation for its imminent surrender, she still hadn't returned. Paet had waited for her until he could wait no longer and had then gone after her.

"We won't hold the lock for you," Ambassador Traet had told him diffidently. Everything about Traet was hesitant and noncommittal; his appointment had been a sinecure, and laughably so. In happier times, Annwn had been a cozy assignment. Now Traet was in over his head, but at least he had the sense to realize it. "If you're not back by sunrise," Traet had said, stuffing a valise haphazardly with documents, "you're on your own."

Paet breathed deeply ten times. He consciously slowed his heart and forced out the remainder of the prickly heat that filled his blood. The fear of the body could be controlled easily, but for the fear of the mind there was no cure. Only action, despite it.

At the end of the street someone smashed the window of a bakery and grabbed a basket of bread amid surprised shouts.

Paet let himself into the tenement building and hurried up the stairs, making no sound that any Fae or Annwni could hear; of course, the things he was most concerned about were neither, and had excellent hearing. Still. The stairway was filled with cooking smells and body odor. When he reached the third floor he stepped carefully out of the stairwell. The narrow hallway was empty; several doors along its length were open, their inhabitants apparently not seeing the point of locking up behind them. Many of the older, poorer residents of Annwn had fought against Mab's Army in the Sixweek War twenty years previously, and had apparently had enough of the Unseelie for a lifetime.

The apartment Paet was searching for was near the end of the hall. Its door was open as well, though light still burned within. Paet took a long, serrated knife from within his cloak, testing the blade with his thumb by force of habit. He pushed the door open gently and waited, listening. His hardlearned caution warred in his mind with his sense of urgency. If ever there was a time to take a risk, this was it. He swore under his breath and stepped into the apartment.

It was small, a single room lit by a lone witchlamp sconce set into the wall. The long-untuned bilious green light cast harsh shadows over the furniture, placing imagined adversaries in every corner. A tattered cot slumped beneath the waxed-paper window. A chipped chamber pot sat in the corner. Books and bits of paper and parchment were everywhere, piled on the floor, leaned in uneven stacks against the wall, scattered across the cot. There was no sign of Jenien.

Stop and think. Breathe. Relax and smooth the edges of consciousness. Paet picked up a book at random and opened it. It was written by Prae Benesile himself, a work of philosophy, something to do with the history of the Chthonic religion. He put it down and picked up another. This one was a collection of Thule religious poetry, prayers to the bound gods, hymns of supplication, prophecies of liberation and doom. A sampling of the rest of the books revealed most of them to be of a kind: works of philosophy, sacred texts—many regarding the Chthonics, but also some Arcadian scrolls, a few codices from the Annwni emperor cult. Some were written in languages that Paet didn't recognize. There was nothing here to indicate that Prae Benesile was anything other than a reclusive scholar.

Paet sniffed. Blood. Blood had been spilled in this room, and recently. He knelt down and examined the dusty floorboards. Too many shadows. Paet glanced toward the window, shrugged, and created a stronger, pure white witchlight that suffused the entire room. The blood on the floor was tacky and brown, smeared in a scuffle. Paet heard the choking cough from beneath the cot just as his eyes followed the trail of drying blood toward it. He tested his grip on the knife and then channeled Motion and drew the cot quickly backward with a twist of his mind.

Jenien lay curled in a fetal position, clutching her abdomen, breathing raggedly. She looked up at him, and her eyes went wide in her pale face.

"Watching," she whispered. "Bel Zheret are here."

Paet's heart leapt forcefully at the name. He stood and whirled, brandishing the knife. Nothing moved.

He turned back to Jenien and knelt before her. "If they were here I either slipped past them, or they're long gone."

"Said they'd be back for me," Jenien wheezed. She was having trouble breathing. Paet gently pulled her hands away from her belly, pulled aside her shredded blouse. Jenien was going to die; there was nothing he could do for her. These were wounds that not even a Shadow could recover from.

Paet found a pillow on the overturned cot and put it under Jenien's head. Her hair was wet with perspiration. She reached for his wrist and grabbed it with weak fingers.

"Mab's coming," Jenien observed. "Thought we'd have a few more days."

"Things at the embassy have become frantic to say the least."

Jenien chuckled softly. "Traet running around like a headless chicken?"

"Yes."

"Is that knife sharp, Paet?" she said after a brief pause.

"I'm getting you out of here," he said. "Just rest a moment longer."

"Remember that night in Sylvan?" she asked. She was starting to slur her speech. Her body trembled. "The little theater with the terrible play?"

"I remember," Paet said, smiling.

"I bet if we were normal we could have fallen in love that night," she said, sighing.

Paet felt his emotions receding as she spoke. The world became flat. Jenien was an object, a bleeding thing with no impact. A problem to be solved. Was this lack of feeling something he'd always had, or something he'd developed? He couldn't remember. Had he become empty like this when he became a Shadow, or was it the emptiness that qualified him for the job? It didn't seem to matter.

"It was the mulled wine," he said, sitting her up. "It was strong. Hard to tell through the cinnamon and cloves."

She winced as he maneuvered himself behind her. "You looked very dashing. You had one of those red cloaks that were so popular back then."

"Just blending in," he said. Then, after a moment, "What was so important about Prae Benesile, Jenien?"

She shook her head sadly and worked to speak clearly. "Someone from the City of Mab had been to see him. Five times in the past year. I was just curious. Bel Zheret showed up when—" She winced.

Paet brought up the knife. "They take him?"

Jenien nodded. "He struggled; they killed him."

"Ah."

"I don't want to die," she said. It was a statement, merely an observation.

"We've been dead for a long time," he whispered in her ear. He drew the knife across her throat in a quick, sure motion, and pulled her neck back to hasten the bleeding. She shook; her chest lurched once, then twice. He waited until he was certain she was dead, checking her eyes. He looked into them until all the life had gone out of them. It took time. Dying always took time.

Paet took a deep breath and braced his knee against her back. He put the serrated blade of the knife to Jenien's throat again, using the original cut as a guide. He buried his other hand in her hair and pulled, hard, as he began to saw.

Ligament popped. Metal ground against bone. With a sickening crunch, vertebrae parted. A few more strokes and the remaining skin tore loose soundlessly. Jenien's head swung obscenely in his grasp.

He laid it gently on the floor and reached into his cloak. Among the few items he'd brought with him from the embassy was a wax-lined canvas bag, for just this purpose. He unfolded the bag and placed Jenien's head, dripping with blood and sweat, gently inside.

That's what you got for being a Shadow.

He didn't hear them so much as feel the disturbance of the air as they flowed into the room.

Paet turned and saw two tall, dark figures flanking the door. For an instant they looked as surprised as he, but to their credit, they recovered more quickly than Paet did. The first one had his sword out before Paet could begin to react.

Paet stepped back, feeling the position of the corpse behind him and moving easily around it. He stepped into a ready stance, his knife already warm in his hand.

The first swordsman closed on Paet, and Paet got a good look into the man's eyes. Black, empty black, stretching inward to infinity.

Bel Zheret.

Paet was a dangerous man. But going up against two Bel Zheret in a closed space was suicide. He backed up, toward the dingy window of waxed paper.

"You're a Shadow, aren't you?" said the first swordsman. He smiled pleasantly. "My name is Cat. It would be my sincere pleasure to kill you."

"It would be my sincere pleasure for you not to."

"Just so. But I must insist. I have never killed one of you."

"Oh. In that case I'm not going to fight you," said Paet, sheathing the knife.

The Bel Zheret stopped short, flicking his blade in the air. The grin faded, replaced with sincere disappointment. "Why not?"

"If I'm going to die anyway, I'd prefer to give you neither the pleasure nor the experience of engaging me in combat. The next time you come against a Shadow, I'd prefer that you have no personal knowledge of our tactics, our speed, or our reflexes. That way, you can be more easily defeated then by one of my colleagues."

Cat pondered this, never taking his eyes off of Paet. "Well," he said, shrugging, "we can still torture you."

He waved the other Bel Zheret forward. "Restrain him, Asp," he said.

Asp moved with astonishing fluidity and quickness. He didn't seem to tread through the room so much as unfold across it, his limbs elastic, perhaps even multijointed. No matter how many times Paet saw this skill employed, it unnerved him.

Paet took a deep breath and unsheathed his knife again, rearing back for a sudden forward attack against Cat, carefully weighing the cloth bag in his other hand. Cat prepared to block Paet's attack, but no attack came. Paet instead added to his rearward momentum by shoving off with his back foot, launching himself toward and through the window. The third-story window.

Falling backward, unable to see the ground, Paet considered his chances for survival. The descent seemed to go on for eternity. He concentrated and slowed his heart again, deliberately letting his muscles go slack. He even willed his bones to soften and become more flexible, though he had no sense of whether it was a good idea, or whether it would even work.

Finally, he hit the cobblestones on his back, at the angle he'd desired. Jenien's head made a sick, muffled thump as it struck. In his hurry, Paet had forgotten the knife in his left hand, and he felt the snap of his wrist as it was wrenched by the hilt's impact. How many of Paet's wrist bones broke simultaneously he couldn't guess. More than one. There was no pain yet, but that would come in a few seconds.

More prominent at the moment were the pain along his spine and his inability to breathe, the sharp crack of his skull against stone. So perhaps not exactly the angle he'd intended. He was still alive, however, and his legs felt fine; that was all that mattered.

Paet climbed slowly to his feet, looking up at the window. Cat was already drawing his head back inside the room. The waxed-paper windowpane fluttered down crazily in the shifting breeze of the cul-de-sac. He could already hear the steps on the stair, Asp already dispatched. He picked up the sack containing Jenien's head and ran.

Blindly at first, Paet raced out of the cul-de-sac and turned right, for no particular reason. He would need to make his way back west, but not by the most direct route, nor by the most secretive. He would have to split the difference, taking random turnings and inconvenient doublings in order to throw off a pair of Bel Zheret, who would already be considering all of the things that Paet was currently thinking. They outnumbered him, they weren't fleeing, and neither of them had just fallen out of a third-floor window. These were tangible assets that Paet couldn't at the moment figure out how to turn into disadvantages. On the positive side, the night that he fled into was growing more chaotic by the minute.

He kept running, the ringing in his ears from the fall replaced by the sounds of battle, ever closer, the clatter of feet and hooves on stone, shouting. He smelled smoke; somewhere nearby a building was burning. On some of the faces he passed, worry was being replaced with panic. The Unseelie were no longer *coming*; they were *here*. Life in Annwn was about to change significantly.

As Paet turned another corner into the wide avenue leading back toward Kollws Kapytlyn, his left hand, still somehow grasping the knife, slammed hard into the post of a pottery merchant's cart being pushed in the other direction. His vision dimmed and his gorge rose as the pain from the broken wrist leapt up his arm, into his brain and then his stomach. Continuing to run, though slower, he considered dropping the bag. He couldn't defend himself while he carried it.

Looking back, he saw Asp now entering the market from the same alley that Paet had. The Bel Zheret caught his eye and moved toward him, shoving a fruit vendor's cart aside with a strength that made Paet wince. Empress Mab's operatives were getting stronger, faster, more intelligent. Whatever the black art was that grew them in the bowels of her flying cities, it was improving with every year.

So there was one. Where was the other one? Had he run ahead, plotting a tangential course, or was he behind the one he'd just seen? Which had been at the window? Which at the stairs? In the pain and hurry, Paet couldn't remember.

Scattered thinking kills quicker than poison. That was one of Master Jedron's favorite adages.

Paet ducked into a doorway and risked closing his eyes just long enough to concentrate and cut off the pain from his wrist, slow his heart, and clear out the essence of fear in his blood. Better to lose a moment of his head start than to give up his mind to panic and pain.

Again he ran, now turning into a blind alley that was dark and cool, the walls close together. It was quieter here; the commotion beyond became a homogenous roar. The smell of smoke, though, was stronger. Nearer the fire.

Condensation dripped down the moss-covered stones. Though Paet knew Blood of Arawn well, and had spent hours poring over maps a few days earlier, he wasn't exactly sure where he was at the moment, or whether this alley would take him to another street or to a dead end. Still, it was the unexpected thing to do, and that was his primary defense at the moment.

The alley opened on a wide street, and Paet hurried into the center of the city, where the giant obelisk atop the Kapytlyn rose up and vanished into the blankness of night. Asp was nowhere to be seen. The crowds were thicker here, the city's dependents waiting for news or instructions. Paet knew that those instructions wouldn't come until Mab's officers took control of the place. The rightful governor was long gone, having taken refuge in the Seelie

Kingdom earlier that day, along with a score of top officials. Most everyone else in government had already fled to the countryside.

Paet stopped a moment to get his bearings—he'd actually been running away from the Port-Herion Lock, not toward it. Inwardly cursing himself, he turned and began again. Thankfully the chaos surrounding him, which would normally have been a hindrance, worked in his favor. At any other time, a limping, sweating Fae brandishing a bloody knife would undoubtedly be noticed. The first rule of Shadows was to draw no attention; that was the ostensible meaning of the nickname. Though not the true one.

Paet breathed deep and concentrated again, hoping to heal the wrist enough to fight. He was running low on *re*, having used up much of his stored magical essence in his various reachings-in today. He did the best he could, then headed toward a side street that led to the Kollws Ysglyn, and the Port-Herion Lock beyond.

The Bel Zheret named Cat was there waiting for him, sword drawn.

Paet dropped the bag and rushed him, praying that his momentum would be enough to take the man down, but the Bel Zheret stayed on his feet and, though unable to bring his blade to bear, punched Paet hard in the stomach. There was something on his hand, turning his knuckles into spikes, and the Bel Zheret twisted those spikes into Paet's midsection, not hard enough to draw blood through Paet's cloak, but still painful.

Paet pulled back, stepping hard on the side of Cat's knee, a lucky move, and the Bel Zheret crumpled, falling backward against the wall. Paet knew from experience that having your knee kicked out of its socket was one of the more painful things that could happen in a fight, short of being run through, and he was amazed that Cat was still standing, let alone continuing to swing his blade.

For an instant, fear tumbled into Paet's mind and he was certain that he was going to die. Right here in this alley, carrying the severed head of a woman with whom he'd once made love. All his regrets spilled onto the dank cobblestones. Where was Master Jedron with a homily against the inevitability of death? Certainly one existed, and it was something stoic and tough. Well. Better to die here in an alley than in a dimly lit room with the Bel Zheret. They would torture him slowly and effectively, and despite his training they would cut his knowledge out of him. With their teeth.

There was a sound in the alley. A pair of burly city guards were approaching, their clubs out and ready. Both looked tense and afraid. They'd been given instructions to remain and to keep the peace until the bitter end. Neither one appeared happy about it.

Cat spun Paet around and shoved Paet's face hard against the wall. A knife pierced his back, went deep, and Paet felt something in his body give. A kidney? The knife traced a path across his back and caught on something hard, a vertebra. With Paet's enhanced sensitivity toward his own body, he felt it in excruciating detail, felt the nerve tissue shredding like spiderweb. Another hard shove and Paet's nose smashed into the bricks of the wall.

Paet slid down the wall and watched Cat begin a methodical slaughter of the two guardsmen, who barely had time to shriek before he began hurting them. One of the Bel Zheret's few weaknesses was that they took a bit too much pleasure in causing pain; perhaps it was an unintended side effect of whatever it was that created them. Perhaps, worse, it was intended.

With the very last of his *re*, Paet attempted to repair those nerves, to find his way into the kidney and send healing toward it. These were still killing wounds, but perhaps they would kill a bit more slowly now, and give him time to reach the lock before he died. Paet now reached out, out of his body and out into Blood of Arawn, looking for life, looking for *re* that he could steal. Two children in an adjoining house, huddling in bed. He drew as much from them as he could without killing them. They'd be sick for a few days, nothing more. It would be the least of their worries. He would kill the children if he had to, but not unless it was absolutely necessary. And it wasn't absolutely necessary. Not yet.

While the Bel Zheret continued its work on the guards, Paet exited the alley in the other direction as silently as possible, picking up the bag as he ran. The knife wound seared through his back, making the broken wrist seem mild in comparison. He could sense fluids in his body mixing that should not mix, blood leaking into places where blood did not belong. Despite his best efforts, he might not make it.

Again he considered abandoning Jenien. A loose cobblestone would do the trick, crush her brain until it was utterly unreadable. But he couldn't do it. Killing her had been bad enough. Nor could he simply toss the cloth bag into one of the now-many burning buildings that lined the street along which he staggered.

A clock in the main temple struck the hour, and Paet felt what blood remained in him drain toward his feet. The Port-Herion Lock would be shut down soon. Any minute now. They would not wait for him.

Running. Breathing hard in his chest. Now no longer caring whether he was seen or what kind of impression he made. Get to the gate, through the lock, onto Seelie soil. This was all that mattered now.

There was a side street that ran along the base of Kollws Kapytlyn, where the Southwest Gate stood, and Paet reached it, out of breath, after what seemed like hours. The street was empty. It ran along a ridge line, overlooking the endless prairies of Annwn. In the distance, one of the giant, tentacled boars, the Hwch Ddu Cwta, raised its head to the sky in the dark, amidst the noise.

Paet's legs felt like they'd been wrapped in cold iron; his breath came like knife thrusts. Blood dripped down his back, thickening along the length of his thigh. He stumbled once, then again. He should have killed those two children; it had been necessary after all. He was sworn to protect the children of the Seelie Kingdom, not the children of Annwn.

He struggled again to his feet. The pain in his back, in his chest, in his wrist—they all conspired against him, hounding him. Each had its own personality, its own signature brand of hurt.

The city gate was up ahead, left open and unguarded. Beyond he could see the lock glowing in the distance. The portal was still open!

One of the Bel Zheret tackled him hard from behind, his shoulder biting into the knife wound. The bag containing Jenien's head tumbled away. Whether his attacker was Cat or Asp he couldn't tell; not that it mattered now. If it was Cat, then he'd get his wish to kill a Shadow after all.

But he wouldn't get Jenien. Paet crawled toward the bag, allowing the Bel Zheret free access to his back, which his assailant readily exploited, kicking him hard in the kidney.

Paet collapsed on top of the bag and, with the last of his strength, crushed Jenien's skull with his hands. It was harder than he would have thought. Mab wouldn't learn any of her secrets now.

The Bel Zheret knelt over Paet and began delivering efficient, evenly timed blows to Paet's spine, then turned him over and dealt equally with Paet's face. Paet felt his nose crack, his lower jaw split in two. Teeth rolled loose on his tongue; he swallowed one. He felt ribs crack, first one, then two more. Something popped in his chest and suddenly he could no longer breathe. There was no sound except the dull rush of blood in his ears. The world spun; the beating, the pounding receded, then faded altogether.

A few minutes later Traet, the Seelie ambassador, followed by a pair of clerks lugging baggage and valises thick with papers, literally stumbled over Paet's body.

"Oh, dear!" Traet cried. "How awful!"

"Is he alive?" asked one of the clerks, kneeling.

"We don't have time for that," Traet muttered, walking past. "There will be casualties."

"Sir, it's Paet!"

The ambassador quickly turned, his eyes wide. "Gather him up, then! Quickly!"

The kneeling clerk felt for a pulse. "He's dead, sir. Perhaps we oughtn't to bother. . . ."

"Don't be a fool," said Traet. "Hand me your bags and take him. Now!"

Neither the clerks nor Traet noticed the cloth bag that had fallen from Paet's hand, now resting in a clump of bushes just outside the gate.

Once the ambassador's party was safely through the lock, the Master of the Gates opened a small door on the side of the massive portal. He adjusted the ancient machinery, and a loud hum joined the cacophony of flames and the percussion of war from across the city. While a sextet of extremely fierce-looking members of the Seelie Royal Guard held back the small knot of would-be refugees that had surrounded the lock, the Master closed the door, carrying a heavy part of the lock's inner workings with him. He stepped through and beckoned the guardsmen to follow. They backed slowly into the silken portal, not so much disappearing as gliding out of existence. The tips of their swords were the last things to vanish. The instant the last of them was through, the portal went dark, revealing behind it only a veneer of highly polished black stone. The desperate crowd banged their fists against it, some weeping, others shouting.

Just before dawn a tocsin sounded in the city and the Unseelie flag was raised upon the obelisk. All was quiet. The crowd at the Port-Herion Lock hesitantly turned away from the dead portal and went their separate ways—some back into the city, their heads hung low; some out into the pampas, not looking back.

chapter two

Titania is the land and the land is Titania. She reads the song
of birds and feels the brush of the plow upon her skin.

—Anonymous, "Ode to Titania"

Today

Regina Titania, Fae Queen of the Seelie Lands, Purest Blood of Pure Elves,
sat upon her stone chair, chin in hand, swinging her feet. The lights
were dim in the throne room, and the sound of her heels clicking against the
floor echoed in the gloom.

She looked at her husband, King Auberon, the son of Aba himself, who
slouched insensate in his own seat. He had not spoken in centuries, not since
she had stolen his power and his mind on the day of their marriage.

"A change approaches, husband," she said softly. "Long ago you warned
me this day would come, and I scoffed. Now I stand chastened."

Auberon's head lolled to the side, and he sobbed quietly.

chapter three

All Gifts are Gifts of Aba, who is God beyond gods. To him who sees clearly, this is not a matter of faith; it is axiomatic.

—Alpaurle, *The Magus*,
translated by Feven IV of the City Emerald

Silverdun sat in the antechamber to the abbot's office, shivering. Tebrit had forced the novice robes over Silverdun's head without giving him the opportunity to dry off first. He was dripping onto the floor.

After a few minutes, Abbot Estiane opened the door to his office and ushered Silverdun in, groaning at the sight of him. The office was cramped, but warm—the abbot was allowed a small brazier in his office, due to his rheumatism. Or, at least, that's what he told everyone. Silverdun knew, however, that Estiane simply didn't like to be cold, and had, in his words, "spent enough years as a coenobite freezing my ass off for no reason."

Estiane said nothing for a minute or two, busying himself with digging through the dozens of scrolls and books littering his desk for something in particular, then giving up and reaching beneath the desk for a metal flask, which he unstoppered and handed to Silverdun.

"Here," he said. "This'll take the edge off."

Silverdun took a pull from the flask and was rewarded with a swallow of some of the best brandy he'd ever tasted. "The queen's tits, Father, where did you get this?"

Estiane smiled. "We all have our little secrets, Silverdun. Do you think I'd still be running this place after all these years if I didn't have a few strings to pull?"

Silverdun nodded and took another sip.

"You've pissed off Tebrit again, I see," said Estiane.

"Not a difficult task."

"Missed morning prayers, did you?"

"I think it was the hangover in particular that got me sent up to you." Silverdun shrugged. "Just between you and me, I don't think Tebrit likes me much."

Estiane waved the thought away. "Nonsense. Tebrit is simply fulfilling his obligations as Prior to ensure that your novitiate is a period of cleansing, separating you from the things of the world in as complete a fashion as possible."

He took the flask back from Silverdun and had a nip from it himself before returning it to the desk. "Oh, who am I kidding? The man despises you. And with good reason."

"I don't think it's very holy of him to take such pleasure in it." Silverdun sniffed.

"Allow the man his small comforts. He has a very difficult and thankless job. Believe it or not, you're far from the least holy novice that's ever passed through this temple."

"Oh, really?"

"I was much worse. Why, during my novitiate I actually snuck a pair of twin sisters into the sacristy and got them drunk on the holy wine."

Silverdun slapped the desk. "You cad! And they still ordained you?"

"They never found out."

"I knew there was a reason I liked you," Silverdun said. "Well, I suppose you've got to punish me. Garderobes for a month, is it?"

"Two, actually. One for missing morning prayers and one for drinking in the presence of your abbot." Estiane smiled and leaned back in his chair. "Ha! Didn't see that one coming, did you?"

"You old bastard. How you ever got to be a religious leader is beyond me."

"It's simple, really," said Estiane, leaning forward, the smile fading. "Look around you. Do you see any parishioners? Any lost souls other than your own coming to me for spiritual guidance? I'm a civil servant. If I was any good at being religious then I'd be out there practicing religion." Estiane sighed. "Being promoted to abbot isn't a reward; it's more of a punishment, really."

Silverdun felt his body finally beginning to warm in the lovely heat of the brazier. "Ah, so you say. But I knew Vestar at the Temple Aba-E in Sylvan. A more holy man I've never met in my life!"

What remained of Estiane's smile vanished and he looked down. "Oh, you had to bring the old man into it, didn't you, Silverdun? Just when I was having such a lark with you.

"Sometimes we in this business put on a bit of a blasphemous face when we can in order to fend off the ills of the world with good humor. We're all corrupt in the eyes of Aba, who sees all. But some of us hew very, very close to the ideal. Some of us are so strong that they don't need any robe betwixt them and the wind. Vestar was one of those."

"So you admit you're a lousy abbot," said Silverdun, smirking.

"I admit no such thing!" said Estiane. "Vestar was a saint. It's just that there are more churches than there are saints, that's all. We do the best we can with the gifts we're given. Most of us are forced to make compromises in order to maintain our sanity. The fact that Vestar never did so is a testament to his unique virtue."

"His unique virtue got him murdered," said Silverdun. "He stood up to Purane-Es when he could have run and saved himself."

"There's that," said Estiane. "There's that."

"Will that be all then?" asked Silverdun. "Or do you have any pies or custards hidden back there that I might have a bite of before I head down to the Frater for my morning gruel?"

"As if I'd share my pie with you," Estiane said, adjusting his robe.

Silverdun stood to go, and the abbot waved him back down again. "Listen, Silverdun. Since I've got you here, there's something I've been meaning to discuss with you."

"If it's twin sisters you're after, I'll need a few days and the key to the sacristy," said Silverdun.

Estiane said nothing; all the humor had left him.

Silverdun pulled his robes around him. "Well, what is it then?"

"I've been debating whether or not to mention it at all, but I suppose it's best if I do. I've received word that Lord Everess would like to speak with you."

Silverdun sat up. "Really? And how does Everess even know that I'm here? Isn't my presence here supposed to be something of a sacred trust?"

"Settle down, Silverdun. You must be aware that Lord Everess knows what he wants to know. The truth is, I told him you were here."

Silverdun scowled. "Why would you do such a thing, Abbot? I don't want to be involved in the affairs of the world. I just want to be left alone. That's why I came here in the first place."

"Yes, and that's the wrong reason for coming here, and that's also why you're such a rotten novice. If it's solitude you're after, there are any number of uninhabited islands in the Western Sea you could have chosen."

"I want to follow Aba," said Silverdun weakly.

"A man can enjoy telling a joke without joining the circus, Silverdun."

"What's that supposed to mean?"

"It means that just because you want to please Aba doesn't mean you have to become a monk. And you know it."

"Enough, enough. What does any of this have to do with Everess? What does he want with me?"

"I'll let him tell you," said Estiane. "And I suggest you hear him out. Now shall I let him know you agree to see him, or shan't I?"

Silverdun thought in silence. The fog in his head was lifting, but his mind didn't want to think—it wanted to be carried off by the warmth into a comfortable silent place. This was, he thought ironically, the closest thing to true prayer he'd experienced since coming to the monastery.

"Fine. I'll see him," said Silverdun. "But I reserve the right to ignore everything he says."

"Excellent," said Estiane. "I'm glad you feel that way, since I already invited him. He'll be here tomorrow."

Silverdun glared at the abbot. "You really are a bastard, you know."

Estiane's smile returned. "I believe you've got some garderobes to clean, Novice. I suggest you get started now, or else you'll have to spend all of midday prayer smelling like a latrine."

The next day was windy as well as cold, and the rain came even stronger. Autumn had settled over the monastery and seemed intent on making its presence known. Thus, Tebrit gleefully assigned Silverdun to the gardens, where he dutifully, if angrily, weeded the cabbage. After an hour his back ached, he was covered in mud up to his shins, and he could no longer feel the tips of his fingers. He tried to stir up a bit of witchfire from time to time, but on each occasion the wind rose up and immediately extinguished it—Aba was watching, it seemed, and wanted to make sure that Tebrit's punishments were exacted in full.

The Temple Aba-Nylae stood on a wooded hill just outside the walls of the City Emerald, so there was no protection from the Inland Sea wind that blew over the hill, leaving the grounds wet and cold even when the sun was shining brightly in the city.

Silverdun was down on his knees, yanking away at a recalcitrant root, when he heard a familiar voice boom from across the yard.

"By Auberon's hairy ass! Is this Perrin Alt, Lord Silverdun, or a rude villein?" The voice then broke out into laughter.

Silverdun looked up and saw Edwin Sural, Lord Everess, standing beneath the cloister loggia, beaming and waving.

"Well, come in out of the rain, Silverdun!" goaded Everess. "I didn't come all this way to watch you play peasant."

Silverdun stood slowly, spitting out rainwater. His hair was soaked through, lying in thick tangles around his neck. His novice's robes, likewise, were drenched, and his hands and feet were thick with mud. He closed his eyes for a long moment before beginning the long squelching trudge across the garden.

"I must say, Perrin Alt," chuckled Everess, once Silverdun was within easy speaking distance, "I do not think the religious life agrees with you."

Silverdun had never much liked Everess, who enjoyed his taunts a bit too much for Silverdun's taste. "One gets used to it," he said. Whatever witty rejoinder he might normally have come up with was drenched as surely as his witchfires.

"By her teeth, Silverdun! It's true what I've heard—you are changed!"

Silverdun automatically touched his face. He could feel the nose, once straight and patrician, now angled with a slight bump. The cheekbones were lower now as well, and the chin not quite so prominent. He had angered the wrong woman, and she had taken her revenge on his appearance. Faella, the young mestine, who for some reason he could not get out of his mind. Queen Titania had told him that Faella was special, that she possessed the so-called Thirteenth Gift, the Gift of Change. He had a feeling that Titania had not told him this merely as a point of information.

"It's the country air," said Silverdun. "It does wonders for the complexion."

"Oh, come in out of the wet and stop sputtering inanities. We've important business to discuss." Everess waved Silverdun toward the calefactory, for which Silverdun was inwardly grateful. The warming-room was the only space in the entire monastery in which a fire was allowed to be lit at all times.

They stepped into the calefactory and almost immediately Silverdun's wet robes began to steam. There was a washbasin filled with hot water in one corner of the room, and before Silverdun could even begin to acknowledge Everess again, he washed his face and hands and feet in the basin, wincing with pleasure as the feeling returned to his extremities with sharp needles of pain.

The calefactory was empty other than the two of them, which was remarkable for this time of day—it was a rest period, and on a cold afternoon one could expect to find easily half the monks of the abbey clustered here, playing cards, drinking the watered-down swill they called wine, or just sitting idly. The fact that it was empty told Silverdun that Estiane had gone out of his way to ensure that the meeting between him and Everess was a private one.

Once Silverdun felt himself to be sufficiently presentable, he sat down at the long table by the fireplace, where Everess was already seated. Everess had his pipe out and was carefully stoking it.

"I'm pleased that you agreed to see me, Perrin," Everess began warmly, all trace of banter put aside. "What I have to speak with you about is a matter of great importance."

"I see," said Silverdun. "Though I should tell you that I did not, in fact, agree to see you. That bastard Estiane agreed on my behalf without consulting me on the matter."

"And yet here we are face-to-face, are we not?"

"There's a fire in here." Silverdun sighed. He found the repartee tiring.

Everess looked little different from the last time that Silverdun had seen him, which had been in the House of Lords some five years earlier. Still stout and red-faced, with the same bristling brown whiskers spotted with gray. His eyes were narrow and partially hidden beneath bushy eyebrows, giving him a permanent squint. He sucked on his pipe, and a small tendril of smoke emerged from it. Silverdun waved a finger at the smoke, and it formed itself into interlocking rings, twisting and spinning up toward the ceiling.

"Oh, do stop fooling around, Silverdun," said Everess. "There's much to discuss, and I'd like to get back to the city before the road out there washes out entirely."

"You have my complete attention," said Silverdun.

"It's time for you to come out of hiding," said Everess. "I understand your need to get away from things for a time, but you're needed elsewhere."

"Quite the contrary. I'm happy here."

"Oh, don't be stupid, Silverdun. You've had your fun playing monk, but that time is over and you and I both know it. You don't belong here. You never have and you never will. You're not meant to be confined like this."

"I was confined for quite a long time at the prison of Crere Sulace. And you never once came to visit me."

"Yes, and when Mauritane offered you a way out, you took it, even though by all accounts you were riding off to your own death."

"Mauritane told me he'd kill me himself if I didn't go."

"Stop acting like an idiot!" said Everess, suddenly angry. "The point is that you *did* go. You left Crere Sulace a criminal, and you emerged from the Battle of Sylvan a hero. You've proved that you have the ability to do what must be done for the good of the kingdom, and that's what I need from you now."

"I disagree. I'm quite content where I am."

"Really?" said Everess. "Look around you, man. From where I'm standing, all you've done is trade one cell for another."

No witty response from Silverdun's typically bottomless well of them was forthcoming, so he simply stood and began to turn away.

"Come into the city, Silverdun," Everess called after him. "Hear what I have to say. And then if you don't like it, you can come back here and keep rotting for all I care."

That stung.

A messenger on a sturdy mare watched Lord Everess's carriage vanish into the rain from the hilltop overlooking the temple. Once he was certain that Everess's departure was assured, he gingerly walked the horse down the grassy slope to the temple's stable.

He handed the reins to a passing monk, assuring the man that he'd be back momentarily. Good to his word, a few minutes later he returned from the monastery, mounted, and rode off without another word.

Silverdun left the calefactory feeling warm, but also a bit dizzy. He and Everess had never been friends—they'd known each other in passing in the halls of Corpus, and Silverdun's second cousin had married a nephew of Everess's, but Silverdun hadn't even attended the wedding. So why was Everess coming for him now?

Silverdun sneaked carefully through the refectory and back into the dorter. All of the monks' rooms were empty now—rest period was over, and afternoon prayers had already begun. Silverdun couldn't have cared less. He sunk onto his cot and leaned against the wall, letting the cool stones calm him.

On a shelf above the bed was a duffel bag that contained the day suit he'd worn when he'd entered the place ten months earlier. It had been washed and pressed. His boots, polished and supple, were lined up carefully next to the bag, and beneath them both was the sword that Mauritane had presented him at the celebration following the Battle of Sylvan. Engraved in the blade was the Silverdun crest surrounded by five stars: one for each of his companions on the journey that had led him out from exile at Crere Sulace and back into life.

Of those five, two were dead: Honeywell had given up his own life to save them at the beginning of their journey. Gray Mave had betrayed them, and died for his sins. Brian Satterly was off somewhere rescuing human babies from Changeling traders, and good riddance. Raieve, now Mauritane's wife, had returned to Avalon to help win the peace there. Mauritane was on leave from his post as captain of the Royal Guard, no doubt fighting alongside her.

Or so he believed. He hadn't seen anyone from his former life in months. He missed them. He even missed the foolish human Satterly. That was depressing.

There was a knock at the door and Silverdun braced for another assault by Tebrit, but instead it was Estiane who stepped into the cell. The abbot shut the door quietly, an odd expression on his face. He held an envelope in his hand, and Silverdun recognized the broken seal as that of Marcuse, the queen's chamberlain. Estiane sat at the edge of Silverdun's cot, turning the envelope in his fingers. He held it delicately, as if it were a dried flower or a piece of fine china.

"Let us be perfectly honest with one another, shall we?" said Estiane. "No banter, no gamesmanship. No hidden agendas. We are both men of Aba, who do our best to serve the Good, and often fail miserably along the way. Agreed?"

Silverdun sat up. A witticism reared up in his mind and he choked it down. "Fine," he grunted.

"I know why Everess came to see you today," said Estiane. "He and I have had a number of rather serious conversations over the past few months."

"Really?" said Silverdun. "Is Everess an Arcadian? He never struck me as the type."

"No, no," said Estiane. "These conversations were of a purely political nature. We don't like to advertise it, of course, but the Church is as immersed in the world of politics as any other large organization. We have power and influence and knowledge, and it has to be wielded."

Estiane tapped the envelope gently against his fingers. "As you may know, the Church has a rather sizable network of believers among the Unseelie. Not even we know exactly how many of us there are across Mab's empire because the Bel Zheret enjoy torturing names out of Arcadians, and we like to offer them as few as possible.

"Much of the useful information our queen possesses regarding the Unseelie comes from us. We have believers at almost every level of government and at every rank in the military. Sometimes their consciences guide them to reveal certain things."

Silverdun smiled. "And you barter that knowledge for influence at Corpus and with the queen's court."

"Of course we do," said Estiane, his voice rough. "We'd be fools not to. This all has very little to do with serving Aba, but the Church is not itself holy. The Church is an organization that exists in space and time, and it must do what it must in order to survive and thrive. If you'll recall, when you were a boy, Arcadianism was practically illegal." Estiane unsuccessfully attempted to hide the guilt he clearly felt. "And that brings us to you, Perrin Alt, Lord Silverdun."

Silverdun sighed. "I was wondering when something would bring us to me. What's this about?"

"I'm not exactly sure, to be honest," said Estiane. "I know that Everess is very keen to bring you back to the capital, but I don't know why. Something to do with the Foreign Ministry, I should imagine."

"Honestly, Abbot!" said Silverdun. "Where's the holiness in that?"

"Holiness?" Estiane hissed the word. "Holiness is a privilege granted to blessed souls like Tebrit, your tormentor. Tebrit doesn't have to make decisions about how the Church's influence is used to direct affairs, or whether those affairs ought to be directed, or what the dire outcome for the Church and its followers will be if those affairs are ignored. Tebrit will not have any blood on his hands if a new war begins because there is nothing he could do to help prevent it.

"I, however, am required to make those decisions. There is no way for me to do this without getting blood on my hands. I don't have the luxury of being spotless."

Silverdun leaned back again, nodding. "I understand now. Everess needs your information, and you've decided to exact payment. He agrees to take me on in whatever role he's dreamed up for me, knowing that I'll be acting as your proxy, and in return you'll provide information."

"Not just information," said Estiane.

"Money as well?" Silverdun was shocked.

"We're being honest, are we not? Silverdun, you don't read the reports that I read, the list of martyrs' names that come across my desk day in and day out. The Unseelie take perverse joy in hunting down and murdering Arcadians. What do you think would happen if they were to take down Regina Titania? The Church would cease to exist. Aba's work in Faerie would be finished."

Estiane leaned in, and Silverdun could detect the faintest trace of brandy on his breath. "I will not allow that to happen."

Silverdun stood and pulled his sword down from the shelf above the bed. He unsheathed it and flicked it back and forth in frustration. "And what if I refuse? What if I just want to be a monk?"

Estiane stood and smoothed his robes. "You never wanted to be a monk, Perrin. You just needed a place to hide for a while. Your hiding time is over—I'm kicking you out."

"You can't do that!"

"I'm the abbot. I can do whatever I want."

Silverdun swung the sword harder in the air, striking at an intangible foe.

"Fine," said Silverdun. "Kick me out. I'll go back to Oarsbridge and live out my days as an eccentric country gentleman. Find a pretty, dumb daughter of a nearby baron to marry to keep me warm at night. How's that?"

Estiane smiled. He walked to the door. "It's not that simple, Perrin. Life never is."

"It can be."

"Here," said Estiane, holding out the envelope. "This was delivered just after Everess left. There were two notes inside. One was addressed to me, the other to you. My note simply asked me to pass yours along to you before I allowed you to leave here."

Silverdun took the envelope, again noting the chamberlain's seal. Inside was a single sheet, printed in a flowing, beautiful hand. It was not the script of Chamberlain Marcuse. Silverdun knew whose script it was, though. He knew it without needing to be told.

Perrin Alt, Lord Silverdun:

When last we met, I warned you that there would come a time when I would call on you by name. That time has come. Consider well what has been asked of you. You are one who, like a prize racehorse, thrives only when placed upon the track. Go where you will thrive.

The note was not signed, but it didn't need to be. It had been penned by the queen herself.

"Shit," said Silverdun. "Shit! Shit! Shit!"

He reached up to the shelf and pulled down his boots.

chapter four

The difficulty, which has yet to be resolved, is as follows. For an Elemental unbinding at a distance, the standard formulation requires the spoken trigger (i.e., the unbinding word) to interact physically with the binding. Given a distance, d, and the speed of sound, r, the effects of an unbinding word should require time t, where $t = d/r$. It has been demonstrated in controlled circumstances, however, that the unbinding occurs *simultaneously* with the trigger. Thaumaturges have debated this question for centuries, but no satisfactory explanation has ever been offered. Since reitic force decreases exponentially over distance, this is rarely a problem in practice. Students are encouraged to use the standard release-chain formulation in most circumstances.

—*Dynamics*, chapter 7:
"Indirect Mechanisms of Release in Distributed Systems"

I t was dawn, and Ironfoot was still awake, his head throbbing, poring over the map. The thing was so big that he'd had a local craftsman create a table for the sole purpose of holding it unrolled. It was a topological map, commissioned some number of years ago by a local governor with a penchant for geography and dreams of wealth from silver mining. The map had been of no use whatever to the governor, save perhaps feeding his ego. But to Ironfoot it had become invaluable.

The readings came in from across the site, and Ironfoot meticulously added them as points of data, using a ruler to draw perfectly straight lines of radiance from one point to the next. A pattern was beginning to emerge, but it still wasn't enough.

He slammed the table with his fist. Years as a scholar had never tempered the wild part of his nature. He knew it and it infuriated him.

He rubbed his eyes and took a long sip of coffee. His mug had been holding down the lower left corner of the map, and now it tried to roll up a bit. He absently smoothed it with his hands. He reached for the next slip of paper and there were none left.

He stood, feeling the ache in his shoulders and back, feeling the fatigue that flowed through him. He could have himself spellrested by the on-site medic, but that false rest affected only the body and not the mind. He needed sleep. Real sleep.

He opened the flap of the tent and was assaulted by the dusty wind that assailed the site day and night. The dust got into everything: clothes, boots, instruments. Some of it was blown south from the Unseelie steppes, but some of it—and this he tried carefully not to think about—was the incinerated remains of Fae men, women, and children. The descendants of the founders of the oldest Elvish city.

"Armin," he called out to his assistant, who stood at the edge of the crater, sipping water from a metal cup. Armin was young, still a student, but already teaching classes of his own at the university and almost certain to be made full professor once they returned to the City Emerald.

"Over here, Master Falores," Armin said, still looking down into the crater. Ironfoot joined him.

"I wish you'd call me Ironfoot like everyone else does."

"I'm sorry; my mother wouldn't approve," said Armin. He was a careful, dutiful student. It was fine if he wanted to be a bit old-fashioned.

Below, the team of students walked the remaining sections of the site, testing each bit of rubble, bone, and metal. Each student carried an intensity gauge, and every few moments would lean down and carefully take a reading, noting the result on a slip of paper that would go to feed Ironfoot's map. The students had caviled at the assignment at first, having not really understood what it was they were volunteering for, but they quickly got over their reservations. The promise of free food and even the smallest of stipends would, Ironfoot was sure, convince any common student to freely give up a limb.

"Shall we have a look?" asked Armin. "See how things are progressing?"

Ironfoot nodded. "It won't be long now. Another day or two and we'll have all we can get."

They had both unconsciously begun breathing through their mouths; they started down into the crater that had, a year ago, been the Seelie city of Selafae.

There was a peculiar smell down in the crater, one that nobody could quite recognize, though it had components upon which everyone could agree. There was a hint of cinnamon to it, a bit of roasted pork, almost pleasant but undercut with an ugly tarlike stink that lingered in the nose. They'd been here for six weeks and no one had yet gotten used to it. Some of the students wore cloths tied around their faces, but these didn't seem to help much. A visiting professor of Elements had offered to remove the odor with a simple transmutation, but Ironfoot had refused, not wanting to contaminate the site.

The students and researchers knew better. At Ironfoot's insistence, not a single breath of *re* was to be expended at the site. No little luck charms, no cantrips to sing the pain out of aching muscles.

Walking among the ruins, the smell crept into Ironfoot's senses and he flinched away from it. There was something about it that he couldn't quite put his finger on, something that might be important. It was a memory, an experience from long ago; he could sense it in the way that any unique smell might recall a memory of younger days, but he couldn't place it and it was driving him crazy.

"How goes it, Mister Beman?" Armin said to one of the students, a tall pale boy who looked as if he hadn't had a decent meal since his schooling had begun, and was only now beginning to fill out under Ironfoot's auspices.

"Coming along, Professor. I hope to have my section finished by lunchtime." He beamed, patting his intensity gauge.

Ironfoot scowled and took the gauge from him. "You're not holding it quite right," he said, demonstrating. "It needs to be held as far from the body as possible, so your own *re* doesn't affect the readings. See?"

The intensity gauge was something Ironfoot had developed in his own student days, working under the Master Elementalist Luane, who had almost single-handedly invented the field of inductive thaumatology. The instrument consisted of a brass tube, about the height of Ironfoot's waist, with a silver tip on one end and a series of graded markings lining the outside of the tube. Inside was a silver plate, opposite a plate of cold iron. In the absence of *re*, the silver and iron plates nearly touched, their natural repulsion negligible. But when the tip was applied to an object or creature that was imbued with the magical essence, the silver plate repelled the iron plate in proportion to the strength of the field, moving a needle along the graded markings. Ironfoot was more than a little proud of it.

He handed the gauge back to the student, who seemed relieved when he and Armin continued on their way. He knelt to inspect a few of Beman's readings. Each item, from the tiniest pebble to the largest section of wall, had been marked with runes designating the direction and intensity of *re* embedded in it. All food for the map.

Once everything had been marked, all the data cross-checked and analyzed for errors, and the artifacts corrected for the many interlocking auras of *re* that permeated any Fae city, then Ironfoot's work could begin in earnest. Fortunately for him (though clearly not for the citizens of Selafae), the blast that had destroyed the city was massive, its reitic force so potent that it had nearly annihilated any background essence that existed in the city before its impact.

Ironfoot was eager to have this done. Eager to solve the problem and move on. Solving problems was what Ironfoot did. The specific problem didn't usually matter to him, so long as it was interesting and got him out of the city. But this one was different. This one would linger.

Once the map was complete, then, he would return to Queensbridge, and would perform what he sincerely hoped would be the greatest feat of investigative thaumatology to date: He would reverse-engineer the monstrous magic that had destroyed an entire city in an instant. He would recreate the Einswrath weapon using only its aftermath as a guide.

And after that? Then what? Would anything seem as important after this? That part of him that was the source of his anger and impatience was singing to him again lately, as it had more and more often over the last few years: time to move on.

He and Armin continued their walk, listening to the sounds of the instruments clinking against the rubble, and the light conversation of the students at their work. Someone was singing an old, sad Arcadian hymn:

> *Lower me down into the hallowed earth.*
> *Let your spirit cover me.*
> *Guide me through the changes that lead me to rebirth,*
> *and through soil, wind, and wave recover me.*

The tune was haunting and lovely, and it struck Ironfoot that what he was strolling through was not simply a project, not merely a research site. It was a massive graveyard, a charnel house of unprecedented proportions. Those white bits of debris scattered among the torn-up cobblestones were not pebbles—they were fragments of bone.

He left Armin with one of the students who had a question about an anomalous reading and continued walking, careful not to tread on anything other than dirt.

Ironfoot was a scholar, but he had at one time been a soldier as well, and these echoes of violence stirred thoughts of revenge and aggression that he liked to believe belonged to his younger self. The drive to win that had never quite left him. And there was no good that could come of thinking about *that*.

So he pushed it away, all of it. There was work to be done, and he had no time for his old regrets.

When Ironfoot returned to his tent an hour later, there was a middle-aged nobleman waiting for him, holding a cloth over his face against the smell. Armin was nervously preparing tea over the small camp stove.

"A Lord Everess to see you, Master Falores," said Armin.

Everess bowed slightly toward Ironfoot. "A pleasure to meet you, Falores. A genuine pleasure."

He wasn't the first noble to come sniffing around the site. Most wanted a tour of the wreckage and a brief talk with Ironfoot regarding his theories about the weapon. Some of them appeared to have genuine concerns about the Einswrath weapon, though some others seemed to have come out of nothing more than ghoulish curiosity. He couldn't tell from looking at him which one Everess was.

"The pleasure is mine, Lord Everess," said Ironfoot, with the requisite deeper bow. "How can I be of service?"

Everess smiled. "Ah," he said. "That's the question, isn't it?"

"It's certainly the one I just asked," said Ironfoot.

"A scholar, and a wit as well." Everess smiled. If he was insulted by Ironfoot's somewhat insolent comment, it didn't show. "I can see that you're a busy man, so I'll be as direct as possible. Come walk with me, won't you?" He picked up a walking stick that had been leaning against his leg and pointed outside.

Ironfoot took Everess through the camp to the edge of the crater, and waved him forward. "This is the best place to go down," he said.

"Oh, I don't need to go down there," said Everess. "I've been here once before, the week after it happened. Once was enough for me, I can assure you."

Ironfoot was stymied. "Sorry, Lord Everess, but if you're not here to tour the site, what is it you're here for?"

"You," said Everess. "I'm here about you, Master Falores."

"Please, call me Ironfoot, sir. Most everyone does."

"Indeed," said Everess. "Well, where can we walk where it doesn't smell like a tannery and we may speak in private?"

"In the mornings the wind comes from the north; it smells nice down by the river."

"Lead the way," said Everess. "Ironfoot."

They walked down the path toward the river, to the spot where the team did their laundry. The river snaked around the wreckage of the city to the north, and Ironfoot headed in that direction.

"You're a very interesting fellow, you know," said Everess. "A study in contradiction, as they say."

"Thank you, sir," said Ironfoot. "I like to think myself unique."

"A shepherd's son from a tiny village who managed to parlay a single tour in the Gnomic War into an admission to Queensbridge. And now here you are years later, a respected thaumaturge, and a tenured professor at the most prestigious university in all of Faerie. That's beyond interesting. That's damnably impressive."

"Thank you," said Ironfoot. "Though fortune played a large part in it."

"Fortune only takes one so far," said Everess. "You've got a fine mind and you're a fine soldier."

"I don't mean to be critical, sir, but I'm well aware of who I am and what I've done. May I ask what it is you're leading up to?"

Everess laughed, a barking noise that made Ironfoot uncomfortable. Ironfoot smiled in return.

Everess let his smile fade. He looked out over the river. The light from the rising sun behind them skipped across its surface. "I'm aware of what it is you're doing here, what it is you're trying to accomplish," he said.

"Is that so?"

"I also know that the dean of your college at Queensbridge thinks it's impossible, and is attempting to have the project suspended."

"It's expensive," said Ironfoot. "And for all I know it may come to nothing."

"For all your talent, son, you're not the best politician."

"Not something I've ever aspired to be."

They came to a steep rise in the path, and Everess stopped talking for a moment to pick his way up it, using his walking stick to climb. When they reached the top he stopped, admiring the view. The ruined city was behind them, and the river valley below them was farmland, much of it gone fallow now that the city it once fed was gone.

"Do you know what my position is, Ironfoot?" asked Everess.

"I don't, I'm afraid. As you pointed out, knowledge of politics isn't among my many astonishing qualities."

"I'm the minister of foreign affairs, which means I have a great responsibility to this land. And in order to execute that responsibility I must have only the best and most talented men and women working under me."

"Are you offering me a job, sir?"

"What if I told you that if you were to come work for me, I would fund any thaumatic research you chose to pursue while at the same time allowing you some physical diversion as well?"

"Sir?"

"It was you who stole across the border through the Contested Lands in order to examine an ancient Arami excavation, was it not? An Unseelie expedition, at that?"

"It *was* interesting."

"Indeed! We thought you were a spy for the longest time until we vetted you."

"You've been watching me? I don't understand."

"Only the best and most talented," repeated Everess. "I don't approach just everyone with these offers."

"What makes you think I'd leave the university?" asked Ironfoot.

"I know exactly why you'd leave it, and that you're considering leaving already."

"You do? And why is that?"

"Because you're bored."

Ironfoot had no rejoinder to that.

"I appreciate the offer," said Ironfoot after a moment, "but as you're well aware, I'm in the middle of something fairly important here."

"Oh, I quite agree," said Everess. "And one of my preconditions for your coming to work at the Ministry would be that you complete that work. As you can guess, we're more than a little interested in its outcome."

"I know," said Ironfoot. He turned away from the river and looked down at the crater. "I'm not sure I know how I feel about potentially handing the plans for the thing that did *that* over to anyone."

"If it's to be used," said Everess, "I prefer that it be used on the Unseelie rather than us."

"Yes," said Ironfoot. "I suppose I do, too."

"Good then. When you get back to the City Emerald, I'll send you a sprite."

They stood silently together, looking down at what was once Selafae, and then turned and walked back down the path.

Four days later it was finished. Ironfoot collected the last of the readings, which would be mapped in the comfort of his rooms back at Queensbridge. The tents were struck, the army guard removed. The Arcadian priests and loved ones, kept away for so many months, streamed into the ruined city— the priests to administer beatitudes; the relatives looking for keepsakes, bones, trinkets . . . anything to remind them of what they'd lost. It was an emotional moment, and Ironfoot had no desire to get caught up in it any further than he already was.

Returning to the Queensbridge campus was like coming home. He couldn't remember the air in the City Emerald smelling so fresh, or the colors being so vivid. For weeks and weeks his entire life had been gray dust and acrid tar, and nights spent hunched over the map. Despite his urgent need to finish the project, he was almost pleased that the minor emergencies that had cropped up in his absence took him away from it for a time. He needed to get some distance from it.

There were message sprites lined up against the office window, bored out of their little minds, all of them clamoring to be the first to deliver its message and disappear. He took them all in turn, scribbling little notes to himself. A dinner invitation from a love-struck female colleague; a meeting request from the dean that could certainly wait. And a simple message from Lord Everess.

"He says he wants you to come over to his office and talk and so on and so forth," said Everess's sprite.

Ironfoot took the tiny creature in hand and said, "Maybe you could just tell him I'm busy."

The sprite's face took on an air of abused hospitality. "Well, he's not going to be too pleased with that, I can tell you. He's a lord, you know. Very fancy. He wears a hat and smokes a pipe. I don't see you with a hat or a pipe, so I guess he wins. Ha!"

Ironfoot had a soft spot for message sprites, though he wasn't quite sure why.

"You think so?" he asked. "You think I don't have a pipe and a hat around here someplace?"

The sprite sniffed. "I know you don't because yesterday I got really bored and I rifled through all of your stuff."

"Clever sprite."

"You think so? You really think so? Because nobody else thinks so, that's for sure. Do you have any roast beef?"

"Excuse me?"

"I like roast beef. I like the smell of it, and I like people who like it. But I can't eat it myself because sprites are herbivores, and it's the greatest tragedy of my life except for when my family died that time."

"Sorry," said Ironfoot. "No roast beef."

"Darn," said the sprite.

"Go on," said Ironfoot. "Send back my message. I think I have some parsley somewhere around here. You can have that."

"Uh, yeah, funny thing about that parsley," said the sprite, flitting up toward the open window. "Remember what I said about rifling through your stuff?"

Ironfoot had done every errand he could think of, returned every message, even cleaned his apartments and straightened the papers in his office. What was he trying to avoid? He'd been so impatient to get back to the city, and now that he was here, he couldn't stop stalling.

The map loomed from the corner of his office. It was rolled up and stored in a tube that was taller than he was, sealed with his own university signet. It called to him, and part of him wanted to answer it, but part of him wanted to set fire to it.

Why? Was this guilt? Was he worried about working on a weapon, about providing the key to re-creating the thing? He didn't think so, to be honest. As much as it might bother him intellectually, it didn't spur this gut reaction. Was it the eeriness of it, the smell of death and tar and gray dust that seemed to emanate from it, even though it produced no actual scent? No, that wasn't it, either.

He knew what it was, but couldn't admit it.

The next morning he awoke early, poured a strong cup of coffee, and forced himself to face the map. He unrolled it in the small parlor of his apartments, where it took up the entire floor, requiring him to lug the settee into the kitchen. He had the final measurements from the intensity gauges stacked neatly on a small stool next to his mug. He took quill and ruler in hand, and began working.

Once the data were entered, there were calculations to be done. These he did on lined sheets of linen paper that he ordered specially from the campus stationery. With each result, a new line appeared on the map. A web was emerging, a pattern. That was good. But still, that unsettling feeling would not leave him. The feeling was linked to that tar smell that he couldn't quite place, the memory it spurred that he could not recall. As the pattern grew, so did the feeling of dread inside him.

When he next looked up, the clock on the mantel read after midnight. The fire had died down in the fireplace, and he realized that he was cold. He stoked the fire, poured himself a whiskey, and went back to work.

He finished the formulaic interpolations around dawn. He'd lost count of the pots of coffee he'd drunk, now measured only in the level of queasiness in his stomach and the frequency with which he'd had to visit the privy. The web was complete, more or less. Some of the data had been lost. Some of the measurements, he was certain, had been faked. One region in particular was a total loss, the readings totally inconsistent with any of the others. It had been handled by the son of a lord whose father had pressed him into the assignment believing that it would reinforce the boy's character. Ironfoot could have told him that there was nothing there to reinforce.

Regardless, what he had was enough, and now the work could begin in earnest. He copied the pattern from the map onto a new sheet of linen paper—large, but not so big as the original map. Only the pattern remained, with detailed figures noting the invocative spectra, the normalization factors. The web stood in front of him, begging to be understood. It was a pattern, yes, but what did it mean? In his imagination about this moment, he'd assumed that the answer would leap out at him at this point. These exact physical components. This precise juggling of Elements, Motion, and Poise, and perhaps any four other Gifts that he could theorize being involved. He was damn clever. It should all have been there, leaping out at him. But it wasn't. The pattern implied nothing. The pattern meant nothing. It was only itself. It suggested things, certainly, but only impossibilities.

Ironfoot awoke. It was late afternoon. He'd fallen asleep at some point, still contemplating the pattern, still frustrated. He opened the shades and let the (morning? afternoon?) sun illuminate the pattern. Still nothing. He stood it upside down. Nothing. He held it up to the window, viewing the pattern through the back of the page. Still nothing.

It gnawed at him, this sensation that the key to its mystery was just outside his grasp. The Einswrath was an explosive—there had to be an Elements component to it. It was a delayed reaction, so it had to use the Gift of Binding as well. But what components? Which bindings? There was no binding ever created to hold in that amount of Elemental force, and no way to trigger it from such a distance. So what, then? It was right there in front of him. So why couldn't he see it?

The dread inside had grown into a fever. This was what he'd truly been afraid of. This was the source of the dread that had been welling up inside him ever since he'd returned to Queensbridge.

He had the pattern complete in front of him.

And he didn't understand it.

He turned toward the wall and lashed out with his fist, making a strangely satisfying crack in the plaster, though the pain that followed wasn't worth it. Raw failure sunk into him like a stone through mud.

You can do better than this, came the voice from inside.

He was disturbed from his misery by a message sprite tapping at the window. It looked familiar.

"Hey, handsome! Open up!" the thing shouted.

He tried to ignore it, but it just kept rapping on the windowpane, calling, then shouting, then howling expletives. He pulled himself out of the chair and shuffled across the room, stepping on the map and not caring. He opened the window, and the sprite flew in and alit on the edge of the chair in which he'd been sitting.

"What do you want?" he said.

"Wow, it took you long enough," said the sprite, sticking its tongue out for emphasis. "What are you, deaf or something? You weren't deaf last time. Did you stand too near something really loud? Because that can happen sometimes."

Ironfoot stared at the sprite, all of his fondness for it having evaporated in his desolation.

"I have feelings too, you know!" said the sprite, stamping its foot soundlessly. "Of course, my feelings are quite shallow, and can easily be repaired with a yummy stalk of parsley, or better yet . . ." The sprite paused, rubbing its tiny hands together. "Celery!"

"Enough already!" Ironfoot shouted, stunned at the anger in his voice. The sprite fell backward, swore loudly, then flitted up again, raising its head gingerly above the back of the chair.

"Wow, you sure got mean."

"I'm sorry," said Ironfoot, trying to be patient. "I've had a hard day. What's your message?"

"Lord Everess replies that he's extra sad you won't come see him. Except he said it in a less nice way."

The sprite thought for a moment, tapping its finger on its forehead. "There was something else, too. Something important. Let's see. Lord Everess . . . extra sad and so on . . . celery . . ."

It snapped its tiny fingers. "Oh, yeah! He wants to know if you're done with your map-thingy yet. He was just blah blah blah about that map."

"I see," said Ironfoot. "Thank you."

"Oh, happy day, you like me again!" it said, looking at him with a loopy grin. "You want to be my boyfriend? I realize that there's a serious size difference that could present some interesting physical challenges, but I'm willing to work through it if you are."

Ironfoot sighed. Maybe this was what he liked about message sprites: their absurdity. Nothing could ever truly upset them because they had no real feelings to begin with.

The sprite flew up and wrapped its arms around his finger. "I want to have your big fat Elvish babies!" it cried theatrically.

"Tell Everess I'll come and see him tomorrow," he said.

"Okay! This is the best day ever!" shouted the sprite, and it zipped out of the window.

chapter five

The city is old, older than anyone knows or suspects, save its ruler. There are myriad tales of the founding of the Seelie Kingdom and the birth of the City Emerald. Some are religious explanations; some are histories cobbled together by scholars based on the evidence of stones and documents so ancient that to expose them to light is to destroy them. Still others are the writings of retrocognitives, though even they will admit that theirs is an art rather than a science.

There is the official history, of course, taught to schoolchildren, that Regina Titania caused the ground to be leveled and the stones of the Great Seelie Keep to rise into place during the *Rauane Envedun-e*, the Age of Purest Silver. Like most legends of the *Rauane*, however, the story is often told with a wink, and the queen's official biographers parrot it with a telling blandness.

The city's original name was Car-na-una, which in Thule Fae meant "the first true thing," or perhaps "the basis of reality," and whatever the origin of the name, it is evocative of the feeling that the city often arouses in visitors; there is a weight, a feeling of solidity and eternity that resonates in the stones and in the art of their arrangement.

The poet Wa'on remarked in his *Journals* that "it is not the city itself that provokes this emotion, this unconscious awe. Rather, it appears as if it is something *beneath* the city, a deeper truth upon which it was built. The City Emerald is ancient, yes, but what lies beneath it is older still. Something older than Fae, older than words or memories. A giant that slumbers, while the city and its inhabitants crawl across its massive frame like fleas on a dog, each unaware of the others' presence. As I passed through the gates I had a sudden fear that the leviathan might awake and stretch its limbs and I would be crushed. By the morning, however, the feeling was gone, and I would not have remembered it save that I had noted it in the margin of a book."

The City Emerald has a reputation as the most beautiful city in the Seelie Kingdom and perhaps in the entire world of Faerie. Even its most ardent admirers, however, have sometimes felt a momentary chill within its walls, sensing the presence of something just outside the edge of perception; something too large to be real; something that has already swallowed them whole.

—Stil-Eret, "Unpopular Reflections on the Capital," from *Travels at Home and Abroad*

The Evergreen Club was the most exclusive in the City Emerald. As a Seelie lord, Silverdun was granted a lifetime membership, and had spent a considerable amount of time here during his all-too-brief years as a carefree young noble.

A quiet servant met him at the entrance and guided him down a hallway of polished mahogany paneling that glinted in the light of perfectly tuned witchlamps in silver sconces. They passed through the main dining room, a sea of white tablecloths and expensive clothing and aristocratic half-smiles. Heads rose as he passed, but few of the diners recognized him, and even these looked away, uninterested. Before his imprisonment at Crere Sulace, before his long journey with Mauritane, before his disfigurement at the hand of Faella, they would all have known him, the ladies especially. But those days were gone.

As always, thoughts of Faella haunted him. Despite what she'd done to his face, he could not blame her, or be angry with her. He'd deserved it. And if not for breaking off their brief affair, then for any number of similar insensitivities in his checkered past.

The servant stopped at the entrance to a private dining room, where Lord Everess sat with a man Silverdun recognized as Baron Glennet, who held one of the highest posts in the House of Lords, and an elderly woman he didn't recognize. They were sipping on a floral broth that smelled wonderful.

Everess and Glennet rose when Silverdun entered, and the woman nodded. Her sash identified her as a guildmistress.

"Am I late?" asked Silverdun.

"Not at all," said Everess, pumping his hand. "Right on time!"

Silverdun bowed. "Baron Glennet I know by reputation, but I'm afraid the guildmistress and I haven't had the pleasure."

"Of course," said Everess. "Perrin Alt, Lord Silverdun, may I introduce Guildmistress Heron, our illustrious secretary of states."

"I hardly think myself illustrious," said Heron. "The foreign minister exaggerates, as is his wont." She was elderly, just this side of ancient, but her eyes shone with intelligence. She cast a slight disapproving glance at Everess, who did not miss it. Silverdun liked her already.

"Come, Silverdun, sit," said Glennet. "We've much to discuss!" Glennet had a long reputation as a conciliator; he'd engineered any number of compromises within the House of Lords, and between the House of Lords and the House of Guilds, two bodies that could scarcely agree on the time of day, let alone governance. He too was old, but his exuberance gave him a semblance of youth.

"I'm afraid my conversational skills have atrophied in recent months," said Silverdun, sitting. A waiter noiselessly placed a bowl of broth in front of him.

"Ah, yes," said Glennet. "The aristocrat monk! I'm pleased we were able to steal you from your contemplation for dinner."

"It would appear that monastic life does not suit me," said Silverdun, a bit embarrassed and trying not to show it.

"Well, you are to be commended for attempting such an . . . unusual path," said Heron. "But I believe that the wider roads are wider for a reason, if you take my meaning."

"Of course," said Silverdun, taking her meaning and liking her somewhat less as a result.

"I'm just glad Baron Glennet was able to pull himself away from the card table in order to join us," said Heron.

Glennet's easy smile faltered. "We all have our little sins, Guildmistress." Not "Secretary."

Secretary Heron was about to comment further when waiters appeared, removing the broth and replacing it with roasted quail, in a sauce of raisins and bee pollen and a liquor Silverdun couldn't identify. He took a slow bite and waited for someone to tell him what the point of this dinner was. Not a social gathering, to be sure, as Everess and Heron clearly disliked one another.

Glennet dabbed at his chin as though it were a fine art. "Secretary Heron," he began, "what news have we of Jem-Aleth? Has his social life improved at all?"

"No," Heron said primly. "Our beloved ambassador to Mab continues to be politely tolerated at court, mostly ignored, and never invited to state dinners. Or teas. Or children's spinet recitals."

"He told me that a city praetor invited him to a mestina once," said Everess, "but it was one of the bawdy type and he left ten minutes in."

"Yes," said Secretary Heron, rolling her eyes, "but what Jem-Aleth didn't tell you is the that the only reason Praetor Ma-Pikyra invited him in the first place was that he'd confused him with somebody else."

Silverdun watched the back-and-forth, mildly interested in the idle chatter, but his thoughts were more concerned with the reason for his own presence here. "I knew Jem-Aleth in school," he said, reminding them that he was still in the room. "Nobody liked him then, either. The reason for the Unseelie cold shoulder may be personal as well as political."

"Quite the contrary," Everess said, unable to allow Silverdun to have useful information that had not come from him. "Before last year's Battle of Sylvan chilled our relations with our Unseelie neighbors substantially, Jem-Aleth was quite well liked in the City of Mab. Though whether that's a compliment to Jem-Aleth or an insult to the Unseelie, I can't say." He chuckled, looked around for an answering chuckle, got none, and plowed ahead. "Regardless, we've received not a whit of useful information from him in a year. He sends his dispatch each week, filled with scraps of information culled from publicans, maids, and would-be courtiers and sycophants, but even if there were anything useful buried in them, we have no method of responding to them in . . . useful ways."

Everess shot a glance at Silverdun and narrowed his eyes, smiling at Silverdun as though he were a prize pupil. "And there could not be a more urgent time to follow up, I fear. Don't you agree, Silverdun?"

All eyes turned to Silverdun. He flashed his trademark charming smile, but he found Everess's look discomfiting. What was Everess getting him into?

"I've been indisposed, Lord Everess," he said after a long sip of wine. "Perhaps you'd care to educate me."

Everess sighed, annoyed.

"You are aware, perhaps, that the Seelie Kingdom was nearly dragged into a full-scale war with Mab last year. You were there when it happened, after all."

"I seem to recall, yes."

"And you recall further that during the course of that altercation, the Unseelie unleashed a weapon so powerful that it destroyed the entire city of Selafae in a single blast?"

Silverdun's smirk faded a bit. "Yes. I remember that as well. The Einswrath, I believe they call it?"

"Yes," said Secretary Heron, scowling. "After the Chthonic god of war. Most unseemly."

Everess ignored her. "Then you are aware, Silverdun, that things have changed."

"Here we go," said Heron, her scowl widening. "Foreign Minister Everess's stock lecture has begun in earnest."

Now it was Silverdun's turn to ignore her. "What things, exactly, have changed, as you see it?"

Everess clenched his teeth, looking at Silverdun as though he were a child. "Everything, man. The balance of power, the status of relations between our kingdom and the other nations of the world and other worlds. The very nature of warfare itself."

It was true, Silverdun knew. The implications of a weapon powerful enough to level an entire city were enormous. No one, however, seemed to agree on what those implications might be. But clearly Everess was about to tell him.

"Go on," Silverdun said.

Everess reached for a glass of brandy, took a generous swallow, and launched into what Silverdun assumed was the stock lecture to which Heron had referred. "Certainly you can see that we have reached the end of an era, Silverdun. A cornerstone of propriety has been annihilated before our eyes. Your compulsory army days were long after my own, but you were certainly taught as I was: cavalry, battle mages, infantry in evenly spaced lines politely slaughtering one another on the battlefield. All those pretty tactics and stratagems, all those brilliant battles of old, always applicable. We used them against the Western Valley upstarts the first time they rebelled; we used them against the Gnomics a dozen years ago, and against the Puktu barbarians in Mag Mell a thousand years before I was born. But now all that has come to an end."

"I understand what you're saying, Everess," said Silverdun. "But what of it?"

"If Mab had one of those things, then she's certainly got more of them. We can only assume that she hasn't got a flying city full of them, or we wouldn't be having this conversation today. We'd be in an Unseelie work camp fetching water, or we'd be ashes in a hole somewhere."

"It tells us nothing of the kind," said Heron. "I believe that what it tells us is that she *hasn't* got any more of them."

"What this tells us," continued Everess, "is that the kind of war we were trained to fight has become obsolete in a single blaze. This new weapon of Mab's means that an army is no longer necessary at all! All one needs is a trebuchet and a tailwind and he can lay waste to anything he sees fit, from a safe and happy distance."

"Nothing will stop war," said Heron. "And war with Mab will soon be inevitable, as it has been twice before, and nearly was a year ago.

"I could not disagree more," said Everess. "We are entering the age of a new kind of war. What matters now is not just where our troops are placed.

What matters is information and influence. We need to know what Mab's game is. We need to know what Mab's allies are up to, and where our own allies stand. We need to know how many of these accursed things Mab's got, how many she plans to build, and how long before she decides to fly south and begin incinerating the Seelie Kingdom. And we need to do whatever we can to disrupt that process at all costs."

He stared at Heron. "With the right tools, we *can* prevent that war."

Everess smiled at Silverdun. "And I believe that you are just the man to help in that endeavor."

"You want me to be a spy?"

"More than that," said Heron drily. "He wants you to become a Shadow." Heron made a melodramatic spooky face at him.

"You mean the mythical spies from the Second Unseelie War?" asked Silverdun. "I was under the impression that they didn't actually exist."

"Oh, but they did," said Everess. "And they shall again."

"This is a lovely fantasy," said Secretary Heron. "But the way to stop Mab is through diplomacy and, if it comes to it, war. All of your playing at spies won't change that, Everess."

Glennet had been observing without comment. "I understand your objections, Madam Secretary," he said, leaning in. "But I'm afraid that the Foreign Committee in Corpus is willing to give Lord Everess the benefit of the doubt." He paused, giving Heron a conciliatory look. "For the time being."

He looked at Silverdun. "And for what it's worth, I agree that Lord Silverdun would be an excellent choice."

"Fine," said Heron. "Play your games. But understand that I will expect complete reports of all your activities."

"Done," said Everess. "I'd be a fool not to keep you apprised of our progress."

"And if I find out you've been keeping vital information from me," she said, "there will be repercussions."

"If all goes as you believe, Secretary Heron," said Everess, sniffing, "then there will be nothing of value to withhold."

The conversation moved on to other topics, though the chill between Everess and Heron never thawed. Silverdun, however, barely paid attention.

"What the hell was that all about?" said Silverdun. They were at a table at a café on the Promenade, just outside the Foreign Ministry building, a few blocks from the Evergreen Club. It was night, and the Promenade Green was filled with musicians, jugglers, and solo mestines. It was dark, the Green illuminated only by witchlit lanterns. Nightbirds sang from hidden perches.

"If there's one thing that ought to be obvious," Silverdun continued, "it's that I have no interest in politics or governance. When I left school and took up my title, I sat in Corpus exactly once, and I was so bored I stopped paying attention after about ten minutes. I voted on six bills, and to this day I have no idea what they were."

"Oh, stop it," said Everess. "That's not why I asked you here."

"Then why am I here? You come to the temple with vague presentiments of doom, talk me out of my cozy monastic life, and now suddenly you're offering me a job as a spy?"

Everess took two glasses of brandy from a passing waitress, a wisp of a girl with conjured wings who fluttered a few inches off the ground. He handed one of the brandies to Silverdun.

"Calm down, lad. There's someone I'd like you to meet before we begin the sales pitch."

Everess looked up over Silverdun's shoulder. "Ah. Here he comes now."

Silverdun turned and looked. At first he saw no one. No one that Everess might be referring to, anyway. A jongleur, a skald, a mestine conjuring dancing bears. "Who might that be?"

As he said it, he noticed someone approaching, someone vaguely familiar. The recognition of his presence was like that of an optical illusion in which the eye is required to swap the foreground of an image for the background. Two faces or a vase. No one there or someone.

This no one was nearly upon them before Silverdun recognized him. Odd. Not only did his dress and manner cause him to stand out boldly in the mostly upper-class Promenade, but he also walked with a heavily pronounced limp, dragging his left leg behind him, using a thick wooden cane in its place.

"Lord Silverdun, I'd like you to meet Chief Paet. Paet, Lord Silverdun."

"Hello," said Paet simply. His expression was affectless, his eyes slightly squinted though it was night. The winged waitress was passing back by, and Paet took a drink from her tray without her noticing. He sat.

"I'm no expert on manners," said Silverdun drily, "but I believe you're supposed to bow and tug a forelock when you meet a lord of the realm, Paet."

Paet looked Silverdun in the eye and shrugged. "Drag me before the Sumptuary Court then."

Silverdun looked to Everess, who was saying nothing. "Well, this is a kick in the teeth, isn't it? Insolent one, this Paet."

"That's 'Chief' to you, milord," said Paet. His expression hadn't changed at all during this exchange.

Silverdun frowned. "I believe I'm supposed to kill you for talking to me like that. I'm an iconoclast, however, so I'll wait to hear why Everess here has inflicted you on me before I do."

Everess laughed out loud. "Ignore him, Paet. He won't really kill you."

Paet shrugged. "He's welcome to try."

Everess sighed. "Now, now. This isn't how I wanted this meeting to go at all. Paet, calm yourself. Silverdun, shut your mouth for a moment and listen."

Paet and Silverdun eyed each other carefully. Silverdun wasn't as disapproving of Paet as he'd let on. The impropriety was nothing; he'd been treated far worse at Crere Sulace, by prison guards who, due to their low birth, could have been hanged for looking him in the eye. It was important to keep up appearances, however, lest someone mistake him for a tiresome social reformer. Still, there was something disquieting about Paet.

"Earlier this evening," said Everess, "we discussed the Shadows. The 'mythical spies,' as you put it."

Silverdun pointed at Paet. "Are you telling me that this fellow here is a Shadow?"

"Not *a* Shadow," said Paet. "*The* Shadow. There's only one. Now, anyway."

"This is true?" asked Silverdun.

"He's quite serious," said Everess, nodding. "When the group was disbanded after the Treaty of Avenus, it was decided to keep one Shadow in service into perpetuity. In case they were needed again."

"And you believe they are needed."

"It requires a certain type of person to do the work that must now be done. And I know that you are exactly that sort of person."

"I?" said Silverdun. "The 'rude villein' whose most recent distinction was being the first monk in history ever to be given the sack?"

Paet smiled at Everess. Under the squint, which appeared to be a permanent feature, the smile looked rueful, whether it was or not. "He makes a fair case against himself, Everess. Perhaps he's not the man you thought."

"Yes he is," said Everess, who had developed his own squint now. Silverdun had a feeling this wasn't a good thing. "And despite his endless protestations, he knows it. He only needs to realize it."

"So, what? You want me to become the new Shadow? Take over from Paet here?"

"No," said Everess. "You're going to lead a small team of Shadows. The group is being re-formed. Chief Paet here runs the day-to-day affairs of the Information Division. You'll be the lead Shadow."

"You want me to work for him?" said Silverdun, incredulous.

"You need him," said Everess.

"More than you can possibly know," said Paet.

Silverdun scowled. "Are you always this . . . ominous?"

Paet tapped his cane on the ground. "You'll be hearing from me shortly," he said.

Silverdun and Everess watched him leave. Silverdun blinked, and that same odd trick of the eye occurred, foreground into background, and Paet was gone.

"Interesting fellow, isn't he?" said Everess, once he'd vanished.

"I can't say I'm in love."

Everess chuckled. "Give him time. Paet's a good man. His experience has made him what he is. All for the love of Seelie. The Seelie Heart; isn't that what Mauritane called it?"

"Mauritane excels at convincing others to fling themselves at death in the service of abstractions." Silverdun sighed. "You're not helping your cause."

"This is good work," said Everess. "We need you. And let's be frank. You need us."

A remark leapt to Silverdun's lips, but he suppressed it. Perhaps if he stopped arguing the point, Everess would shut up about it.

"Tell me this, Everess," said Silverdun, quiet. "Was I chosen for this because of my strengths or because of my ability to get intelligence from the Arcadians?"

"I never do anything for only one reason," said Everess. "Either way, it's time for you to stop pissing around and get to work."

Silverdun wanted to disagree, but couldn't.

chapter six

"You're mad," said the goat, hopping up and down.
"I am indeed," the bear replied. "But there is strength
in madness."

—from "The Goat and the Bear," Seelie fable

The Copperine House sat on an estate nearly a day's ride outside the City Emerald, set back from the Mechesyl Road, just beyond a small ridge dotted with spruce and fir trees. This was the beginning of the Western Valley, where the high mountaintops held snow year-round, and the evergreens were the only trees that grew. Here, though, the conifers mixed in with deciduous life, speckling the landscape with points of darkness in a world of color.

The house was relatively new, less than three hundred years old. It had been donated by the sixtieth Lady Copperine after the unfortunate incident that claimed both her son's life and the lives of the twelve others in the café with him when he'd lost control of his Gift of Elements and turned them all into sand, including himself. The incident was hushed up by the Royal Guard, a fire set, and the heir apparent to the Copperine title was mourned appropriately. Devastated, his mother donated the family estate to the Crown, with the explicit instructions that it be used to prevent other such tragedies. Once her affairs were settled, Lady Copperine drank poison and joined her son in death.

The house itself was large and rambling, having been added on to and spellturned rather haphazardly in its day. The unfortunate lady's great-uncle had been something of an amateur turner and had made a number of questionable choices regarding the estate's architectural layout. Now the house was three times as large as it had been when built, though there were rooms in it that had been lost forever. The residents of Copperine House had it that an unlucky niece had been inside one of the lost rooms when it was badly turned, and haunted the building into the present day.

Sela's favorite place was the tiered terrace that overlooked the small valley behind the house. There was nothing artificial in this view. Only trees, sky, earth, and small animals that could sometimes be cajoled into eating corn from Sela's hand. If she were able, Sela would have waited for a rainy day, then stepped down each stone tier, walked barefoot through the grass as the rain plastered her hair against her face, and disappeared into the forest, never to be seen again.

This was a fantasy, of course. Beyond the terrace was a fence of pure Motion that would stop her in her tracks, and unpleasantly so, were she to take more than a few steps into the lawn. That the small animals could come and go through it while she could not was some small comfort to Sela. The part of her that was them, at least, was free. This was something she knew intellectually, but could not bring herself to feel. Not in this place. Not with the Accursed Object wrapped around her arm.

The Accursed Object was a band of cold iron, three inches thick, that encircled her upper arm, resting snugly against her skin. It was coated with the barest plating of silver to keep it from burning, but its presence disrupted her *re* enough that she could barely think, let alone employ her unique skills.

Some others in Copperine House attempted to escape from time to time. Horeg the Magnificent, a mestine of some great former renown, once chewed off his own arm at the shoulder, but the attendants discovered him bleeding to death halfway to the road and dragged him back in. All the way he shouted to them that he had a performance at the Principal Theater that could not be missed. Once it was all over, the attendants had whispered in Sela's hearing that the Principal had been closed for over six hundred years, and Horeg the Magnificent wasn't *that* magnificent. He was only forty-five.

Panner-La, a military commander, had been able to dig a tunnel forty feet long beneath the house before he was caught. He'd managed the feat by whittling away at his own Accursed Object just enough to use Elements to turn the earth to air, an inch or two a day, over the course of twenty years.

Many attempts at escape had been made, but Sela didn't know of any that had succeeded.

The cold iron bands kept most of them in check, but there were some whose Gifts were so strong that they could not be fully stifled. There was Brinoni, the daughter of a courtier in Titania's court, whose Premonitory Gift was so powerful that she lived her entire life in the future, several hours ahead of reality. Her body jerked and dragged as she attempted to move in time with her future actions. Her speech was so much nonsense, always responding to words as yet unsaid, and thus disrupting her own visions. Brinoni lived in a future that no one else would ever experience, the future that would have been had she not been there to see it.

Some of the patients' Gifts were so extreme and so dangerous that there was nothing for them but to keep them sedated at all times. Prin had once been a Master of the Gates, but had been caught between worlds and lost his mind. Left fully conscious, Prin was capable of transporting the entire house and a good portion of the countryside to another world entirely, or to one of the dark places, or of spellturning the house into itself. Sela thought his case was unbearably sad, and would have put Prin out of his misery if she'd been able to work out a way to do it without being caught. Because even with the band around her arm, Sela could feel Prin's anguish despite the drugs they gave him. His misery ran so deeply that she'd almost managed to form a thread toward him. But not quite. There hadn't been any threads in quite some time.

In Sela's case, the band was highly effective. Her talent required concentration, and the Accursed Object kept her just off-kilter enough to render her essentially powerless. Of all the patients at the Copperine House, Sela was the only one who was not mad. Nor was she a danger to herself. What kept Sela at Copperine was the simple fact that nobody knew what else to do with her.

Sela understood that she could not be allowed free. Or at least, she understood that her keepers believed that to be the case. Sela knew—or remembered knowing, as her mind was one of the many things that the band hampered—that, if free, she could find a way to be of no danger to anyone. But given her history, it would be difficult to convince anyone of that.

Thinking of her history led her to thoughts of Milla. The thoughts of Milla, on those occasions when they came, overtook her and she broke down. Today was no exception. While the rain pattered down just past the terrace awning, Sela experienced Milla's pain all over again, still fresh no matter how many Accursed Objects they wrapped around her limbs or how much bottled forgetfulness they forced down her throat. Milla was real, and Milla was dead, and it was Sela's fault. It was truth; a hideous truth. One that could never be undone.

Oh, Milla.

An attendant, seeing Sela weeping on the terrace, rushed to offer a handkerchief, a cool drink, a cucumber sandwich. Anything to calm and please. The conceit was that the patients at Copperine were, in fact, guests at a proper country estate, and the staff all behaved as though this were the case. Many of the patients chose to believe it, and those who didn't, like Sela, saw no reason to spoil the fantasy. It was nice being treated like a lady, even if the lady couldn't leave her estate. It was far better than what she'd grown up with.

The manor house is very large, bigger than anything Sela has ever seen. Bigger than anything she's ever dreamed of.

Mother told her that she was a very lucky girl, that she must do everything that Lord Tanen and his servants told her. She was Lord Tanen's ward now. Sela didn't know what that meant. Mother had said that she would come to visit Sela soon, but later Sela heard Mother and Father whispering in bed, and Father said, "Why did you lie to her? We'll never see her again." And Mother only cried and said, "What can I do?"

A beautiful room in the manor house has been prepared for her. It's so beautiful and fancy that at first she forgets all about Mother and Father, and the farm, and her friends in the village. At night, though, she cries and misses her family.

Lord Tanen calls the three old women "crones." He says that she is to do everything they tell her, and that if she does not, he will come back and punish her.

"Where will you be?" asks Sela.

"I will be in the city," he says. "But I will come to visit from time to time."

Lord Tanen is old, and his skin looks like Father's old saddle. His breath smells sour. She does not like him, so she is glad he is leaving.

"Don't you want to know why I've brought you here?" he asks her.

Sela hasn't thought about it. She doesn't know what a ward is, but she is a good girl and does as she's told.

"Why?" she asks, because he wants her to.

"Because I have searched far and wide for a special girl like you," he says. "Did you know that you were special?"

"No."

"Do you want to know what makes you special?"

"Okay."

"There might be something inside you called a Gift. Do you know what Gifts are?"

"Magic," says Sela. Everyone knows that. "There are twelve Gifts. But children don't have Gifts and, and farmers don't have them, either."

"That is mostly true," says Lord Tanen. "Children do not express their Gifts; they only manifest during puberty. But there are ways of knowing in advance. And while it is true that the lower classes show a far lower rate of manifestation, it is not unheard-of."

Sela doesn't understand what Tanen is saying, and is getting bored. She looks around her bedroom for something to play with.

"May I have a doll?" she asks.

"You won't have time for dolls," he says.

Sela was sitting quietly in the tearoom when Lord Everess stepped through the door, still shaking the rain from his hair. He was the sort who seemed jolly but, upon closer inspection, was anything but. Even with the Accursed Object damping her down, Sela could see it.

"Sela," said Everess with a curt bow, the benevolent recognition of a nobleman to a woman with no status whatsoever. Under normal conditions, it would have been impossible for Everess even to address her, so there was no appropriate greeting.

"Lord Everess," said Sela, rising and curtseying automatically, as she'd been taught since her earliest childhood. Always ready to please. Always ready to obey.

No. This was not Lord Tanen. All lords were not the same. That's what Everess had told her.

She looked him directly in the eye. "How may I be of service to you, Lord?"

Everess cracked a smile. He took a large pipe from the pocket of his voluminous overcoat and lit it, puffing quietly for a moment before speaking.

"Let me ask you a question, miss. How do you like it here?"

If Everess was expecting a polite response, he wasn't going to get one. "I despise it here," she said simply.

Everess laughed out loud. To him, she was a puppy nipping, nothing more. "Brutally honest as ever, yes. This place hasn't drained that out of you."

"I am what I was made to be," Sela said.

Everess watched her, puffing on his pipe, saying nothing. Letting the silence between them grow dense.

Finally, he spoke. "What is it that you want?" he asked.

"Excuse me?"

"For yourself. What is it that you want for yourself?"

"I've never been asked the question before." Sela thought back. No, it was true. At no time in her life had anyone ever asked her what she wanted; not about anything that mattered.

"Well, it's not a complicated question, however novel," Everess huffed. "If you despise Copperine House, as you say, then where is it that you'd prefer to go?"

Sela glared at him. "You of all people should know that I can't answer that question."

Everess smiled. Of course he knew. And he wanted to be sure that she was focused on what she owed him before he made whatever strange request he was about to make of her.

She decided to answer the question anyway. "I want to be useful," she said, crossing her hands on her lap. The muslin of her skirt settled softly. "I want to be . . . good. Do good."

"Ah," said Everess. "Meaning what, exactly?"

"I want for my life to . . . mean something. I sense the hours and days and years going by, and nothing I do means anything to anyone. I might as well not even exist. Sometimes I wish that I didn't."

Everess dragged a chair toward the love seat where she sat and planted himself in it, leaning forward. He took her cold hands in his, which were warm and meaty. She smelled tobacco and liquor on his breath.

"Sela," he said. "What if I told you I had an opportunity for you to be useful and good? More useful than you can possibly imagine?"

What game was Everess playing? What fancy of his was this? While Sela had been at Copperine, Everess had visited from time to time. They'd played draughts. He'd checked up on her, asked after her health, made sure she was being taken care of and treated properly. But she had never been under the illusion that he loved her or even cared for her as another Fae. She was a duty of his, and though she'd never understood the exact nature of that duty, she knew the reason for it. It was not the same reason that Lord Tanen had raised her, had invested so much in her upbringing, but it was not far different, she felt now.

"You misunderstand me, Lord Everess," Sela said, stiffening. "I did not say I wished to be used. I said I wished to be useful."

Again the smile. Sela could not think of anything she'd ever said to Everess that had wiped that smile off his face. Someday, she found herself thinking, she would find a way.

"I apologize profusely, miss," said Everess, leaning back and releasing her hands. "I did not mean to imply that."

"Then let us stop circling around it," said Sela. "What is it that *you* want?"

Everess stood and began making a lap around the room, inspecting the mantelpiece, sniffing at the condition of the wallpaper. "How long have you been at Copperine, Sela?"

More circling, then. "Ten years." She could just as easily have told him the number of days.

"Do you know why I brought you here?" he said.

"I have an assumption," said Sela. "At first, I simply assumed you were being kind, knowing so little of kindness as I did. After a time I came to believe that it was because you could simply think of nothing better to do with me. But now I know why."

"And why is that?"

"Because you believed that at some point I would become a valuable asset to you. And now that time has come."

"Well," said Everess, drawing out the word. "All three of your assumptions are true, to a greater or lesser degree. I did and still do feel very warmly toward you, Sela. And at the time, I certainly had no idea what was to be done with you. You don't really belong here, but I could never figure out where you did belong. And as for your being an asset, Sela . . ."

He paused, perhaps thinking of the right way to say it, then gave up. "It's true, of course. One doesn't get to where I am without understanding people and how they can be maneuvered into serving one's own ends."

"How noble," she said.

He ignored her. "But believe me when I say, Sela, that I do care for you. More than you think. And I want you to be happy."

Was this true? Maybe he thought it was true.

"Regardless, I've found a place for you. A place where you can use your talents. Where you can be of use to me. And where you can be truly useful. Does that interest you?"

Sela scoffed. "What difference does it make? I have no control over where I'm sent."

"Well, of course not. You're a ward of the Crown. I am, as a matter of law, your guardian and master. That is a matter beyond my control, and I wouldn't change it even if I could. But even though the choice is mine to make, I offer it to you. I require you to choose what I'm going to offer you of your own free will."

"Why?" she said, raising her voice. "What is this? What is it you want of me?"

Everess smiled again. "I want you to save the world, my dear. How useful would _that_ make you?"

Sela left the conversation with Everess feeling as though she knew less than she had going in. When she returned to her room, she discovered a pair of servants packing her things into new suitcases. Or, rather, one new suitcase, as there was nothing to put in the other. Four dresses, a hat, a book of poems, a hand mirror. Underthings. Not much else. That was all she owned in the world. Without a word, one of the servants closed and latched the one used suitcase and carried it out of the room. The other motioned her to follow him.

Outside, the rain had slowed to a drizzle. Everess stood by his carriage, an elaborate thing, fit for a nobleman of his stature. He was waving her forward.

This was Everess in a nutshell. He spoke to you of choices, of caring. But while he was offering you choices, your bags were being packed in the other room.

The carriage ride was bumpy and unpleasant. The new dress that Everess had purchased for her was stiff, and it scratched at her neck and wrists, though she had to admit she adored the glamoured pattern of poppies that gently waved across the skirt in a nonexistent breeze. The shoes were another matter. Detestable, evil things that pressed her toes together and bit at her heels. In Copperine House she'd worn slippers every day, and had forgotten that such evils as dress shoes existed. She'd once had hard calluses on her feet from wearing even more fashionable shoes than these, but that was in the past.

After nearly a full day's travel, the Mechesyl Road began to widen into a highway with several lanes of traffic on either side. Most were leaving the city. Peddlers with donkeys loaded with pots and pans, cheeses, sausages, intricately woven charms, potions, boots, belts, tiny birds, mice, wooden toys. All returning from the Grand Bazaar just outside the gates of the City Emerald. Soldiers on horseback riding in formation—the blue-gray coats of the Seelie Army, the deep red of the Royal Guard—carefully and nonchalantly keeping out of each other's way. A few pretty carriages such as the one in which she rode, off to nearby villas, mostly closed with curtains drawn, pulled by matched teams of white mares (these, explained Everess, were currently all the rage, taking care to point out his own pair). Men on horseback, groups of rough-looking men wearing swords and knives. Farmers with their carts carrying the day's leftover produce.

Then came the City Emerald. The carriage turned the corner at the crest of the hill and began to descend, and the city came into view, the sinking sun exploding from the surface of a wide lake and bathing the Great Seelie Keep in light. The keep was at the direct center of the city, built atop a hill that it was said Regina Titania raised from the ground with a wave of her wrist. Surrounding the keep were Titania's pleasure gardens, acre upon acre of real estate accessible only to the queen and her eunuch gardeners. From there the city radiated out in all directions. Spires of temples and cathedrals reaching to the sky, their windows flashing with sunlight as the carriage began to move downhill. Towers made of glass spirals that defied gravity, whose purpose was unknown to any save the queen herself. Buildings of every shape and size and age, some erected thousands of years in the past, some brand-new.

The City Emerald was ever changing, of every age, seemingly eternal. Sela had read about it many times, but had never seen it.

Surrounding the city like a projection of the Seelie Keep was the wall, a thing of deep and perplexing magic. It appeared to be no more than twenty feet tall, but by all accounts it was impossible to reach the top of it. Anyone was invited to climb it if they so wished, but no matter how much time they spent ascending it, the battlements remained forever out of reach. Or so Sela had been told. No place in all of Faerie was more steeped in legend and myth than the City Emerald, and the truth about it, whatever it was, was so deeply buried that it was impossible to sort out from the stories. Sela imagined that Regina Titania kept it that way on purpose. Who would be foolish enough to assault such a place? It was moot, because no foreign power had ever been allowed the opportunity.

The carriage continued down the hill, and over the course of an hour, the City Emerald continued to grow larger and larger in Sela's sight. Just when she thought it could not appear any grander, the carriage would pass through a stand of trees and it would emerge again in her vision, seeming twice as large as before. She had never seen a thing so enormous, but then, she had seen so little of the world. Only Lord Tanen's estate and Copperine House, and neither, apparently, was representative of the Seelie Kingdom at large.

Finally they reached the North Gate and were waved through without comment by the guards stationed there. The gate was not high, but it was very wide and allowed multiple lanes of traffic to pass side by side. For a moment there was darkness as they passed beneath the wall, and Sela felt a brief chill that was not merely a drop in temperature. Then they were through, and the City Emerald lay sprawled out before her.

The most recent buildings lined the streets nearest the gate. These streets were filled with shops and inns and stables. A sweet, almost pleasant smell drifted into the carriage—beer, sawdust, manure. A whiff of roasting pork found its way to her nose and she felt her salivary glands contract, realizing that she hadn't eaten since leaving Copperine House. Everess's nose twitched at the smell, and he adjusted the blinds on his side, lighting a scented candle in a sconce next to the window.

"Do you think we might eat soon?" Sela said, breaking the silence between them that had lasted almost the entire trip.

"What?" Everess said, starting. "Oh, yes. My apologies. I myself never eat more than one meal a day—I find eating to be a singular waste of time and do it as seldom as possible."

Looking at Everess's round belly, Sela imagined that his single meal must be quite something to behold.

"We'll be at my city home shortly, and I'll have the chef prepare a little something for us."

A little something turned out to be a feast the likes of which Sela had never seen: roasted grouse, a ham, a side of beef, with turnips, squash, pumpkin, potatoes, and beets. Bowls of rose petals and chrysanthemums were constantly refilled by servants—Sela stuck mostly to these, having never developed a taste for meat.

Everess's city home was at least the size of Copperine House, and in the middle of the city—on the Boulevard Laurwelana, which, Everess had pointed out, was the most exclusive street in the city. All Sela knew was that she felt comfortable here.

The street outside was loud and confusing. Strangers were everywhere. She would have to get used to strangers. She'd known everyone at Copperine House and understood how they fit. Even when new residents or staff arrived, she had a context in which to place them. But here in the city, everyone was new all the time. They came and went. She barely had time to get a sense of one before that one was gone and another came along. It made her head hurt.

"Are you well?" said Everess, pausing over a bite of ham.

"Yes," she said. She touched her forehead and it felt clammy. "I'd like to see my room, please."

The bedroom was papered in dark damask, and the bedclothes were a deep burgundy. Everess had remembered, at least, how she preferred her surroundings. Her clothes had already been unpacked and put away. Her few personal items were on a table by the bed.

She lied down, fully clothed, fingering the Accursed Object on her upper arm, wondering whether they were going to take it off of her. The thought both frightened and excited her.

But mostly frightened.

chapter seven

The Promenade extends from the southern (and always open) drawbridge of the Great Seelie Keep to the Houses of Corpus, where lords and guildsmen argue and maneuver and, from time to time, legislate the workings of Seelie government. Though Titania's rule is absolute, the complexities of day-to-day affairs she leaves to those who are affected by them more than she. The Seelie queen presides primarily over matters of state and, to a lesser extent, the management of the social aspect of Seelie life, which is, to the Fae mind, at least as important as the affairs of state, if not more so.

The drawbridge passes over the Grand Moat, which is more impressive for its beauty than for its defensive capabilities, especially considering that the Great Seelie Keep has never in recorded history been the target of an attack. The moat is home to a hundred species of fish and frog, and other creatures that are unseen but whose song emanates in a hush from the water, a sonorous plea that induces poets to weep.

The Promenade is the home to the many offices of Seelie government. The Foreign Ministry and the Secretariat of State reside in a stately, if dull, pile of stones on the Left Walk, and the Barrack, which houses the high command of the Seelie Army, sits opposite. The fact that these two buildings sit opposing one another is metaphorical fodder for political wags who frequently point out that the government and the army have been known to work at cross purposes more often than not.

The Barrack is a recent structure, a mere hundred years old. For many thousands of years, the army was housed in the Great Seelie Keep itself, but its oft-adversarial relationship with the Royal Guard, also (and still) quartered there, resulted in its removal to a safer distance.

—Stil-Eret, "The City Emerald,"
from *Travels at Home and Abroad*

Silverdun, having regained his taste for the dress of nobility, if not its pretenses, presented himself at the Barrack the morning after his dinner with Everess, Heron, and Glennet. A surly corporal took his calling card and bade him wait, then directed him to follow, walking at such a pace as to require that Silverdun trot along behind him. The corporal led Silverdun to a small meeting room, ushered him in, and closed the door. Alone, Silverdun sat drumming his fingers upon the table, looking out the window down at the Promenade where Seelie without any seeming cares strolled the wide avenue, laughing and talking in the noonday sun.

The door opened and Mauritane strode in, wearing a uniform that Silverdun had never seen him wear: that of the commander general of the Seelie Army.

"It's good to see you again, old friend," said Mauritane, gripping Silverdun's hand. In the year since they'd last met, Mauritane seemed to have aged five. Despite the few runnels of gray in his long braided hair, however, he looked content, perhaps even pleased. Silverdun couldn't remember ever having seen Mauritane appear content in all the years that he'd known the man.

"Married life and martial supremacy agree with you," said Silverdun. "How is Raieve?"

"Still in Avalon," said Mauritane, his look of contentment faltering. "We don't see each other often, but we make do."

"Still in love, then?"

"Very much." It was odd hearing Mauritane talk about love in the same voice that he used to talk about killing. He had a fairly narrow range of emotions, Silverdun recalled.

"And you?" said Mauritane. "I'm frankly surprised to see you here. The last I heard you'd devoted your life to Aba and were swinging censers at a temple." A hint of mockery?

Silverdun shifted uncomfortably in his chair. "That didn't work out quite as planned," he said. "Apparently I'm not cut out for the religious life. Or so everyone seems to believe."

Mauritane chuckled. "I could have told you that," he said. "Though I was always willing to give you the benefit of the doubt." He paused, then said, "When men fight together, they come to know each other in ways that are otherwise impossible. You play at the disaffected rogue, but there's a depth to you that you can't always hide."

Mauritane's judgment, concise and declarative as ever.

"I'll take that as a compliment and move on."

Mauritane finally sat. "It was meant as a compliment," he said.

He patted Silverdun on the shoulder, a gesture that didn't entirely work, but with Mauritane's Gift of Leadership, it was difficult not to be affected by it. "Now, what brings you to see me? Interested in joining the ranks? We're always looking for infantrymen, though I suppose we could bring you on as a chaplain."

A joke! Who was this fellow, so like Mauritane and yet so . . . pleasant?

"I assume, then," said Silverdun, "that Lord Everess hasn't told you about his plan to resurrect the Shadows?"

Mauritane's smile vanished. "What are you talking about?"

"Only last night I dined with Everess and a few other dignitaries. There was talk of war and an impassioned speech by Everess on its changing nature. Then Everess tried to recruit me into a merry band of spies, a revival of the Shadows. Very interesting stuff."

"I see." Mauritane tapped a finger on the table in a perfect rhythm. "And what did you say?"

"I told him I'd consider it. But there's a catch, which is that Regina

Titania told me on our triumphant return to the City Emerald last year that one day she'd call upon me for a service." Silverdun scratched his nose. "And this appears to be it."

Mauritane said nothing for a long moment, peering out the window. "Did Everess introduce you to anyone . . . unusual?"

"You mean Paet? The very Shadow himself?"

"Ah. Then this is no game. Everess has finally managed to pull this off."

"You don't seem especially pleased."

"Pleased?" asked Mauritane, his voice rising. "Why would I be pleased that the foreign minister has been granted his own small private army, off chasing figments and possibly precipitating wars?"

"The intent, as I understand it, is to prevent one. Further, he very strongly implied that the Seelie Army is in no position to fight Mab as it stands."

Mauritane scowled, clearly torn. Now *this* was the Mauritane Silverdun was used to.

"You must understand, Silverdun, that in some regard I agree with Everess's position. He's correct that at present we would be outmatched by the Unseelie. Mab has her own troops, and in addition she's managed to conscript forces from Annwn and a few other tributary states in her 'empire.'"

"And the Einswrath," said Silverdun.

"Yes, there is that."

"I take it we have no like weapon of our own?"

"No, nothing even remotely like it. But Mab's only used the thing twice. Once on her own people at Gefi, and once on Selafae. So the question of the year is—"

"Why hasn't she used it since, or threatened its use?"

"Precisely. We have our theories, of course, but the consensus seems to be that she's merely biding her time until she can plan a full-scale invasion of the Seelie Kingdom, with little chance of failure."

Silverdun actually gasped. "Is this possible?"

"Our best guess is that within a year, given our understanding of her troop movements and placement of her cities, we would be powerless to stop it."

Silverdun knit his brow. "You and Everess seem to be in agreement, then. Something must be done. Mab must be stopped by any means necessary. Why not the Shadows?"

Mauritane snorted. "Everess cares about nothing aside from his own position. To him, re-forming the Shadows is part of a strategy to build power for himself. He'll play upon whatever fear, whatever threat is necessary to pursue it. Don't trust him."

"Oh, I never intended to trust him," said Silverdun. "Among nobility, trust is rarer than a hard day's work."

Mauritane chuckled.

"Then you think I should find a way to wriggle out of this? I admit that I have no more confidence in Everess than you do."

"No!" Mauritane almost shouted. "You must accept. You must be a part of this. If he's received approval from Corpus and the queen's blessing, then it's going to go ahead no matter what I do. My best hope is to have someone on the inside, someone who can keep an eye on Everess and his ilk and do his best to ensure that the needs of the kingdom come before his ambition."

"And to report back to you."

"Yes."

The whole thing was beginning to seem hopelessly tangled. But Silverdun could see in Mauritane's eyes that war was not a hypothesis. It was a certainty. A war that could not be won.

"Do you think the Shadows can change things?"

"I certainly hope so. If you do the right things. I shudder to think what those things might be." Mauritane looked down at his hands. "And by allowing it to go forward, not fighting it, then I share an equal measure of guilt in whatever those things may be."

"We do what must be done," said Silverdun.

"Then do this thing, Silverdun." Mauritane looked him in the eye. "Make sure that the end justifies the means." This was not a request. This was an order, with the full weight of Mauritane's Gift of Leadership behind it. Ordinarily, Silverdun would have been offended at the hint of manipulation that went into such a thing, but in this case he supposed it was forgivable.

"Don't worry, Mauritane. I'll keep all of my most heinous acts to myself."

"No," said Mauritane. "You'll tell me everything. I want to know exactly what it is that I need to be forgiven for."

"And Paet. What's your opinion of him?"

"We've crossed paths once or twice over the past year. From aught that I can tell, he's a good man, if a bit strange. But I wouldn't trust him, either."

Silverdun left the Barrack feeling deeply uneasy. He watched the pretty Fae stroll up and down the Promenade, shading their eyes from the sun under parasols. Luxury.

He'd never felt as though he was truly a member of Seelie society; he'd always existed on the edge. He could frolic and strut with the best of them, but something about it had always seemed hollow. There was a hole in him that had never been filled.

And now he was about to become part of something that would only set him apart further. But would it fill that hole, or only widen it? No way of knowing.

He squared his shoulders and stepped into the sunlight, merging perfectly with the perambulations of Seelie life.

Everess wanted to use him. The Arcadians wanted to use him. Mauritane wanted to use him. Even the queen herself had her own hooks in.

For a failed monk, Silverdun was beginning to feel extremely popular.

chapter eight

Sailors call the Inland Sea the One True Queen, and when a
man joins the crew of a ship on that sea, he takes part in a
secret ceremony in which he renounces his allegiance to his
native land and swears to pay fealty only to the waves. It's
said that a sailor who refuses the oath is certain to drown
and fall into the abyss, to float downward into eternity.

—Stil-Eret, "At Sail on the Inland Sea,"
from *Travels at Home and Abroad*

A small ship struggled across the surface of the Inland Sea, tacking toward
the island of Whitemount. In the sky, formless masses of late-autumn
clouds moved in pompous procession, now blocking, now revealing the sun.

Silverdun stood in the bow, gripping the railing and trying to remain
steady on his feet. He tried to recall the little cantrip he'd learned in prison
to subdue nausea; it was a useful thing to know there, given the quality of
the food. The syllables faltered on his tongue—best not to say it rather than
foul it up, as it would no doubt make the feeling worse.

The ship was called *Splintered Driftwood*. All ships of the Inland Sea were
so named, the captain had told Silverdun, laughing. In the harbor Silverdun
had seen a three-master dubbed *This Way to Drowning*. Gallows humor, he
supposed. Hilarious.

There were five crewmen on the ship, not including the captain; they
went through their duties without speaking, ignoring Silverdun completely.
When a swell came and tilted the deck up to a sincerely alarming angle, the
quiet sailors paid it no notice whatsoever.

He gripped the rail tighter.

The railing was of smooth, polished wood, furbished to a rich luster, secured by gleaming brass fixtures. Silverdun clung to it as though it were the only steady thing in the universe. The harder he clutched, however, the more he felt the rolling gait of the ship beneath him. And if Silverdun looked too long at it, the bile began to stir in him again. He followed the advice he'd been given and fixed his gaze on the island toward which they were headed. It helped a little.

"Enjoying your voyage immensely, I can see," came a smooth voice behind him. Captain Ilian strolled toward Silverdun, having no trouble crossing the rolling deck. He was of middle age, though it was difficult to tell just how old. As young as forty, maybe as old as sixty. He was trim and broad-shouldered, and had clear green eyes that evoked the surface of the sea.

"I've never enjoyed another more," Silverdun said, scowling.

Ilian patted him on the shoulder. "That's the spirit," he said. He looked up at the sky. "Long crossing to Whitemount, but not too bad. We'll be there before nightfall."

"With all this wind I'd have thought we'd get there faster," said Silverdun.

"Plenty of wind, yes, but all blowing in the wrong direction, I'm afraid." One of the crewman brushed by Silverdun, pulled hard on a rope, and tied it back. The dance of canvas and rope was a type of wizardry unto itself, one that Silverdun would never comprehend.

"What if," said Silverdun, "I could get the wind blowing in the proper direction? Would that get us there faster?"

"Aye," said the captain, a curious smile working across his face. "That it would."

Silverdun stepped toward the stern of the ship and looked up at the sails. There were two of them, wide and full, canted heavily toward starboard to force the boat across the current of the wind.

Despite his nausea, Silverdun was well rested, full of energy and essence. It would be nice to actually do something. For far too long, he realized, he'd allowed life to simply happen to him. After his long year of military service, Silverdun had been happy to be at play in the court of Queen Titania, wooing every lady-in-waiting he could get his hands on and steadfastly ignoring his duties at Corpus. He'd wanted nothing more than what life handed him.

Unfortunately, Silverdun's uncle, who had been managing his estates of Oarsbridge and Connaugh in his absence, had decided that he'd prefer to be lord himself, and had had Silverdun exiled to the prison of Crere Sulace.

There, he'd been drafted into service by the great Mauritane, and had followed the man on his mission for the queen, barely understanding why he was doing it. They'd landed themselves in the middle of an Unseelie invasion at Sylvan, after Mab had used the Einswrath weapon just to the north, at Selafae. Mauritane had led them into battle, and Silverdun had become a war hero.

But again, Silverdun hadn't become a war hero through much choice of his own; Mauritane had practically led him out of Crere Sulace at knifepoint. Silverdun had allowed Mauritane to drag him across half of Faerie, just as he'd allowed his uncle to steal his inheritance out from under him.

And after Mauritane, then what? He'd wanted nothing to do with life at court any longer; prison and adventuring had faded that particular blossom well and truly. He'd had no interest in returning to his family lands to try to wrest his estate from his uncle. No interest in regaining his roguish reputation at court.

During his travels with Mauritane he'd met the abbot Vestar at the temple Aba-E in Sylvan. There was no disputing that Vestar was a holy man, that he'd found a spiritual peace beyond knowing. Meeting him and spending time among the monks at the temple had revived Silverdun's longing for something, a longing his mother had implanted in him, and which he'd struggled with all his life. Silverdun had always wanted to believe in Aba, the way his mother so effortlessly had, but he'd never been able, no matter how hard he tried.

And so he'd ended up at the Temple Aba-Nylae, enrolling as a novice, hoping that a steady diet of prayer and instruction would be enough to ignite something in his soul. It had become abundantly clear, however, that his soul had been in no way set aflame. It was clear to everyone . . . including, Silverdun reluctantly admitted, himself. And Prior Tebrit was a git, pure and simple. If nothing else, Silverdun could revel in the fact that he never had to see Tebrit's smug face ever again.

And now here he was, following someone else's plan for him. And as before, he had little idea of what it was he was getting himself into.

Silverdun leaned into the wind and reached out toward it with his mild Gift of Motion. Using *re* felt good, especially when he was full to spilling over with it. It was a kind of warmth, not physical, but almost spiritual. He'd tried to explain it to the human Satterly, but it was like describing color to a blind man. *Re* was simply *re*. There was no describing it.

With Motion he inexpertly reached out and caught hold of the wind. He grabbed it hard with his mind and pushed. There was no binding, no words, nothing formal about this; his will against the wind and to the victor go the prize. He hurled the wind against the sails and waited for the boat to lurch forward, to begin racing toward the island.

Nothing happened.

He tried again, pouring himself entirely into the task. He was strong, and it felt good to flex. With a colossal effort he flung what felt like the entire atmosphere of the world at the sails.

The ship seemed to rock slightly, although that might have been his imagination.

Silverdun looked down at the ship's deck. The captain was there, watching him, laughing.

"How goes it?" shouted Ilian.

"You whoreson!" Silverdun called back. "I believe I've been set up!"

Ilian strolled toward him, smug laughter fading to a friendly grin. "You university boys are all the same," he said, gesturing up to the sails. "You see the sail, big and white, and you assume that you've got to bridle the wind in order to get the job done."

"And I take it this was the wrong thing to do," said Silverdun.

"It was the obvious thing to do," Ilian answered. "You cannot wrestle the wind, son. The wind is connected to everything: the waves, the sun, the moon. You can blow a breeze on land by twiddling your fingers, but out here you're just pissing into it."

"So what do you recommend I do instead?" Silverdun asked.

"Sit and wait, and let the wind do its job." Ilian chuckled and walked away.

The sun was just touching the horizon, its light melting into the water, streaming across the sea toward them when the *Splintered Driftwood* touched up against the empty wooden dock at the island of Whitemount. The island was a great slab of granite thrust out from the sea, speckled with the few scrub pines in Faerie foolhardy enough to attempt to grow from it. On the island's highest point was an ungainly heap of stones in the shape of a castle. A steep trail had been cut into the rock leading up the rocky hillside toward it.

Ilian leapt from the ship at the bow and caught the mooring line that one of the silent crewman threw at him. He tied it with practiced grace, then walked to the stern and did the same thing. The *Splintered Driftwood* now nestled against the dock, its motion subdued. "We've arrived," called Ilian. "Come ashore!"

A rattling noise sounded behind Silverdun, from multiple directions. He turned to see the crewmen, all five of them, coming to an awkward standstill, their limbs relaxing, bowing at the waist. The air shifted as multiple glamours faded away, and in the sailors' places stood five automatons, constructions of silver and brass in the shape of men. Silverdun was impressed.

He stepped carefully onto the dock and looked at Ilian, nodding toward the ship. "Interesting crew," he said.

"You like them, do you?" said Ilian. "Master Jedron doesn't like visitors of any kind to the island. Only his students, whom he barely tolerates, and I, whom he loves dearly."

"Shall I simply go up and announce myself, then?" said Silverdun, pointing at the castle.

"Oh, no. I'm to come and present you. I'm Master Jedron's valet, after all. It's part of my job."

Silverdun frowned at Ilian. "I assumed that you were only the ship's captain."

Ilian waggled his fingers in Silverdun's face, his eyes wide, mocking. "Nothing is as it seems!" he said.

The trek to the castle was steep and dismal; a brisk, wet wind licked at them all the way, now at their faces, now at their backs, as they struggled up the switchbacks on the mountainside. By the time they reached the castle, Silverdun was exhausted and damp. It was dark, and the wind here at the island's summit was even stronger.

Up close, the castle Whitemount was more intact than it appeared from a distance. It consisted of a single tower surrounded by a square courtyard. The outer walls were fallen, but beyond them the courtyard was well maintained. The interior walls of the castle were straight and in good repair; the glass windows clear and unbroken. The courtyard was deserted. If Master Jedron had any retainers other than Ilian, they were nowhere to be seen, though Silverdun would not have blamed them for remaining indoors on such a bleak night.

"Come on, then," said Ilian, waving Silverdun on. He pushed open a heavy wooden door and entered the castle without further comment.

Inside, the castle was dry and cool. The main hall was decorated, though sparsely, in a style from decades past—clearly there was no lady at Whitemount. Ilian passed briskly through the spacious hall toward a set of wide spiral stairs that hugged the tower's interior. Silverdun followed. The stairs continued up several flights, with witchlit sconces evenly spaced along its length. Their light was tuned to orange, providing a glow that appeared warm but provided no actual warmth.

At the top of the tower, the stairs ended at a stout wooden door. Ilian knocked, and for a moment there was silence. Then a voice rasped, "Come!"

Master Jedron's study occupied the entire top floor of the tower. It was comfortable without being lavishly appointed; tapestries hung on the walls; tapers were lit and placed in sconces around the room. A well-stoked fireplace burned opposite the door. In the center of the room Master Jedron sat at a large desk made of ebony, his boots propped up on the corner of the desk. Jedron's salt-and-pepper hair hung to his shoulders, neatly combed. His face was deeply lined, giving the semblance of extreme age, but there was clearly nothing frail about him. He had a glass paperweight in his hand, which he tossed absently up and down.

Jedron squinted at Silverdun for a long moment and then said, "Who the fuck are you?"

Silverdun looked back at Ilian, who chuckled but said nothing. Ilian retreated casually to a spot near the door and motioned Silverdun back toward Jedron with a nod of his head.

"Are you stupid?" said Jedron. "I asked you a question. Who are you?"

Silverdun cleared his throat. What was this? "I am Perrin Alt, Lord Silverdun. I'm here to present myself to you for training."

Jedron looked baffled for a moment; then he burst out laughing, as if Silverdun had just told him the funniest joke he'd ever heard.

"What? You?" Jedron pointed at Silverdun, shaking with mirth. "Oh, that's a good one! Who put you up to this?"

The tips of Silverdun's ears began to burn. "I can assure you, sir, that this is no jest. Lord Everess himself sent me to you."

"Oh, did he?" Jedron's laugh settled down to a chuckle. "You can understand my amusement, of course."

"I'm afraid I can't," said Silverdun. He was going to kill Everess for this.

"Well, look at you! You're so fancy and sensitive, you're practically a woman!" Jedron took his feet down off the desk and leaned forward. "Not that I haven't trained women, of course," he said. "That's not what I mean at all. But most of the women I've trained are quite a lot more manly than you, I'm afraid."

The old man shook his head. "And I thought the *other* new student was a disgrace."

Silverdun rolled his eyes. "I see. This is some kind of test, to see if I'll lose my temper under stress or some such. Am I right?"

With blinding speed, Jedron reared back and hurled the glass paperweight, which slammed into Silverdun's temple with astonishing force. Silverdun stumbled back; the pain was unbelievable. He reached out for something to support himself with, as he suddenly felt dizzy, but there was nothing there. Red and blue spots began to speckle his vision and his knees buckled. He sat down hard.

Silverdun's head throbbed; his entire skull hurt. When he looked up, his vision was blurred and slightly doubled. Jedron stood over him, looking at him with an appraising eye.

"Well, you were right about one thing, boy. That was your first test, and you failed it miserably, I'm sad to say."

"Oh," groaned Silverdun. "And what test was that?"

Jedron looked at Silverdun as if Silverdun were the stupidest person he'd ever met. "Dodging paperweights," he said.

Silverdun awoke in a strange bed, fully clothed, his head throbbing. He touched his temple and grimaced at the tenderness of the welt that had grown there while he slept.

Carefully, he sat up and winced, the previous evening slowly filtering into his mind. The sea voyage, the climb, the old bastard with his paperweight. After that, everything got a bit fuzzy.

The bed was comfortable, the mattress stuffed with down and the pillow large and soft. When he swung his feet gently onto the floor, a plush rug rather than cold stone met his toes. He stood carefully; the rush of pain to his skull was even worse than he expected.

When his vision cleared, he looked around the room. It was small but not cramped; the furnishings of good quality but not ostentatious. A fresh set of clothes was draped over a chair, and his boots were on the floor nearby, cleaned and polished. His sword hung from a hook on the wall.

Silverdun dressed slowly and looked himself over in a mirror of perfectly smooth glass. Despite the purpling knot on his temple, he was still roguishly handsome, in his way. He'd been even more handsome, once. A length of ribbon had been hung from the mirror frame, and Silverdun tied his hair back with it.

Only then did he realize that he was starving—he hadn't eaten since the bowl of fish chowder he'd choked down on the dock yesterday morning.

When he bent to pull his boots on, the throbbing in his skull had already dwindled a bit.

"Let's get trained then," he said. "Time to become a spy."

The door was locked.

He tried it several times, shaking the latch hard, but the door was heavy and the lock solid; it refused to budge.

He pounded on it and called out. "Ilian? Care to let the new trainee out for a bit of food?" There was no answer. He knelt down and peered through the keyhole; only the bare stone of the passageway's far wall was visible.

He pounded harder. "Jedron? Is this another test? Going without breakfast?" The shouting made his head ache.

The window was small; too small to climb out of, but at least it opened, rotating out with a tiny brass crank. Silverdun cranked it all the way open and stuck his head out. The salt breeze was bracing.

Silverdun's room was on the side of the tower opposite the courtyard. The wall here practically jutted out directly from the turgid water. Only a few sharp rocks and a narrow hint of a path separated the tower from the sea.

"Auberon's balls," said Silverdun. He sat down heavily on the mattress. Here was yet another cell.

At least this one had a soft bed for a change.

Perrin is nestled in his mother's lap, her arms wrapped around him against the sudden evening chill. They are on the veranda overlooking the south lawns. Beyond the row of peach trees, a group of men from the village are repairing the low wall that surrounds the manor. Perrin likes walking along that wall; he can go the entire length of it, and even once made it all the way around the giant rectangle without falling off.

Mother leans in, kisses the top of his head, and inhales. "Your hair smells like sunlight," she says.

Iana comes to speak to Mother. She's one of the servants, and is always kind to Perrin. "Lady," she says, curtseying. "A moment, if I may." She nods meaningfully at Perrin.

"It's all right," says Mother. "Go ahead."

Iana doesn't seem to approve, but she goes on anyway, and suddenly she no longer acts like a servant. "I've decided that you will lead prayers tomorrow morning, so be ready."

"Oh," says Mother. Perrin turns in his mother's arms to look at her face. Iana has just spoken to Mother as if *she* were the servant, and Iana her mistress! But Mother is smiling. "I am honored, Mother."

Why is Mother calling Iana Mother? Perrin is confounded.

"I trust your judgment, Daughter," says Iana. "If you believe the boy is ready . . ."

"I believe it."

"He may not attend until his tenth birthday, you know."

"That is only two years from now."

Iana smiles. "It is a good thing. For him to be brought up in Aba's light. But we must be careful."

"Yes, Mother."

Iana curtseys, and she is a servant again.

When she is gone, Perrin asks, "Is Iana really your mother?"

"No, silly. Grandmama is my mother. Iana is my teacher in the Church."

"Aba," says Perrin. He knows about Aba. "Aba is a god," he says.

"Aba is God beyond gods," says mother. "He is first among kings."

Perrin is confused again. "I thought Uvenchaud was the first king."

Mother laughs. "Uvenchaud was the first king of Faerie, yes," she says, "but he was not a god."

"We are descended from Uvenchaud."

"Your father likes to say that, yes. But that was many thousands of years ago. I think at this point in history, more Fae are descended from Uvenchaud than not."

Perrin thinks about this. He points down to the villagers working at the wall. "Mother, are they descended from Uvenchaud too?"

"So many questions you have!" scolds Mother, smiling.

"Are they?"

Mother makes a funny face. "I suppose."

"Then aren't they noblemen as well?"

Mother laughs again, this time out loud. He loves the sound of her laughter. "Yes, I suppose they are."

"Then why don't they live in a manor like we do?"

Mother's smile fades. She looks at Silverdun. "Being noble has nothing to do with living in a manor, Perrin. That is the *world's* way, not the true way."

"Are you an Arcadian then?"

"Yes I am."

"Will I be an Arcadian too?"

"When you are older, you will go off to school in the city and you will learn many things, and then you will decide what sort of man you want to be."

Perrin doesn't really know what she means. "Can I go with you to the prayers? I want to hear you read them. Please?"

Now mother becomes very serious. "No you may not, and you mustn't ask again. And Perrin," she says, almost in a whisper, "you are *never* to speak of Aba, or of my conversations with Iana, or of our prayers to anyone. Do you understand?"

"Even Father?"

"Especially Father."

"But why?"

"Your father and I agree on most things," says Mother. "But on one very important subject we have a fundamental difference." She looks so sad when she says this, and Perrin hugs her tight.

"Can't you compromise?" says Perrin. "You always say if I have a disagreement with another child I should compromise."

"In some matters there is no compromising."

Perrin feels a tightness in his stomach. "Do you want to watch me go all the way around the wall?"

"Of course I do," says Mother, and her smile returns. She stands him up and brushes his hair with her fingers. "You're getting so very big."

"Make sure you watch," Perrin says.

"Come here," says Mother. She hugs him, puts her face against the top of his head, and inhales. "My sunlight."

He turns to run off, but Mother catches his collar. "Remember what I told you. It's very important, and I must know that I can trust you."

"I promise," he says.

As he's running down the south lawn, she calls out, "Don't disturb the noblemen fixing that wall!"

"I won't!" he shouts back.

He makes it almost all the way around, but falls by the back gate, scraping his knee. He cries, and Mother comes and scoops him up, carries him into the house, and there is warm supper and music and play and the softness of sleep.

Silverdun sat up; at some point he'd drifted off to sleep again, but now hunger roused him. The door was still locked, and pounding on it still produced no response from Ilian or Master Jedron.

This was ridiculous; the mental equivalent of the paperweight to the head. A tactic meant to do what? Unnerve him? Test his patience? Annoy him? If so, it was succeeding admirably.

Clearly Jedron had no intention of allowing him out of the room, so it was going to be up to Silverdun to escape. Surely Everess and the odd, brooding Paet hadn't gone to all this trouble only to have Silverdun starve to death in a tower room like a doomed princess in a tale.

He began with the door. The bands around the wood and the lock were of iron plated in silver. Silverdun's attempts to use Elements or Motion against the door only succeeded in worsening his headache. Several painful shoves with his shoulders proved that it couldn't be forced, and he nicked the blade of his rapier trying amateurishly to pick the lock. If he'd had a bit of wire he might have tried picking the lock, although he wouldn't have had any idea how to do that given all the wire in the world.

"Damn you, Jedron!" Silverdun shouted, punching the door and immediately regretting it.

Breathe. Think. Be calm. Losing his temper wasn't going to accomplish anything. And if Jedron was watching him through a peephole or with clairvoyance, Silverdun felt sure that his anger would only give the old man pleasure. Clearly no one was coming to help him. He couldn't force the door.

The window was of no use. He certainly couldn't spellcraft his way through the stone of the walls or the ceiling.

There must be something in the room that might help him. If nothing else, that stray bit of wire for him to practice his lock-picking skills with. He knelt and looked under the bed, finding nothing. He opened the drawers of the small bureau and felt around inside them, then pulled each drawer out and inspected it top and bottom. He pulled the bureau out from the wall and felt the back. He tipped it over and examined its bottom. Nothing. He took the mirror from the wall and found that it was indeed hung on its hook by a length of wire, but after a moment's experimentation it became clear that the stuff was far too flimsy to be of any use at lock picking. The bed frame was of wood, fitted with pegs, not nails.

After several minutes, Silverdun had been over every solid item in the small room and found nothing that might help him in any way. All that was left were the pillow and the mattress. Angrily, Silverdun stabbed at the pillow with the tip of his sword, sending goose down flying. The sight of the feathers floating aimlessly to the floor incensed Silverdun for some reason he could not explain, and he began to hack furiously at the mattress with the edge of his blade, sending clouds of down into the air. Again and again he struck at it, ignoring the pain in his skull.

He'd nearly shredded the entire mattress when he both heard and felt his sword strike metal. There, in the midst of the now-ruined mattress, was a silver key. It had been hidden in the mattress. Silverdun snatched it up and put it in the lock. It fit perfectly.

Master Jedron and Ilian were standing in the hallway. Jedron was smirking.

"Took you long enough," he said.

"And what, pray tell, was the point of that exercise?" Silverdun barked. "To teach me how to disarm bedclothes?"

"No," said Jedron. "It's to teach you to stop waiting around for other people to tell you what to do and think for yourself for a change."

Jedron peered into Silverdun's room. A layer of goose down covered the floor. "I hope you don't mind sleeping on wood slats," he said, smiling. "Because that's the only mattress you're getting."

chapter nine

In the Secret City the sky is madness.

This is Mab's world. This is Mab's sky.

In the Secret City the past rolls down gutters and into sewers.

This is Mab's past. These are Mab's sewers.

In the Secret City the citizens are long gone, replaced by the secrets they once knew.

These are Mab's people. These are Mab's secrets.

—Ma Tula, "The Secret City"

Timha awoke in his tiny chamber freezing, with the same pit of dread lodged in his stomach that had been there for weeks. Despite the chill, his chest and arms were covered in perspiration. Every day now he awoke feeling the same way. The cold, the unease, the sweat. Timha dressed quickly, pulling on his robes and a long cloak that did something to keep the chill out, but the robes absorbed the sweat and left him feeling a bit slimy.

It was always cold in the city. Always cold, always gray. No matter where Timha went, the wind always seemed to find its way at him, invading his robes, making him shiver anew, a hundred times a day. Even the fires in the common rooms seemed to burn colder, with a sickly blue aura around them. Timha couldn't remember the last time he'd felt warm.

He left his chamber, taking care not to look out the windows that he passed in the hall on the way to the stair. He kept his eyes on the floor, concentrating on the millennia-old patterns in the tiles, faded and cracked, but still clearly visible; a vision of an earlier era. Timha and his colleagues were led to believe that the city had been built even before the *Rauane Envedun-e*, the Age of Purest Silver, when magic filled the world like sunlight. Well, it was certainly old. It needn't be *that* old in order to impress Timha.

Timha made it to the staircase without glancing out a single window. It was strange how they attracted the eye, despite the deep unpleasantness that looking outside engendered. It was the sky. Timha did not need to see the sky today. Not today when the dread was so bad that it felt as though his insides were liquefying.

All night the intricate dance of the Project paraded before him in dreams. He could not escape those motions; the precision and complexity of them consumed his waking hours and his sleeping ones as well now. Not that he slept much, or well.

Timha was still seeing those motions when he emerged in the dining hall, glowering at the other journeyers and their apprentices. They seemed at ease, restful, even content as they sat lingering over their breakfasts before the stoves that were never quite hot enough. Well, why shouldn't they be content? Each had his or her own little bit of the overall structure of the Project to contend with, and it was challenging, rewarding work for them. They knew that their presence here meant that they were the best and most respected thaumaturges in the empire, long may it sail. They knew that when their work here was done they would retire, wealthy and respected, to villas on the fore moorings of the fairest cities, perhaps even the new City of Mab itself.

What they did not know was the thing that made Timha sweat at night, that made him lightheaded and anxious nearly every moment of the day. They were spared this knowledge because it would do no good for any of them to know.

"Morning, Timha," said Giaco, one of the Elements experts, leader of the group who were working on improving the outer shell. "How are things in the heart of the beast?" Giaco and his team were close with one another; several of them had taught together at a university in one of the flag cities. They were working on the project of their lifetimes, with access to only the best supplies and research materials, a limitless budget, and an army of apprentices who would gladly do anything they asked. Moreover, they were doing all this in Mab's own Secret City, one of the most hallowed locations in all of the empire. This was Mab's redoubt. This was where she had come to have her children, where she mourned the loss of her husbands. This was where Beozho wrote his *Works*. Giaco and his friends were in paradise.

Timha hated them for it.

"Things are progressing very well, thanks," said Timha primly. He sat at a table by himself, took tea from an apprentice without looking up, and tried to ignore the dance that twirled in his mind. The cruel irony of his position struck him now as it often did, that he was suffering not because he was a poor worker or because he was intellectually inferior to his fellows, but rather because he was their better. Master Valmin had taken Timha under his wing early on, brought him into the core team, gone over the more esoteric and taboo portions of the Project with him. At the beginning, they had all been excited, and none more so than Timha. It was the position of a lifetime. And while he certainly had reservations about the use of the Black Art, Valmin had assured him that it was for a noble cause, that evil could indeed be harnessed for good.

For the sake of the empire, Valmin had said, an encouraging smile on his face. Think of the soldiers who gutted their enemies on the battlefield, of the generals who sent their troops into the fray knowing that not all of them would return. All great enterprises, Valmin had told him, have some element of darkness at their heart. Better to name it and know it, to contain it so that it did only the harm it was intended to do.

What Valmin had not told Timha, or perhaps had not known himself, was that working the Black Art was not something one did lightly. It was powerful but draining, both mentally and emotionally, and the feeling of . . . Timha could only describe it as *sinfulness* never left him, though Timha believed in neither Aba nor the Chthonics, nor anything else for that matter. The Black Art wormed its way into your bones. Its harsh workings yielded impressive results, but each day Timha had felt as though a part of his soul were draining away.

And that was before all the trouble had begun.

It started with a realization that Timha himself had made, reviewing an extremely complex passage in the notes of Hy Pezho, the Project's original creator. Timha had read the passage over and over again, trying to deduce its meaning and finding himself unable. He'd brought it to Valmin, who had

retired to his own quarters with it for most of a day. When Valmin had
emerged, it had been with a dour face. Their task was going to be much more
difficult than they had at first believed.

Valmin had been given the most prestigious portion of the work, and he
had shared it with Timha and a few select others because they had proven
themselves the best of the best in their respective fields of study. And now
they were the ones who would have their throats cut by the Bel Zheret if they
failed. The others would be sent home, perhaps with a bit of disgrace, or more
likely with no comment at all, and Valmin and Timha and a few others would
be gutted like fish and left to rot in the stinking basements of the Secret City
where the raw materials for the Black Art were kept.

Timha shuddered at the thought. The basements were the only things
that bothered him more than the sky.

Nothing was what it was supposed to be.

Timha lingered over breakfast, but it still ended too quickly. He made his
way down a twisting corridor to Master Valmin's chambers. The doors were
manned by a pair of armed guards who opened the door for Timha, waving a
deglamouring wand over him, relaxing their grips on their weapons only
when they determined that Timha was indeed Timha.

Valmin's office smelled of burnt tea, chalk, and bitter herbs. Valmin was
already at his desk when Timha entered. The room was filled with stacks and
stacks of books, most of which were unavailable to the general populace.
Some were proscribed by Mab, forbidden even to Master Valmin himself, and
the fact that these books were currently resting open in front of Valmin was
as good a sign as any that the Project was in deep trouble.

The walls and floor of the spacious chamber were surfaced in smooth
slate, installed by journeyer Elementalists who no doubt had been annoyed at
the task but had done an excellent job nonetheless. Nearly every free bit of
space on the walls was filled with arcane sigils, mathematical equations,
apothecarian symbols, and diagrams of the dance at the heart of the Project,
drawn in white chalk.

During the night, Timha noticed, Valmin had erased some of the equations relating to the stored energy bindings. For a moment Timha's heart rose in hope, but then he realized that Valmin had simply replaced yesterday's unworkable mathematics with those from the day before. Every light they shone on some aspect of the Project seemed to cast some other part more deeply into shadow.

"Good morning, Journeyer," said Valmin, not looking up from his text. This was the Red Book, so called from the color of its binding; books on the Black Art were required to be nameless. Valmin had been spending more and more time studying this particular volume. Was he onto something?

"Anything, master?" said Timha. His voice came out thin and reedy, almost rasping.

Valmin looked up briefly from his book. "Trust me, Timha, if I have glad tidings in the middle of the night I will drag you out of bed myself."

Timha suddenly felt like crying. How shameful would it be to burst into tears in front of Master Valmin? The thought of it chilled Timha enough to let the tears subside. But it wasn't fair! It wasn't fair!

The Project simply ought to have yielded up its secrets to them by now. After all the work they'd put in, the long hours poring over the plans, the detailed instructions, the philosophical notes that Hy Pezho had left. Every separate part of the thing made sense, if an esoteric and abstract sense. But when put together in the way described in the plans, the interaction of alchemy, bindings, and the essence of the raw materials, the totality of it became so complex that no one could hope to understand it all. It was simply impossible for a Fae mind to hold together all at once.

Valmin and Timha had been forced to admit that Hy Pezho was a genius, perhaps the greatest thaumaturge of his age, if these plans were to be believed. But there was nothing in Hy Pezho's history that indicated where he might have come across such knowledge. The son of the great Black Artist Pezho, he had spent his early years wandering from city to city, squandering his father's small fortune and giving the world no reason to afford him any regard whatsoever. Then he'd disappeared for several years, and the next thing anyone knew he'd become one of Mab's inner circle. And the next thing anyone knew after that, he was gone, the mention of his name forbidden at court. His only legacy, as far as Timha knew, was the Project. The Einswrath. Citykiller. But what a legacy it was. A thing of such elegance and power, such might.

If only Hy Pezho were here to explain it.

"What can I do?" said Timha, dreading the answer.

Valmin looked up wearily. He waved at a stack of books on the table opposite him. "The answer is in there somewhere," he sighed. "Find it."

Outside, the portal lock shimmered and choked out two tall, gaunt figures in blue robes. The guards at the lock started at their sudden entrance, reached for their swords, then dropped them when they recognized the robes.

The arch of the lock stood on a lonely rocky promontory connected to the Secret City by a long, narrow bridge of chalky stone. All around was the roiling, slithering sky. Guards for this posting were handpicked for their ability to avoid looking upward.

One of the men had skin as pale as moonlight. The other was so dark that his eyes seemed to glow from an empty void. The guards looked away. It was not permitted to speak to Bel Zheret unless spoken to. And neither of them had even the slightest desire to be spoken to.

The pale-skinned Bel Zheret was named Dog. His partner was Asp. Dog and Asp strode toward the bridge arm in arm. They were in a fine temper. They loved each other.

At the entrance to the city, the sentries likewise lowered their eyes and their weapons to allow Dog and Asp to pass. The Bel Zheret flowed through the entrance, robes sweeping across the stones in a most aesthetically pleasing manner.

As soon as they'd turned the corner past the sentry booth, the sergeant took a message sprite from its jar, gave it careful instructions, and then released it. It flew with an urgency typically unknown among sprites.

Above, at the entrance to the research facility, the head guardsman received the sprite and took its message. His eyes widened. He gave a hand signal to the second-in-command, and she ran.

Bel Zheret were coming.

Dog and Asp went slowly up the steps to the converted palace where the researchers worked on their project. They stepped deliberately, artfully. All of life was art, viewed properly. Bel Zheret understood this instinctively. *Aesthetics is the highest order of understanding.*

The city was cold and dry. Its narrow, winding streets were deserted, had been for centuries. It was spotless. Dog commented to Asp on it, and Asp agreed that it was a pleasing sight. Satisfying.

At the top of the steps, the palace stood out against the sky. Dog and Asp did not find the sky particularly pleasing, but then, no one did. Perhaps Mab did? She must have, or she wouldn't have left it that way. The guardsmen on the palace walk were standing at stiff attention, staring straight ahead. They'd been warned that Bel Zheret were coming. This also pleased Dog and Asp. Fear was appropriate.

Inside the palace, Dog and Asp both stopped briefly. The smell here, of cooking, Fae sweat, traces of garbage and offal. Unpleasant.

Dog turned to one of the guards. "This palace has an unwholesome odor. See to it." The guard turned and ran as fast as his legs would go.

They flowed into the common room, where flabby, sweaty, hairy research thaumaturges and their assistants and servants acted as though they hadn't spent the last five minutes in a frenzy of preparation, cleaning, hiding, or destroying those things that Dog and Asp might object to. Again, appropriate. They were happy to go along with the farce. Another instinctive habit. *It is a privilege to be feared. Do not abuse that privilege.*

Dog turned to the most cowardly smelling of all the cowards in the room. "Where might I find Master Valmin?" he said, his voice smooth and precise.

The coward shook, but his voice was admirably strong. "Through there," he said, pointing. "Last door on the right."

Dog and Asp found Valmin and his journeyer Timha pretending to be hard at work on their assignment.

"Welcome," said Valmin, offering no other pleasantries. He had dealt with Bel Zheret in the past.

"Tell us," said Asp. It was economical; Valmin already knew why they were there. Economy was important. *Do the most with the least.*

"Yes," said Valmin. He cleared his throat, holding out a prepared document in a leather binding. "Here is the complete report, of course." Asp took
the thing without looking at it, and it disappeared inside his robes.

"Summarize for us, won't you?" asked Dog.

"We have made significant progress with the casing system, and the containment fields. And we are very close to reaching a hypothesis about the
underlying mechanism."

"Very close?" said Dog, his voice still smooth as silk. "To a hypothesis?"

Asp chimed in. "In other words, you have built a pretty box. You still do
not understand what goes in the box, but nearly have an idea about one of
many ways in which it might possibly work."

Valmin said nothing.

Dog strode calmly toward Valmin and grabbed him by the wrist. To
Valmin this motion had happened nearly instantaneously; Bel Zheret experienced time rather differently than the typical Fae. Dog turned the wrist
slowly, pushing Valmin to the ground. From this position he could snap
Valmin's elbow backward, break his wrist, reach into the small of his back
with extended claws, or any of a hundred other things. But physically
harming Valmin was currently forbidden. Injured thaumaturges were not
productive thaumaturges.

"We will return in six months," said Dog. "If by then you have not produced a functioning Einswrath, the two of you will be killed."

"But . . . one cannot rush the process of inquiry! It takes as long as it takes!"

"We understand," said Asp. "And if this particular inquiry takes longer
than six months, then you will die and we shall promote others into your
positions. I am simply alerting you to your time frame."

Dog released Valmin, and the old master fell to the floor, clutching his
arm in pain. The elderly were disgusting. Dog resisted the urge to wipe his
hands on his robes.

"Good-bye," said Asp. Without any further ado, Dog and Asp turned
and left the room.

They swept back through the common room and out of the palace. At
the palace entrance, Dog sniffed the air. He picked out the guard to whom
he'd spoken earlier about the odor.

"It still smells bad," he said. "Can't you smell it?"

Dog watched the guard's face carefully. He knew what the man was thinking. *Do I admit that I can't smell what the Bel Zheret smells, or do I agree with him to please him?*

Dog didn't wait for an answer. He held up two fingers. "Your nose must require cleaning," he said. He grabbed the guard's neck and plunged the two fingers into his nostrils, digging into the soft membranes there with his fingernails.

"Perhaps there is some foreign matter encrusted within?" he said, clawing up and down. Blood began to pour from the guard's nose. The guard began to shriek. Musical!

"Maybe your sense of smell will improve now," said Dog, letting go. "You write and let me know if that's the case, won't you?"

Dog smiled at the thought of the guard sitting down to compose the letter. He couldn't wait to read it.

The guard fell to the ground, clutching his face. Blood dripped down his fingers.

"All right, then," said Dog. "Have a lovely day."

As they walked toward the lock across the narrow stone bridge, they locked arms again. "That was fun," said Asp.

Dog could only agree.

. . . after loud complaints from the House of Guilds, I was asked to pen an official statement on the matter. It read, in part, "The so-called Shadow Office does not exist, and never has. The notion of a secret group of spies, strangers to propriety, and invested with powers granted by the Black Art, is repugnant to Her Majesty. It is a fantasy promulgated by seditious elements within the very body who proposes that said office be expunged."

The statement was, of course, a lie. The Shadows existed then, and exist to this day. One small portion of the statement, however, is factual. The very notion of the Shadows is indeed repugnant to the queen. This, however, has never stopped her from employing them.

—Cereyn Ethal, *Autobiography* (unexpurgated)

Studying with Master Jedron was like a cross between military training and torture, using techniques of both disciplines in equal measure. Jedron's idea of a training exercise was to have Silverdun practice the crossbow for an hour, and then—with no warning whatsoever—release a half dozen hunting dogs for him to fend off. Another "exercise" was to tie Silverdun's wrists and ankles together and then have Ilian throw him into the ocean from the rocky cliff at the north side of the island. Jedron would then casually toss knives off the cliff until Silverdun caught one and used it to free himself.

"What's the point of this?" Silverdun blustered, after the second of these, clambering out of the water. He stumbled in turbulent surf that beat against the black stones whose edges had cut Silverdun more than once.

It was a gray day, about two weeks into the training. Low, gray sky, turgid sea. It was highsun but felt like dusk. Silverdun's clothes clung to him, flapping against his prickling skin in time with the wind. He brushed his hair out of his eyes.

Jedron and Ilian, who'd walked down from the tower to meet him, looked at each other. Jedron threw Silverdun a towel. "You don't need to know the lesson in order to learn it," he said.

"Not the test," said Silverdun angrily. "The cruelty. I was under the impression that I was being trained for a job, not being punished for my sins."

"It's both," said Jedron.

"Where's the other recruit you mentioned before?" said Silverdun. "Do you treat him as badly as you do me?"

Jedron thought about it. "No," he said. "He's not quite as stupid as you are."

"Well, where is he?"

"He's around," said Jedron. "I don't want him to pick up any of your bad habits."

Later, after Silverdun was dry, Jedron came to his quarters. "Come with me," he said.

Outside it had begun to rain, and Silverdun's fresh clothes were soon as sodden as his previous ones had been. Jedron led Silverdun and Ilian down to the quay, where the *Splintered Driftwood* rested, rolling in the waves. A storm out to sea somewhere was wreaking a mild havoc here. Jedron climbed aboard and beckoned Silverdun to follow.

On board, the silver-and-brass automatons had been covered with canvas tarpaulins that were tied around the things' ankles. Jedron untied one and pulled the canvas free, gesturing for Silverdun to have a closer look.

Silverdun leaned in and whistled appreciatively. The structure of the automaton's body matched that of a Fae body perfectly, only with the skin removed. Muscles of silver, tendons of brass. Eyes of glossy, polished marble.

"This is saturated argentine, isn't it?" said Silverdun. Spellplastic silver, the stuff could be manipulated easily with Elemental hook sequences.

Silverdun had never seen so much of it in one place; it was astonishingly expensive.

Jedron shrugged. "Not my area of expertise," he said. "And not the point."

Ilian took a small knife and, before Silverdun even realized what he was doing, swiped it across one of the many cuts on Silverdun's left hand.

"Ow!" said Silverdun. Ilian and Jedron shared a quick glance: *What a baby!*

Ilian pried open the automaton's mouth, and its tongue, a lump of argentine, lolled out. Ilian wiped the knife blade clean on it and shut the thing's mouth.

"Why do you think I have these spellwork sailors, when real ones would be far less expensive, and easier to maintain?" asked Jedron.

"Ilian said it was because you didn't like visitors."

"True," said Jedron. "But that's not really it. It's because I live in a different world than the one you live in."

He stared out to sea. "Faerie is a more dangerous place than most suspect, and Faerie is perhaps the most civilized of all the many worlds. The real threats out here aren't bugganes or soldiers. Those are obvious. You can see them coming."

Jedron turned his gaze on Silverdun. It was piercing, and somehow deeply off-putting. Almost bestial. But not that; something else that Silverdun couldn't name.

"The real threats are the people whom you do not realize you can't trust until it is too late. Trust is perhaps the most deadly weapon that can be used against you. I have none. And neither must you.

"That is why I will not be your friend, or anything like one. I don't want you to like me. I don't want you to think you can trust even me."

Silverdun glanced at the automaton. Its face began to cloud over, as though seen through a misted mirror. "You're hardly making a case for yourself. Everess said that—"

Jedron laughed out loud. "Everess? That pompous bag of gas? He'd step on his own mother to get another rung higher on the ladder. Do you think he's gathering his own personal gang of spies purely for the love of the Seelie Heart?"

"Are you saying I shouldn't work for him?"

"Of course not. I'm only saying you shouldn't trust him."

"Well, that's one thing you didn't need to teach me. I never trusted him."

"And yet you came all the way out here solely on his word."

"I'm not doing this for him."

Jedron chuckled again. "Well said."

The mist around the automaton's face began to slowly resolve itself into skin, making a face. Dark hair began to flow out of its bald head.

Silverdun pointed at Ilian. "What about Ilian? You trust him, don't you?"

Jedron rolled his eyes. "Him I could kill in a heartbeat."

Ilian flicked his knife open and, more quickly than Silverdun could register, put it to Jedron's throat. With almost no effort, and just as quickly, Jedron snatched the knife from Ilian's hand and hurled him overboard, into the roiling water.

"Look," said Jedron, pointing to the automaton with his knife. Silverdun looked and shuddered. The automaton now looked just like Silverdun, an almost exact duplicate. It glared at Silverdun warily.

"There's the only one in all the worlds that you can trust, Silverdun," said Jedron.

Silverdun stood before his mechanical double. This was one of Jedron's less subtle lessons; the theater of it hardly seemed up to the old man's standards.

The automaton stepped back warily as Silverdun approached. Silverdun looked in its eyes, and a shudder of revulsion went through him. They were Jedron's eyes.

"Not quite an exact copy, though, is it?" said Silverdun. "Something about it isn't me. How it looks at me."

"No, and that's because it isn't you. I didn't say that *you* were the only one you could trust. You're weak and confused."

"No," said Silverdun. "Then who's he?"

"He's who you'll be when you leave here. He's who you'll be after you've completed your training."

Silverdun frowned.

"You don't like him, do you?" said Jedron. His face looked sour.

"No, to be perfectly honest."

"You'll like *being* him even less," said Jedron. He muttered a syllable under his breath, and the automaton's glamour vanished, leaving it a dead machine again. Jedron covered it with the tarpaulin. Silverdun, in a none-too-subtle frame of mind, couldn't help thinking that it looked like a shroud.

"You have no idea what you've gotten yourself into, lad," said Jedron, smiling.

On the dock, Ilian was pulling himself up out of the water, shaking sea-water out of his hair. Jedron walked past Silverdun toward the dock. As he passed, he grabbed Silverdun's shoulder.

"Hold on," he whispered, "and listen closely."

Jedron nodded toward the dock. "Ilian is a traitor. We'll have to do something about him."

Three weeks passed, during which Silverdun's training became a bit more what he'd expected upon his arrival. He learned to move without making a sound, though some of the means by which he was asked to do so seemed patently impossible. Feel the floorboards with your mind before you step on them? That would have been difficult even for someone with a well-developed Gift of Insight. Silverdun possessed the Gift, but had never studied it.

There was Silverdun's problem in a nutshell. Insight was a Gift of the Head, and Glamour was of the Heart. Silverdun had poured all of his efforts into Glamour as a youth because he had always fancied himself an artist. Insight was a Gift for research thaumaturges and alchemists. Men who sat in chairs and pondered. Silverdun's father had pushed him toward Insight as a more noble form of study. Silverdun knew that he could have been great at Insight. As it was, he was a mediocre Glamourist at best. But at least he'd gotten what he wanted.

In the mornings were the daily drills with Jedron. They drilled with knives and the *petite arbalète*, a small, short-range crossbow. Silverdun learned how to kill without making a sound, how to kill painfully, how to disable without killing, all with a calculating precision that teased at his scruples more and more with each passing day.

Silverdun took his meals with Ilian, who said little but always seemed to keep an eye on him. Ilian was always nearby, always ready to assist in training, or stepping in to clean something, or bringing Jedron his meals. Jedron and Ilian appeared to have no relationship that Silverdun could divine. They almost never spoke to one another.

Silverdun asked about the other trainee a few more times. Ilian assured him that he was around somewhere, but that Silverdun wouldn't meet him until he was ready.

Every few days, Jedron would invite Silverdun to his study for an evening drink, but these evening drinks likely as not turned into hours-long study sessions. And Jedron never ceased to be amused by his habit of unexpectedly hurling blunt objects at Silverdun's head.

Silverdun had managed to reshape what was left of his bed into a makeshift pallet, which was far from the least comfortable arrangement he'd ever had (sleeping outdoors in the dead of midwinter after a full day's ride took the prize by a long shot), but was a far cry from paradise. Most nights, though, Silverdun was so tired that by the next morning he didn't remember his head hitting the pillow, and he rarely dreamed.

"We haven't talked about swords at all," said Silverdun one day, after a long practice session of hand-to-hand fighting with Jedron. Silverdun was sweating and huffing, but Jedron wasn't even breathing heavily. Astonishing for a man of his age.

"No," said Jedron. "And we won't."

"Why not?"

"A sword is a weapon of last resort in our work. If you find yourself drawing one, then you've done something terribly wrong."

"And what if someone draws on me?"

"Throw a knife in his neck and run," said Jedron, matter-of-factly.

"That hardly seems within the bounds of propriety," said Silverdun.

"Propriety is a millstone around your neck, boy. The man with propriety is the one who dies first. The sooner you get used to that idea, the better off you'll be."

"But," began Silverdun. He paused, carefully choosing his words. Had he heard correctly? Jedron might as well have told him to get used to the idea of kicking puppies and slitting the throats of milkmaids. "If our goal is to protect the Seelie way of life, how do we achieve the goal by abandoning the very thing that makes us Seelie?"

"Your precious propriety is for the safe ones. We provide the luxury of civilized ideas like personal honor by eschewing them."

"I don't understand," said Silverdun.

Jedron pointed east, toward the City Emerald. "All those pretty Fae over there, all those *civilized* Fae, live in a giant cocoon spun of the silk of ignorance."

It was the most poetic Jedron had ever been, and Silverdun said so.

"Go to hell, Silverdun. I'm being serious. It is a grand thing to believe oneself safe. All of the great things of civilization are crafted by those who are free from danger. Their error—the one we are employed to hide from them, and rightly so—is their belief that they can uphold civilization by acting civilized. The reason the Shadows have existed for so long, despite the public hue and cry about their rumored existence, is that those in positions of power are continuously reminded of that error when it kicks them in the face."

"If you're so apathetic about honor and propriety and civilization," Silverdun spat, "then why bother protecting it at all? Why risk your life to protect something for which you seem to have little use?"

"Because if I don't, who else will? We are beset on all sides by ignorance and savagery, Silverdun. The bestial Gnomics to the south. Mab's legions of blind, devoted 'citizens' who might as well be slaves. Or worse, really . . . at least a good slave owner values the life of his investment. I may not have much use for the finer things in life, but I loathe the alternative.

"And," he said, smiling wickedly, "I love my job."

A week later, Jedron had Silverdun in his office, studying maps. Most were maps of Faerie: city maps, diagrams of the movement patterns of Unseelie cities, topographical maps. Others were of Mag Mell, the world of ten thousand islands; Annwn, its vast lands almost unpopulated except for the one great city called Blood of Arawn; the Nymaen world, mostly water, mapped to an astonishing precision. Jedron, of course, expected him to memorize every detail of every map and quizzed him throughout the evening, hurling paperweights and books at him if he answered incorrectly. He seemed in an especially surly temper tonight. Even Ilian seemed unsettled, which Silverdun couldn't remember ever having noticed before.

Finally Jedron bid him put the maps away. He poured them brandy from the decanter and they shared a silent drink. When Silverdun finished, Ilian appeared from the shadows and escorted him to his bedroom.

In his room, Silverdun began to feel strange. He knew this feeling. At university, he'd taken a class on poisons. He'd dropped out of it after a week, and never gotten credit for it. The reason he'd dropped it was that he'd accidentally ingested a potion called iglithbi. Not a poison, exactly—it was created for recreational purposes—but in a large enough dose easily lethal. Odorless and tasteless, favored by careful thieves and rapists. If he'd been stupid enough to accidentally sip it, he'd be stupid enough to accidentally kill himself.

And now there was no question about it: He'd been drugged with iglithbi. The effect was unmistakable. But how large a dose?

Silverdun's faculties began to abandon him. He thought wildly for the composition of iglithbi, its organic ingredients and reitic bindings. And there in his mind, amazingly, was the formula; one of the few things he'd actually retained from his university days. He reached out with his Gift of Elements, searching for the binding called *Elesh-elen-tereth*. It was easy to locate using only the Gift, and easy to unbind. He found it and could sense its particular color of *re* flowing through him. He reached out and pushed it with his Gift, changing *Elesh-elen-tereth* into water and *spiritus sylvestre*.

Unfortunately, a good deal of the potion had already found its way into Silverdun's mind. He was still awake—that was something—but unsteady. The room seemed to breathe around him, the walls quavering.

Was Ilian truly a traitor? Had he done this? Or was this another of Jedron's mean-spirited tests? Jedron had drunk from the same bottle of brandy, true. But it was easily possible that Jedron possessed Elements as well.

Silverdun wanted badly to lie down and sleep. His bed, or what was left of it, suddenly seemed like the most appealing place in all Faerie.

But he wouldn't allow himself the pleasure. Jedron's demonstration on the *Splintered Driftwood* had affected him more deeply than he'd thought. If Ilian had spiked the brandy, and if Jedron didn't possess Elements, then Jedron could be dying in bed at this very moment, and Ilian doing whatever treachery he had planned.

But still—the bed.

Silverdun heard a scream outside the window. Or thought he did. Time and space seemed to plummet in random orbits. Silverdun stumbled to the window and looked out. All was a blur. Down below there were flickering lights, waving in the night. Torches. Fireflies. Witchlight. Embers.

He ran toward the door and missed, hitting the wall instead. He corrected and stole out of his bedroom into the passage. A few minutes later, he stood at the main gate, peering out into the overcast, empty night. He wasn't quite sure how he had navigated the stairs down to the floor level of the castle. He knew he'd done it, but couldn't remember how.

The scream again. Silverdun plunged into the darkness. Out through the main courtyard, down toward the rocks. A set of steps Silverdun hadn't seen before. He took them down, down, toward the water's edge. At the bottom of the steps was an expanse of stone, a circle of torches, a pit. Fire. A man tied to a table, screaming. He looked up at Silverdun. A stranger. His face, filled with fear, burned itself into Silverdun's mind. Out of the ring of fire another face. Ilian. Ilian annoyed. A word of binding. Silence. Blackness.

Silverdun came awake again, his face pressed against the cold, wet steps. Wet bruised chill of early morning. He tried to raise his head, and a dull sick pain rocked him. Down in the stone clearing, Ilian lifted a blackened bundle out of the pit. Charred sticks? No.

Bones.

Silverdun wanted to cry out to Ilian, but his tongue felt swollen in his mouth. He couldn't form the words. But Ilian saw him anyway.

Ilian placed the bundle of sticks (bones) gently on the ground and walked slowly up the steps.

"Your file didn't mention anything about you having studied potions," said Ilian. "That complicates things a bit, I'm afraid."

Silverdun summoned *re*, channeled it through his Gift of Elements, but nothing came. The required concentration was beyond his grasp. Ilian lashed out with his boot, knocking Silverdun's head against the stairs, and Silverdun blacked out.

Spring term has just begun, and already Perrin is overloaded with schoolwork. He's been tested for Elements and Glamour and passed both with ease. Wouldn't Father be livid if he chose to study Glamour at university! University is still two years away, though; it seems like forever.

Perrin walks through the old school garden, tucked between the library and the upper dormitory, imagining life as a famed Glamourist. He would live in a hovel in the city and smoke cigarettes and fashion glamours in a studio during the day and drink wine and make love to dangerous women at night. He would hide his noble heritage the way Rimaire had, only revealing his lordship on his deathbed.

Perrin sits on a stone bench and looks around; the garden is deserted. He's bought cigarettes from one of the school cooks and is working out how to smoke them the way the men in the city do, with the wrist extended, tapping off the ash with a flick of the thumb.

There's a shout by the garden gate and Silverdun tosses the cigarette as fast as he can into a camellia bush.

A boy comes running into the garden, smacking the gate hard against the wall, the sound reverberating in the enclosed space. Hard behind him are four other boys, chasing him.

The boy being chased runs toward Perrin and trips, falling down at Perrin's feet. It's Bir, the son of a tea guildsman from the Western Valley. His parents donated a fortune to the school to get him accepted, Perrin's been told.

"Help," pleads Bir. Then the boys are on him. They're fifth years, all tough boys, and Perrin has no interest in getting involved.

The leader of Bir's pursuers is Tremoin, the Baronet Dequasy, who is a pompous ass and, Perrin notes with satisfaction, utterly useless at Glamour. Tremoin gets Bir down on his back and straddles him, holding a fist up to strike.

"Go on, say it!" says Tremoin. "Just say it and I'll let you go."

"I won't," says Bir.

Tremoin looks up at Perrin, noticing him for the first time. "Oh, Perrin. Lovely seeing you. Were you aware that Bir is not only common, but an Arcadian as well?"

A spike of fear plants itself in Silverdun's belly. "I was not aware of that, no."

Bir struggles, but Tremoin is much larger than he is.

"As an experiment of sorts," Tremoin continues, "I've asked him to openly deny his god to see if he's struck by lightning, thus demonstrating whether Aba is a wrathful god or not."

"I take it he's refused," says Perrin, trying to keep his voice steady.

"Natural philosophy does not appear to be an interest of his," Tremoin observes.

Perrin hopes that Bir will do the smart thing and deny Aba, but Bir has chosen to be a martyr. He shouts, "I will not deny Aba, not for you, not for the queen herself!" His voice echoes in the garden.

"A man of principle!" says Tremoin, pleased. "Boys, let's show Perrin here what we do to men of principle."

After the spectacle is over, Perrin goes to the library and creates a casual rampart of schoolbooks around him. He takes pen and paper from his bag and writes his weekly letter.

"Dear Mother," he writes. "I watched a boy at school get beaten senseless today because he refused to deny your god. But all is well, I suppose, as Aba will no doubt forgive the boy who administered the beating, and Bir (this is the boy who was beaten) will get his reward in Arcadia, when She Who Will Come arrives clad in alabaster armor or satin robes or whatever it is she's to arrive in.

"While this is all well and good, it no doubt comes as little comfort to

Bir, who currently lies delirious in the infirmary. Or perhaps it comes as all sorts of comfort. I must admit that I find it difficult to comprehend a god so overflowing with love who yet stands idly by while one of his adherents is getting his face smashed in.

"Please say hello to Father for me, if you ever see him, and to Iana as well. You are, I assume, still taking orders from the laundry maid, so be sure to treat her with due respect when you pass along my salutations.

"I remain your devoted son."

He signs the letter and stuffs it quickly into an envelope, not reading it over. He gathers his books, walks straight to the school office, and drops the letter in the post box.

And immediately regrets it.

For the next week he goes through his classes filled with dread, imagining his mother receiving the letter, opening it, reading it. What will she do? Will she take her own life out of grief and disappointment? Will she come to the school and scold him in front of his friends? Will she simply refuse to speak to him again?

She does none of these things. When her letter arrives, Perrin takes it back to the garden and opens it with trembling hands. It reads,

"Dear Perrin,

"You may fear that I am upset with you for the tone of your recent correspondence, but I am not. I have placed a heavy burden on you, and for that I apologize.

"Perhaps I should have done as so many other parents have and simply raised you to fit in, passed along to you values typical to your class without comment and let you grow to become whatever society would have you be. If I had done so, however, it would have been a grave disservice to you. So perhaps I withdraw my apology.

"You expressed in your letter some confusion as to why Aba stood by and allowed that foolhardy young Arcadian to be hurt. Here is my response: Aba created a beautiful, kind boy named Perrin and gave him strength and the understanding to do what is right, and then He placed that boy exactly where he needed to be in order to help your young Arcadian. I am not sure what more you would have Him do.

"Who, then, stood by and did nothing?"

Perrin's face is hot and his eyes burn. With great effort he produces a flicker of witchlight—his first and only mastery of Elements to date—and burns the letter.

The next day Perrin learns that Bir has been dismissed from the academy. He is called into the headmaster's office and is asked to sign a statement to the effect that Bir is a deeply troubled boy and that he attacked Tremoin without provocation. It will be best for everyone involved, the headmaster tells him, if Perrin would agree with this interpretation of the story. Perrin signs the statement gladly; the knowledge that Bir is gone fills him with relief.

Silverdun awoke in his shambles of a bed, still dressed in his damp clothes, though his boots had been removed. His head throbbed; the worst hangover he'd ever had, with none of the concomitant fun.

Last night was a blur. Something had happened, something bad. What was it?

Darkness. Torches. Steps. Bones. Ilian's boot.

Ilian!

How much damage had Ilian managed to do while Silverdun had slept? He'd murdered the unknown man at the stone clearing. Was that the other recruit? Had he been drugged just as Silverdun had? Had Ilian murdered Jedron as well? Jedron had drunk from the same bottle Silverdun had.

Silverdun bounded to his feet and instantly regretted it. His gorge rose, but thankfully Silverdun the Professional Drunkard had more control over his gag reflex than most. He dunked his head into the washbasin on the table and felt more awake, at least.

He headed toward the closed door, moving silently as Jedron had taught him. The small bodkin came out of his boot without a sound. Silverdun had been no mean threat before coming to Whitemount; after six weeks studying with Jedron, he was now a true menace.

The corridor outside was empty, the witchlight sconces dimmed. The only real light came from the small windows set into the wall, and the wall was so thick that very little light actually found its way in.

The sound of steps clattered on the stair. Whoever was coming was making no attempt to mask his approach. Silverdun gripped the knife firmly but easily and faded back against the wall, unmoving, just as Jedron had taught him.

A figure reached the top of the steps; Silverdun watched his weak, muted shadow approach around the curved passage. The figure was holding something. A weapon? Silverdun waited until the figure was just upon him and then leapt, intending to sweep his opponent's knee and bring the knife to his throat.

He realized as he was being thrown to the ground, his arm bent backward in a most painful fashion, that his potential assailant was Jedron. Once he was on the ground, Jedron—for good measure, Silverdun assumed—bludgeoned him on the head with what turned out to be a silver tray. The contents of the tray spilled onto the ground: bread, bacon, coffee.

Jedron stood over him, scowling. "Don't do that to me ever again."

"I thought . . ." began Silverdun, confused, and in more pain than ever.

"I know what you thought," said Jedron. "But no worries. I've taken care of the Ilian problem for the moment. He's in the basement."

"What was he up to last night?" croaked Silverdun. "I saw a man, I think. He killed a man."

"That's none of your concern," said Jedron. He pointed at the food on the floor. "There's your breakfast," he added, then turned and walked away.

chapter eleven

There is such a thing as too much power.

—Fae proverb

Sela awoke full of expectations and impatience. Today she would go downstairs for breakfast, and Everess would meet her there and explain all of the wonderful things that she was going to do, and then she'd get started doing them. The Accursed Object hugged her upper arm, feeling more like a manacle than ever. She wanted it gone, but she was also afraid of losing it, afraid of knowing what she might do without it.

She was so frustrated she wanted to destroy something. But that wouldn't have been polite. She'd been taught all about propriety: Don't slurp your soup; don't speak with your mouth full; don't destroy things simply because you're impatient. She waited.

A few hours later, Everess finally appeared, with an elderly doctor. The doctor carried a worn leather bag that smelled familiar, like the hospital wing of Copperine House. It made her smile. The doctor, however, was not a pleasant man. Even with the Accursed Object in place, she could sense it.

The doctor looked her over appraisingly. "Amazing," he said finally, reaching out gingerly and touching her face. She wanted to flinch, but did not.

"She seems so tame," said the doctor. "So sane."

"She's a rare find," said Everess.

"She's also right here in the room with you," said Sela. "And she would prefer if the two of you would speak to her, rather than about her."

The doctor looked at Everess wide-eyed, as if unsure whether it was safe to laugh. Everess gave him a warm smile, and the doctor let out a chuckle.

"My my," he said. "Simply amazing. Consider my fears allayed, Lord Everess."

Sela maintained her composure, but inside she fumed. This was exactly the sort of thing that they'd said about her when she was first brought to Copperine House, after the horrors of Lord Tanen and Milla. After the deaths and the loud sounds and the look on Lord Tanen's face at the end.

Everess nodded to the doctor's bag. "So you agree that it's safe?"

The doctor knelt and opened the bag. "Oh, that I cannot guarantee, milord. But it will do what it was intended to do, that's for certain. And whoever made her this way appears to have succeeded admirably."

"I am right here," said Sela, gritting her teeth. "I am not a thing. I am not a creation."

The doctor looked again to Everess for guidance, and Everess gave him that confident smile and put an arm around him. "Perhaps you might wait outside for a moment," he said. The doctor did so, leaving Sela and Everess alone.

"It's not proper for the two of us to be alone together, Lord Everess."

Everess waved it away. "Propriety! That's something, indeed."

He motioned her to the bed and she sat. "Now listen here, Sela. I understand that you don't like being poked at and treated like a prize horse. But you must understand that you are something rare and unique."

"I'm not any kind of thing. I am Fae. That is all I am."

Everess looked at her. Even with the Accursed Object she could sense the momentary sadness that flashed through him. "You are Fae, yes. But that is not all you are." He sat next to her.

Everess took her face in his hands, but it was not a tender gesture. "Now we've gotten off on the wrong foot. The good doctor is here to lift a heavy burden from you, to give you a present. But you must promise to use it responsibly."

Sela's eyes widened. A present? Sela did not have a good history with presents.

"Let's let the doctor come in and go about his business and then you can see. Fair enough?"

Sela nodded, and Everess let the doctor back into the room. He looked into her eyes with a magnifying glass and blew some kind of powder into her ears. He pricked her finger with a needle and let a drop of blood fall into a tiny glass vial. From his bag, he took a small box the size of a stick of butter and dropped the vial into it. The box rattled for a moment and then produced a series of musical tones that appeared to satisfy the doctor.

"She's in perfect condition," he said to Everess. "Physically, anyway."

"Then let's do it," said Everess.

The doctor reached into his bag once again and took out a circular object wrapped in muslin. He held it out in front of her and unwrapped it slowly, showing it to Sela. "What do you think of this?" he said, finally speaking to her.

Sela looked. It was another Accursed Object. She wanted to cry. This one was much narrower, and it was trimmed with fine, filigreed silver, unlike the solid, featureless ring currently encircling her arm.

"What is that?" said Sela.

"Neither the doctor nor I believe that you're ready to have this thing removed entirely. We're not sure how powerful your Gift is without it, and I'm not sure I want to find out."

He paused, taking the band from the doctor's outstretched hand, and his face grew suddenly very serious. "This is power, girl. Power and freedom that I've decided you're capable of controlling." He held it up for her to see, and he gripped her forearm tightly. "If you ever, for a moment, abuse this freedom," he said, "I'll put you down like a buggane in heat."

Sela knew that threats were supposed to be upsetting, and she had seen others cowed by them. Sela assumed that the portion of the heart that cringed at being threatened must have been cut out of her. It was at moments such as this one that Sela frightened herself, when she got glimpses that she was so very unlike the others around her. She knew she was different, but that didn't make it any easier.

What passed through her mind next was a list of the ways that she could kill Everess where he stood. Not that she had any intention of doing so. She actually quite liked Everess; he was going to teach her how to be useful. But it made her feel better to think of killing him.

"We should lay her down for this," said the doctor, indicating the bed. "I imagine she may thrash around a bit."

"Should you give her a physick of some kind?" asked Everess.

The doctor only shrugged in response. He unscrewed the lid from a small jar and sniffed the contents. The smell seemed to satisfy him. "Lie down," he said. It was the first time he'd addressed her since he'd entered the room.

Sela did as she was told. Freedom? Power?

The doctor held up the replacement torque in both hands and turned it around in the light. "Such fine workmanship," he said. He handed Everess the small jar. "When I give the word, pour this over the existing torque."

"What does it do?" said Everess, sniffing the jar just as the doctor had done.

"It will dissolve the iron; the thing should just fall right off."

The Accursed Object? Fall right off? Surely this wasn't right. The Accursed Object was never to be removed. Never, never, never!

"No!" she shouted. She jerked herself up off the bed, twisting her arm out of Everess's grasp. Everess stumbled backward, spilling the liquid contents of the jar onto Sela's shoulder. The liquid ran down her shoulder, and she scrambled away from Everess and the doctor, screeching, her hands over her ears.

When the liquid touched the Accursed Object, it began to sizzle and sputter. Sela looked and saw acrid smoke and a fine red foam erupting wherever the jar's contents touched the Accursed Object. There was a cracking sound, and she felt something strange, something that made her stomach drop deep and clouded her vision.

The Accursed Object fell off of her arm.

She felt naked and exposed, but only for an instant. She touched her arm and the corrosive from the jar burned her fingers, but she didn't care. She felt the indentation in her skin where the Object had been for as long as she could remember.

"Get her!" shouted the doctor, and she looked around. Everess and the doctor were trying to get at her, the doctor in front, holding the Object's replacement. He was coming at her. He was trying to hurt her. And everything was clear, and everything was bright, and the thing that was inside her reared up and grinned from imaginary ear to imaginary ear because there was no more Accursed Object and it was free free free! And it licked out ever so lightly and . . .

The doctor was gone, the only trace of his presence the currents of air that rushed in to take his place. The air currents were lovely. She could feel them. She could feel everything. Oh, it was beautiful! She sat back, reveling in the perfection and the connection of everything and all and ever!

And then she was dragged back from her reverie by Everess, who grabbed her roughly by the wrist and forced the replacement Object on her arm before she could react. It encircled her, brought her down, brought her back into control of herself.

She stood up, wavering. Everess helped her stand. "I've made your doctor go away," she said. "I'm very sorry."

"It was his own fault," said Everess. "He should have known better."

"Will you send me back to Copperine House now?" she asked, worried.

"No," said Everess. "But you must promise never to do anything like that again."

Sela looked down at the new Object and gulped. It was very pretty. It felt nice against her skin. It didn't encircle her as fiercely as the Accursed Object had. She could think. She could feel. She looked at Everess, and a thread leapt, *leapt* out of him, and she could feel him, and for the first time she realized that not only was he frightened of her, he was disgusted by her.

"I think I'd like some tea," she said coldly.

"Fine. Come along," said Everess. He led her downstairs for tea, and when she returned to her room an hour later, all evidence of the doctor and of the old Accursed Object was gone.

The crones are not nice. When Lord Tanen is at the manor, which isn't often, they are respectful to him, and tell Lord Tanen how well they are treating her. But when he is gone they are cold and cruel. There is no one to play with. No one to sing to her or tell her stories. The crones are always there, but all they do is stare into her eyes, poke and prod her. They say strange words and paint pictures on Sela's body and watch her and wait. Sela knows that they are waiting for her to manifest her Gift, and they say the words and paint the pictures to make it come faster and be stronger. She wants to manifest her

Gift because she wants to please them. But she soon comes to understand that nothing she says or does will please them.

She learns to sew and knit, and learns to read and write in Common and High Fae, and she learns poetry and singing. She learns how to hold a knife and how to kill cats. She learns how to move quietly. She learns how to hurt a man by kicking him in a certain place. It will also hurt a woman, but not as much. The crones make her learn all these things, and if she makes a mistake they slap her.

The only one who is nice to her is the big man named Oca. He towers over the crones. He moves slowly and has a high voice. Oca is the only one who is ever allowed to be alone with Sela, and that makes him special. He brings her meals and stands over her while she eats, tut-tutting if she refuses to finish her entire plate. He is kind to her, but only when the crones are not around. If they catch him being nice to her, he will be punished. He says it is a shame what they are doing to her, but she doesn't know what that means.

Lord Tanen does not come often, but when he does, the manor house comes alive. The maids are given extra chores; a special chef comes to the kitchen. All of this belongs to Lord Tanen. The house, the land, even the village at the bottom of the road, which is like Sela's village. She would like to visit there but is not allowed. Sela understands that Lord Tanen owns her as well, though when she tells Oca this, it upsets him. She doesn't want him to be upset.

Everyone is frightened of Lord Tanen, and the crones pinch Sela and warn her to be on her best behavior whenever he comes to visit.

Lord Tanen is coming today, Oca tells her. When he arrives, the crones meet him, and the butler comes and gives him a drink. There is a lavish meal in the dining hall that's kept locked at all other times. The staff have been busy all day in preparation, but Lord Tanen never thanks them that Sela can tell. Oca has taught her that it is always polite to say "Thank you" when someone does something for you. But Lord Tanen is the owner, and the owner does not have to say thank you if he doesn't want to.

After Lord Tanen finishes his dinner, he asks to see Sela. Oca and the crones have dressed Sela in a stiff white dress, with flowers woven into her hair. Sela likes the attention and the dresses and the flowers, but does not enjoy being presented to Lord Tanen. She must curtsey, then stand quietly, saying nothing and not moving, until dismissed. He stares at her silently, nodding his head. He motions her closer and takes her chin in his hand and looks deep into her eyes. His hands feel like paper. He is neither kind nor unkind. Like the crones, he is waiting for her Gift. Until then, there is nothing to do but wait.

The next morning, Sela awoke in her new room expecting Everess to appear and take her somewhere, somewhere where she would do something other than have tea and sit and read. She began to feel as though she were still at Copperine House, that nothing had really changed.

There was a quiet knock at the door, and a chambermaid appeared carrying a washbasin and clothing.

"Good morning, Miss Sela," said the maid, in an accent that Sela had never heard before. Sela looked into her eyes; they glinted in the morning sunlight that drifted in through the diaphanous curtains on the windows. She was not very pretty, and there was also something sad and damaged about her. Nothing unusual for Sela—she was used to seeing sadness and damage at Copperine House—but she'd assumed that people in the outside world were all like Everess: confident, direct, unbroken.

"Is something wrong?" the maid asked. Her name was Ecara, Sela realized with a start. She touched the new Object on her arm, and it was cool to the touch. Accursed no more.

"No, Ecara," Sela said, smiling. This was a smile that would win over Ecara, she knew. Ecara felt invisible most of the time. Looking around her, Sela couldn't see any threads stretching out from the girl. It was so sad; she was just like Sela herself.

Seeing the hint of confusion in the girl's returned smile, Sela added, "I asked Lord Everess what the maids' names were last night. I like to get to know people."

Ecara curtseyed, clearly uncertain what to say. "We don't have to be formal with one another," said Sela. "We're just two girls with jobs to do."

Something in Sela's mind slid into place, and Sela could see a thin blue thread spring into existence between her and Ecara. The maid couldn't see it, of course. It wasn't something you saw with your eyes. Blue felt like trust and friendship.

Ecara was fairly weak willed. With only a tiny effort, Sela could convince Ecara to fall in love with her, to die for her, or to kill for her. It would be easy. She hoped no one would ask her to do that, though, because she thought that Ecara was a very nice girl.

"I'm sure we'll be great friends," said Sela.

The blue thread wavered; that was the wrong thing to say. Why was it wrong? What had she done?

Awkwardness flowed out of Ecara. She wasn't on a level with Sela; it was impossible for them to be friends.

Sela corrected. "Now then, let's get me washed and dressed. I'm sure Lord Everess has a great deal for me to do."

That did it. Even if she hadn't been able to feel inside Ecara, she could see the relief on her face. Sela was the kind mistress; Ecara was a favored servant. All was well. The blue line snapped into place that much more firmly. This was one of the saddest things that Sela knew about people; sometimes frightening them made them love you more.

She allowed Ecara to dress her without another word. It was a complicated gown with hoops of whalebone and petticoats and all sorts of lace pieces that Sela couldn't even name.

Sela sensed that Ecara thought her beautiful; she moved her eyes over Sela's soft, unblemished skin, her lustrous hair, her curves. This wasn't the sexual attraction that Sela sometimes got from women; it was something more innocent, a kind of adoration. Sometimes tinged with jealousy, but not in this case. It was very sweet.

Yes, Ecara would die for her if it became necessary. Oh, how she hoped it wouldn't!

"So today's the day, then, is it?"

"For what, miss?"

"The day that I'm to be taken out to do . . . whatever it is that I'm supposed to be doing."

"I don't know about any of that," said Ecara, frowning. "I'm just here to check the fit."

"Oh?"

"Aye. His Lordship says he wants you to look just right for the lads."

Something cold pierced Sela's thoughts. "Does he?" she said.

The blue thread wavered and turned a deep violet. She'd frightened Ecara.

"I'm sure he doesn't mean anything by it, miss." The girl trembled.

"Are we quite finished then?" asked Sela, with as haughty a voice as she could muster, stretching that violet line nearly to its breaking point. But not past it.

"Yes, miss."

Ecara helped her out of the complicated dress and left the room without another word. Sela wanted to call after her and apologize, but on some level knew that there was nothing to be done about it. So she sat.

And waited.

chapter twelve

Alpaurle: Who, then, is the trustworthy man?

The High Priest: Why, one who can be trusted, of course.

Alpaurle: And how do we know that a man can be trusted?

The High Priest: Such a man does not engage in deceit.

Alpaurle: And how do we know this of him?

The High Priest: Because in all his dealings he is honest.

Alpaurle: But what of a man who is simply never caught in deceit? Would he not appear to be trustworthy? How, then, do we know the trustworthy man?

The High Priest: I see that you are again trying to confuse me.

Alpaurle: Not at all! I am only trying to resolve my own confusion. That is why I ask.

—Alpaurle, from *Conversations with the High Priest of Ulet*, conversation VI, edited by Feven IV of the City Emerald

After the incident with Ilian, Jedron became more surly and combative than ever. Silverdun couldn't tell whether he was angry at himself for allowing himself to be used by Ilian, or whether he was genuinely dismayed at the loss of his only companion. Whatever the reason, he took out his extra aggressions on Silverdun. Not only did he increase the intensity and frequency of their practice sessions, but he also unloaded a great deal of Ilian's chores onto Silverdun. So in addition to his grueling workouts, Silverdun now found himself cooking meals and scrubbing floors.

Nice work for the Faerie lord of Oarsbridge and Connaugh manors. Not that he'd ever been much of a lord. Looking back, Silverdun had to admit that the lordship was only really good for two things: giving him access to women of every station, and providing enough income to keep him off the streets. Being bowed at was all well and good, but Silverdun had discovered over the years that he found commoners and bourgeoisie much more pleasant to be around than his alleged peers.

"Not enough!" shouted Jedron one morning as Silverdun failed to climb the tower by hand in the amount of time that Jedron deemed fitting. "You've got Elements, schoolboy! If there aren't any handholds, then *make* handholds! Just make them so no one will notice them."

A few evenings later, during one of their map studies, Jedron—completely out of the blue—snapped Silverdun with a cloth map, using it like a whip. It caught Silverdun in the eye, blinding him for a full day.

Jedron refused to discuss Ilian, or the man Ilian had killed (or indeed whether this was the other recruit), or even mention Ilian's name. After the first day, he had Silverdun take Ilian's meals to him, while Jedron decided what to do with him.

The basement was small, with a cell in one corner. Ilian had been dumped in the cell, beaten and bloodied, wearing only a loincloth.

The bars of the cell were of cold iron. When Silverdun was a boy, he'd thought that cold iron was actually cold. He was disabused of that notion when he touched a bar of it on a dare at boarding school. Upon touching it, the flesh of his fingers leapt away, seemingly on its own, tearing itself in its hurry to avoid the touch of the metal. The amused school physician had explained that *re*, the magical essence, had a deep disaffinity for cold iron, was intensely repelled by it. Silverdun had developed a huge blister on his finger and hadn't been able to use *re* for a week.

At first, Ilian simply took the meals, which were mainly bread and water, without speaking, and handed Silverdun his waste bucket in exchange. He looked Silverdun in the eye, questioningly, but said nothing.

Then one morning two weeks later, when Silverdun brought him his breakfast, Ilian spoke.

"How is he?" he asked, taking the small dry loaf through the bars.

"What?" asked Silverdun.

"How is Jedron? His moods. Has he become more withdrawn? Begun drinking to excess, that sort of thing?"

"What is it to you? If I recall correctly, you were attempting to murder all of us a few weeks ago. Your concern seems misplaced."

"I care deeply about Jedron. He is my oldest and truest friend. But you must understand that he is not what he once was. He sometimes becomes irrational, paranoid. As a teacher and a former Shadow himself, he has no peer, but the truth is that his advancing age, the isolation, and the guilt over his actions have taken their toll."

Silverdun let this sink in for a moment. Could Ilian be telling the truth? His heart began to sink in his chest. If Jedron was truly mad . . .

"I saw you kill a man," said Silverdun. "And you tried to poison me."

"Are you sure that's what you saw?" said Ilian. "Did you actually see me kill Ironfoot?"

Ironfoot. The other recruit. Silverdun thought back. He'd seen torches. He'd heard screaming. The smoking pit, the bones. "I saw enough."

"And how do you know it was I who put the iglithbi in your brandy? Did it ever occur to you that Jedron did it himself? One of his little tests?"

Silverdun had to admit that Ilian was convincing. But wasn't this exactly what a clever liar would say?

"Tell me what happened to this Ironfoot, then. The one I saw. The one whose bones you collected from that pit."

"Why don't you ask Jedron that question?" said Ilian. "If that doesn't convince you of his madness, I don't know what will."

This conversation was beginning to unnerve Silverdun. He liked to know what he was dealing with.

Silverdun looked down and realized he was still holding the tankard containing Ilian's water. "You're a fairly good liar," he told Ilian. "But I've been a nobleman long enough to see through even the best liar."

"Not the best liar," said Ilian. "For Jedron is the best of them all."

Ilian leaned close. "Soon his paranoia will turn toward you, Silverdun. When the old madman tries to murder you in your sleep, don't say I didn't warn you, you idiot."

Without thinking, Silverdun hurled the tankard between the bars with all his strength, catching Ilian on the temple. Ilian's knees buckled, and he fell to the floor.

Silverdun stormed out of the room and up the stairs to the top of the tower, where he found Jedron sitting at his desk, with a glass of brandy in his hands.

"Dammit, Jedron," Silverdun barked. "I want you to tell me what the hell is really going on around here."

Jedron made no response. He had fallen asleep at his desk. In all the time he'd been at Whitemount, he'd never seen Jedron unconscious.

"Jedron!" Silverdun called. The old man stirred and sat up, fixing a dark gaze on him.

"Get out," he said. When Silverdun began to protest, Jedron hurled the glass of brandy at him. This time, however, Silverdun managed to duck.

After leaving Jedron's room, Silverdun left the tower and returned to the stone steps he'd discovered on the night Ilian had drugged and beaten him. It was sunny and breezy out, and in the light of day the stair seemed far less ominous. There was no railing, he saw, and he wondered that he had made it to the bottom that night without killing himself.

The sea was loud at the base of the steps, where the stone expanse overlooked the water. The stone table was still there, as was the pit. Silverdun peered down into the pit. It was about four feet deep, and empty save for a layer of caked ash. It was scorched on the bottom and the sides.

He jumped in, and his boots sank into the muddy ash. He knelt and took some of the stuff in his hands. It was thick, like clay. The inside of the pit smelled damp and somehow cruel, a malevolent acridity.

Something white glinted in the sun, and Silverdun stepped carefully toward it. Half buried in the sodden ash was a tiny white object. Silverdun picked it up and held it up to the light. It was a bone, a small one. A toe or a finger bone, perhaps. Apparently Silverdun had seen exactly what he thought he'd seen.

Silverdun brushed off the bone and slid it into his pocket. The last evidence of Ironfoot's existence. Whoever he was. Something was going on here, something that neither Ilian nor Jedron would admit, and Silverdun was going to find out what it was.

When he returned to the tower, he found Jedron in the main room, oiling the crossbows. When Silverdun entered, Jedron carefully returned the weapon he'd been cleaning to its peg on the wall and boxed Silverdun's ears. "Where in the queen's hallowed hole have you been?"

"Looking for answers," said Silverdun. "I had a very interesting conversation with Ilian earlier."

"Did you," said Jedron, a statement more than a question. "And what, pray tell, did my erstwhile servant have to say for himself?"

"He told me to ask you what happened on the night I was drugged. The night I saw Ironfoot killed."

Jedron laughed. "Ironfoot killed, eh? Ilian is trying to confuse you; can't you see that? It's the oldest trick; divide your enemies and have them do your fighting for you."

"Then tell me what happened that night." Silverdun held up the bone he'd discovered earlier. "Tell me why I found this in that pit!"

Jedron slapped the thing out of Silverdun's hands. "That does not concern you!" He shoved Silverdun against the wall, hard.

"There is a conspiracy at hand, boy," said Jedron. "There are dark forces at work throughout Faerie. Mab's Einswrath is only a symptom."

He began breathing quickly. "There are the religious fanatics: the Arcadians and the Chthonics. The rebels in the Western Valley. There are certain actions that must be taken that might seem shocking. Things that will cleanse."

"What are you talking about?" said Silverdun.

"When you're ready, you'll understand," said Jedron. "But don't you dare question me in my home. Do we understand one another?"

He didn't wait for Silverdun to answer, but instead stormed upstairs to his office, and didn't emerge for the rest of the afternoon.

It was dark when Silverdun returned to the dungeon carrying the tray for Ilian's supper. Ilian stood against the wall of his cell, eyeing Silverdun with a curious expression that Silverdun couldn't fathom.

"That was a nice shot you took earlier," he said, pulling back his hair to show off the crescent-shaped welt where the tankard had struck his forehead. "I didn't see it coming."

"Your master trained me well," said Silverdun.

At this, Ilian smiled. "You've been an apt pupil," he said.

Silverdun reached through the bars and placed the fresh bread and water on the floor while Ilian stood against the far wall. "Eat," he said.

Ilian ate, looking at Silverdun all the while.

"Would you like the pisspot now?" Ilian asked politely.

"No. I want to show you something." Silverdun took the bone from his pocket and held it up in the dim witchlight of the cellar. "What do you make of this?"

Ilian's frustrating smile returned. "I suppose you could make a necklace out of it, or a very small whistle."

Silverdun ignored the witticism. "I found it in the pit, the one in which you claim no one was murdered. And yet this is a bone, is it not?"

Ilian's smile faded. "Let me see it," he said.

"Tell me what it is."

"Give it to me and I'll tell you what it is."

Silverdun sighed and reached carefully through the bars, the bone in his fingers. Ilian reached for it, then instead grabbed Silverdun's wrist and pulled, hard. Silverdun had no way to brace himself and so plunged face-first into the cold iron bars.

The pain was intense and immediate. Just as he'd remembered, it felt as though a legion of lightning-fast ants were fleeing from the points of contact, down through his body, away, away from the cold iron. This time, however, they didn't stop; the ants continued down his arm and leapt from his wrist into Ilian's hand. Here was a different kind of pain, a pain of rapid depletion, as if something inside him was draining out of him.

It was *re*. Ilian was stealing his *re*, using the cold iron bars to flush the magical essence out of Silverdun's body.

Silverdun felt the way he did after overusing the Gifts in too short a time; physically depleted, yes, but emotionally and spiritually depleted as well.

Before Silverdun could react, Ilian had taken what *re* he needed and used it. Silverdun felt a nauseating sway, and the world tilted sideways and backward. Ilian let go of Silverdun's hand and Silverdun fell back. There was a deep, sickening feeling of vertigo. He looked around and realized that he was inside the cell, not outside it. Ilian had used *re* to do this. Ilian possessed the Gift of Folding.

Silverdun breathed heavily. Ilian was no mere manservant; that was for certain.

Silverdun backed as far from the bars as he was able, until his back was pressed against the cool stone wall of the cellar. He'd been behind iron bars before, trapped in the wastes of the Contested Lands with Mauritane and his merry band of fools, by *humans* of all things. If he could get far enough away from the iron, concentrate, he could breathe in enough *re* to get himself out of the cell.

But it was no use. The bars were too close, and there was no *re* to be had.

"Dammit!" shouted Silverdun, smashing both fists against the wall behind him. Ilian was loose in the tower, and perhaps this time Jedron wouldn't be able to best him. And there was another part of Silverdun that knew that Jedron would be furious with him for allowing Ilian to escape. Maybe it would be better if Jedron *didn't* make it.

Shut up, Silverdun.

He eyed the bars of the cell glumly; he could almost feel their repulsion, even from here. There was something curious about the way the dim light in the room hit the bars at chest height. They looked as though viewed through a prism, or through a glass of water, the bars seeming to jog slightly to the right for a few feet, then resuming their course above. As sometimes happened to him during times of stress, Silverdun found himself focusing on this odd optical illusion rather than the problem at hand. A trick of the mind, perhaps, to stave off despair.

Silverdun stepped forward to examine the trick of light more closely, his curiosity momentarily dispelling his discomfort. When he looked more closely, he smiled.

This was no trick of the light; the bars had actually been shifted by Ilian's fold. When Ilian swapped with Silverdun, he'd simply rotated the space around them in a half circle. But the bars didn't quite line up properly when reversed.

Silverdun's face and shoulders still burned where Ilian had pulled him against the iron. Wincing, Silverdun ran at the off-kilter section of the bars and kicked out with all his might. The pain was intense, the same crawling sensation, now running up his leg, twisting his scrotum. The bars bent and cracked, but didn't break.

He stepped back for another kick. By the queen's tits, he did not want to do this again. He did it anyway.

Silverdun's second kick sent a huge portion of the cell door flying backward with an ugly metallic clatter. He pulled his leg back too quickly, however, and caught his shin on the sharp edge of one of the bars that had been cut apart. The cold iron dug into his flesh, creating an entirely new kind of pain, like barbed ice in the blood. Silverdun staggered backward, falling to the floor. He screamed.

There was a creaking noise. Silverdun looked up. The lock of the cell's door was now on the floor, part of the portion that Silverdun had kicked away. The creaking was the sound of the door swinging open on rusted hinges.

He stood, shaking, eased himself through the opening with extreme care, and hurried up the stairs, taking the knife from his boot with a shaky hand.

Silverdun hurried up the stairs to the main floor and stopped. Silence. Silverdun replaced the knife in his boot, exchanging it for the *petite arbalète* on the wall of the main room. He cocked it as quietly as possible, ensuring that the quarrel was set properly, just as Jedron had taught him.

Where would Ilian have gone? Upstairs? Or would he have attempted to escape in the *Splintered Driftwood?* Silverdun headed for the stairs, if for no other reason than the fact that the wound in his calf was still screaming, and the thought of running all the way to the quay filled him with dread. Each step toward Jedron's office, however, was like a knife thrust in his leg. There had never been anywhere near as many steps in this staircase as now, even at Silverdun's most exhausted.

As he rounded the stairs to the level of his own bedroom, there was a loud crash from above, and a muffled shout. Silverdun forced himself forward, his body protesting with every movement.

Just when he thought he couldn't take another step, he reached the top, and the wooden door to Jedron's office. He pushed it open.

Jedron and Ilian were inside, facing each other. They'd been grappling with one another. The desk was broken, on its side. Books and maps were strewn everywhere. Jedron and Ilian circled one another, both unarmed. Ilian's face was red and he was sweating profusely. Jedron was flushed, but no sweat appeared on his brow. Neither man turned when Silverdun entered the room.

"Glad you're here, Silverdun," said Jedron. "Perhaps you'd like to pitch in? Test some of those skills I've drummed into you?"

Ilian scowled. "You know that he's mad, Silverdun! If you don't believe me, ask him what happened on the night you were drugged! Ask him!"

"He's just trying to confuse you, boy. He knows you wouldn't understand."

"That man you saw," said Ilian, "the one on the table. His name was indeed Ironfoot. He *was* the other recruit. Jedron—"

Jedron lunged at Ilian, tackling him and pushing him backward. He was strong, Silverdun knew. But Ilian seemed evenly matched with him.

Silverdun held the *petite arbalète* up, aiming at the two men. This was clearly a serious situation, but it was also utterly preposterous. Part of him wanted to shoot both of them and try to sail the boat back to the mainland himself, where he would find Everess and kill him using one of the nearly infinite methods that Jedron had taught him. Unfortunately, the tiny crossbow contained only one bolt, and Silverdun doubted he could take either Ilian or Jedron hand to hand even when his entire body *wasn't* racked with pain. So he'd have to pick one or the other. But which?

Ilian got his feet between himself and Jedron and shoved hard; Jedron was flung backward, into a bookcase, smashing it, sending books and scrolls flowing onto the floor. Jedron pushed himself up into a standing position.

Jedron glared at Silverdun with the fierce rictus that passed for his smile. "Just like I told you at the dock, eh boy? Nothing is as it seems!"

"Ah," said Silverdun. He aimed the crossbow at Jedron's head and pulled the trigger.

The bolt in the crossbow was bound with a healthy dose of Motion, vectored in the direction of the bolt's flight. When the trigger was pulled, the binding was released and the bolt flew astonishingly fast; then a separate binding of Elements was released and the bolt's head exploded.

All this happened so quickly that to Silverdun it appeared that him pulling the crossbow's trigger and Jedron's head erupting in flame were two separate, unconnected events. It was not flesh and bone, however, that sprayed outward, but rather bronze and gold and bits of silver.

Jedron was not alive—he was one of his own automata. His headless body swooned and fell smoothly to the ground, its glamour evaporating, leaving no doubt as to its true form.

Ilian stood, dusting off his shirt and trousers. "Good shot," he said. "Though I hope you realize the replacement cost for that thing is coming out of your wages."

"Your name's not Ilian," said Silverdun.

"No," he said simply.

"You're Jedron."

The other man clapped, smiling. "Very good, Silverdun! Not everyone figures that part out at first."

The real Jedron righted two chairs and bade Silverdun sit in one of them. "So tell me," he said, "when did you figure it out?"

Silverdun sat, laying the crossbow on his lap, not quite comfortable letting it go. "I wasn't absolutely certain until he mentioned something that he'd said at the quay. But it wasn't something *he'd* said; it was something *you'd* said. He wasn't there." Silverdun sighed. "But I suspected it earlier."

"Oh, good. Because that verbal slip was my last-ditch attempt to keep you from shooting me. When did you first suspect?"

"It was when I knocked you out in the cell, and when I went upstairs, Jedron was asleep. But he wasn't really asleep; he was only inactive, the way the automata on the *Splintered Driftwood* are."

The real Jedron smiled and nodded. "Hm. Well, I hate to admit it, but you really put me through my paces. You weren't supposed to wake up the night that I inducted Ironfoot. That required some truly inspired improvisation on my part."

"That wasn't part of the test," said Silverdun. "Or whatever it was."

"No. You were supposed to begin to suspect Jedron over a slightly longer period of time, ultimately leading to a final confrontation in which you killed him in order to save yourself. Killing the teacher is a very important part of the training."

"Why's that?" said Silverdun. The pain in his leg was beginning to subside, finally.

"Like I said—and by 'I,' I mean that fellow on the ground over there—it's important for you to understand that you cannot trust anyone. Not anyone. Not ever again. It's the sort of thing one hears but must experience firsthand in order to truly grasp. Better you learn it here where it won't get you killed."

"But," said Silverdun, "what if I'd shot you instead of him?"

Jedron waved the question away. "It would take a lot more than one of those little quarrels to stop me. As you'll soon discover for yourself."

"What does that mean?"

"You want to know what happened that night, don't you? The man you thought you saw killed?"

"It was going to be my next question, yes."

"Let's go see then, shall we? I think you're ready."

Jedron stood and motioned for Silverdun to follow. Silverdun's head was spinning. Again he asked himself: What the hell had he gotten himself into?

At the bottom of the steps, the torches were already lit. Jedron led Silverdun down the stairs and onto the stone expanse. There was a man standing before the pit, holding a black robe.

Silverdun started to sweat, the pain in his body now replaced with a shivering dread. What was about to happen?

The man in the robe stepped forward, and Silverdun recognized the face immediately. It was the man he thought he'd seen Ilian murder.

"Hello," the man said. "My name is Styg Falores. But you can call me Ironfoot."

"I'm not certain what the proper greeting is for this occasion, so I'll just say hello back," said Silverdun, attempting to regain his composure.

"Strip down and put this on," said Ironfoot, holding out the robe. Silverdun looked over at Jedron and Jedron nodded.

Why not? How much stranger could this day possibly get? Whatever was happening, this Ironfoot fellow had gone through the same thing. Some kind of initiation ritual, perhaps? Silverdun thought about the bone, and the ash.

He looked toward the pit, but inside all he could see was darkness.

He stripped off his clothes and pulled on the black robe. It was made of silk. It made him feel like a part of the night.

"Walk to the edge of the pit," said Jedron. Silverdun did so. He squinted, still seeing nothing.

"Look down and tell us what you see," said Jedron. He said the words as though they were part of a ritual, with a musical cadence.

Silverdun looked down. At first he saw nothing, but then he noticed something moving, something barely distinguishable in the glint of the torchlight. But it was only black on black. Perhaps it was nothing.

"Perrin Alt," said Jedron, "what do you see?"

"Nothing," said Silverdun.

Jedron and Ironfoot pushed him then, hard, into the pit. There was something inside, waiting for him. It received him. Enveloped him.

The pain that came next made the touch of cold iron seem like a lover's caress.

Part Two

For reitic energy compressed into a contained binding, the formula is consistent regardless of the specific physical Gift involved, be it Motion, Elements, or even Folding. There is a practical limit to the amount of energy that can be compressed in a given container, as the required binding energy increases exponentially with the volume of the container. For any given volume v, the required binding energy is $\frac{1}{2}ev^2$, regardless of the bound form. Thus it is recommended that when large energy bindings are required, sufficient space is allotted in the design.

Since it is often impractical to contain energies of multiple Gifts in a single binding, the problem often arises when it becomes necessary to mingle the products of multiple Gifts prior to the full unbinding of a closed system. Students often attempt to rechannel such products across a binding in order to avoid the difficulties that arise with nested binds. Unfortunately, this is not possible.

To understand why it is impossible to channel one Gift through another, it is necessary to understand the formulae for channeling Gifts through a medium. The standard formula for that energy is, in its most basic construction, $c = 2/(e - m)r$ at any point during the transition, where c is the required channeling energy, e is the energy to be channeled, m is the total energy of the channeling medium, and r is the inductive resistance factor of the channeling medium. The problem that arises when both e and m are reitic energies is that during the channeling, e inevitably increases at the sourcepoint of the channel, while m inevitably decreases, such that at a determinable point during the channeling process $(e - m) = 0$. At this point, the equation fails, as the bottom term becomes undefined.

It is tempting to imagine that one might avoid this problem by channeling ever greater amounts of energy into e, but regardless of the value of m, the required value of e will inevitably approach infinity before the sourcepoint completes the transition.

—*Dynamics*, chapter 8:
"Channeling Methodology in Closed Bindings"

chapter thirteen

A shopkeeper from one of my villages came to me with a problem; he'd been advertising an opening in his shop and had thus far received only two applicants. One was a penniless drifter, the other a retired mestine.

I counseled him to hire the drifter, his being the slightly more reputable profession.

—Lord Gray, *Recollections*

The first rehearsal following a tour was always the worst. The props had been put away roughly after the final show in the last city, and the sweaty costumes were dumped in trunks without being washed or folded. Everyone was sick of it all, and nobody wanted to come back to work.

The Bittersweet Wayward Mestina had finished its sweep of the southern cities and had finally returned home to Estacana after four weeks on the road. They'd then taken a well-deserved week off, having done a brisk business while away. But now the week was over, and it was time to get back to work.

Faella let herself into the theater early and stepped up on the stage, alone. The theater was called The Snowflake, and it had been her father's dream. Father, however, hadn't lived to see it.

Ironically, it seemed that all this time, Father had been the one standing in the way. While he was running the Bittersweet Wayward it had only ever been marginally profitable. Usually they could afford to eat; usually they had comfortable lodgings. But it wasn't unheard-of for them to sleep in the wagons outside the walls of a city, crowded up on makeshift beds of costumes and curtains.

It wasn't until after Father had died, and Faella had inherited the business, that she realized how incompetent he'd been. Always the showman, always the promoter, he'd managed to secure business across the kingdom, but he'd mismanaged the funds horribly, given away too much of the gate to unscrupulous theater owners, squandered money on expensive theatrical detritus: props, amplifying cabinets, real velvet costumes when felt would do just as well.

No, Father had been a deeply impractical man. Faella had loved him, and had grieved when he'd passed away just after the end of midwinter, but now she rarely thought of him. And now, just a year later, The Snowflake was hers. The down payment had been made with gold that she herself had earned through hard work and perseverance.

The problem was, it wasn't anywhere near enough.

She stood upon the stage and bowed deep to the empty theater. Legions of imagined adoring fans applauded her. She stretched and sang a few scales.

Faella had been a brilliant mestine since she was a little girl; that was common knowledge. She'd been the star of the Bittersweet Wayward since she'd been old enough to speak. All the other mestines in her employ knew it and grudgingly accepted it.

It had never occurred to Father, though, that Faella might not have wanted that for herself. He'd just assumed that because she was so talented, and because she enjoyed it so much, that she'd never want anything else.

Faella knew she was meant for more. She just *knew* it. She'd hoped that owning the theater, being in charge of the mestina, would do the trick. But quite the opposite was true: It only made her feel more constrained, more trapped in her tiny life.

There must be more than this. It was as though there was a living thing inside her that yearned for greatness, that lived inside her heart and pummeled at her to be released from the tedium of her days.

Such thoughts always led to thoughts of Perrin Alt, Lord Silverdun. She'd met him on the way to Estacana, during the dead of midwinter. She'd fallen in love with him on sight. Foolish girl that she was, she'd assumed the feeling was mutual because he was attracted to her.

Silverdun was everything she'd ever dreamed of. Gorgeous, talented, intelligent. And important.

Silverdun was a lord. A nobleman. He could sweep her away, make her a lady. Surely that would fulfill her longings? In her headstrong desire, she'd made an ass of herself, thrown herself at him. And when he'd done what any man would have done—that is, bed her and then leave her—she'd become furious. Beyond furious. If only she'd known then how vile other men could be, she might have been a bit more forgiving. But not so then.

Then something very strange had happened. The thing inside her that knew she was destined for greatness had *leapt out* at him. It had done something. It had made him ugly. Changed his face somehow. Not that there was really a *thing* in her. It *was* her. The part of her she'd been pushing down all her life.

At first she'd thought it was just a very well done glamour that she'd done, despite the fact that she knew deep down that it was something else entirely. She'd written a spiteful note on the mirror: *Be as ugly out as in*. That would show him!

Then he was gone, and she wished she'd done something different. She played back every minute of their time together and realized that at every turn she'd played the desperate common girl to the hilt, that she'd been petty and foolish. He'd liked her, and he'd slipped through her fingers, and his last memory of her would be that stupid glamour. And yes, it *had* simply been a glamour, nothing more. What else could it have been?

Yes, he was gone, off on his secret mission or whatever it was with gruff, gruff Mauritane and that scary woman and the human and the sullen fat one. Off they'd gone, into the Contested Lands, and she'd never seen him again.

A month or two later, though, she'd been paging through one of the court papers, reading gossip about people she hated to admire but did anyway, and there was a likeness of Silverdun. He was a hero now. A true war hero from the Battle of Sylvan.

Of course. Just her luck. The one she let go would turn out to be not just a nobleman but a *war hero* to boot.

But then she'd noticed something even stranger, that had made her forget all about her own self-pity.

Silverdun's face was still changed. It wasn't quite the hideous face she'd given him in her rage. But it wasn't the face she'd met him with, either. It was something in the middle. Oddly, she liked it a bit better than the pretty face he'd started out with.

But if he was still wearing it, then it was no glamour. There was no way to elude that nagging feeling anymore. The thing—no, not a thing—*Faella* had done something that she wasn't sure anyone knew how to do. Certainly not an uneducated girl from a second-rate mestina in a second-rate city on the wrong side of the kingdom.

But there it was.

Faella reached out her hand and began the motions of a new mestina she'd just begun to write. It was called "Twine." She glamoured two thin strands of pure color: one red, one gold. The two threads weaved around her in the darkened theater, bathing her face in their light. She moved her wrist slowly in rhythm and the strands began to move more quickly, circling one another.

Once she'd begun to believe that she'd truly done something unusual to Silverdun, it seemed to set something off in her. It started small. Little things: The very item she needed would find itself to hand without her having to look; a dress she'd been longing for would turn up drastically on sale at the boutique on the Boulevard. That sort of thing.

But soon inexplicable things had begun to happen. One night, when the first month's mortgage payment had come due for the theater, she'd opened the cash box to find precisely the amount she'd needed to pay. What made this even more remarkable was that it was at least twice the amount it should have been, given the ticket sales that night.

Never anything astonishing. Never more than what she needed at a given moment.

The red and gold strands circled each other, then dove toward one another, twirling around and around. They dipped and dodged and wove in and out. Twining about in a perfect braid and then—

The two strands became tangled; they hitched in the air above her, in a snarl. She let them go and they fell limply to the floor in a disappointing knot, then faded away.

Certainly the others should have started appearing by now. Mestines weren't known for punctuality, but they were seldom this late.

"Miss Faella!"

Faella looked up and saw Bend, one of the stagehands, running into the auditorium.

"Bend?" she said crossly. "Where is everyone?"

"Apologies, miss. I looked for you at your home but you'd already left."

"Why? What's going on?"

"It's Rieger," said Bend. "He's hurt bad, stabbed."

"Oh, hell," said Faella. She and Bend ran from the theater together. Rieger was Faella's on-again, off-again lover, but more to the point he was one of her best mestines.

Estacana was an unusual city, having been built for giants; its roads were too wide, its windows too large, its steps too tall. Faella liked it. She liked things that were larger than life. But today the city didn't hold her interest as it usually did. She followed Bend through the streets to the fourth-floor garret where Rieger lived.

The room was crowded with players and hands from the Bittersweet Wayward, all standing around looking worried. Leave it to mestines to become melodramatic and useless in a crisis.

"Everyone out," she barked. "Go to the theater where you can be useful." She began shooing them out.

Once the room was cleared she found her way to Rieger's bedside and looked down at him. A physician, an elderly woman in a starched-neck black dress, was tending a wound in Rieger's abdomen with herbs and smoke, blowing the white healing vapor into the cut. Rieger's sister Ada sat next to him on the bed, holding his hand.

The physician looked up at her. "Who are you?" she said.

"I'm Faella," she said. "I'm his employer."

"Will you pay for my services?" asked the physician.

"Yes. Use whatever cures you have at your disposal."

The physician nodded, reached for her bag, and rummaged through it.

Faella knelt next to Rieger and ran her fingers through his hair. He was unconscious, breathing rapidly.

"What happened?" she whispered to Ada.

"You know him," Ada said. "Out drinking and carrying on until daybreak. He and another fellow at the tavern got into a drinking competition, and somehow a fight started. Rieger went into it with his fists, but the other fellow had a knife."

"Do they know who it was?"

"Oh, sure," said Ada. "Malik Em. But he's with the Wolves, so they won't touch him."

The Wolves were a band of thieves who were clever enough to invest a portion of their earnings with the City Guard. Untouchable.

"I see," said Faella. She looked at Rieger, and a sudden wash of pity ran through her. She didn't love him, and he certainly didn't love her. But she did care for him. He was tender and talented and he made her laugh.

She looked down at him. The physician had cleaned away the dried blood, leaving the ragged knife wound fully exposed on his belly.

She took the physician aside. "What do you think?" she said.

The physician looked at Rieger, thinking. "I have a few preparations I can try, but I won't lie to you. It doesn't look good. I'd say he'll likely die as not, no matter what I do. The cut's too deep and has done too much damage."

"I see," said Faella.

She knelt again by Rieger, looking again at the wound. She couldn't take her eyes off of it. One tiny little cut, no longer than a finger. That's all it took to kill a man.

It seemed absurd. Laughable. How could something so small accomplish so much?

She wanted to touch it; she didn't know why. Ada was on the other side of the room with the physician, who was showing her how to apply a new poultice. Feeling guilty, Faella reached out and ran her fingers along the jagged red opening.

Things that were cut could be sewn. Faella's mother had been able to mend a dress so that you could never tell that it had been ripped. It was just a matter of concentration, she'd always said.

Faella concentrated on Rieger, and her mind shifted into a kind of daydream, imagining what sorts of things lay beneath a man's skin. Blood and bone, flesh, meat. She'd never seen those things, but she assumed that he must look rather like a side of beef inside.

Strange about healing. The body knit itself from the inside, like a torn hem taking a needle and stitching itself up. It was mysterious and wonderful. A kind of magic unlike the Gifts. The deeper magic of nature, which always desired to make itself whole. And couldn't such a thing be nudged in just the right direction? Faella had no idea how a body mended itself, but she understood desire.

"Remove your hand from the injury, miss!" came the physician's voice. Faella opened her eyes; the physician was standing over her, scowling. Faella looked down and saw her palm pressed against Rieger's belly, massaging it.

"You're killing him!" shouted Ada. She grabbed Faella's hand away.

The wound was gone, as Faella had known it would be.

The physician bent over and stared at Rieger, then at Faella. Rieger's breathing was already beginning to slow.

"I don't know what kind of trickery you mestines have gotten up to, but I don't appreciate being fooled!" the physician snapped. "Play your glamour pranks on someone else!" She stormed out of the room, slamming the door.

When, an hour later, Rieger regained consciousness, he asked Faella what had happened. Neither she nor Ada had an answer.

A week later, Faella was shopping in the bazaar when she saw Malik Em out roaming the aisles with his friends in the Wolves. He laughed and winked at the stallkeepers, taking a piece of fruit here and a silver ring there, paying for nothing but thanking the vendors profusely in a mockery of propriety.

The body desired to heal itself, she had discovered. But what if it didn't? If that desire could be increased, could it be decreased as well? Removed altogether?

Faella watched Malik Em go, lost in this thought. When she learned a few days later that Malik Em had died of a simple ague, she shrugged. Albeit with a grim satisfaction.

Probably just a coincidence.

No, probably not.

Faella knew desire, and no matter how much she tried to enjoy her life as the proprietor of the Bittersweet Wayward Mestina, she knew that she never could.

More was waiting out there. More would come to her, whether she wanted it or not.

Someday Silverdun would return to her, she began to think. And she wondered, if it did someday happen, would it be because she herself had caused it?

It was something to ponder, but in the meantime there was always work to do.

chapter fourteen

In matters of war, as in love, things rarely go as expected.

—Lord Gray, *Recollections*

Paet was waiting at the dock when the *Splintered Driftwood* nuzzled into its slip, guided flawlessly by Jedron, now back in his role as Captain Ilian. Paet had a satchel slung over one shoulder and held it close to his body. Silverdun looked over at Ironfoot. Neither of them had spoken much during the brief trip back to the mainland. Silverdun had been lost in his thoughts, and apparently so had Ironfoot. "Captain Ilian" hadn't spoken to either of them at all, seeming to understand that they needed the space.

The boat touched the dock with a light thump, and one of the automata tossed a line to Paet, who tied it. Jedron leapt from the boat onto the dock; he and Paet regarded each other, but neither spoke.

"Come on, then," said Jedron, waving to Silverdun and Ironfoot. "We don't have all day."

Silverdun rose and took a step forward, and stumbled. Since the night that he'd been tossed into the pit of blackness, a night that he did not care to remember, he'd felt uncomfortable in his own skin. Oddly, though, at the same time he'd never felt better. Whatever they'd dunked him in appeared to have done him some good, but still . . . it was impossible to describe. Jedron had told him that the feeling of strangeness would pass. It was all "part of it," but he refused to say what "it" was, and Ironfoot claimed not to know either.

Silverdun followed Ironfoot onto the dock and stood blinking. The sounds of the seaside assailed him all at once: the shouts of the fishermen, the shushing of the wind through a hundred sails, the calls of gulls overhead. Farther up the pier, a legless man played the ocarina for passersby.

"All went well, I assume?" Paet asked Jedron.

"As well as can be expected," Jedron said. "This one," he added, jostling Silverdun's arm, "gave me a bit of a turn, though. Someone forgot to tell me that he'd studied potions at Nyelcu."

Paet's expression didn't change. "He didn't."

"I dropped out after a week," said Silverdun. "It wasn't for me."

Jedron glared at Paet, who shrugged. "Were they successful or weren't they?"

"They were," said Jedron. His look said *don't test me.*

"Then we're finished here. Her Majesty thanks you for your service."

There was a moment of deep tension between the two. Then Jedron laughed. "You little shit." He untied the line and then leapt with an astonishing nimbleness back on board the *Splintered Driftwood.*

For a while Paet stood and watched as Jedron and his crew of mechanical sailors eased out of the marina and into open water. Silverdun and Ironfoot watched with him. No one spoke.

Once the boat had vanished in the waves, Paet turned and looked at Silverdun. "You think you hate him now?" he said. "Wait until you've known him as long as I have."

"Now what?" said Silverdun.

"Now you go home and get settled," said Paet. "Both of you. If your training was anything like mine, you're exhausted beyond belief."

"True," said Ironfoot. "I can't remember ever having been so tired."

Paet opened his satchel and handed them each a sheaf of documents. "Each of you has a new valet at home," he said.

Silverdun looked at the documents. On top was a Copyist Guild–certified likeness of a man named Olou, whose title was given as "Special Services Officer" of the Foreign Ministry.

"Olou's a good man," said Paet, pointing at the likeness.

"What is he for?" asked Silverdun.

"He'll do all the things that an ordinary gentleman's man would do, and a few things he wouldn't. He'll help you select the proper attire for a given assignment, clean and maintain your weapons, that sort of thing. He'll also supervise the maid and cook. His job is to look out for you when you're at home."

"A nice perk," said Ironfoot.

"When you get to your home, give him the sign 'The master has returned.' He will offer the countersign, 'And there could not be a lovelier day for it.'"

"Seems a bit paranoid," said Silverdun. "Do you really expect a faux valet might strangle me in my sleep?"

"Stranger things have happened," said Paet. "You've become a serious investment of the Ministry. We like to look after our investments."

"I see."

"Oh," added Paet. "Olou told me your rooms are a shambles, and that he expects you to take better care of your things while he's in your employ."

"It's not my fault," said Silverdun. "I had a girl, but she resigned in a dispute over wages."

"Really?" asked Paet. "Olou gave me the distinct impression that you'd bedded her and that her husband found out about it."

"That is true," said Silverdun wistfully. "But that's not why she quit."

"I don't really need a valet," said Ironfoot. "I've been a bachelor for many years now."

"I didn't ask if you needed one," said Paet. "But if you insist on dressing yourself, that's your business."

Paet pulled another sheet from the sheaf in Silverdun's hand. There was an address written on it: Blackstone House. One Sevetal Lane.

"Be at that address tomorrow at sundown," he said. "That's where you'll be working. Don't be late."

With that, Paet turned and walked off up the dock, leaving Silverdun and Ironfoot to find their own ways home.

Blackstone House rose out of a walled garden overgrown with nettles, wild roses, and moss-covered willow trees. Sevetal Lane was just inside the north wall of the city, in a neighborhood peopled mostly by those who valued their privacy and could afford to maintain it. Thus its secretive appearance was less out of place than it might have been elsewhere. A bronze gate was set in the wall just to the right of the house, its bars offering a view only of a chaotic line of shrubbery that might once have been an orderly hedgerow.

The second story jutted out above the garden, a bleak promontory, its dark bricks worn and vine-covered, its windows shuttered.

When Silverdun's hired cab dropped him off, just before sunset, he was certain there was some kind of mistake. He double-checked the address with the driver, who shrugged and whipped his horses on without a word.

This couldn't possibly be right. The headquarters of the all-powerful Shadows was in an abandoned ghasthouse? Surely Paet was having a joke at his expense.

It was chilly out, but Silverdun's new cloak, provided by his equally new valet Olou, was just the thing to keep out the cold. Olou had turned out to be a young man, probably fresh out of the army, who'd drawn a short lot somewhere along the way. Regardless of how he'd ended up there, he tended to his duties with panache. And Silverdun had never looked better.

Silverdun approached the gate, but before he could peer in, another carriage turned onto the road. It too stopped in front of Blackstone House, and Ironfoot emerged from it. He examined the house with the same reservation that Silverdun felt.

"Strange place for a government office," he said.

"Ministry of Ghosts, perhaps?" offered Silverdun.

Ironfoot smiled. "So what happens? We go in, get accosted by a few vengeful spirits, and then Paet shows up and laughs at us while we're wetting our breeches?"

"I was thinking roughly the same thing."

"When I was in the army, they tied new recruits in burlap sacks and rolled them down the hills in the Gnomics," said Ironfoot. "Big, tall things, these hills. They'd have races with them."

"And how did you fare?" asked Silverdun.

"I won four out of five," said Ironfoot. "It's all in how you arch your back."

"Universal, I suppose. In my first session of Corpus, the senior hall minister handed me a four-hundred-page stack of bills and told me I'd be voting on them the next day, so I'd better read them all."

"How far did you get?"

"I never even glanced at them," said Silverdun. Seeing the look on Ironfoot's face, he added, "I wasn't much of a legislator."

"Do you find yourself wondering if we've made a terrible mistake?" asked Ironfoot.

"Every day. But then, I've made a career of joining the wrong team," said Silverdun. "One gets used to it after a while."

"That's encouraging," said Ironfoot glumly.

"Right on time, I see," came Paet's voice behind them.

Silverdun turned. Paet was standing in the street, leaning on his cane. There was no carriage anywhere nearby.

"Where did you come from?" said Silverdun.

"I'm a Shadow, Silverdun," said Paet. "It's part of the job. Shall we go in?"

Paet approached the gate and placed his palm on one of the bronze bars. He said a word of unbinding, and the gate swung open.

Paet led them up the walk. It was darker here than outside, the moss-hung willow branches filtering out what remained of the daylight. It smelled of roses and loam.

The front door of the house was black; the paint on the door and the trim was chipped and peeling in places.

"The servants have clearly been on holiday for some time," said Silverdun.

"You can grab a paintbrush and take care of it if you like," said Paet. He took a ring of keys from his pocket and placed one in the front door.

The door opened into a totally empty room. Dust lined the windowsills and blanketed the wooden floors. A soot-blackened fireplace hulked on one wall. Very little light found its way through the drawn shutters. Paet produced a tiny witchlight torch from his pocket and lit their way toward the stairs.

"Come on," he said. As they walked, Silverdun noticed that while their steps kicked up dust from the floor, they left no footprints.

They climbed the stairs to the second story, which was as dusty and empty as the first. Their steps made hollow echoes. Paet led the way to a back bedroom, where an empty bed frame lurked in a corner.

"Through here," said Paet, indicating a closet door. He opened the door and stepped in, beckoning for Silverdun and Ironfoot to follow. Silverdun stood in the closet, crowded against Paet and Ironfoot, feeling foolish. Paet smelled like pipe smoke. He closed the door and they stood in the cramped space for a moment while Paet found another key on his ring in the torch-light. He placed it in the closet door lock and turned. The closet seemed to turn upside down, and Silverdun's stomach heaved. Ironfoot gulped.

Silverdun looked down, and now he could see light coming from under the closet door. Paet opened it and they stepped out of the closet into a small reception room. A pretty young Fae woman stood when they entered.

"Good evening, Chief Paet," she said.

Silverdun looked around, disoriented at first, until he realized what was going on. The entire house had been quite expertly spellturned. They had simply stepped into a turned version of the bedroom they'd just left.

"Good evening, Brei," said Paet. He removed his cloak and handed it to her. "I'd like you to meet Ironfoot and Silverdun, our newest Shadows."

"A pleasure, gentlemen," said Brei, reaching for Silverdun's and Iron-foot's cloaks as well. She smiled at Silverdun. "I've got keys for the two of you, and there's tea or coffee if you'd like some."

Silverdun and Ironfoot looked at each other. Perhaps this wasn't going to be so bad after all. "Tea, if you please," said Silverdun.

Paet led them from the reception office into what should have been the hallway. In this turning of the house, however, all of the other upstairs inner walls had been removed, creating an open office space that was filled with desks.

"Welcome to the Office of Shadow," said Paet. "Your new home."

Paet walked them through the office, briskly introducing them to a dozen different office workers: two copyists, a translator, and a cluster of ana-lysts, whose job it was to read all of the documents and memos pertaining to intelligence, and to prepare briefs. One shelf along the wall was lined with message sprite jars; all the other walls were covered with maps. Papers were stacked high everywhere, on desks, in baskets; more bulged from a row of special drawers along the wall beneath the message sprites.

One of the analysts was a young woman with a strong Eastern accent, a lilt that Silverdun had grown accustomed to in his days at the prison of Crere Sulace, and now found that he missed. When Ironfoot was introduced, she smiled, her eyes wide. "I've so been looking forward to meeting you," she said. "I've read all of your monographs on forensic thaumatics."

"Well, I'd be happy to discuss the subject with you anytime you like," said Ironfoot.

"Come along," said Paet. "You can flirt with the help another time."

Ironfoot shrugged. "We'll talk later," he told the analyst, who grinned at him.

Paet pointed to the stairs. "My office is down there, as is the mission room and the Shadows' Den, which is where you'll be spending most of your time."

They went downstairs. Here, the layout of the house hadn't been altered. The main room with its fireplace was here, but it now held several tables surrounded by chairs, all covered in maps and scrolls. A row of books—atlases, almanacs, and censuses—lined one wall.

"The mission room," said Paet. "This is where you'll be briefed on your various assignments."

Through one door was a large office that was Paet's. It was sparse and neat. Another door opened to a smaller office with three desks in it, all three of which were empty. The room smelled a bit musty. Paet turned on the witchlamp on the wall, and the office filled with a warm yellow glow.

"This is the Shadows' Den," he said. "This is your office."

Silverdun ran his finger along one of the desktops, leaving a line in the dust there. "Hasn't been used in a while," he said.

"It's been a while since we've had anyone to use it," said Paet. "It's about time, too."

"Where does the front door lead?" asked Ironfoot.

"Turns back in on itself," said Paet. "Very handy if you need to induce a gag reflex."

"Three desks," said Silverdun.

"Hm?" said Paet.

"In the so-called Shadows' Den. There are three desks, and only two of us."

Paet smiled. "Ah, yes. I thought Everess would have told you. You've got a colleague. She'll be joining us shortly. Everess is bringing her."

Ironfoot and Silverdun shared another glance. *She?*

"In the meantime I've got work to do. Get yourselves acquainted with things; have Brei show you where to find things like pens and ink and so forth. When Everess shows up, we'll talk."

"Excuse me, Paet?" asked Ironfoot.

"Yes?"

"Where's my laboratory?"

"I'm sorry?"

"My lab. Everess promised me a lab. For my research."

Paet smiled. "Did he?" he said.

"Yes, he did."

"Hm."

Paet went into his office and shut the door, leaving Ironfoot and Silverdun alone in the mission room.

"That was interesting," said Ironfoot.

"Pens," said Silverdun.

"Indeed."

"I was expecting something quite a lot more sinister, weren't you?"

"I was expecting a lab."

"It seems nothing is quite what we expected."

Ironfoot smiled. "It'll all fallout. Now, if you'll excuse me, I believe I'll go consult with Brei about those pens." He made for the stairs.

"Like hell," said Silverdun, following. "I saw her first. Besides, you've got your Eastern analyst on the hook already."

There were footsteps on the stairs. Silverdun looked up and saw Everess descending, followed by a vision in a white dress who was, quite simply, the most beautiful woman Silverdun had ever seen. Their eyes met, and Silverdun nearly lost his breath.

When Everess had told her that she'd be working with two men, Sela hadn't thought much about it. She'd assumed that these men would be like Everess himself, fat and officious, though it occurred to her as she stood on the steps, staring, that it was a foolish notion. The man at the bottom of the stairs was nothing like Everess. His hair was long and dark, and it flowed beautifully when he turned his head to look at her. When she looked into his eyes, she felt dizzy. Those eyes.

Was this love? Did it really happen this fast?

There was another man standing next to him, but Sela barely noticed him. She stared until the dark-haired man finally tore his eyes away from her, but even before he did, a thread wove itself between them, red and orange and gold. When it connected, it felt as though it were pulling taut, drawing her physically toward him. It was silly, of course; the threads existed only in her imagination. She could neither feel nor actually see them. But still.

She noticed that Everess was looking at her strangely. "Have you and Silverdun met already?" he asked.

Silverdun. His name was Silverdun.

"I'm sure I would remember," said Silverdun, approaching as she and Everess continued down the stairs. The other man rolled his eyes from some reason that Sela couldn't quite make out. No matter how deeply she was able to read those around her, there was still so much they did that baffled her.

"Well then, I suppose introductions and brandy are in order all around," said Everess. "Where the hell is that gravedigger Paet?"

"Right here," said Paet, stepping out of his office. Paet had no love for Everess, that was clear, even without a thread to read. And when a thread finally did connect the two, it was green and brown both ways, with a hint of violet fear emanating from Everess. He was afraid of Paet, only a little, but she knew he would never let it show.

She watched the connections form between all of the men in the room; it was a fascinating, nascent web, but she didn't have time to consider it all because Everess was introducing her all around. The sad, angry man with the

cane was Paet. The confident, intelligent one was Styg Falores, but she was
to call him Ironfoot. And the breathtaking one was Perrin Alt, Lord Silverdun. A lord, no less!

"But not much of a lord," said Silverdun, after Everess gave his title.
"You can simply call me 'Silverdun.'"

Sela suppressed a silly grin. She would call him whatever he liked!

Then fear soaked her. Surely these weren't the appropriate emotions for
someone in her position. Although the more she thought about it, the more
she realized she didn't actually know what her position was.

"Have a seat here in the mission room," said Paet. "Now that we're all
assembled, it's time to talk about why we're all here."

"Just so," said Everess. "You may begin, Chief Paet." Everess wanted Paet
to remember who was in charge. Paet behaved as though he didn't realize it,
but Sela knew he did.

Sela sat as far as possible from Silverdun, who seemed to be studiously
ignoring her. The thread between them was so strong that she could almost
feel his thoughts. She was adrift on the sea of him, trying to ignore him and
failing.

He looked at her, an eyebrow raised. He smiled a faint, almost impercep-
tible smile and shook his head ever so slightly. *No.* He waved his hand in a
quick gesture, and the thread between them simply vanished. He was gone.
She almost lurched in her chair at the sudden loss of him. She looked down,
and when she looked back at him he had the oddest look on his face. She had
no idea what it meant. Sadness? Confusion? Curiosity?

No one had ever done that to her before. It was disarming and dis-
tressing. At least now, however, she could concentrate on what Chief Paet was
saying. And just in time, it appeared, as he was now addressing them all.

Paet sat on the edge of one of the tables and looked across at Silverdun,
Ironfoot, and Sela in turn. "I cannot tell you how happy I am to see the three
of you sitting here before me," he began. Which was strange, since Sela could
easily sense that he was in no way happy. What he was feeling was more like

a grim satisfaction. But it had been Sela's experience that people rarely said what they truly felt.

"It has been five years since there was another Shadow in the building other than myself. Five years since my . . . injuries precluded me from performing active fieldwork. For most of that time, I've been afraid that there would never be another.

"The events of the past year, however," Paet said, tapping his cane against the edge of the table, "have demonstrated to the Crown just how crucial our efforts are. And despite the objections of some members of Corpus, who believe that what we do is unsavory at best and morally reprehensible at worst, Lord Everess has convinced the queen that our work ought to continue."

Everess beamed. There was a time when Sela might have thought him a fool for being so easily flattered, but she realized now that there was nothing that Everess said or did that was not calculated. He was a fascinating man.

"I realize," continued Paet, "that the three of you have been kept mostly in the dark as to what it is the Shadows actually do. There are two reasons for that. The first is that we have strict rules about secrecy, and we do not discuss our missions, tactics, or strategy anywhere outside this building. There are no exceptions to this rule. Thus, we could provide only the vaguest of notions about what it was that you've gotten yourselves into.

"And the other reason," he said, not smiling, "is that if we *had* told you the extent of our work, there's a chance that you wouldn't have agreed to join us."

Silverdun and Ironfoot chuckled, as did Everess. Sela, however, did not. "That wasn't a joke," said Paet. The chuckles stopped.

"I will not equivocate," said Paet. "You will be asked to lie. To cheat. To steal. To kill, when necessary. You will be sent to the most dangerous places in the known worlds. If you are caught, we cannot in most cases admit publicly that we are aware of your existence. You will routinely be asked to perform duties that would be, to even the hardiest Fae soldier, impossible. And in return you will receive a bit of money, but almost nothing in the way of prestige, or honor. Quite the contrary, in fact; you may over time lose whatever sense of honor you once had."

"Somehow I don't see that being much of a problem for Silverdun over there," quipped Everess.

Silverdun made an extremely rude gesture toward Everess. "Pray, continue," he said to Paet.

"In short," said Paet, clearly annoyed at the interruption, "you have been conscripted into the most difficult career in all of Faerie."

"And after all this," said Ironfoot, "what if we decide it's not for us?"

"That is not an option," said Paet.

"You can't be serious," said Ironfoot.

"I *am* serious. I do not recommend that you test me on this. As a result of your . . . training at Whitemount, you are no longer permitted a life outside the Shadows."

"This is madness," said Silverdun.

"You've spent time at Crere Sulace, Silverdun," said Paet. "If you decide life as a Shadow isn't for you, perhaps you could renew some old acquaintances. I'm sure Everess told you when he approached you that once you agreed to enlist with us, there was absolutely no turning back. Did he not?"

Everess smiled a cold smile. "You wanted the best," he said to Paet. "I got you the best. Sometimes certain allowances must be made in the recruiting process."

There was silence in the room for a moment. Sela could feel Paet's fury, and Ironfoot's astonishment. Everess was so good at masking his emotions that very little trickled out into the extraordinarily thin thread between him and Sela. Silverdun she still could not read at all. His mood, however, was not difficult to fathom.

"Son of a whore," he muttered. "It's Mauritane all over again."

"For the time being," said Sela, "perhaps we ought to let Chief Paet continue. Whatever the future may be, we're all here now, and there is work to be done. Is that not so, Chief?" As she spoke, she pushed hard against the thin threads connecting her with Chief Paet and Ironfoot. She barely knew either of them, so she had little to work with, but she wove as much trust and acceptance into the skeins of those threads as she was able. It seemed to help a bit. Ironfoot calmed perceptibly, and Paet appeared to relax as well. Silverdun was glaring at her. Did he suspect what she was doing?

Surely not. There wasn't anyone else in all of Faerie who could do what she did, as far as she knew. Empathy was only supposed to work in one direction: toward the Empath. But Lord Tanen had ensured that she was unique.

"We are," said Everess, trying to take control of the situation, "at a watershed moment in the history of the Seelie Kingdom, and indeed of the entire world of Faerie, if not the rest of the worlds to boot.

"Now is the time for boldness and decisive action," he said. "This is no mere philosophical exercise. This is the future of the land. We are gathered here to contend against the very destruction of our way of life. It may be that we in this room are the ones who prevent that destruction."

Everess turned to Ironfoot. "Tell them what you saw at Selafae, Master Falores."

"'Ironfoot' will be just fine, thanks," said Ironfoot. "And Everess has a point. I've been at the center of what was once Selafae. If we can prevent another attack like that one, it's worth all of our lives."

"It's difficult to sit in this cozy house and seriously ponder the fate of the whole world," observed Silverdun. "And hardly a comfort."

"It is indeed difficult," said Paet. "You're absolutely right, Silverdun. There is no comfort now. But there will be."

Paet looked at Silverdun. "What we do is difficult, and it is painful, and it is deadly. But it gives us the power and the opportunity to make the greatest difference that a single Fae can make in the world. To me, that's worth it."

Paet stood, leaning on his cane. "So I ask you. No, I *beg* you. Join me in this endeavor."

There was another silence. "Oh, why not? What the hell else have I got to do?" said Silverdun. Everess laughed out loud, and Sela joined him. Ironfoot looked at Sela. His look said, *What the hell have we gotten ourselves into?*

Sela wished she knew.

"There's one more thing we must do tonight," said Paet. "The final step in your initiation. Once it is complete, then I will personally complete your training until I believe you are ready to be sent out on assignment."

"What's the final step?" asked Everess.

"That's between me and my Shadows," said Paet. "I'm going to have to ask you to leave, Lord Everess."

Everess seemed about to say something unkind to Paet, but he restrained himself. "I suppose it's good for you to have your little rituals," he muttered.

He walked to the stairs and saluted to Sela, Ironfoot, and Silverdun. "I salute you, good Shadows. I bid you serve your kingdom well."

He nodded to Sela. "Have Paet call you a cab when you're finished with whatever it is you're about. He'll pay." He went up the stairs, and his footsteps faded away above.

"Come into my office," Paet said.

Once everyone was inside, Paet closed the door behind them and locked it. He took a small wooden box from his desk drawer and opened it, revealing a simple metal ring lying on the box's velvet lining.

"Do any of you know what this is?" he asked. No one did.

"What does it do?" asked Sela.

"No one outside of this room knows of its existence," said Paet, "except perhaps for Regina Titania herself; the claims of her omniscience are, in my experience, not unfounded. This ring is part of what sets us apart from others, and a part of our strength."

He held up the box to let everyone see it. There was nothing remarkable about the ring at all. It was just a band of iron.

"This," he said, "is a binding ring."

Sela had no idea what this meant, but Ironfoot apparently did, because his eyes widened. "Astonishing," he said. "I've read about these, but I never knew they truly existed."

"The existence of things believed to be fictional is our stock-in-trade, Ironfoot."

"What does it do?" repeated Sela.

"What its name implies," said Paet. "It binds us to one another, makes it impossible for any of us to betray the others."

"But it's made of iron," said Ironfoot. "Are we supposed to wear one everywhere we go?"

"No. You only need put it on once and say the incantation."

"Does it hurt?" asked Sela.

"Oh yes," said Paet. "Quite a lot."

"Well," said Silverdun. "We've come this far. What's one more bit of madness?"

Paet took a pair of bronze tongs from his desk drawer and lifted the ring out of its box. Beneath the velvet lining was a small slip of parchment, with the Elvish incantation sounded out in Common. Silverdun read over the incantation, practiced it a few times, then held out the forefinger of his left hand.

"I'll go first," he said.

Using the tongs, Paet raised the ring over Silverdun's outstretched finger and let go. The ring fell into place and Silverdun screamed. He jerked backward, stumbling against the wall, wringing his hand in pain.

"Say the incantation!" said Paet.

Silverdun rasped out the words; as soon as he finished, his body jerked again. The witchlamps in the room dimmed briefly, and then Silverdun flung the ring onto the floor.

"That was extraordinarily unpleasant," he said once his breathing slowed enough for him to speak.

Ironfoot was clearly none too interested to go next, but a quick glance in Sela's direction showed that some chivalrous instinct demanded that he precede her. Paet retrieved the ring from the floor with the tongs and repeated the procedure on him. Sela instinctively dropped the thread joining Ironfoot to her.

Ironfoot didn't scream; rather he growled low, like an animal, his face red, and he hissed the words of the spell through gritted teeth. Again the lights dimmed, and Ironfoot too flung the thing across the office, this time directly at Paet, who quickly dodged it.

Silverdun clapped Ironfoot on the back. "Feels nice, doesn't it?"

Ironfoot grimaced. "The really painful part will come when he admits that the bloody thing doesn't actually do anything."

"My turn," said Sela. Paet looked at her and hesitated. Then he offered her the ring. After seeing what her two comrades had just suffered, the anticipation was growing unbearable, and she simply wanted to get it over with.

She held out her finger, and Paet dropped the ring on it.

It hurt. Very much. She did what was required, and hurled the ring as far from her as possible.

"Are you all right?" asked Silverdun. She wanted to tell him that no, everything was not all right, and would he please put his arms around her?

"I'll be just fine," she said.

Paet put the ring back in the box, and the box back in the drawer. He regarded them with satisfaction.

"Forget what Everess said. *Now* you are Shadows. *Now* we are brothers and sisters. We share a bond unlike any other.

"Now the work can truly begin."

"What about you?" said Silverdun. "Aren't you going to put it on?"

"I put it on a long time ago," said Paet.

Sela had hoped she'd get a chance to speak with Silverdun after the meeting, but he seemed preoccupied, and Sela was so torn by her own confusion that by the time she got up the courage to speak with him, she discovered that he'd already gone home.

As promised, Paet hired her a cab and she went home alone, confused, elated, worried. All of these emotions clung to her like one of the formal dresses that Everess liked for her to wear: awkward, ill fitting, oppressive.

Everess was in his study when she arrived at Boulevard Laurwelana.

"Quite an evening, eh?" he said, looking up from his work.

"It was, at that," she answered.

"Well, go on up to bed," he said. "It's late, and I'm sure Paet has all sorts of things to hurl at you tomorrow. Both literally and figuratively, if I know him."

"Of course, Lord Everess."

After a moment Everess looked up and found her still there. "Yes," he said, annoyed, "what is it?"

"You didn't tell us the whole truth," she said.

Everess leaned back in his chair. "You're right," he said. "I didn't. I'm sorry."

"Apology accepted," said Sela.

She went upstairs to her room and lay on the bed, fully clothed. Ecara came to undress her, but Sela sent her away. She tossed and turned but couldn't sleep.

About an hour later, there was a loud knock on the door downstairs. A few seconds passed, and then another. Sela heard footsteps, the opening door. She heard muffled voices. Quiet at first and then louder.

Sela crept out of her room and down the hallway. She stood on the landing and peered over the banister that overlooked Everess's parlor. Paet was here, pacing, while Everess sat in a wingback chair with a large goblet of wine, watching him.

"Angry?" said Paet. "I'm furious!"

"Calm down, man," said Everess. "Have a seat. I'd offer you a drink, but you've clearly had some on your own."

"You asked me for recommendations," said Paet. "I gave you a list. Twenty-five names. Excellent candidates, chosen from within the Ministry, the army, the Royal Guard. Any of those would have been perfect. But do I get any of those?"

"Now look here—"

"Of course not!" Paet interrupted. "Instead you give me, what, a university professor! And a sarcastic monk! And that *thing* you've got locked upstairs!

"You expect me to do what I do, to work miracles, and yet it seems that in every instance, you do everything in your power to hinder me!"

"If I may speak for a moment," said Everess coldly.

Paet ignored him. "And then, as if that weren't bad enough, you lie to them, tell them that this will be something that it isn't. It's the first day, and I'm fairly certain that these brilliant new Shadows you've selected for me all want to quit."

He paused. He took the decanter on the sideboard and poured himself a glass of whiskey.

"And I wish I could let them!"

He sat down in a chair opposite Everess and took a long drink from his glass.

Everess cleared his throat. "Where to begin?"

He leaned forward. "First, and most important, did Silverdun and Ironfoot return from Whitemount successfully? Or did they not?"

"They did."

"Good. At least you're willing to admit it. Second, that university professor was a war hero in the Gnomics. He fought with valor and distinction and was awarded the Laurel four times over for excellence in combat. He's no mere scholar and we both know it.

"Now Silverdun. You know that Silverdun was with Mauritane on whatever bloody secret mission that Titania sent him on. He fought at the battle of Sylvan. He's a very clever fellow, and no slouch with the Gifts, either.

"And as for that *thing*, as you have so gallantly put it, I have expressed to you on more than one occasion not just how valuable she *is*, but how much more valuable she may *become* with the proper training, which I expect you to provide."

Sela realized they were talking about her. She was that "thing." She had known for a long time, ever since she'd been taken from Lord Tanen and brought to Copperine House, that she was different somehow. Perhaps even special. She even understood why she was "valuable." She had skills: She could read others; she could kill. All of the things that Tanen had brought out in her; those things that she'd tried hard at Copperine House to forget. Now these things determined her worth.

Tonight she did not want to be different. She wanted to be like anyone else. A pretty blonde girl who Silverdun might see and fall in love with.

Not a *thing*.

"But there is one more piece of information that you do not have, and which I have reserved in anticipation of this very moment."

"And what is that?" asked Paet, seething with anger. Sela did not need to read a thread to know what Paet was thinking. This was Everess's favorite game: to withhold a vital piece of information, hide it behind his back like a club, and then beat you over the head with it.

"That I did not choose Silverdun, or Ironfoot, or Sela."

"No? And who did? Was it Aba's guiding hand? Regina Titania herself?"

Everess smiled. "The latter, actually."

Paet's eyes widened. "You expect me to believe that the Seelie queen reviewed your request for personnel and personally selected these three to be Shadows? During her rest period while hearing petitions, perhaps? Or in between drinks at a ball?"

"I can only tell you what she told me. I went to her to discuss the matter of reopening the Office of Shadow. We spoke briefly, perhaps five minutes. At the end of the meeting, she wrote three names down on a slip of paper and handed it to me."

"And you are only just now telling me this?" said Paet. "Why?"

"As you are so fond of telling others, Paet, it was not necessary for you to know."

Paet seethed.

"One last point," said Everess, pouring himself another drink. "You accused me of lying to our recruits. Did you not just this evening admit to doing the same thing? I fail to see why you have singled me out for opprobrium on that count."

"What I did," said Paet, "and will always do, is conceal that information which has been deemed classified. That is not quite the same as lying, unless you'd like to spend the rest of the evening arguing the semantics of it. What you have done is deliberately mislead them.

"Of course you fail to see the distinction. You're so comfortable with falsehood that you can't tell the difference."

Everess's face had slowly reddened throughout Paet's brief speech. "There is a line I suggest you do not cross, Chief Paet. I allow you to speak to me freely, and not as the commoner you are to the nobleman that I am. But I will only take so much abuse from you."

"Then I'll add only one more thing, *my lord*," said Paet. "If you ever keep me in the dark about something so critical as the selection of my officers again, there will be hell to pay."

"I'll take it under advisement," said Everess. "Now, are we quite finished?"

Paet stood. "For now. Until the next time you find a way to be a thorn in my side. And before you take any more umbrage, be advised that I will speak to you any way I damn well please."

He strode away and out of Sela's vision. Her heart was racing. She tiptoed back to her room and lay down, willing herself to be calm.

She had known that Paet and Everess weren't on the best of terms, but now it seemed as though they detested one another. She had never trusted

Everess. Did that mean she ought to trust Paet? He was difficult to read, almost closed to her.

That reminded her of Silverdun's trick during the meeting earlier. How had he managed to shut her out so easily? No one had ever done that to her before. And what had he been thinking when he'd done it?

There were so many questions, so many puzzles. Just when she thought herself an expert on Fae nature, she realized that she really knew nothing at all.

Sleep was a long time coming.

Silverdun's body wanted sleep, but his mind wouldn't allow it. He lay in bed, tossing and turning, the details of the meeting replaying themselves in his head.

What had he gotten himself into? Could Everess and Paet have been serious? Would they truly toss him back into Crere Sulace if he tried to back out now? When Mauritane was recruiting allies to take with him on his mad mission across Faerie at the queen's behest, he'd told Silverdun more or less the same thing: Go with me or I will kill you. How many of Silverdun's great life choices had been made at knifepoint?

And Sela. She was beautiful, to be sure. And alluring. There was something almost mystical about her, something mysterious and primal. But there was also something very wrong about her, a hardness, something dark that suggested she'd seen things that no one should see. The look in her eyes, at the same time keen and confused, as if she were from another world entirely.

She had gotten inside his head somehow, using the Gift of Empathy. Silverdun had experienced Empathy; the counselors at Nyelcu all had a bit of it. But this was something different altogether. She hadn't just read his mind; she'd somehow become one with it. When she reached into him, something of her was there with it; they mingled somehow. And what he'd felt of her had been deep and dark, the Inland Sea at night, an endless abyss. The water of her was pure and clear, but what swam beneath its surface chilled him.

One of the things that Mauritane had taught him during the long weeks of their trek across the kingdom was how to guard himself from Empathy. What a typically Mauritane skill, Silverdun realized.

Still, Sela *was* beautiful. He was pulled to her. He wanted her.

He began to drift off to sleep, dreaming of kissing her, but as his mind wandered toward dreaming, her face became Faella's in his mind, and it was Faella's name he whispered just before he lost consciousness.

chapter fifteen

The difficulty of the fool's errand is that it is typically the
fool who undertakes it.

—Master Jedron

The first day of the month of Hawk dawned sunny and bright, but despite
the weather, Blackstone House was still as oppressive and imposing as it
had been on their first visit. The inside of the house was, perhaps, bleaker
than it had been then; the early morning light that eked its way past the
heavy shutters cast a pall on the empty rooms. Silverdun climbed the stairs
and stepped into the closet in the back bedroom. He paused with his key in
the lock, hesitating the way one would before jumping into a cold pond. The
disorientation was of the kind that one never got used to.

The instant Silverdun stepped into the turn, the house came alive with
sound. Copyists and amanuenses hurried through the office carrying scrolls
and bound documents, and a pair of message sprites were brawling in one of
the corners, fighting over a scrap of pink silk fabric. In the main office, every
desk was occupied, the intelligence officers preparing briefings or translating
intercepted documents or whatever it was that they did. A few heads turned
when Silverdun entered, then went back to whatever they'd been doing. Silverdun went downstairs feeling oddly light and at ease.

Ironfoot and Paet were waiting in Paet's office, sipping tea in awkward
silence. Paet glanced with practiced accusatory subtlety at the clock on his
desk, showing ten minutes past the hour. Silverdun ignored him.

"No Sela this morning?" Silverdun asked, as innocently as possible.

"She's on another assignment," said Paet, expressionless.

"Of no concern to me, I take it?" asked Silverdun.

"Not at this time."

Silverdun sighed and sat. This was going to be the way of things. Well. Information had a way of getting around. At court, as in politics, as in most everything else, information was always the most precious commodity.

"I'm sending the two of you to Annwn," said Paet, handing each of them a leather binder holding unpleasantly thick sheaves of documents. Ironfoot reached out eagerly for his, but Silverdun wavered, experiencing again the strange, embarrassing shame at taking orders from his social inferior. This had, of course, become a pattern with him since his days as a prisoner at Crere Sulace, but he'd never quite gotten used to it. If there were a medal for least respected nobleman in all of Faerie, he'd have won it hands down. Maybe it was a good thing. "Humility is the soul's sustenance," Estiane had told him once. Smug bastard.

Silverdun took the binder and opened it. It contained dossiers on a number of government officials, a briefing on the political situation, the names and addresses of friendly contacts among the populace, and a brief mission document, written in Paet's tidy scrawl, a bit blurred by a copyist who was either harried or incompetent.

"Obviously you can't travel directly, so we'll be sending you via Mag Mell. The ambassador in Isle Cureid will provide you with the documentation you'll need to cross into Annwn." The Port-Auvris Lock, the gateway connecting the Seelie Kingdom directly to Annwn, had been closed five years earlier, during the Unseelie invasion.

"Your primary mission," said Paet, "is to make contact with several of the local authorities in Blood of Arawn who we believe may be particularly resistant to the current political situation. Since Mab conquered Annwn five years ago, the populace has become more and more restless. There have been four separate rebellions quashed by the Unseelie contingent there. All of them minor, but there does seem to be a trend."

"What are we after?" asked Silverdun. "Annwn is a bit of a backwater, isn't it?"

"Yes," said Paet, "but it's a backwater that provides a massive amount of tribute in the form of gold and a fair-sized army that can be mobilized against the Seelie Kingdom should Mab see fit to do so."

"Do we have intelligence that leads us to believe she might?"

Paet nodded. "We have evidence that proves she already has. One of our spotters along the border near Wamarnest spied two companies of Annwni cavalry training alongside their Unseelie counterparts."

Ironfoot frowned. "Why train so near the border? Wouldn't it make sense to hide that kind of force?"

Paet made a noncommittal gesture. "It may be that they wanted us to see it, to frighten us."

"It's also the only place they've got to drill cavalry," said Silverdun. "Any farther north and the ground is too unstable to risk horses. They build those cities in the sky for a reason."

"Regardless," said Paet, "if we can find some way to undermine the Unseelie in Annwn then we're that much closer to surviving a war."

"You'd like the two of us to whip up an armed insurrection? That shouldn't be too difficult. We'll hand out a few sharpened sticks and some pamphlets and that'll be the thing done."

Paet sighed. It was childish to needle him, but it was also gratifying.

"There are other methods that may prove more effective," said Paet, ignoring him. "As you may know, the political system in Annwn is rather unlike ours. Overall, they're ruled by the Unseelie, but Mab typically doesn't dismantle the existing structure unless it suits her to do so, and in the case of Annwn, it did not."

"So what's the existing structure?" asked Ironfoot.

"The city of Blood of Arawn, and thus the world at large, is run by a number of elected magistrates, who themselves elect seven of their number to act as a high council."

"Who elects them?" asked Silverdun. "The people?"

"Yes," said Paet. "Property holders, anyway."

"Very progressive," said Silverdun.

"Anyhow, this system of elections is rife with corruption, and any given election can be bought fairly easily. A few bags of gold distributed to the right people—"

"And we can help place in power those favorable to our cause," finished Silverdun.

"Precisely," said Paet. "As Everess has told you both, our battles aren't fought on the field. Our offensives are a bit more judicious."

"I imagine it would be fairly expensive to buy out the entire body politic," said Silverdun. "Or do your pockets run deeper than I suspect?"

"Any trouble we can cause," he said, "even enough to disrupt troop movements between worlds for a while, could give us a useful advantage. And if we can help arrange a rebellion with the vague promise of Seelie assistance . . ." Paet let the words linger in the air.

"But there wouldn't be any real Seelie assistance, would there?" said Ironfoot.

"Not unless we wanted to start the war on our own, no. But allowing a few rebels to believe it is a different matter altogether."

Silverdun smiled. "I see that Everess's way of thinking has rubbed off on you," he said. "Anything for victory."

"Yes," said Paet. "For this victory, yes." He leaned forward. "For this victory I will lie and cheat and steal and kill if I must. If the choice is between a single life and a *way of life*, then there is no contest."

He glared at Silverdun. "Spend some time in Annwn under Unseelie rule and then tell me what you think about it."

Paet had a fine way of making even the most ruthless actions seem reasonable. No wonder Everess had him in charge.

Paet waited for what seemed a calculated moment and then added as if in afterthought, "There's something else I'd like you to check into while you're in Annwn."

"What's that?" asked Ironfoot.

"When I was there five years ago, I was working with your most recent predecessor, a woman named Jenien. She was killed at the home of a man named Prae Benesile on the night of Mab's invasion."

"The trail of her killer may be a bit cold after five years," said Silverdun.

"I *know* who killed her," said Paet, a bit more severely than seemed necessary, even for him. "I want you to find out about Prae Benesile. I want to know why she was investigating him and why it got her killed by the Bel Zheret."

Silverdun and Ironfoot glanced briefly at each other. Ironfoot's face was stony, but Silverdun could almost see the words "Bel Zheret" hanging on his lips.

"And what do we do if we encounter Bel Zheret ourselves?" asked Silverdun.

Paet laughed, a short bark that echoed in the room. He stood slowly, leaning on his cane. He turned around, facing the wall, and lifted up his shirt. A long, purple scar made an artful swirl across his back.

He let the shirttail fall and looked at the two of them. "You?" he asked, sighing. "You die."

He paused. "That reminds me of something," he said.

Silverdun wasn't quite sure he wanted to hear whatever it was the thought of his death reminded Paet of.

"When you go on this mission, it's likely that you'll find yourself in a stressful situation before too long," Paet said.

"That's kind of the point, isn't it?"

Paet smiled his thin smile. "I suppose so. Regardless, when that happens, you may find yourself experiencing . . . certain reactions that you have not felt before."

"What does that mean?" asked Silverdun.

"I can't say," said Paet. "You must be ready for anything. Just be aware that if you find yourself suddenly more capable than before, that this is to be both expected and encouraged. There's no way of telling exactly when or how this will occur."

"How can you be so sure that whatever this is, is going to happen?"

"It always happens to newly minted Shadows. It's the way of things."

"Jedron never mentioned anything about it," said Ironfoot.

"I imagine that half of what Jedron told you was outright lies, and the other half was misleading."

Silverdun couldn't argue with that.

"Be warned," said Paet. "That's all."

"Paet," said Ironfoot. "When we were on that island, something very strange happened. There was a pit, and it was black—"

"I know what you're going to say," said Paet. "And I'm afraid I'm not at liberty to discuss it. What happened on that island is not for you to know. For the time being."

"And when will that time cease to be?" asked Ironfoot.

"When it becomes necessary for it to be otherwise."

Paet stood and shooed them out of his office.

"Now go into the den and wait. I'll be down in a few minutes with the mission specialists, and we'll go over in detail exactly what I expect you to do."

chapter sixteen

Mag Mell is a place of circles and mirrors. The world is a spiral archipelago of round volcanic atolls, with calm waters within and raging seas without. The waters within the island grottoes are preternaturally, magically still, and because the sand beneath them is black, they provide a perfect reflection of the sky above. In Mag Mell, mirrors are holy; to break one is to break the symmetry of life itself.

It is a segregated world. The men live aboveground on the islands in houses of wood, and the women live beneath the water in villages of rock and woven seaweed. They come together in the shallows to court and to mate, but the majority of their lives are spent separately.

Children in Mag Mell are born androgynous and amphibious, capable of living either above or below the water, but when they reach puberty they must decide on a gender. When that time is reached, a special ceremony is held during which the child declares itself either male or female. If the child chooses to be male, then it remains on land and after several months it loses its gills and takes on masculine attributes. If it chooses to become female, it goes to live beneath the waves and loses its lungs instead. It is said that when a native man peers into the coastal waters of Mag Mell, he sees the woman he

might have been. He can ask her questions and she will
answer with the wisdom of the woman he is not.

—Stil-Eret, "Mag Mell: World of Mirrors,"
from *Travels at Home and Abroad*

Silverdun had visited the world of Mag Mell once as a very young man.
He'd traveled here with his father on holiday. Now that it occurred to
him, he was fairly certain he owned the house on Isle Dureicth where they'd
stayed. Or at least he should.

Silverdun remembered Mag Mell as being warm and bright, but when
they stepped through the Port-Herion Chancery Lock, they were greeted
with dim light and a stiff chill. The arch on the Mag Mell side of the gate
was located underground, Silverdun remembered. When the warping mists
of the lock left his eyes, he saw a long stone ramp leading upward toward a
stout metal gate, and more dim light beyond. Powerful witchlight chande-
liers hung from the ceiling, but they weren't quite capable of dispelling the
sepulchral feel of the place.

Or perhaps that was only Silverdun's imagination. The delegation of jewelry guildsmen who stepped through the gate just behind them were jolly
enough. They had laughed and spoken loudly all the way through the customs check on the Faerie side of the gate, which seemed to have lasted for
hours, and their temper hadn't changed now. One of them, in fact, was still
speaking to Silverdun about his guild's mission to negotiate mineral rights
with a mining consortium on one of the southern islands. Silverdun and Ironfoot were both dressed as minor government officials, and Silverdun supposed
that this was the sort of thing that such people were forced to endure on a
daily basis.

As they proceeded up the ramp toward the gate, Ironfoot looked around
brightly, taking it all in. They could have done much worse in their selection.
He barely knew Ironfoot and already he felt as though they'd been working
together all their lives. The binding ring? Perhaps, but if so, it was a wonderful spell, because Silverdun found that he genuinely liked the man.

Had Silverdun ever had a friend of his own social rank? Maybe he wasn't cut out to be a lord after all.

At the top of the ramp, they were subjected to Mag Mell customs agents who were, sadly, quite a lot more efficient and friendly than their Seelie counterparts. They looked more or less like Fae, although they were darker of skin, and had rounded ears like the Nymaens, like Silverdun's old traveling companion Brian Satterly. The agents inspected Silverdun's and Ironfoot's Foreign Ministry identification closely, but waved them through without question.

Past the metal gate at the top of the ramp, they rounded a corner and stepped outside into a light rain that dotted the sea like ground pepper all around the tiny island that housed the gate. A ferry waited to take them to Isle Cureid, the capital.

"Lord Silverdun!" came a voice behind them.

Baron Glennet, Silverdun's dinner partner from a few months before, had just emerged from the gate and was hurrying toward them, followed by a small retinue of aides and attendants.

"Baron," said Silverdun. He was aware of Everess's approval of the man, but he couldn't decide whether that made him trust Glennet more, or less.

"I saw you on my way through the lock, but I just missed being in your group. I'm glad I was able to catch up with you."

He turned to Ironfoot. "You must be Master Falores from Queensbridge. I've heard a lot about you."

"A pleasure," said Ironfoot.

Glennet leaned in and whispered, "I wanted to wish you luck on your errand in Annwn."

Silverdun smiled. "We'll do our best," he said. "What brings you to Mag Mell?"

"Work, as always," he said. "Trying to negotiate a better price for silver ore on behalf of the Smiths' Guild."

"Your works sounds like all sorts of fun," said Silverdun.

"Less dangerous than yours, anyway," said Glennet with a knowing smile.

They were all met at the ferry by a matronly woman named Glienn, who was the Seelie ambassador's second-in-command. The jewelry guildsmen had met their contact on the island, and they were already happily getting drunk on the other side of the ferryboat.

Glienn was welcoming, but a bit circumspect, and exchanged only pleasantries while they were at sea. When they reached the docks on Isle Cureid, there was a hansom cab waiting for Glienn, Silverdun, and Ironfoot. Glennet had arranged his own transportation, and they parted with the requisite pleasantries.

Silverdun, Ironfoot, and Glienn piled into the cab, thankful for the shelter and warmth, and the cab moved quickly away. Isle Cureid was a pleasant enough place despite the rain: The homes and buildings were all of brightly painted wood, the streets of volcanic rock, silver in the rain. Everything looked new and clean. It was certainly odd to look out onto a busy street and see not a single woman; Silverdun was glad they weren't staying long.

The Seelie Embassy was located on a quiet side street. It was built of imported Faerie marble, and seemed dour and out of place in the gayness of Mag Mell. The rain, however, seemed appropriate to it. As they piled out of the hansom, Silverdun smelled calendula and capelbells, Faerie flowers from the garden fronting the embassy, mixing with the odor of earthworms and horse dung.

The Seelie ambassador was a Fae gentleman named Aranquet, who dressed in the colorful linens of Mag Mell, with his Seelie Army medals pinned directly to the pink blouse. He welcomed them to the embassy, smiling. Glienn passed out powerfully strong drinks that smelled of mint and were served in cups made of tightly woven reeds.

"Welcome to Mag Mell, gentlemen!" Aranquet sang, shaking their hands briskly. "Come, come!"

He led them to his office, which was airy and spacious, filled with furniture also woven from reeds of some kind, and satin pillows in the color of peaches and limes. A riotously colored bird sat on a perch in a corner, its beak tucked beneath its wing. Glienn left them, shutting the door behind her.

Once the door was closed, Aranquet's demeanor hardened. He drained his drink and set the cup aside, his eyes on the two men in front of him.

"So," he said. "You're Paet's replacements, eh?"

"You know him?" said Silverdun. "Has he always been so charming as he is now?"

Aranquet laughed out loud. "Ah! I can see we're going to get along famously." He reached for his drink cup, found it empty, and scowled. "No, Paet has never been renowned for his wit or charm. Then again, he's done things for the Seelie that . . . well, he's accomplished some astonishing things in his time and received no credit for it. Not publicly, anyway. And never asked for any."

Aranquet tapped the cup on his desk. "Still and all, though, a bit of a bastard."

"We were told you'd have some documents for us," said Ironfoot.

The ambassador looked sideways at Ironfoot. "You're the diplomatic one, I take it?"

"No," said Ironfoot. "I'm just more scared of Paet than he is."

Aranquet took two sets of papers from a drawer and handed them across the desk to Silverdun and Ironfoot. Passports and travel documents.

Silverdun looked at the passport, which was a perfect forgery as far as he could tell. The glamour imprinted on the page looked exactly like him, but gave his name as Hy Wezel, with an address in Blood of Arawn.

"The two of you could hardly pass as Maggos or Annwni," said Aranquet, indicating the passport, "so we wrote you up as Unseelie Fae instead. A bit more dangerous, perhaps, but these are quality documents. They'll hold up to close scrutiny. If you get detained with them, however, they'll probably cut your heads off."

Silverdun glanced at the travel documents and laughed. "Eel merchants?" he said.

"Lot of eel going back and forth between worlds. The Annwni can't get enough of them. The Maggo variety, I mean. Decent Fae eel they turn up their noses at."

"I was an eel merchant once before," said Silverdun. He thought of his trip across Faerie with Mauritane, who had tried with a total lack of success to pass them off as eel merchants to a traveling mestine named Nafaeel and his troupe, the Bittersweet Wayward Mestina. And the star of that show had been Nafaeel's daughter. Faella.

Now was no time to be thinking about Faella. She'd been bad for him.

She'd ruined his face. There'd been something strange about her, as well: She'd manifested a Gift that Queen Titania had referred to as the Magic of Change, the Thirteenth Gift. Silverdun liked to think of himself as a worldly fellow, but he'd never heard of such a thing, and hadn't really felt like asking his sovereign to elaborate on the subject. But his thoughts kept coming back to Faella at the oddest moments. Seeing her face in his mind, he felt a subtle pang, a queer sense of loss.

Aranquet sniffed. "I don't suppose it's any good asking you two the nature of your errand in Annwn? If you were to give me some clue, I might be able to . . . assist somehow?" He looked significantly at Silverdun.

"Her Majesty's business, I'm afraid," said Ironfoot. Silverdun only shrugged. Information was as precious a commodity in Mag Mell as it was back home.

"Well, then," said Aranquet. "If there's nothing else, I'll need to be getting along. I've a dinner with Baron Glennet tonight, and the wife expects me to help her browbeat the cooks."

If Annwn had ever been a pleasant place, that time had been prior to Mab's rule. Beyond the city center of Kollws Kapytlyn, the streets of Blood of Arawn were filthy, strewn with rotting garbage and horse dung. Beggars lined the streets. Some played tiny harps and sang, in a distinctively nasal, plaintive wail. Others simply sat on street corners rattling cups. Most nonofficial buildings were desperately in need of repair.

"I've been in some foul-smelling places," Silverdun told Ironfoot as they stepped warily down the main road in the district of Kollws Vymynal. "But there's something truly awful about the stench here. It's like despair mixed with . . . rotting fish."

"Villages on the Gnomic borders smell worse," Ironfoot said. "Like feet. Nobody knows why."

"Never been," said Silverdun. "Never seen a Gnomic. Though I was told by a young lady at university that they're really quite noble and deeply misunderstood."

"Put her alone in a room with one for ten minutes and she'll be telling a different story."

The street they were on climbed steadily upward toward the summit of the hill upon which the district was built. As they climbed, a slight breeze blew, taking some of the smell with it, and the sun peeked out from behind a cloud. Silverdun looked back; from here he could see most of the city. The Unseelie flag flew limply here and there; outside the walls was a tent city blown by the dust of the plains.

They found the address they were looking for at the end of a cul-de-sac, a claptrap four-story building that had seen much, much better days. They looked around, saw nothing suspicious, and went inside. As they climbed the stairs, Silverdun took a small leather notebook from his jacket pocket.

The door of the third-floor apartment was opened by a tiny woman in a faded linen dress who didn't look them in the eye. "What is it?" she asked in a small voice.

"We'd like to talk to Prae Benesile, please," said Silverdun, mimicking an Unseelie accent and trying to sound as pompous and official as possible. He and Ironfoot had agreed to pose as bureaucrats from the Unseelie Revenue Office. It wouldn't endear them to anyone, but the Annwni would be afraid not to speak to them.

"Prae Benesile? He's been dead for years," said the woman.

"Ah," said Silverdun. "Well, there's a tax matter we need to discuss with his next-of-kin then. Do you happen to know where we can find him or her?"

A man came to the door. He was small but muscular, wearing only breeches. His beard was clipped short but ragged. "What's this about?" he asked.

"They're here for your father," said the woman. "Something about the taxes."

"Dead men can't pay taxes," spat the man. "Or do you Unseelie bastards intend to dig him up and go through his pockets?"

"Tye!" hissed the woman, her eyes wide. "Please."

Tye Benesile examined Ironfoot and Silverdun. "Come in then," he said. He waved them in. As Silverdun passed him he could smell the brandywine on the man's breath.

The apartment was small, the air stifling. Tye Benesile's wife stood looking at them, suspicion worn into her features. Benesile himself sat on a pasteboard chair and indicated a stained sofa for Ironfoot and Silverdun. "If it's revenue you've come for," he said, "you came to the wrong place. I'm out of work. You should have that written in your book." He pointed at Silverdun's notebook.

"It's information we're here for, not money," said Silverdun. He took a fountain pen from his pocket and unscrewed the top. "We'd like to know what your father was doing when he died."

"My father?" said Tye. "My father was a scholar. He studied at a famous university. You should have *that* written in your book as well."

Silverdun and Ironfoot shared a brief glance. Silverdun tried again. "Do you happen to know if your father was working on anything of note at the time of his death?"

Tye Benesile's eyes widened. "They said that he was killed in the riots on the night you lot showed up, by the looters. But I always knew it was a murder. I told them when they came; I said there was nothing here anyone would want to loot. This was his place then, you know. All he had was his books, and they aren't worth a copper slug."

"Do you have any idea why someone would have wanted to murder your father?" asked Ironfoot.

"I'm going out," said Tye's wife. She had a basket over her shoulder. "They said there might be eggs at the market today."

"Go then," said Tye, resenting the intrusion. She stamped her foot and slammed the door behind her.

Tye Benesile pointed at his chest. "My father always said *I* should go to university. He said if I worked hard I could do it, but I never wanted to. I was young; I didn't want to do anything for my own good. Too late now, though, right? He said the brandywine would rot my brain, and I took it as a personal challenge."

Silverdun sighed, rolling his eyes. This was going nowhere. But Ironfoot held up his hand. "Go on," he said to Tye. Ironfoot seemed to grow taller and stronger when he said it. Ah. The Gift of Leadership. Interesting fellow, this Ironfoot.

Tye responded to Ironfoot instantly, seeming to forget that Silverdun existed. "Like I said, all he had left was those books, and I know they weren't worth much because I tried to sell some of them after he died, and I couldn't get anyone to even look at them. Some of them are in different languages, even. He could read Thule Fae as well. Can you imagine that? There's but ten or eleven in all the Known who can read the Thule Fae these days. But he could. He was retired; you know that. He spent all of his last days up here reading and writing."

"Did he ever speak to anyone?" said Ironfoot. "Did anyone ever come to see him?"

"Just the one fellow," said Tye Benesile. "Another scholar. Unseelie. That was before, of course. Before the war and all. My father didn't care for that scholar, though. He was the wrong sort, if you know what I mean."

Silverdun leaned forward, now interested. "I'm not sure I do," said Silverdun. "What sort would that be?"

"Black Artist," Tye Benesile whispered. "That's what Father said. I never met him. But if Father knew things that a Black Artist wanted to know, then you can put that in your book for certain."

"What was this Black Artist's name?" said Silverdun. He supposed it was possible that there were still Black Artists among the Unseelie, though Tye Benesile was clearly not the most reliable witness.

Tye thought for a moment. "Father never said it. If he had, I would have remembered, because I've got a fine memory, even now. You can't imagine how fine it was then. But he *was* a Black Artist, even if you don't believe me."

"When was this?" asked Ironfoot. "How long ago?"

"That was before, I said. Before all this," he said, waving his hand around. Silverdun assumed that by "all this," he meant the Unseelie invasion.

"How long before?"

"It was when I was still working at the mill," said Tye Benesile. "I remember it, of course. That was three months to the day before."

"And did the Black Artist continue visiting your father until he died?"

"No. They had a falling out; something Father had that he wanted. Tried to buy it off of him, but Father refused. Funny thing with lights in a box. So he beat Father up and took it."

"I don't suppose you've kept any of your father's books?" said Silverdun.

"Well I couldn't sell them, could I? So I threw some away, burned some. There are still a few left, though. The really expensive-looking ones. Figured maybe a book dealer in Mag Mell might take an interest if I could ever find the time to make the journey."

Tye led them to the tiny bedroom, where a sunken mattress sat on the floor and a wooden box served as a bedside table. There was an antique wardrobe pushed up against one wall. A nail had been hammered into its crest and a clothesline strung from it to the wall. Tye nodded at the wardrobe; then his face fell.

"Stupid! Stupid! Now you're going to take them, aren't you? I never should have said anything!"

"Don't worry," said Ironfoot, the Leadership resonating in his voice. "We aren't going to take anything."

That seemed to satisfy Tye. He sat down heavily on the bed and watched as Silverdun opened the wardrobe.

It was stuffed with books. Silverdun picked one up and read from the spine. *Inquiry into Matters Philosophical and Theological.* Prae Benesile's own *Thaumatical History of the Chthonic Religion.* Another was in High Court Fae, and Silverdun struggled to translate its title. Something like *A School of Thought Regarding the Gods of the Earth, Bound, and Their Origins.* The next books he examined were in languages he couldn't read. One appeared to be from the Nymaen world, a human tongue. Another was in Thule Fae, like the inscriptions on the Tuminee burial mounds north of the river in Oarsbridge, where Silverdun had been raised. Ironfoot, scholar that he was, seemed to be having an easier time with the translation, but still looked confused.

"I don't supposed you're versed in Thule?" Silverdun asked Ironfoot.

Ironfoot looked up from the book he'd been flipping through. "I am," he said. "But I can't imagine what a Black Artist would have wanted with someone who studied all this stuff."

Silverdun scanned a few lines of verse from *Prinzha-La's Days and Works.* A story about one of the daughters of the god Senek, who fell in love with a mortal Fae. Senek turned him into a ram. You always had to be careful messing around with a powerful man's daughter. Some things never changed.

"I suppose," said Tye from the bed, "if you wanted to *purchase* a few of them I'd be willing to let them go for a reasonable price. You gentlemen being representatives of the government." What had happened to the angry man who'd greeted them at the door? Had Ironfoot's Leadership changed all of his spleen to ardor with a single glance?

"That won't be necessary," said Silverdun. He fished in his pocket for a few coins and slapped them into Tye's hand. "For your trouble."

Tye looked to Ironfoot to make sure the transaction was acceptable. It was.

"I don't think we're going to learn anything else of value," Ironfoot whispered. Silverdun nodded.

They thanked Tye for his time, and the man bowed to Ironfoot a bit more deeply than was required by custom. Now it was just getting annoying.

"If there's anything I can do for you, sir, day or night, I'm your man," he said, his voice slightly wheedling. "Just call on me."

Ironfoot looked a bit puzzled, but thanked the man.

Outside in the stairwell, Silverdun said, "That's quite a Gift you've got there. With that much Leadership in you, I'm surprised you weren't commanding a battalion back in your army days."

Ironfoot stopped on the landing and faced him. He looked troubled. "I've always had it," he said. "A bit, anyway. But on my best day, I could possibly convince a good friend to go along with a suggestion he was already inclined to favor, if I pushed with all my might. I've never done anything like that before."

"Why do you suppose that is?" said Silverdun.

"Whitemount," said Ironfoot. "Don't you feel it?"

"Every day," Silverdun said. "I haven't slept much. I've felt strange. A bit unbalanced sometimes."

"So have I," said Ironfoot. "I just assumed it was the stress of the new job, you know? All of Jedron's tricks, then straight into Paet's service."

"You think it's more than that?"

"I don't know. When we were in Tye Benesile's apartment just now, I was getting nervous. I was worried we were about to fail our first assignment. It kept growing inside me like a panic. Did you notice it?"

"No."

"I did my best to hide it," said Ironfoot. "And then something . . . happened in my head. It was as though I had far more capacity for *re* than I've ever had before, and it all just surged into me. But when it happened I pushed with the Leadership, and it was like a dam had burst. I think Tye Benesile practically worships me now."

"He's in love with you, if you ask me."

Silverdun wanted to ask Ironfoot about that night at Whitemount. The fire, the pit, the blackness. But something inside him wouldn't allow it. He decided to force the issue.

"Ironfoot," he began.

There was a crash below, and the sound of boots on the stairs.

"Tye's wife," said Silverdun, scowling. "She must have given us up."

"We can go down or up," said Ironfoot. "Any preference?"

Silverdun listened. There were at least four sets of boots. "We're to avoid notice at all costs," he said. "We go up."

They hurried up the stairs as quickly as possible, past Tye Benesile's floor and higher. The stairs continued above the fourth floor, but instead of terminating on the roof, they opened onto a low, narrow attic that stretched the entire length of the building. It was hot and close, smelling of dust and mouse droppings, and was cluttered with odd bits of lumber, broken furniture, and the like.

There were voices down below, but Silverdun couldn't make them out. Assuming that the men were after them, they'd be at Tye Benesile's door by now. Tye would do his best to protect Ironfoot, but he was drunk and not particularly bright. It wouldn't take long for them to realize where Silverdun and Ironfoot had gone.

"Now what?" said Ironfoot. It was one thing to have the Gift of Leadership, Silverdun noted, but quite a different thing to lead. Not that Silverdun was much of a leader on his best day. Why had they been picked for this assignment, exactly?

"We want to get out of this building without being seen," said Silverdun, quietly shutting the door to the attic behind him.

There was a small window at the far end of the attic. Weak light dribbled through it and pooled on the floor. "Let's have a look."

Downstairs there was a crash and another shout, this time of someone in pain. Tye Benesile?

Silverdun and Ironfoot moved carefully, picking their way through the tiny attic. Batlike creatures slept in the exposed rafters. They wriggled when Silverdun brushed up against them. The going was painfully slow as they wove their way through the narrow space, trying to be as silent as possible.

Now there was more noise on the stairs, and pounding from beneath them. The men were knocking on doors. Silverdun and Ironfoot were nearly to the window now.

The door to the attic crashed open. A pair of Annwni guardsmen peered into the attic. They were armed with short swords and wore dark blue uniforms with black leather helmets and boots. Silverdun and Ironfoot crouched down, but there was nowhere to hide.

"There!" shouted one. He ran toward them, shoving a broken chair aside.

Silverdun ran toward the window and tried it. It was locked, but the lock gave with a hard shove. He opened the window and looked out. It opened directly onto the cul-de-sac below, a forty-foot drop with nothing to break the fall. On the street, five more guardsmen stood at the entrance to the building.

"I think doing this silently is going to be quite a lot more difficult now," he said, turning back around.

Ironfoot already had a knife out. He hurled it at the guardsman in front, and the point found its mark in the Annwni's throat. The man dropped without taking another step. Silverdun bent, took a knife from his boot, and heaved it at the remaining guard. The man raised his hand reflexively, and the knife lodged in his palm. He screamed, but it was more a scream of rage than pain, and he kept coming.

Ironfoot was already moving, running toward the guardsman. He reached the other one first, the one he'd killed with his thrown knife. Rather than jump over the man, however, he bent down and removed his knife from the guard's neck with a fluid motion, then raised it just as the second watchman leapt at him, Silverdun's knife still lodged in his palm. Ironfoot made a brutal upward jerking motion and the second watchman went over his shoulder and crashed into the wall.

All of this happened in the moment it took Silverdun to catch up to him. By the time he reached Ironfoot, both watchmen were dead. Ironfoot wiped his knife on the leg of one of the dead men and handed Silverdun's back to him, still slick with blood.

"I imagine someone heard that," said Silverdun. He looked down at the fallen watchmen. "To hell with Jedron and his advice on swords," he said, taking the closest one's blade. It was light and unbalanced, but it was sharp. That was fine; there wasn't going to be a lot of finesse required in the next few minutes.

"Suit yourself," said Ironfoot. He held onto his knife.

Now there was more noise on the stairs. Silverdun led the way out of the attic, his heart thudding in his chest. It had been a long time since he'd last killed anyone. The Battle of Sylvan, in fact. Over a year ago. His heart was pounding and his palms were beginning to sweat, but it was also familiar and, frankly, a bit of a relief to be in action.

There were four men on the landing, and they ran straight at Silverdun and Ironfoot without preamble. As soon as Silverdun engaged the first of them, he realized his mistake. It was difficult to swing a sword in such a narrow space, and he was forced to resort to jabbing with it like a tiny spear. His opponent had the same problem, of course, but his opponent also had three friends.

Ironfoot, however, did not have this problem. He flitted past Silverdun and took the second man on the stairs, dodging his blade. Once Ironfoot was inside the man's guard, he was able to use his knife freely. His opponent was down in an instant, and Ironfoot shoved him roughly backward, tripping up the man behind him.

Meanwhile Silverdun managed to take out his own opponent with a lucky thrust. He pushed his man aside and followed Ironfoot. Against the two of them, the last of the guardsmen didn't last long.

The noise of the fight, however, had drawn the attention of others, and now three more appeared below.

"Why so many?" asked Silverdun. "Two upstairs, the four we just did, five on the street, and now these fellows?"

"Worry about it later!" called Ironfoot. He lunged at the man closest to him, who appeared to be in charge. But this one had apparently earned his promotion, because he sidestepped Ironfoot's lunge and smashed him hard on the back of the neck with the hilt of his sword as he went past. The men behind him grabbed Ironfoot but didn't kill him. Interesting.

Silverdun turned to run back upstairs, but there was a man above him as well. Well, one was better than three, even if fighting from below. He jumped up and immediately tripped on one of the men he'd just killed. As he fell forward, his opponent chopped down, flailing.

And lopped Silverdun's sword hand off at the wrist.

Silverdun watched it happen, trying to reel backward, moving as if through water. There was no pain at first, just shock. Blood, deep deep red, flowed thickly from his wrist. Silverdun couldn't remember ever having seen blood so thick.

Without thinking, Silverdun reached with his left hand and lashed out with witchfire, the simplest bit of Elements he could muster. He hoped, at best, to blind his attacker momentarily with a flash of flame.

Instead, the narrow stairwell exploded with heat and light. The man in front of him was incinerated. He fell, twisting and smoking, in front of Silverdun.

Silverdun turned and looked down. The watchmen's leader hesitated on the landing below him, his sword at the ready. Silverdun let the *re* well up in him again, but there was none. He'd used it all in that one burst. Impossible. Using every bit of essence in his body in an instant ought to have killed him.

The pain from his wrist finally figured out how to reach his mind and he gasped in agony. He stumbled, fell, tried to stand. A fist connected with his skull and he dropped, unable to move. He was still awake, but his arms and legs wouldn't respond. There was quite a lot of swearing; Annwni had interesting swears, thought Silverdun.

chapter seventeen

In mounted combat, it is preferable to shoot the rider out of the saddle. Sometimes, however, it is easier to put your arrow in the horse, and just as effective.

—Cmdr. Tae Filarete, *Observations on Battle*

Sela had her maid Ecara dress her in a simple gown; today she fancied herself a free-spirited girl, waiting-maid to a Duchess, perhaps, or a guildsman's daughter. Regardless of how she felt about Lord Tanen, he had certainly taught her many things, and one of them was how to fit in just about anywhere. It didn't matter if she didn't know a thing about the kind of woman she was pretending to be. It all came to her as she went along. She watched the dance of the colored threads that spread among those around her and simply danced among them.

Life in Lord Everess's household was both more and less pleasant than she might have imagined. Everess was rarely at home, and that was fine with Sela; she found the man's company ever less pleasant the more she knew him. But she was lonely. For so long she'd been used to her fellow residents at Copperine House. They were strange and damaged, but they were known. Her only regular company was Ecara, and Ecara wanted only to please her, and so had begun to grate on Sela's nerves.

After that first night at Blackstone House, she'd assumed that her new life was starting, finally. The air smelled of possibility as she rode in the open carriage back to Lord Everess's apartments. But that had been days ago. And in the interim, she'd heard nothing except for Everess's assurances that she ought to enjoy the peace and quiet because it wouldn't last.

To occupy herself, she thought about the ways in which she could kill Lord Everess using only the objects readily at hand in the apartments. He was so fat and soft that there were a plenitude of options. The quickest way: silver filigree letter-opener plunged deep into the eye socket. Instantaneous. The most painful: tie him down in the parlor, start a nice fire, heat the poker just the perfect shade of red. Eyeballs, then tongue, then anus. She had learned that one when she was thirteen. And then there was the way that she'd killed Milla. And the doctor.

Oh, Milla. But she wasn't real. No, Milla wasn't real. The doctor wasn't real. It was all pretend. All pretend.

Take a deep breath. Don't think. Good girls don't think: They respond.

Anyway. She much preferred Paet to Everess, and wished that she could live with him instead; he was simple and straightforward. He had known pain, deep pain, and that connected them by a thin black thread, even if Paet didn't realize it. She'd asked Everess whether she could move in with Paet, and Everess had laughed as though she'd told a funny joke.

It was all so confusing sometimes.

And Silverdun. Oh, my.

At Copperine House there had been a very wealthy actress named Starlight, who'd been the recipient of a bad Ageless treatment. She never aged, true, but her mind was lost in time, and she never seemed to know what day it was. In one of her more lucid moments, she'd talked to Sela about love. Love was what made everything else worthwhile, she said. Passion, romance. To hold and to be held by a strong, handsome man, to be enveloped in him: That was the best thing in life.

Sela hadn't had the faintest idea what Starlight had been talking about. She knew about love, of course. She saw the threads of love spun between others; those threads were bright, bright colors: red and orange and gold, sometimes fiery, sometimes only glowing. But Sela had never experienced that sort of love herself. The only person she'd ever loved had been Milla. And that had been something different altogether.

When she came downstairs, Paet was waiting for her in the parlor. Lord Everess was nowhere to be seen.

"I have a task for you," he said.

"Oh, thank you," said Sela.

Lord Tanen has a gift for Sela. She is ten years old and cannot remember ever having received one. It is small, wrapped in cotton paper, tied with a real silk ribbon. He sits her down in her bedroom and puts the box on her dressing table.

"Open it," he says. "Today is a special day."

But she doesn't want to open it. The wrapping is so beautiful and the suspense so exquisite. She looks at Tanen, but his expression is, as always, impossible to read. He simply stares at her until her fingers reach for the bow.

"Is it my birthday?" she asks.

"No. You do not have a birthday."

Inside, her heart is swelling. Is this how it feels to be cared for? She remembers her parents, but she's been warned many times never to think of them, so she puts them out of her mind. She pulls delicately on the bow, and it comes undone with a soft slipping noise, barely audible.

The paper is smooth, its folds perfectly straight. Once the ribbon comes off, the paper unfolds itself and lies flat on the table, revealing a silver box.

"Open it," says Tanen. With trembling hands, she does.

Inside is a tiny figure of a swan, made of tin, painted blue. There's an even smaller tin key. She picks up the swan, holding it gingerly in both hands, turning it over.

"Oh, it's lovely," she whispers. Should she give him a kiss on the cheek? In books, when a father brings a daughter a lovely gift, she kisses his cheek. But Tanen is not her father and has told her so many times.

There's an opening in the swan's back. Tanen points to it. "Put the key in there and turn it. Hold the wings down while you do so."

The key fits perfectly in the swan's back and she turns it, the wrong way at first, then properly. As it goes around it clicks, the way the clock in the hall does when the maid turns it. She is not allowed to wind the clock, and she has always wondered how the clicking must feel. It's even better than she imagined; the mechanism inside the swan offers the perfect amount of resistance to her touch.

"Don't overwind it," scolds Tanen. "You'll break it." She stops, nearly letting go.

"Now place it on the table and watch."

When she lets go, the swan begins to flutter its wings. It bounces on the table, once, twice. Then it takes flight, shaky at first, then more certain, turning in wide, lazy circles near the ceiling.

Sela laughs and claps her hands. She watches, rapt, as the swan dips and sways and finally comes to rest on the dressing table, just where it started. Its wings flutter a few times more and then stop.

"May I do it again?" she says, reaching for the key.

Tanen places his hand on hers. His touch is cool, his skin dry. He takes the swan and drops it on the floor, crushing it under his boot. He points. "Pick up the pieces," he says.

Sela wants to cry, but knows that if she does then one of the crones will punish her. So she kneels and picks up the swan's remains: impossibly small gears and springs and a spiral of metal that burns to the touch.

She places the pieces gently on the table before her. She should have known. She should never have let herself believe that there would be kindness. Only Oca was kind, and then only when no one else was around.

"Some people," says Tanen, "are like this swan. They are not real. Not elves, but machines. Carefully crafted, they appear to be just like us. They speak and cry and bleed, and their insides are not gears and springs but flesh and bone, ingeniously created by our enemies."

"How will I know which is which?" asks Sela, breathless.

"I will tell you. I will point them out to you."

"And then what?" Do not cry. Do not cry.

"And then you will stop them, just as I have stopped your swan. The swan feels nothing. It is nothing. It is only a clever machine."

"Some people are clever machines," says Sela.

"Yes," says Tanen. "And nothing more."

"You said today was a special day," say Sela, remembering.

"Yes, indeed I did. The crones tell me that today is very important."

The crones have told her about this. They have told her that it is the beginning of a great change, that she will have to be ready. They feel her forehead several times a day. They place strange instruments on her belly and back and listen intently to them. This morning, she remembers, one of them lifted her head and said, "It's time."

"Stand up and come with me," says Tanen. "I want to have the crones examine you again."

She stands and realizes that it is warm and wet between her legs. Something thick is running down the inside of her thigh. She steps back, nearly tripping over the leg of her chair. On the floor are three drops of blood in a perfect triangle.

She feels dizzy. "What's happening?" she asks. "Am I dying?"

Tanen smiles, the first time she has ever seen him do so. His smile makes her more nervous, not less. "Quite the contrary, Sela."

He takes her face in his hands and looks hungrily at her. "Today your life has finally begun."

The city at night, after a rainstorm, was a glittering wonderland. Kerosene lamps and witchlights twinkled on rain-glazed cobblestones. Distant thunder from the retreating storm rattled beneath the tip-tip dripping from eaves and the muted slap of boots on wet stone. Here in the alley, earthy smells and human smells and dank smells and chimney smells mingled into an aroma different from all of the others, the after-rain smell.

The dress Paet had given her was constricting and uncomfortable. He'd given her scented powders for her skin and hair, and painted red circles on her cheeks. She hated it.

She knocked on the door at the end of the alley. "What do you want?" came a muffled voice from inside."

"Bryla sent me, she did," said Sela. She was talking in Ecara's accent, the way common city Fae talked.

The door was opened by a sullen stump of a man with thick arms and legs and silver tips on the points of his ears.

"Didn't send for anyone tonight," said the man.

She smiled a helpless smile and shrugged. "Bryla said to me go to Enni's place, and so that's what I done," she said.

She smiled a lopsided smile and waited, waited. The man looked at her. Wait. She felt the click and a thread sprung up, seething, bloodred.

There were two kinds of male lust, Sela knew. One was a desire to possess, to grab, to take something away. The other was an opening up, an exquisite longing for communion. This was decidedly the former.

Sela stepped forward a bit and the thread deepened. Sometimes when it was this thick she found herself knowing things. "You're . . . Obin, right?" She reached out and touched his collar.

"All right, come in," said Obin. "But don't get your hopes up. It's dead in here tonight."

"The rain," she tried. Yes, that was right. Rain was bad for business.

The door opened onto a narrow hallway. Obin led her through it and into a small parlor where three women sat, all heavily perfumed and tightly corseted, as Sela was. They all looked tired and bored. When they saw Sela, a tension sprung up in the room. A green-brown web of suspicion and contempt formed among the women.

"Who's she?" said one. She was thin and pale, with dark hair and delicate hands. There were circles under her eyes.

"Bryla sent her," said Obin. "Don't know why."

"She can't just come in here on a night like this," said the dark-haired woman. "That's silver out of my purse."

"Now now, Perrine," warned Obin. "Let's be ladies, shall we?"

Sela sat primly on a vacant love seat and waited, ignoring the glares from the other women. After a minute or so, their attention drifted and they began a desultory conversation that Sela ignored.

A knock came at the door and Obin went to answer. A young guildsman, nervous and polite, entered the parlor and looked at the women. Sela waited for him to find her with his gaze. The instant his thread appeared, she pushed back against it. *Not me.* His gaze slipped past her, the thread evaporating. The guildsman settled on the dark-haired woman, Perrine, and she led him through an arch in the back of the room.

Two more men came, and each time Sela pushed them away. For a little while, she was the only girl in the parlor. Obin tried to strike up a conversation with her, but she pushed back against him as well, and he lost interest in her.

Perrine reappeared after half an hour, followed by the young guildsman. His eyes were glazed, and he had a dopey smile on his face. Perrine looked haggard and stumbled a bit. She flopped down on the couch and took a cigarette from a box on the center table.

"Young ones," she said after he'd gone. "Hate the nervous young ones."

They sat in stony silence for several long minutes. Then another knock, and in came the man Sela had been waiting for. He was just as in his portrait, with cape and cane and a wide mustache. He bowed low when he saw the dark-haired woman. "Lady Perrine," he said in a booming voice. "So good to see you this lovely evening."

Perrine smiled and waved, suddenly alert and attentive. She stood and curtseyed, and Sela followed her lead.

The man looked Sela's way. When his thread sprang up she leapt at it, dragged at it. He looked at her, bewildered for a moment, then smiled.

"Ah, whom have we here?" he said. Sela felt Perrine's thread go purple-black. It stung, but she ignored it, smiling.

"Sir," she said.

"Perrine," said the man, "you are first in my heart, of course, but I would very much like to get to know this new friend of yours."

"Of course, Guildsman Heron." Perrine seethed.

Heron took a silver khoum from his pocket and pressed it into Perrine's hand. "You're a treasure, my dear."

Sela smiled and took Heron's hand. To Obin, she said, "Where shall I take him?"

"Upstairs, second on the left," said Obin. "Everything you need is in the room already."

Sela nodded. "Thank you."

They went upstairs without a word. Sela found the room Obin had indicated, and they went inside. There was a bed and a small table upon which were laid out a bowl, a candle, a packet of herbs, and a stoppered glass bottle.

"I trust your preparation is of adequate strength," said Heron, removing his cape. "I prefer an intense level of connection."

"You won't be disappointed, love," said Sela. She unstoppered the bottle and poured its contents into the bowl, then mixed in the herbs. The potion shimmered momentarily. It was an Insight preparation, similar to icthula, but with a decidedly different purpose.

Heron undressed while Sela prepared the draught. He climbed into the bed, and the bedsprings rattled beneath him.

"I'm ready, ready, ready," he said. His thread, bloodred flecked with brown, throbbed.

"Almost there, dear," said Sela.

She knelt on the bed and brought the bowl to his lips. He drank and lay back, impatient. She lifted the bowl and pretended to drink.

"Now come here and give us a kiss," he said.

Sela placed the bowl on the bed and leaned down toward him. She put her hands in his hair and ran her fingernails down his cheeks. He sighed happily, the effects of the potion beginning to affect him.

Heron's eyes closed. Sela took a small knife from her bodice and drew it across his neck. His eyes opened wide. He tried to speak, but only managed a thick gurgling sound. He pawed at her, grabbed at her hair and yanked at it.

"You're not real," said Sela.

Once she was certain he was dead, she stood and walked out of the room.

chapter eighteen

Indirect problems require indirect solutions.

—Fae proverb

Silverdun maintained consciousness as his captors dragged him roughly down the stairs and outside. He felt the sun on his face, but his vision was blurred; he saw only blue sky and moving shadows. He was lifted into the back of a closed wagon, and presently the wagon began to move.

With each bounce over the rough cobblestones, Silverdun's wrist shot pain up his arm. One of the guardsmen had bandaged it, and the bandage was already wet with blood. That deep, deep red blood. The light in Annwn, its red sun? Silverdun shuddered; his body wanted to die, but Silverdun refused to allow it. He'd never experienced anything similar.

The wagon turned, and its wheels rolled onto smooth stones. Silverdun smelled hay and horse dung. He tried to sit up and made it to his elbows. Ironfoot was slumped next to him. His eyes were open, and he looked back at Silverdun.

They were pulled from the wagon and carried inside a cool place that reeked of urine. There were calls and shouts. Silverdun was placed on a straw mat on a dirty stone floor, and he heard Ironfoot grunt next to him. There was the sound of metal on metal. Silverdun raised his head again. He and Ironfoot were in a small jail cell. He closed his eyes and slept, despite the pain from his wrist. A little while later he came awake and felt something cool and soothing on his right hand. He looked over to see someone, an old woman, applying a salve to the stump of his wrist.

"Surprised he's not dead," said the witch.

Silverdun almost wished he were.

Perrin is studying for his fifth-year exams when a message sprite alights on his windowsill.

"Hey, Perrin Alt, Lord Silverdun!"

Perrin looks up from his studies, scrutinizing the sprite. "I'm not Lord Silverdun, foolish sprite," he says. "That's my father."

"Well good news!" shouts the sprite. "You are now! Your father's dead!"

Perrin grabs the thing around its waist. "What? What are you talking about?"

The sprite blanches. "Aw, shucks. I was hoping you were one of those guys who didn't like his dad and was going to be *happy* to find out he was thrown from his horse and killed instantly. Then you'd probably want to offer me candy!"

Perrin throws the sprite at the wall, but it veers off and lands on top of a bookcase. "Hey, it wasn't *my* fault. Sheesh."

"Get out of here!" shouts Perrin.

The sprite pauses at the window. "So . . . where are we on the candy issue?"

The next day a carriage arrives to take Perrin back to Oarsbridge Manor, where his father is to be buried in the family plot. Mother is waiting for him at the front door. She embraces him, and he lets her. Father's body is laid out in the parlor, on the carved wooden bier that has been in the family for hundreds of years.

Perrin feels almost nothing when he sees his father. He examines his emotions carefully, and can come up with nothing other than a bland annoyance at having been summoned away from school during exams.

Mother is standing in the doorway, watching him. "Whatever you're feeling is all right," she says.

"I don't feel anything," says Perrin.

"That's all right, too."

"Everyone always tells me that he was a great man, a great lawmaker," he says. "I never really paid that much attention to his career."

"He never paid that much attention to you, either."

"He was extremely cordial."

Mother laughs, and raises her hand to stifle it. "I suppose he was, at that."

The funeral is well attended—seemingly by every member of Corpus, both lord and guildsman alike—and goes on for hours. It is dusk by the time the last statesman completes his encomium and sits. Perrin watches his father go into the ground, and suddenly he is filled with regret. He squeezes his mother's hand, and she squeezes back. She sees his tears and seems to understand them, even though he himself does not.

Afterward, Perrin's uncles Bresun and Marin take him aside. Bresun is father's twin brother, the younger by ten minutes, and Marin is much younger, the child of Grandfather's second wife.

"My deepest condolences . . . Lord Silverdun," says Bresun, emphasizing the "Lord."

"Thank you," says Perrin. He's known that the title would someday be his, of course, but he'd assumed that it would be many years in the future. "It's all a bit much. I confess I am somewhat overwhelmed."

"And who could blame you?" says Bresun. "Title is a great obligation, and not one to be taken up lightly."

Perrin nods. He has never liked Bresun.

"Since you're not yet of age, you'll need to appoint an overseer for the estate," Bresun continues. "I will, of course, be more than happy to assume that role."

Marin smiles weakly. "It's a fine idea, I think."

"Thank you," says Perrin. "I will consider your offer."

This is not the response Bresun wants. "I can assure you, son, that there is no one better acquainted with your father's affairs than I."

"Fine," says Perrin, suddenly not caring. "I accept."

Over the next few days, Perrin spends most of his time with a quill in his hand: penning thank-you notes to the many attendees of the funeral and signing a never-ending flood of documents for the solicitors. He falls asleep at his father's desk and is woken in the early morning by his mother's touch on his shoulder.

"Come, Perrin," she says. "There is something I want to discuss with you."

They walk out the south entrance, onto the lawns where Perrin played as a boy, and down the grass to the row of peach trees. The trees are in bloom, and they smell sweet and full.

They pass through the small gate set in the wall and continue down the path to the knoll that overlooks the river and the fields. The stone bridge after which the manor is named is still there after all these years, still in daily use.

"These are *your* lands now," says Mother.

"Yes," says Perrin, though he finds it hard to accept.

"Your father managed them well," she says. "He was always fair to his tenants, and they respected him."

"Everyone respected him, apparently."

"And rightly so. But I do not think you have any interest in managing our estates, do you, Perrin?"

Perrin stops walking and looks at her. "Of course I do. It's my responsibility."

"Your *responsibility*, yes. But not your desire."

"What are you getting at, Mother?"

"I want you to donate these lands to Aba."

"To the Arcadians, you mean."

"To *Aba*, I mean."

"Doesn't Aba already own everything anyway?" Perrin smirks.

"You're too old for that snotty attitude, Perrin," says Mother. "You demean us both. I have considered the matter prayerfully for some time."

"Mother," says Perrin. "You can't expect me to just . . . hand over my estate. It's madness."

"You have an enormous trust that will give you income for the rest of your life, Perrin. You don't need the money."

"It's not about the money. I don't care about that."

"The Church will manage the estate with love and care. They will treat the people with respect, even those who do not believe."

"Oh, yes. I'm sure they will. And I'm sure they'll happily pocket the income as well. Don't be naive, mother."

"I am many things," she says, her voice trembling, "but I am not naive."

"Mother," says Perrin. "I'm sorry. I didn't mean to hurt you. Honestly."

"I know."

"You're right, of course. I don't have any interest in being a landholder. Or in being a member of the House of Lords, for that matter. But Bresun and Marin will—"

"Bresun cares about nothing but money and status, and Marin is a fatuous cretin!" says Mother, her voice rising. She's breathing heavily.

"Well, as soon as I'm of age I'll be in charge and I'll make sure that they stay in line."

"By the time you come of age, Bresun will have found a way to take all of this from you."

"He can't, Mother. It would be unlawful."

Mother laughs, but it is not her usual warm laugh. It's more of a cackle. "Oh, Son. There is only one law that cannot be bent by money and influence. That is Aba's law, and it will punish Bresun, but not in this life. Bresun wouldn't dare go after your father, but he'll have no qualms taking *you* on."

Perrin pauses. He has never known his mother to be a cynic.

"Look out there," she says, pointing at the fields. "See those farmers? In two years' time they'll be groaning under Bresun's whip. And if you don't believe me, go visit his little estate and see how happy his tenants look.

"We called them noblemen, remember? Descendants of kings, each and every one of them. Don't they deserve better than that?"

Perrin has no idea what to say.

"I told you then that one day you would have to decide what kind of man you wanted to be. Now perhaps that day has come. Make the right choice. If not for Aba, then for me."

She leaves him there on the river path. One of the farmers spies him and waves, beaming.

The next day, Perrin sits Bresun down and explains that he's considering donating Oarsbridge and Connaugh estates to the Arcadians. Bresun smiles patiently, and explains in no uncertain terms what a terrible idea this is. He is charming and convincing, and within the hour, Perrin and he are sharing a drink and Perrin is laughing at himself for ever having considered such foolishness.

"Your mother is a wonderful woman," says Bresun. "But she's not the most realistic person in Faerie."

Silverdun smiles knowingly. He returns to school the next day and finishes his term with excellent marks.

Silverdun awoke to the sound of singing, the ethereal wail of Chthonic hymns. The tune was an old one, and familiar. Silverdun knew the same tune but with different words; the Arcadian peasants in Oarsbridge had sung it in the fields when he was a child. His mother had told him once that it was the singing that first drew her to Aba. Silverdun couldn't understand these words, sung in the vowelless glottal language of native Annwni, but he assumed it was about more or less the same thing: freedom from suffering, the walk of the soul, release.

There had been a few Arcadians at Crere Sulace, the prison where Silverdun had been held with Mauritane and the others. They sang the same sorts of songs. Silverdun had resented it then, and he resented it now. The notion of freedom in captivity, of the release of earthly bondage. How long were you supposed to keep singing before deciding that nobody was listening? Silverdun had left the monastery, so he supposed he'd reached his limit, assuming he'd ever truly been singing to begin with. Still, it was pretty music.

He opened his eyes and struggled into a sitting position to find Ironfoot awake, and eating. Ironfoot glanced over and pushed a tin plate of bread and greens toward him. Silverdun wasn't hungry, but he ate anyway, taking great care with his right arm.

"Does it hurt?" said Ironfoot, indicating the bandaged stump.

"Not really, no," said Silverdun. "Itches like a bastard, though."

Ironfoot nodded. If he had stories about amputees he'd met during his years of service in the army, he wisely kept them to himself. Silverdun knew that he should be focusing on their present predicament, but his thoughts kept coming back to his missing hand, and how thoroughly his life had been ruined. He couldn't go on with the Shadows like this; if they weren't hanged or imprisoned for life, his career was over. He might well be returning penniless to Oarsbridge to become one of those nobles, "reduced in circumstances," who survived by selling off his titled lands bit by bit until there was nothing left.

"Well, I'd say that our first mission has been an unqualified success," he said. "Wouldn't you agree?"

Ironfoot took a while in answering. "Oh, yes. We'll most certainly be lauded as heroes for this," he finally said.

"I've been a hero before," said Silverdun. "It's a wonderful way to meet women."

A pair of guards appeared in the hallways outside the cell, one aging and grizzled, the other young, barely out of his teens. The older of them opened the cell door, and the other came in to rouse Silverdun and Ironfoot.

"Come on, then," the young guard said, pulling Silverdun to his feet.

"Where are we going?" asked Ironfoot.

"You're being brought before the magyster," said the older guard.

Once Silverdun was on his feet, the young guard grabbed his forearm roughly and smashed the stump of Silverdun's wrist into the stone wall of the cell. Silverdun shrieked.

"You killed two of my best friends," the young guard snarled in Silverdun's ear.

"Now, now," said the older guard, stepping into the cell. "That'll be enough of that."

Chastened, the younger guard allowed the other to lead Silverdun and Ironfoot out of the cell and into the hallway.

"I apologize for young Bryno's conduct," said the old guard. "But you must admit he's got a legitimate complaint."

The guards led them past a row of cells, nearly all occupied. Many of the prisoners were paupers, perhaps caught stealing food or pickpocketing. Some were drunks; some were religious types who'd probably picked the wrong day to inject politics into their worship. They all watched Silverdun and Ironfoot pass with open interest. As far as any of them knew, Silverdun and Ironfoot were Unseelie bureaucrats: something they doubtless seldom saw here.

They were walked through another row of cells, then into a dark corridor and up a dim flight of stone stairs. Guards were placed here and there along the halls. Even if Silverdun had the strength to attempt overpowering his current escorts, there was nowhere to run.

After a few more turns and stairs they were deposited in a featureless, windowless room, where a man in a maroon robe sat on a dais in a high-backed wooden chair. A large book was open on a stand in front of him. A pair of guards stood on either side of the man, who leaned forward when Silverdun and Ironfoot entered. He was in his early middle years, with a bit of a paunch. There was an eagerness in his eyes that made Silverdun uncomfortable. This was a man who wanted something.

The old guard bowed to the man, who nodded back. The younger guard forced Ironfoot and Silverdun to their knees on the floor before the dais.

The older guard spoke. "Be it known that the two unnamed accused Fae have been brought before Magyster Eyn Wenathn."

There was a clerk sitting at a tiny desk in a corner of the room who was writing swiftly on a lined piece of parchment. "So noted," he said.

Magyster Wenathn leaned back in his chair and licked his lips. "Tell me your names," he said.

Silverdun attempted to stand, but the gloved hand of the young guard held him firmly down by the shoulder. "My name is Hy Wezel, and this is my associate En Urut. We are citizens of the Unseelie Empire, and we demand to be released this instant."

"Yes, I've examined your papers," said Wenathn. "They're excellent forgeries. Eel merchants; that was a nice touch."

"There's been a terrible mistake," said Ironfoot. "We've just arrived from Mag Mell in order to—"

"Be quiet," said Wenathn. "If you wish to keep to your story, that's fine. You may do so. As a magyster of this kollws, I have the right to examine you before turning you over to our gracious Unseelie protectors."

A bit of resentment in the mention of the Unseelie? Silverdun believed there was.

Ironfoot licked his lips and began to speak, but Wenathn cut him off again.

"If I do so," he said, "you will most certainly be tried and convicted as spies of the Seelie Kingdom. I can only assume that this is not your desired outcome."

"We are what we say we are," said Ironfoot. "We were attacked by those watchmen without explanation. My partner and I—"

Now it was Silverdun's turn to interrupt. "If we *were* Seelie spies," he said carefully, "that would be extremely awkward for all parties. There could be a serious incident." He looked Wenathn in the eyes as he spoke.

Wenathn gestured at the man in the corner. "Strike out that last statement," he said. Then he spoke to the guards. "Leave us. I'd like to question these prisoners privately."

The clerk at the desk stood, taking his papers with him. He trotted to the door of the room, waving for the guards to follow him. The younger guard, standing behind Silverdun and Ironfoot, began to speak, but the clerk stopped him. "You've heard the magyster," he said. "Come."

The door closed, and the room was empty save for Wenathn, Silverdun, and Ironfoot.

"Let us speak as men of understanding, shall we?"

Ironfoot stood. "Listen to me," he said, just as he'd been instructed by Paet. "We are *precisely* who we say we are." That last had a bit of Leadership in it. Wenathn, however, wasn't easily led.

"Don't worry," said Silverdun. "It's all right. He knows who we really are."

Ironfoot glared at him. "Hy Wezel!"

"No, it's true. We are, in fact, Seelie spies, and we've been sent on a mission by Titania to undermine Mab's rule here in Annwn. Killing good Annwni men was never part of our plan."

"I don't doubt your intentions are beyond reproach," said Wenathn, smirking. He stood, and gestured for Silverdun and Ironfoot to stand as well. "Still, you have killed them, and that puts you in a very difficult position."

"You could turn us over to the Unseelie," said Silverdun. "Why not do so?"

"Why not, indeed? I'd surely be lauded for doing it. And I most likely will, unless . . ." Wenathn drew his pause out for effect, then seemed to change course.

"The situation here in Annwn is a complicated one," he resumed. "The Unseelie rule here as our benefactors, not as our conquerors. And in order to maintain what some very cynical boors might call the *illusion* of autonomy, we Annwni are permitted to conduct our affairs to a large degree without their direct involvement. So when they do become involved, one takes an interest.

"Two days ago, the Unseelie proconsul sent out a message for the guard to be watchful for a pair of Unseelie eel merchants matching your description. You were to be watched closely and detained only when you attempted to leave Blood of Arawn."

They'd been betrayed. By whom? Aranquet, the ambassador to Mag Mell? He seemed the most likely candidate.

"Unfortunately for you, yesterday a woman reported two Unseelie men acting suspiciously in her home to the guardsmen in my district. Eager to share in the reward that I myself offered for these men, a dozen of my guardsmen descended on that home, causing an unfortunate incident that led to the death of a number of them, and the loss of the entire building to fire. In short, it was an utter debacle, and one that has taken a great deal of effort to keep quiet."

Silverdun was starting to understand. Wenathn was in a complicated position. If he turned them over to the proconsul, he'd be rewarded for capturing a pair of Seelie spies. He would also, however, be upbraided by his peers for having created the situation that got so many of his own people killed. He was looking for a way out. But surely the reward outweighed whatever calumny he might receive. What was he after?

Then it hit him. Elections. The elections for magyster were being held later in the year. The landowners of the kollws would be voting soon, and Wenathn wanted to ensure that he was reelected.

"If the circumstances of our capture were made public," said Silverdun, "a potential opponent might seize upon such a situation in order to cast you in an unfavorable light."

"Such things do happen," said Wenathn.

"Let me propose a scenario to you, Magyster Wenathn," said Silverdun.

"Propose away."

"Suppose you determined that we were, as you have suspected, notorious spies of Regina Titania. Having captured us, you would no doubt be warmly regarded by your Unseelie protectors."

"No doubt," said Wenathn.

"Suppose then that having thus determined, you remanded us to the custody of the Unseelie. I presume a small detachment of Unseelie Army officers would retrieve us from your jail and convey us back to the City of Mab, where we would be tried. And in the course of that trial, all sorts of things could come to light that no one in this room would be especially pleased to have repeated far and wide. Correct?"

Wenathn frowned. "Correct."

"Let us suppose even further," said Silverdun, "and this is in the wildest realm of speculation imaginable, of course. Let us suppose that some in Annwn would not be terrifically opposed to having friends in the Seelie Kingdom. Friends with pockets."

Now Wenathn looked definitely interested. "Elections can become very expensive affairs," he said.

"Then I believe there's a very simple solution that can accommodate us all," said Silverdun.

Before dawn the next morning, Silverdun and Ironfoot were roused in their cell by a different pair of guards. They were brought out of the jail in a different direction, out to an enclosed courtyard, where Wenathn stood with a pair of Unseelie Army officers in front of a covered wagon. Wenathn ordered Silverdun and Ironfoot to be shackled hand and foot.

"I'm glad we agreed to do this quietly," Wenathn said to the officers. "There are some elements here in Blood of Arawn that still take offense at your gracious assistance in our local affairs."

"Yes, well. Some people will never accept the way of things," said one of the officers. "The proconsul is grateful to you for your assistance in this matter. It will not be forgotten."

"I hope not," said Wenathn. "It's not every day that one gets the opportunity to foil a foreign plot, is it?"

Wenathn's clerk handed the officers a sheaf of papers, and the officers placed Ironfoot and Silverdun into the back of the wagon, chaining their shackles to a bolt in the carriage's floor.

There were no windows in the back of the wagon, and very little light. Silverdun's right hand hung free, since there was no way to shackle it, and he held it gingerly aloft. Ironfoot was a dark shape in front of him.

"This is never going to work," said Ironfoot.

"We'll see," said Silverdun.

The wagon started and turned out of the courtyard. It proceeded through the winding streets of Blood of Arawn, jouncing on the cobbles and potholes as it went. The Unseelie officers were talking in the front of the wagon, but Silverdun couldn't hear what they were saying.

The wagon pulled up short and stopped, nearly throwing Silverdun against the back of its cab.

"Out of the way!" he heard one of the officers shout.

There was another shout, this one wordless, and then steps on either side of the wagon. Two blades clashed, and then there was silence.

The back of the wagon opened, and a man dressed entirely in black, with a black hood covering his face, stepped in and unlocked Silverdun's and Ironfoot's shackles. "Out," he said.

Silverdun and Ironfoot climbed out of the wagon. They were in a narrow alley. An oxcart was blocking the path in front of the wagon, and standing on the cart were two more men in black, also hooded, holding crossbows. Another held a sword at the throat of the driver of the wagon. The other Unseelie lay either unconscious or dead next to him; in the predawn light of the alley it was difficult to tell.

"Come with me," said one of the men in black. He led Silverdun and Ironfoot around the corner, where two horses were saddled and waiting. Once they were out of sight of the Unseelie, he pushed back his hood. It was the older of the two guards who had brought them to Wenathn.

"Annwn used to be a good place," he said. "Are you truly here to help rid us of the Unseelie?" He peered deeply into Silverdun's eyes.

"We are," said Silverdun.

The guard handed Silverdun the travel documents that had been taken from them when they'd been captured. "Take these and ride directly to the river. There's a boat waiting for you there called the *Magl*," he said. "We'll detain these men long enough for you to get there, but no longer."

Silverdun nodded. He couldn't think of anything to say that didn't sound crass, so he said nothing.

"A little help getting up?" he said to Ironfoot, holding up his stump. Ironfoot helped him mount his horse, and the two of them rode off into the morning.

Once they were safely on board the *Magl*, which turned out to be a dusty mining barge, the crew escorted them down into a small hold that smelled like dirt and lamp oil. It was close and dark, but Silverdun was grateful nonetheless.

"Unbelievable," said Ironfoot. "I can't believe that actually worked."

Silverdun, however, had been certain that it would. Wenathn wanted to be elected to the high council, but if the tale of their exploit was revealed in open court before the Unseelie proconsul, he'd be excoriated for having botched it so badly. The problem was that he couldn't have released them without making the proconsul's office suspicious, and he'd miss the opportunity to curry favor with them by allowing two spies to go free. The third option was to allow them to escape; not from *him*, but from the Unseelie soldiers. That way Wenathn had done his duty as a good little collaborator, and the Unseelie looked stupid in the bargain.

"But," said Ironfoot, "won't the truth of all this come out during the Unseelie investigation of our escape?"

"It would, if there were an investigation. But the Unseelie can't allow themselves to be seen losing foreign spies, so they do what all spineless bureaucrats do when they're in trouble."

"They cover it up."

"Exactly. It's like it never happened. And now Wenathn is our good friend in Annwn, a man who clearly has no love for the Unseelie and can almost certainly be influenced once we help get him elected."

Ironfoot whistled. "You're a devious son of a whore, Silverdun. I'll give you that."

"My mother was no whore, but you're right about the other."

"Well done, then. I suppose our mission was a success."

Silverdun winced. "Tell that to my right hand," he said.

Time on the river crawled. Once the city was behind them they were able to move about freely on deck. The air was fresher, but the view wasn't much better. Outside the city, Annwn was an endless sea of prairie grass, without a single tree or shrub to break up the view. Sometimes they saw animals come to drink at the water, but beyond that, nothing. They took their meals with the crew, who were a taciturn bunch.

On the second day of the journey Silverdun began to feel queasy; his wrist itched. That evening he began to vomit and sweat, and every time the boat rolled in the water he groaned.

On the morning of the third day, he was delirious, remembering things only in bits and pieces. There was the nausea and the dreadful itching and the pitching of the deck. He wanted desperately to scratch at his stump, but Ironfoot kept stopping him. Why did Ironfoot keep stopping him? In a lucid moment he looked at his hand, saw it covered in blood. "Stop it!" came Ironfoot's voice through the haze. He felt something being tied around his arm, something thick and heavy. When he went to scratch the wrist it wasn't there; there was only thick heavy cloth. He burned and choked and itched.

When he awoke on the fourth morning, he felt light-headed, but the delirium had gone. He was lying out in the open, and the sun hurt his eyes. When he looked down at his right arm he saw that it had been wrapped in a piece of sail and belted to keep him from scratching it. The pain and itching were gone, but he still felt the ghostly sensation of the missing hand straining against the wrappings. It felt impossibly real.

He was on the foredeck, his clothes soaked in sweat. A cool wind blew across the bow, and Silverdun reveled in it.

"You're awake at last," said Ironfoot. He brought Silverdun a tin cup of water and a plate of dried fish. Silverdun ate and drank, slowly at first and then faster.

"More water, please," he said, holding out the cup. Ironfoot refilled it once, and then again.

"How do you feel?" asked Ironfoot. "The captain thought you were done for."

"Not I," said Silverdun, pulling himself up slowly to a standing position. "We Lords Silverdun are made of hardier stuff than most. Extraordinarily difficult to kill."

"I need to change your bandage," said Ironfoot. "Sorry about the wrapping, but we couldn't get you to stop scratching at the thing; you kept reopening the wound. The captain says you'll have to get it sewn up properly by a physician as soon as we get to Mag Mell or you're liable to get gangrene."

"Lovely," said Silverdun.

Ironfoot removed the belt holding the cloth in place and pulled the sailcloth off the bandage. Underneath was a bloody mess, but despite the confusion of blood-caked bandaging one thing was very clear.

"Auberon's balls!" said Ironfoot. "Your hand's grown back!"

Silverdun pulled off the bandages and held up his hand. It was there, good as new. He flexed his fingers and thumb; everything worked. There was no itching, no tenderness, no pain.

"That's a nice trick," said Ironfoot, eyes wide. "What did you do?"

Silverdun pinched the skin on the new hand hard and thrilled at the pain. "I have no idea."

He lay on his stomach and reached into the water, washing the blood from his hand. When he held it up again it was as if nothing had ever happened to it.

"Look at this," he said to Ironfoot. "Right here on the palm. That scar. I got it when I was a boy, falling off a wall."

"I see it," said Ironfoot.

"Let's assume for a moment that it's somehow possible to regrow a hand," said Silverdun. "How do you explain regrowing a scar?"

"I have no compelling scholarly response to that one," said Ironfoot.

By boat they traveled south along the river to Glaum, the gold mining center. Dressed as mine officials, they walked on board a transport ship bound through a waterborne industrial lock connecting the river with a shipping port in Mag Mell, a few days' sail from Isle Cureid. When they arrived at the embassy, Aranquet greeted them with open arms.

If the Seelie ambassador was surprised to see them alive, he gave no indication of it. Either he wasn't the one who'd sold them out to the Annwni, or he was an exceptionally good liar. He feted them with shellfish and liquor, and brought them as his special guests to a water ballet in the atoll's lagoon. The male and female partners performed a complex and deeply stylized dance, part above the water and part below. Beneath the water, female spectators watched the bottom half of the dance. Aranquet explained in whispers that there were in fact two different ballets occurring simultaneously; the Dance Above and the Dance Below. Each had its own secret meaning, and no one except the gods knew it in its entirety.

Silverdun tried to pay attention to the performance, but all he could think about was the hand.

chapter nineteen

A Chthonic priest complained to me about the tax on his property. I told him that the tax rules applied to everyone in my lands. He responded that the rules clearly did *not* apply to everyone, as I myself was exempt from them.

I doubled his tax. That shut him up.

—Lord Gray, *Recollections*

When Silverdun and Ironfoot arrived in the City Emerald, it was the middle of the night. That was despite it having been midday in Mag Mell, which they'd just left. The time change was disorienting, but Silverdun was still thrilled to be back in Faerie. The air was cleaner, more pure. Silverdun felt lighter on his feet the instant he emerged from the lock.

They stepped outside onto the street from Chancery Station, and both of them breathed deeply.

"Here we are," said Ironfoot.

"We are indeed," said Silverdun.

"It appears to be just past two in the morning. I can't say I'm particularly sleepy, though."

"No, neither am I," said Silverdun. "And I don't want to wait until the morning to talk to Paet."

"Nor I. Let's go drop off our things at Blackstone and then go to his flat and wake him the hell up."

"Best idea I've heard all day."

Their plan, however, was thwarted by the fact that when they arrived at

Blackstone, Paet was already there, wide awake, waiting for them in the main office. A few analysts, translators, and copyists sat at desks, their heads down, intent on their work.

"Welcome home," Paet said once they were in his office. He looked genuinely relieved. "I can't tell you how glad I am to have you both back." It was the first time Silverdun could remember him expressing an emotion that wasn't anger.

"I lost a hand," said Silverdun.

Paet looked at Silverdun. "What on earth are you talking about?"

"An Annwni guardsman lopped off my hand, and five days later it grew back."

A thin smile crept across Paet's lips. "Is that so?"

"What did you do to us?" asked Ironfoot. "At Whitemount. Something happened to us there. Jedron did something to us. I've been puzzling over it ever since we left, and I can't think of a single thaumatic explanation for it.

"And I'm very smart," he added.

"I think it's time you told us what it was you did to us," said Silverdun.

"Anything else unusual happen?"

"As a matter of fact, yes," said Silverdun. "I burned down an entire building with a single burst of witchfire, and Ironfoot here turned a man into his willing slave."

"I see."

Paet took a bottle of whiskey from the sideboard next to his desk and poured three glasses. He handed one each to Silverdun and Ironfoot and raised his glass. They drank.

"I told you to expect some unusual aftereffects, did I not?" said Paet. "It appears as though these effects have begun sooner rather than later."

"I assumed you meant nausea or headache," said Silverdun.

"I was purposefully vague because it's different for everyone."

"What is?" asked Ironfoot. "*What* is different for everyone?"

"Something happened to us at Whitemount, Paet," said Silverdun. "And you know what it was. So tell us."

"I can't," said Paet. He looked tired, strained.

"And why not?"

"Because the less you know about it, the better," said Paet, raising his voice. "Knowledge is everything in this business. The more you know, the more of a liability you are."

"And here we go with this routine again," said Silverdun.

"Listen, you," said Paet. "I slit the throat of a woman I loved to protect the very same information. Do you think I was happy about it?"

Silverdun had no response to that, besides horror.

"Anyway," said Paet, "what we did to you is less important than what you do with it."

"That's not good enough," said Ironfoot.

"Here's what I *can* tell you," said Paet. "You're stronger than you were. You've realized that, I believe. Both physically, and with your *re*. You are much more difficult to hurt, and you regenerate very quickly when injured.

"There are other . . . advantages as well, but I'm not at liberty to tell you what they are unless it becomes necessary for me to do so."

"And what circumstances would be required to make that a necessity?" asked Silverdun.

Paet drained his whiskey. "You don't want to know."

He poured another glass. "Now if you'll excuse me, there are more pressing matters that I must attend to."

"What would those be?" asked Silverdun.

"I take it you haven't looked at a newspaper since your return." Paet handed a folded copy of the *Register* across the desk. It was folded to a story whose headline read, "The Inquiry into Guildsman Heron's Death Widens."

"Heron?" said Ironfoot. "Is this the husband of the secretary of states?"

"The very same," said Paet. "It's the scandal of the day at court, and there's already pressure on the secretary to resign."

Silverdun glanced down the article. "A murder. Are we to investigate it?"

Paet grimaced. "Oh, no. We already know who the murderer is."

"Who?" asked Ironfoot.

"Our own Sela," said Paet. "Everess put her up to it."

There was a silence in the office.

"Why?" Ironfoot finally said. "Is it within our purview to do such a thing?"

Paet shrugged. "One of the benefits of being a Shadow is that we have no official purview. Though I imagine if this were traced back to the foreign minister, he'd soon find himself looking for another job, if not another head."

"What's his explanation?" asked Silverdun.

"That's what I intend to find out."

The next morning, Silverdun was awoken by the sound of someone ringing the bell at the front door. It was just barely sunrise outside, and he'd had no more than four hours' sleep.

A moment later, his valet Olou strode into his room without knocking, as was his wont.

"Knocking," Silverdun said, "is a civilized practice. In every corner of the realm, Olou."

Olou shrugged. "I may be your valet, sir, but I'm also an officer in the Foreign Ministry. And as far as the ministry is concerned, this is my house, and you're the invalid uncle that I attend to."

"I knew there had to be a catch," said Silverdun. He rose and began dressing, inspecting the clothing that Olou had laid out for him. "Nice outfit," he said.

"I do my best," said Olou.

"Who's knocking at my door—forgive me, *your* door—so hellishly early in the morning?"

"Abbot Estiane from the Temple Aba-Nylae."

"What does he want?"

"It wasn't my place to ask, sir."

Silverdun finished dressing and left the room with a sneer at Olou. By the time he found himself in the sitting room of his apartments, he was in a better mood, and he greeted Estiane with a smile that Estiane did not return.

"What's wrong, Estiane? Did they finally discover your cache of liquor?"

"I am going to speak this morning with Lord Everess," said Estiane. "Depending on the outcome of this conversation, I may ask you to reconsider your choice of employment."

"Says the man who practically pushed me into it."

"A situation has arisen," said Estiane, "that has made me question that decision."

"Trust me; I've questioned it plenty for both of us."

"For what reasons?" asked Estiane. The abbot's eyes were red; he appeared as though he'd been crying.

"I'm not sure if I can say," said Silverdun.

"Ahh," said Estiane, folding his hands in his lap. "Secrecy. You have indeed entered a world of shadows, Perrin."

"This is the way of things," said Silverdun. "I knew that before I joined up with Everess, and I've had it confirmed more than once since."

"We will speak more of this later. I just wanted to let you know."

"Abbot," said Silverdun, "what is the extent of Aba's forgiveness? Just out of curiosity."

Estiane sighed. "The Scripture says it is infinite, child. Let us hope for both of our sakes that the Scriptures do not exaggerate."

Lord Everess's office was spacious and homey, dressed with antiques and old religious artifacts: an Arcadian censer from the Ram cycle; a Chthonic candelabra with twelve candles of different hues, each representing both a god and a Gift; a bronze statue of a Nymaen god, who was a grossly fat man with his hand held up in benediction. Everess himself held no particular religious beliefs, having been raised in the high nobility where such things were typically frowned upon. An Arcadian opponent in the House of Lords had once snidely remarked from the floor that power was Everess's only religion. That had gotten a good laugh from the gallery.

Religious types didn't worry Everess, nor did political opponents given to cliché. There were only two in all of Faerie who sincerely worried him: Regina Titania and Chief Paet. The queen's power was perhaps not what it once was, but that was like saying a dragon's flame was perhaps a bit cooler than it had been; one could still easily be incinerated by it.

Paet bothered Everess because Everess needed him, and Everess did not enjoy needing anyone. But only Paet could do what Paet did. Someday perhaps Silverdun could replace him, but not any day soon.

It was difficult to control someone who cared about nothing save the one thing you dared not take from him. Meetings with Paet were always the low point of any day, and after the Heron affair, Paet was going to be livid. Well, let him come. Paet needed him as badly as he needed Paet.

As if on cue, his amanuensis announced Paet at his office door, and Everess grunted his assent.

"Good morning, Chief," said Everess. "To what do I owe the pleasure?"

Paet flopped heavily into the chair opposite Everess's desk; it was a reader's chair from a Resurrectionist tabernacle, and it had cost a fortune. "You know why I'm here," he said. "This Heron business."

"What about it?"

"When you said you wanted to 'borrow' Sela for a 'small errand,' I did not imagine that you'd be sending her into a halcyon brothel to murder a ranking member of the Smiths' Guild. A guildsman who also happens to be the husband of one of your chief enemies in government."

"Your lack of imagination is the stuff of legend, Paet," said Everess. "But there is nothing in our agreement that says I require your permission to do . . . well, anything."

"It was stupid, and if you'd asked me I'd have advised strongly against it."

"Which is precisely why I didn't tell you."

"What could you possibly hope to gain with such an act? There's going to be an inquiry. And if that inquiry leads the high prosecutor back to the Shadows, we're finished."

"Well, I should think it would be obvious what I hoped to gain," Everess said. "The scandal will drive Heron out of the House of Guilds, and none of her political allies will try to protect her overmuch, not wanting to be painted with the same brush."

Everess smiled. "Even if there were an inquiry, it would never connect Sela to the act. She was heavily made up and heavily glamoured before she went out."

Paet shifted in his chair. Everess knew that despite the chair's attractive appearance, it was hellishly uncomfortable. Which was precisely why he'd picked it.

"What do you mean," asked Paet, "'even if there were an inquiry?'"

Everess smiled, leaning back in his own chair, which was, on the other hand, extraordinarily comfortable. "Despite the outcry among those in Corpus who might gain from a lengthy scandal, an inquiry would be . . . deeply awkward for those who would be in charge of investigating the act. If we'd gone after the secretary of states herself, they'd have no choice. But with her husband, there are limiting factors."

"Meaning?"

"Meaning that the high prosecutor and half of his staff visit that brothel on a regular basis. Why do you think it happened there?"

"Well. You've clearly thought of everything," said Paet. "But why kill the man? That seems excessive, even for you. I was under the impression that we didn't assassinate our own."

"Because the very ones who oppose us most strenuously, those who will suspect that we were responsible for the act, will see Heron's death as a warning. They'll think twice before being as openly critical as Guildmistress Heron has been."

"I give up," said Paet. "You're going to do what you want despite my objections."

"Good. I'm glad you're finally figuring that out."

There was a commotion in the outer office. Everess's amanuensis knocked at the door. "Milord," she said, "I apologize for the interruption, but there's an abbot out here who insists on speaking with you immediately, and—"

"Aba is everywhere, young lady," said Estiane, brushing past her into the office. "And as I am his representative in Faerie, I go where he goes."

"It's fine," said Everess. "Come in, Abbot."

Paet stood. "I'll leave you to your next happy visitor," he said.

Estiane bowed at Paet, but said nothing, his face red with anger. Paet smiled and left, shutting the door behind him.

"I am outraged," said Estiane, before Everess had a chance to speak. "I am stunned! I can barely form the words to express the horror I am feeling right now."

Everess looked at Estiane, trying to hide his contempt. Was hypocrisy a requirement for high religious office? Or was it merely a common accompaniment?

"I trust you do not approve of my methods."

"Your *methods*," hissed Estiane. "You had a man *killed*. It is your *murders* I do not approve of."

Everess stood and walked to the window of his office, which overlooked the Promenade. "*You* came to *me*," he said. "You wished to barter your Arcadian intelligence for a bit of influence."

"That's right," said Estiane. "Influence. Not assassination."

"'Everess,' you said. 'The secretary of states is causing grief for the Arcadians. She refuses to address the persecution of our adherents in the worlds in which the Seelie have influence.' Is this not so?"

"I have a sacred duty to protect those in my charge," said Estiane. "I understand that this sometimes requires compromise. I am willing to accept the moral taint that accompanies such things. I will be held accountable by Aba for that. But I will not be a party to murder!"

Everess whirled on him. "How noble of you!" he said. "You will suffer the ethical opprobrium from on high, on behalf of your people. You will happily make yourself a martyr. But when it comes to the required actions, you suddenly want no part. You want the effect, but you will not be a party to the cause!"

"I demand that you confess to this crime. If you confess then Aba will forgive you," said Estiane.

"You are in no position to demand anything of me," said Everess. "If I resigned today as foreign minister, there is no one to take my place who would give your church the time of day. Your influence in Corpus would drop to zero. And then all of this will have been for nothing."

"Not this way," said Estiane. "I do not want it at this price."

"Of course not. You want your crops to grow, but you do not want your hands in the dirt. It doesn't work that way."

Everess poured himself a drink and took a sip before continuing. "Now listen, Abbot. The most likely replacement for the secretary would be Lord Palial. You know Lord Palial, of course, because he is one of your most ardent disciples. In secret, of course, but such is the way of the world."

Estiane thought this over. "This is not ended, Lord Everess. By no means. And let me be very clear. If I ever hear of you doing something like this on my alleged behalf again, I *will* confess to this act myself, and the consequences be damned!"

Everess laughed. "Such consequences are always damned, Abbot. That is the price we pay as men of action."

Estiane spewed a few more complaints and empty threats and then stormed out just as he'd stormed in. But he'd accepted what had happened just as Everess had known he would. So insidious, this sort of thing was. A slippery slope, as they said. Within five years the abbot himself would be sticking the knife in.

Everess picked up the fat little Nymaen statue. The antiquities dealer who'd sold it to him claimed that rubbing its belly was good luck. "Luck is for amateurs," he told the statue, replacing it on his desk.

chapter twenty

Given time, all wonders become ordinary, and cease to
be wonders.

—Fae proverb

utumn ended with a series of bitterly cold days that brought to mind
echoes of midwinter. But those days passed, and spring began to work its
deep magic in Faerie. The cherry trees on the Promenade blossomed, the rain
slowed to intermittent drizzle, and the City Emerald came to life. Titania's
Spring Pageant took over the city for a full week, during which colorful ban-
ners were hung from lampposts and windows and the streets were strewn
with rose petals, the blossoms taken from Titania's own private garden. Music
blared from the Outer Court of the Great Seelie Keep day and night, and the
pageant itself, at the week's end, was a ten-hour extravagance with a parade,
a show of pyrotechnics, and a grand mestina on the keep grounds open to the
public.

The mestines produced a massive epic, beginning with Uvenchaud
slaying the dragon Achera and culminating with him leading the combined
Fae clans to victory over the Old Thule in the Midlands War. Achera's flames
were so realistic that children screamed when he flew overhead, and the
crowd roared when Uvenchaud's army climbed the ramparts at Drae and
overcame the Thule king Marlace in the last battle. The final scene showed
Uvenchaud being crowned King of Faerie, and the crowd cheered, throwing
flower petals at the mestines who stood on the ground, working the intricate
glamour art above them.

The Shadows did not attend the pageant. That week, Silverdun returned to Annwn to deliver a hefty sum of gold to Magyster Wenathn, who won his reelection bid handily. Wenathn now had his sights set on election to high council, and the Shadows were more than happy to assist him in any way possible. Useful intelligence soon began to flow from him as their relationship deepened.

Silverdun's spring was primarily taken up, however, with the reviewing of an endless stream of intelligence from sources far and wide, looking for any sign of Mab's intentions, and finding scant little. Unseelie forces continued to build near the border, albeit slowly, but no solid indication that this was meant as anything other than posturing was forthcoming. Nor was there any information about the Einswrath weapon, or why it had not been used anywhere since Selafae.

Ironfoot spent most of his time at Blackstone Manor, his maps spread out before him, performing calculations, but his anger at being unable to discern the workings of the Einswrath had turned to despair and then disillusionment as he began to believe that the problem was unsolvable. He developed a rhythm during the spring: He would work the problem until he began to feel violent, and then he would push it aside for a few days and join Sela and Silverdun in scanning intelligence.

Both Ironfoot and Silverdun noticed their Gifts steadily increasing in power, but as they rarely found themselves in significant danger, no more marvels such as Silverdun's regrown hand or Ironfoot's burst of Leadership took them by surprise. They spoke of it often at first, and Ironfoot had undertaken some research on the side to try to determine what had been done to them, but such inquiry went nowhere, and as Ironfoot already had one impossible problem in front of him, he had no great desire to commit to another.

As Everess had predicted, no progress was ever made on the murder of Guildsman Heron; ultimately the official pronouncement came down from the high prosecutor's office that it had been a robbery attempt gone wrong. A patsy had been arrested and hanged, and the matter dropped. Guildmistress Heron had resigned and gone to live with relatives in the East. After her resignation, another of Everess's predictions came true. The Arcadian Lord Palial was appointed by Corpus to take her place.

Sela was sent out on assignments from time to time, usually by herself, usually to cajole information from male informants who had proved less than forthcoming. Due to Paet's constant and strenuous objections, she undertook no more assassinations on Seelie soil.

When not on assignment, she and Silverdun studiously ignored one another. Her feelings for him only grew, however, and while she sensed that he felt the same way, something kept them apart, some reservation on Silverdun's part that caused them never to be alone in the same room together, and never to speak of anything other than work.

As a result, she found herself spending more and more time upstairs, with the analysts. As time passed, she grew to enjoy teasing out information from among the stacks and stacks of disparate documents, working out how to apply it, how to sense patterns. It was a different way to use her skill with Empathy, and she much preferred it to the way she'd been taught.

Paet allowed his Shadows a certain amount of leisure, but that was only because he sensed that rough times were ahead. Cries for war continued to escalate in Corpus, and there would soon come a time when cooler heads would cease to prevail. When war came, as he knew it would sooner or later, the lives of the Shadows would change in ways they couldn't imagine.

Spring grew; Faerie warmed; the waters of the Inland Sea grew calm and lost their chill. Spring, however, was only a season. Summer would come soon enough, and then autumn would be back for more.

chapter twenty-one

The cynosures are objects with remarkable thaumatic properties, though because they are objects of worship the Chthonics do not allow them to be studied. Twelve were created in the wake of the *Rauane Envedun*-e, but it is not known how many of them are still in existence, as the Chthonic priests refuse to discuss them in any detail.

The philosophical significance of the cynosure is multifarious. Its wholeness represents the wholeness of the spirit. Its size, the area of each face, the angle of each vertex, the length of each side, all relate to both the religious and thaumatic aspect of the object. As I will show in the following chapter, the two can be seen as indistinguishable.

—Prae Benesile,
Thaumatical History of the Chthonic Religion

Journeyer Timha sat in Master Valmin's study, stuck on a passage in Beozho's *Commentaries*. It was an exceedingly dense passage in a work well known for its obliqueness. Alpaurle himself had referred to it as "the ravings of a great man in decline." Over the centuries, scholars had debated the value of the work; for a tome ostensibly about thaumaturgy, there was very little spellwork in it. The *Commentaries* was, rather, a massive philosophical work, littered with partial references to and quotations from documents that had been lost to the ages, but which Beozho clearly expected his audience to be deeply familiar with. About these secondary documents, Alpaurle had commented, "some are works of genius, others flights of fancy, and yet others are intellectual self-pleasure."

The passage now plaguing Timha was in one of many sections of the work that appeared to have nothing whatsoever to do with thaumaturgy. It was, however, referenced twice in the notes that the black artist Hy Pezho had left in the margins of his plans. Valmin had gone over the passage twice and found nothing of interest, and now Timha was reviewing it only because he could think of nothing else to do.

The panic among the senior staff had been growing daily in the months since the Bel Zheret's visit. They'd elected not to tell the rest of the group about the approaching deadline. What good would it do? Everyone understood the urgency of the project.

Timha reached the end of the page and realized that he had no idea what he'd just read. He went back to the top of the page and tried to find where he'd left off, but recognized nothing. He had to flip back three pages to find the passage at which he'd stopped paying attention.

"We are bound by division," the paragraph began. "Categories mean nothing at depth. All Gift is flow. Eternal, unchanging. We refuse eternity, refuse what we unsee, and so must make what we can see and judge. It is our nature, but it is also our failing."

What the hell did any of that mean? It was all loopy doublespeak as far as Timha could tell. More to the point, it had nothing to do with reitic mechanics whatsoever. What Timha needed was a derivation of Folding that would solve the energy containment equations. He needed a solution to Vend-Am's inequality with a resulting force greater than the square of its input vectors. The *Commentaries* contained not a single spell, no concatenations of triggered bindings, nothing that might ever be remotely considered to be practical thaumatics.

They were all going to die. There was nothing for it. It had become clear to Timha that Hy Pezho's talents had not only been greater than anyone had imagined, but they were greater than any of them could comprehend. And as a result, everyone here was going to die. Bel Zheret didn't make idle threats. They were Mab's personal secret police, loyal as hounds. The ultimatum had come from Mab herself.

There was no possible way that the Project would be finished in the time remaining to them. Even if Timha had discovered the innermost secrets of the universe in Beozho's *Commentaries*, there wasn't enough time to translate that into a working weapon.

Master Valmin, who'd been sleeping in his chair, sat up with a start. "How goes it, Journeyer?" he asked, already knowing the answer.

"The *Commentaries* are still as opaque and meaningless as ever," said Timha, without looking up.

Valmin leaned back in his chair. "I discovered at university that, in a pinch, I could get high marks in my history classes by writing term papers about that book."

Timha looked at him. "Really?"

"Oh yes," said Valmin with a rueful smile. "None of the professors wanted to admit that they didn't understand the thing, so they never argued with anything that I said."

Timha laughed, weakly. Valmin was looking off into the distance.

After a few minutes' silence, Valmin rose from his chair and stretched slowly. He strode to Timha's side and patted the younger man on the shoulder.

"All will be well, Journeyer. All will be well."

But all would not be well. And they both knew it.

Timha waited a short while, pretending to examine a book by an Annwni lunatic named Prae Benesile. Benesile's tortured writing made the *Commentaries* seem downright lucid by comparison. None of the thaumaturges here in the Secret City had ever even heard of Benesile, but his books were referenced more than once in the marginalia of Hy Pezho's plans for the Einswrath. But if Beozho's work was tangential at best, Prae Benesile's were beyond unconnected. This particular text, for instance, was entitled *Thaumatical History of the Chthonic Religion*.

Pointless. Folly.

"I'm going to go study in my room for a while," he said.

Valmin didn't even look up, just grunted and waved. Timha carefully gathered a very specific set of documents, along with a few innocent books and scrolls, and left the room, breathing hard.

Timha took the books and papers back to his room and dumped them on the table. He would look at them in the morning.

But his desperation would not let him rest. He picked up a book—it just so happened to be the Prae Benesile book again—and opened it at random. The first line completed a sentence from the previous page: "bound like the Chthonic gods at Prythme." Timha sat and stared at that line, which meant nothing to him, until he heard a knock on the door.

It was Master Valmin. "Journeyer, I'm afraid I've just received some terrible news. It's your mother. She's passed away."

Timha broke down crying. But not for his mother. Not much, anyway.

The next morning, Timha's bag was packed and he stood on the threshold of his bedroom, looking back into it. The wooden doll his sister had carved him for his tenth birthday he left on the table by his bed, along with the antique clock his mother had given him as his graduation present from university.

He picked up the clock and turned it upside down. The inscription read, "For Timha, who will do astonishing things." Indeed. He put the clock down gently and began to cry again.

He left the palace and strode down the bone white stairs toward the lock landing. With every lonely step, he looked out across the vast city with its silent spires and vacant shadows, thinking that within those long-empty windows something was watching him. Something old and hungry, with teeth the same color as the stones.

The two guards at the lock landing were Elev and Phyto, neither of whom Timha knew well. Neither was notorious for being especially strict, but that was only a relative comfort; these were Mab's palace guards, the cream of the crop. They were not fools.

Elev took Timha's travel documents, signed by Master Valmin, and studied them carefully.

"Sorry 'bout your mother," he muttered, handing the papers back.

"Surprised they're letting you go for the funeral, to be honest," said Elev. "What with them canceling all leave and everything."

"Well, Master Valmin pulled some strings for me," said Timha. "One of the perks of being a trusted servant, I suppose."

"Must be nice," said Elev.

Phyto reached out for Timha's bag. He opened it and pulled out each article of clothing, waving a tiny wand across each piece. The purpose of the wand was to dispel glamours, to ensure that Timha wasn't attempting to smuggle anything out of the city.

Phyto replaced the contents of the bag neatly and refastened its latches, then turned the wand on Timha himself. He started at Timha's feet, feeling first with his hands, then following with the wand. Up Timha's body he went, paying careful attention to the belt buckle and the brooch that fastened Timha's journeyer robe. As Phyto moved the wand above Timha's neck, Timha held out his hand.

"Please," he said, "not the hair." His eyes pleaded with Phyto to let it pass.

"Bald on top, are you?" smiled Phyto.

"Yes," answered Timha, "and glamoured hair this believable costs a fortune in the city. I'd hate to lose it all just for a security check."

Phyto thought this over.

"Sorry," he said, and passed the wand over Timha's scalp. Timha's beautiful, thick hair vanished, leaving the fine wisps that were his natural complement. He sighed in relief; he'd considered hiding the documents he'd stolen up there.

"Ah, I can see why you went with the glamour," said Elev.

"Thanks," sneered Timha. "Can I go please? I don't want to miss my connection on the other side of the lock, and it's almost highsun."

"Go on," said Elev, looking a bit regretful.

Timha knelt down to tie the bootlace he'd deliberately left slightly loose. It had taken only the slightest touch of Motion to pull it entirely undone. He looked up as he tied. Phyto and Elev had begun quibbling about whose shift ended at highsun. Still watching them, Timha reached back and grabbed at the loop of cord he'd left on the ground. It was glamoured invisible, so he'd had to drop it a few paces back from Phyto and his wand.

Wrapping the cord around his wrist, Timha tugged on it, and the sheaf of invisible documents it was tied to followed along, floating easily on a pillow of pure Motion, the same spell Timha's father had used as a barge-master on the Stripping Sea. Timha nodded to Phyto and Elev and passed through the gate, leading his potential death by treason along behind him like a puppy.

chapter twenty-two

The flying cities of the Unseelie are incredible sights to behold, but the truth is that they were born of necessity. The ground beneath them is constantly riven with earthquakes that open great cracks in the earth on a daily basis. Mab and her people took to the skies not in order to approach the heavens, but rather in order to escape the ground.

—Stil-Eret, "Secret Journeys to the North," from *Travels at Home and Abroad*

The Union Locks—properly known as the Locks of Mab's Glorious Union, though no one referred to them as such—rested upon a massive floating platform in the heart of the Unseelie lands. In the center of the platform was the station itself, with its shops and cafés and its grand marble ticket counter. Surrounding the station were the locks themselves, housed in grand arches designed to complement the curves of the station. Beyond, on a separate tier, were the airdocks, where transports and personal fliers were moored. At all times, day or night, the lock arches flashed silver and airships of all shapes and sizes came and went.

Far below all this, Timha emerged from a small private lock into an atrium on the lowest level of the central platform. There were three arches here, though only the one leading to the Secret City was currently in operation. No one had told Timha where the others led, and he had been sensible enough not to ask. The entire area was off-limits to the public; its very existence was a state secret.

The guards on this side of the lock examined Timha's papers carefully, paying special attention to the release that Master Valmin had signed. A wand was passed over it to verify its veracity. Once the guards had checked the papers, they called a superior down from an upper level to review them all a second time.

Timha waited as patiently as possible, but inside he felt as though he were about to burst. If his invisible bundle were to be discovered here, he would never leave the Union Locks. There would be no public trial. They would simply slit his throat and toss him out a garbage chute, for the birds and the Arami nomads to pick over. They'd probably torture Master Valmin as well, to determine whether Timha's treason was in fact a conspiracy.

The superior officer had the guards strip Timha and carefully examine both his clothes and his bag, running deglamouring wands over every item, piece by piece. As they spread out his belongings, one of the guards stepped perilously close to the hidden bundle on the floor. If he took another step to the right, he'd tread on it. A wand passed a bit too near, and Timha tried not to gasp as a bit of the string was revealed. It lay on the floor, visible evidence of Timha's crime. He tried not to look at it. Breathe. Breathe.

Finally, finally, the guards decided that Timha was fine to proceed.

Timha bent down as nonchalantly as possible and retrieved the exposed string, waving his hand in such a way as to drag the bundle in a wide arc to keep it from accidentally brushing one of the guards when he left the room.

The guards waved him out of the atrium, and he took a small lift up to the main level of the station. He nearly ran to the jakes, where he just made it to the urinal trough before he wet his pants. Before he left, he pulled the bundle to his belly and tied the string tightly around him. As long as no one searched him again, he'd be fine.

An amplified voice rang through the station, calling the name and destination of his transport. He ran from the jakes and out of the building, ignoring the vibrant life of the place that had given him so much pleasure when he'd passed through it on the way to the Secret City. So much had changed since then. The world, he felt, had been altered beneath him. His life had drifted over a strange, hostile landscape, over the very edge of the world, and he had only the vaguest idea which direction to sail in order to save himself.

The funeral for Timha's mother was held at the observation deck atop the pinnacle spire. The city of Nearside arrayed beneath him, Timha tried to concentrate on the funeral, but his eyes kept drifting to the decks below. Proud, tall Unseelie Fae going about their business, the grand Elvish race at the height of civilization. None of them knew about Timha's plight. None of them cared.

They had no idea what lurked at the heart of their world. Timha had been exposed to that darkness, and the city could not fly high enough to bring him into the light.

The priest's elegy droned on; Timha heard none of it. As far as Timha knew, the man had never met his mother, and the speech was merely a string of empty platitudes. In a circle around the bier, Timha's family and friends sat and watched. Timha's brother Hy Foran was next to him. He reached out and squeezed Timha's hand, looking kindly at him. Timha forced a quick smile.

"Fear not, Timha. She's gone on." Hy Foran patted him on the shoulder. Timha realized that his brother had mistaken his anxiety for grief. In truth, Timha had never particularly liked his mother. She was an uneducated lump who had seemed to revel in her own mediocrity. Come to think of it, his entire family was blandly commonplace. Timha had known from childhood that if he were ever to be happy, he'd have to leave Nearside for the City of Mab.

And look where that had gotten him. He'd been there during the abortive attack on the Seelie lands, when the city crashed near the border. Thousands had died that day. Timha had escaped with merely a broken wrist, but the horror had not left him. From there to the Secret City, the pinnacle of his young career. And from there to treason.

He looked over at Hy Foran. True grief gleamed in his brother's eyes. This was not going to be easy.

After the prayers had been said, and the bier set alight and released into the sky, the family returned to Hy Foran's home, which was a respectable if small dwelling with a view of the portside edge. Food was piled on the table in the common room, and candles glowed on a long table where a portrait of Timha's mother had been placed. Timha took a few dumplings and some boiled greens and pushed them around on his plate for a few minutes while the others ate in quiet contemplation. Hy Foran's two small children ran through the house, playing.

After the children had been put to bed and the extended family had returned to their own homes, Timha, Hy Foran, and Hy Foran's wife, Letta, sat on the balcony overlooking the edge. Far below, grasses swayed in the moonlight. A minor quake kicked up dust and a distant thunder. Letta handed out beer in wooden mugs.

"It must have been difficult for you to get away," said Hy Foran. "I know the work you're doing is very important."

"Yes," said Timha, looking out over the edge. "But family is more important than work."

Hy Foran nodded.

"I need help," said Timha. His voice cracked when he spoke. Tears began to well in his eyes. "I'm in terrible trouble."

Hy Foran's eyes widened. "Tell me, Brother. Anything I can do to help I will."

"I need to get out of the country. I have to get to the Seelie Lands. It's the only place I'll be safe."

Hy Foran and his wife shared a look. "Timha," said Hy Foran, "what is it? What's happened?"

"Look," said Timha. "I know the two of you are Arcadians. You can help me."

Hy Foran leaned back in his chair, looking sidelong at him. "Timha, I don't know what—"

"I'm not going to turn you in, damn you. I need you to help me!"

"What is it you think we can do for you, Brother?" Hy Foran's expression had darkened; his voice was flat.

"I've heard that your kind have ways of spiriting people out. Believers who are in trouble with the authorities, that kind of thing."

Hy Foran's eyes narrowed. "But you are not a believer."

Timha paused. "No. But listen to me. I know things. The Seelie will know who I am. They'll know that I have things that they want. Oh, Brother, I'll be killed if I don't go!"

Hy Foran and Letta shared another, longer look.

"Would you give us a moment, Brother? My wife and I need to talk."

"Of course," said Timha. He stood shakily and went inside, closing the balcony door as softly as possible. He went to the common room and sat, his stomach in knots. He nibbled on a sweetcake, but it stuck in his throat.

The door to the balcony opened. "I must discuss your case with another. You will have to tell him everything. Do not tell me; I do not want to know."

Timha cried now. He couldn't help it. "Thank you, Brother. Thank you so much." He put his hands over his face and wept.

"I cannot promise anything, Timha. I do not think you understand what it is you're asking of me."

"I'm sorry," said Timha. "I'm so sorry."

A week later, Abbot Estiane was in his office at the Temple Aba-Nylae, lost in contemplation, when a young monk came hurtling into his office, carrying a letter.

"What's this?" Estiane said, a bit crossly. "I've asked not to be disturbed."

"Father, you must see this at once," said the monk, out of breath.

Estiane took the letter and read it. His eyes widened.

"Send a message to Lord Everess in the City Emerald," he said to the monk. "Tell him I need to see him immediately."

chapter twenty-three

It is always easier to get into trouble than out of it.

—Master Jedron

T he next morning, Silverdun, Ironfoot, and Sela were sitting in the Shadows' Den reviewing a mountain of reports, bored senseless. Paet came limping hurriedly in, carrying a satchel stuffed with papers.

"Go home and pack a bag, each of you," he said in passing. "You're leaving in the morning."

"What, all three of us?" asked Silverdun.

"Be back here in an hour for your briefing," said Paet. He went downstairs to his office and they heard the door slam.

An hour later, they assembled in the mission room. Paet had a map of the Unseelie pinned on the wall. Red pins showed the current known locations of cities, and chalk arrows showed their expected patterns of movement. Paet was pointing at the city of Preyia with the end of his cane.

"This is where you'll be going," he said.

"The Unseelie?" said Silverdun. "There aren't any more dangerous places you could send us?"

"I'm sorry," said Paet. "I didn't realize you'd only signed up for the safe jobs."

"Danger I'm fine with. It's suicide I try to avoid where possible."

Paet waved the notion away. "I've been there dozens of times. The cities are quite lovely, actually."

"I've been in one myself," said Silverdun, recalling his adventure with Mauritane in the City of Mab just before the Battle of Sylvan.

"Yes," said Paet. "This time it won't be necessary for you to destroy the entire city."

"What's the mission?" asked Ironfoot. "What are we after?"

"Ah," said Paet. "A *useful* question. You're going to meet an Unseelie thaumaturge named Timha, who is a journeyer at Queen's University in the City of Mab. Or was, rather. He left about eight months ago."

"Where has he been since?" asked Sela.

"We're not entirely sure," said Paet. "We're hoping he can tell us that himself."

"We're taking him out of the country?" asked Silverdun.

"Yes," said Paet. "He claims to have intimate knowledge about the Einswrath. In fact, he claims to have the plans for it."

"You're kidding," said Ironfoot.

"That's what we've been told."

"We have to get him," said Ironfoot. "I've been through every shred of intelligence on the subject, and we have yet to uncover anything about those plans. I'm getting nowhere with my research. If I could just talk to him for ten minutes!"

"Maybe he can also tell us why they haven't been lobbing the things over the border at us these many months," said Silverdun.

Paet pointed to a map of the Seelie Kingdom on the wall, larger than the one in his office. The known locations of the cities were marked with pins.

"Your briefing documents are being copied as we speak. They contain all the details, but I'll go over the basics with you now."

He pointed to a pin on the map. "The three of you will travel to the Unseelie via lock using false papers, arriving here at the Union Locks."

He moved the tip of his cane from the first pin to another pin farther south. "Once there, you'll travel to Preyia by air. You'll rendezvous with Timha in Preyia." He now drew the tip of the cane to a dot marked on the map just above the Seelie border. "You'll have access there to a borrowed yacht, which you will fly to Elenth, one of the few land-based Unseelie cities, two days' ride north of Sylvan. In Elenth you'll meet with an Arcadian priest named Virum. He works closely with his brethren on the other side of the border, escorting believers who are in danger into the Seelie Kingdom. He'll help you across the border."

"Who's going to fly the yacht?" said Silverdun. "I can't sail something like that."

Paet pointed at Ironfoot. "He can."

"Captain of the sailing club at Queensbridge."

"Pretty fancy for an army man," said Silverdun.

"I like to win at things," said Ironfoot. "Doesn't much matter what."

"Excuse me," said Sela, holding up her hand. "Why can't the Arcadians spirit him out of the country themselves?"

"Good question," said Paet. "They're too afraid. This Timha is a highly placed thaumaturge who's just fled from a top-secret research laboratory. He's carrying on his person the plans for the most powerful weapon ever created. The Arcadians believe, and justifiably so, that if they were caught assisting him, the retaliation against the Church would be apocalyptic. Further, Timha is not himself an Arcadian; some of their members are unwilling to go out on a limb for a nonbeliever. Regardless, Everess tried everything he could think of to convince him, but Estiane refused. As Silverdun may have told you, Estiane and Everess are not the best of friends."

"To put it mildly," said Silverdun.

"Personally," said Paet, "I prefer it this way. I'd much rather have this man's fate in your hands than in those of a bunch of peace-loving monks. When they're caught, they don't fight. They simply surrender and go to their deaths like sheep."

"Only you, Paet, could make peace sound like a bad thing," said Silverdun.

Without warning, Paet took a thick glass paperweight from his desk and hurled it at Silverdun's head. It struck Silverdun's temple, and Silverdun, who had been leaning back in his chair, fell over backward and crashed to the floor.

"Ow!" said Silverdun, picking himself up.

Paet shrugged. "I learned everything I know about management from Master Jedron," he said.

"Bastard!" grumbled Silverdun, clutching his hand to his head.

"Paet," said Sela, tentatively. "What if I didn't go?"

"Excuse me?" said Paet.

"I've got a project going; something I've worked out from going over a number of documents, and—"

"Analysts I've got," said Paet. "But I only have one of you."

Sela looked down at her lap and said nothing.

"Sela," said Paet. "Would you excuse us, please? I'd like to talk to Silverdun and Ironfoot alone."

Sela nodded and stood up. She glanced at Silverdun and smiled primly.

Once they were alone, Paet came around to the front of his desk and leaned back against it.

"You're going to be in Unseelie territory," he said in a low voice. "And that means that it is absolutely imperative that neither of you is taken, dead or alive."

"What does that mean?" said Ironfoot.

"If one of you is killed there, you *must* bring the body back with you."

"Why?"

"I can't tell you that. If it happens, the answer will be obvious, though I don't recommend trying it just to find out."

"What if carrying a body around isn't feasible?" asked Silverdun. "If one of us is dead, it probably means that things have gone badly."

"True," said Paet. "In that case, it is equally imperative that you sever the head, if possible, and return with it. That's better than nothing."

"And why is that?" asked Ironfoot.

"Because Mab has ways of getting information out of you, even if you're dead."

"Failing even that, however," he continued, "you must ensure that the body is destroyed utterly. Preferably by fire."

"Well, this is quite a conversation we're having," said Silverdun.

"What if we're captured alive?" asked Ironfoot. "What do we do then?"

"If one of you is taken, the others must do everything in their power to retrieve him. If, however, that is impossible, the one who's been captured must end his own life. All you need do in that situation is concentrate very carefully on dying. You will not only die, but your body will explode in a most dramatic fashion."

"Um," said Ironfoot, "I'm not aware of any spell that allows that to happen."

"It's not a spell," said Paet.

"With no offense to Silverdun," said Ironfoot, "I have far less trouble lopping off his head than I do Sela's. I just can't imagine doing it."

Paet stared at him. "I thought you understood, I was only referring to the two of you. If Sela dies, leave her."

With that, Paet ushered them out of his office and shut the door behind them.

chapter twenty-four

How great is Mab?

You might ask how deep the sea, how fiery the sun! Perfection itself bows before her.

How gracious is Mab?

Mab's grace and mercy know no limits. To her people she is a mother. To her allies a protector. To her enemies a correcting hand. Even those whom she has slain cry out their gratitude from the afterlife, thankful now their wickedness is at an end.

How wise is Mab?

Mab's wisdom knows no limits. The only thing of which she is ignorant is ignorance itself. Is there anything she has not seen? Is there any secret whose depths she has not plumbed? Look into the heart of any mystery and you shall find the Unseelie flag already planted there.

How powerful is Mab?

All power is Mab's power. All strength is her strength. No enemy can stand against her unless she suffers them to stand. In war she is unconquered and unconquerable. In persuasion, she is truth itself.

How loving is Mab?

To speak of love is to speak of Mab, for they are one and the same.

—Imperial Catechism

O ver the years Mab had overcome an array of foes, but the Great Enemy, the one who could never be slain, was boredom.

Mab had attempted every diversion, delved into every fantasy and fetish and addiction. She had gotten lost in music, in dance, in poetry, in cock-fights, in mestina. Every pleasure to be had, she had tried: wine, men, women, children, orgies. Sweets, fox hunts, fencing, croquet. Sewing, pottery, Elemental sculpture. Each provided its small measure of diversion; each was a coal that burned bright for its season and then went cold, leaving the taste of its ash in her mouth.

For a hundred years she had tried being a man. She had lived as a hermit, as a peasant girl, as a fox in her own fox hunt. She had been and done everything there was to be and do, but it was never enough.

In order to allay her tedium, she had by virtue of necessity been forced to think big. She had wrested control of the Unseelie Lands millennia earlier, conquered all of Faerie north of the Contested Lands. She had spread her influence over worlds, even destroyed one.

The only one who had ever stood in her way was Regina Titania, and Mab both loved and hated her for that. A small part of Mab prayed that the Seelie queen would never be brought down, because then Mab would have everything; the game would end. And what then?

But Titania tested her and taunted her. The ancient rivalry was not enough. What good was a rivalry if not to win it?

Now matters had come to a head. Her new city was built. The Einswrath weapons were being cast in her Secret City. A very special girl awaited her in Estacana, though the girl didn't know it yet. All the stars were in alignment. The time was now. The final battle in the ageless war was about to be joined.

Hy Pezho, that Black Artist, had given her the means of her sure delivery from this endless fencing match. He had been a genius, a man of towering intellect, who divined the secrets that lay beyond common understanding, who opened a window into places Mab herself had never seen. And ultimately, this is likely why she had killed him. He had upset the balance. Now she had no reason not to answer her own challenge. Now she was forced to move against her ancient foe. Now the battle was, if not a foregone conclusion, then a near certainty. Hy Pezho had, without realizing it, forced her hand.

He had tried to fool her, of course, as all ambitious men ultimately did. He believed that his genius extended to his charms and political maneuverings, which for their part were as transparent and mundane as the next man's. For that reason she had been required to condemn him to a place of infinite suffering within the belly of the wraith *fel-ala*. Hy Pezho's own creation. Now *that* was poetic.

The obvious betrayal was the reason she had been forced to get rid of him, but it was his inadvertent destruction of her status quo that had allowed her to enjoy it so much.

So the war would come, and either she or Titania would emerge victorious. There was a small chance Titania would prevail, of course. The Stone Queen, the Seelie Witch, was at least as crafty as Mab and at least as old. She would be difficult to surprise. Down through the centuries, Titania had learned as well as Mab to read the signs in the stars, the rise of nations, the glint in a man's eye.

All that was now drew inward toward a conclusion. And it was all Hy Pezho's fault. Oh, how she loved and hated him for it.

If nothing else, though, at least it wouldn't be boring.

Three Bel Zheret flowed boldly into Mab's private apartments, without knocking or having their presence announced. That was one of the privileges that she allowed them, as they were able to sense from a distance whether she was receptive to their presence at any given moment. They were tied to her with the Black Art's reflection of Empathy, and she could control them with the slightest twist of emotion; she didn't even need to be conscious of it.

Mab's personal secretary Ta-Hila started when they entered; he, of course, had no way of knowing they were coming. Mab knew that the Bel Zheret made Ta-Hila deeply uncomfortable. That was part of their job.

Dog, Cat, and Asp stood before her, without bowing. Bowing was a show of submission, and was not necessary with Bel Zheret, who were submissive to her by their very nature. Bowing would have been redundant.

"Speak," she said.

"One of the magicians in your Secret City, a Journeyer Timha, has disappeared," said Dog. "He left the city for his mother's funeral and has not returned."

"Who authorized the leave?" asked Mab.

"Master Valmin sent a pleading note to the lieutenant of the guard whose task it is to provide security for the city."

"I see."

"You wish the lieutenant to die."

"Yes. But do not kill him. There is no gain in it."

She turned to Ta-Hila. "Have the gracious lieutenant reassigned to less sensitive duties, where his generosity will reflect well upon me."

Ta-Hila nodded, making a note.

"Do you have any knowledge of Journeyer Timha's whereabouts?"

"No," said Dog, smiling. "It is a mystery to us at the moment. A most meaty mystery."

Mab wished she could enjoy such uncertainty as much as her creations did. They were designed to love their jobs and never to despair. Fear and stress were great motivators to the average Fae, but they also caused mistakes, and the Bel Zheret had been crafted carefully to make as few mistakes as possible.

"This incident may perhaps explain another," said Mab. "I received word today from my contact in the Seelie government that three Shadows have been dispatched onto my soil."

"Really?" said Cat. "I would enjoy killing one of them very much. Is one of them named Paet?"

"I do not know," said Mab. "And my contact was unaware of their mission. But I believe your information provides the nature of the mission, does it not?"

The three Bel Zheret nodded in unison.

"Here is what we must do," said Mab. She gave them their instructions, and they left without being dismissed. They knew when she was finished with them.

Once certain plans had been set in motion, Dog, Cat, and Asp had treated themselves to a righteous slaughter in the Secret City. It had been a lovely afternoon. Running, screaming. A merry chase through the bone white streets of the Secret City. Hot blood spilling on cold white stone. Simply beautiful.

Now, Dog stood with his companions in Master Valmin's office. The few magicians who'd managed to survive their ministrations hung by their fingertips from the ceiling. Master Valmin wasn't one of them, sadly. He'd killed himself as soon as they'd arrived. That showed foresight, Dog supposed, though it certainly robbed the Bel Zheret of some fun.

All the begging and pleading was over, which was nice. Desperation wasn't pretty, wasn't aesthetically pleasing in any way. But beyond the desperation was an exquisite, ragged resignation, and that was worth the effort.

Cat was toying with one of the magicians, nibbling on his finger.

"This one is a holy man," said Cat. "I can taste it on him. Devout Chthonic, I suppose. If he were an Arcadian he'd never have made it in here."

"I like holy men," said Dog. "They have a delicate flavor to them, a certain something that's hard to define."

"Tastes like children," said Cat, between mouthfuls.

chapter twenty-five

Disaster is not a tragedy. Failing to plan for disaster is the tragedy.

—Unseelie proverb

"This is madness," said Silverdun.

He, Ironfoot, and Sela stood in the center of the station known as the Locks of Mab's Glorious Union, in the heart of the Unseelie.

"I have to admit," said Ironfoot. "Silverdun has a point."

"Stop it, both of you," said Sela. "We must behave as if we're Unseelie."

"What are we supposed to do?" asked Silverdun, his eyebrow arched. "Love Mab more?"

"You know what I mean," said Sela. "We belong here. This is the center of our world, not the den of a lion."

Silverdun had been in precarious situations before—in fact, it often felt as though his life were merely a lengthy series of them—but this was beyond the pale.

It was hard to believe that it was just this morning that the three of them had met in a café outside the Chancery Locks in the City Emerald. They'd traveled via lock to Mag Mell, from there to Annwn, and from Annwn to this place. Over the course of the day they'd gone by carriage, by boat, by horse, and probably some other means of transportation that Silverdun had forgotten. Twenty-four hours and three worlds later, they'd finally arrived.

"I don't know about either of you," said Ironfoot, "but I'm in the mood to have a nap, not to spirit away a valuable foreign thaumaturge."

"It was easy enough getting here," said Sela. "As long as everything goes to plan, we'll be back home in the morning."

"It was easy to get here because getting here was the easy part," said Silverdun. "If this Timha's been discovered missing already, then security's going to be tight everywhere we go. They'll be suspecting our presence."

"All the more reason to be as inconspicuous as possible," said Sela.

Silverdun looked at her. "Remember, Sela, it's up to you to detect any dangerous suspicions. If you feel we're in imminent danger, make a comment about the camellia blossoms."

"So easy to work into idle conversation," she said.

"Do you have a better idea?" asked Silverdun.

"No, it's fine." She smiled at him. Her smile, as always, both frightened and compelled him. "But let's change it to laurels; camellias don't bloom until the fall."

"Might I point out," said Ironfoot, his fatigue showing, "that it would have been wise to have worked this out *before* coming on the mission?"

Silverdun sighed. "Ah, but where would the fun be in that?"

Sela chuckled. "We're all going to die," she said. Silverdun thought she'd meant it as a joke, but if she had, it fell very, very flat.

Their Unseelie passports allowed them to book passage on a transport ship to Preyia without raising any apparent suspicion. The name of the transport was *Mab's Contempt*.

"So," Silverdun noted, "it's not only ship owners on the Inland Sea who refuse to give their vessels comforting names."

"Hush," said Sela.

When they stepped out of the station onto the main platform, Sela couldn't believe her eyes. The rising sun glinted off a bank of clouds in the distance. Blue-gray mountains rose in the distance, and beyond the platform rocky hills stretched away as far as the eye could see.

But that was nothing compared to the ships. They ranged from tiny skiffs to enormous three-masted leviathans, their billowed sails shining in the morning light. There seemed to be hundreds of them, some at dock on the outer platform, some coming and going. The largest were almost cities themselves, their mainmasts stretching hundreds of feet into the sky, their ruddermasts depending from their hulls to dip into the clouds. In motion they looked like so many giant fish as they plied the skies.

Sela tried to hide her astonishment, noting that none of the travelers hurrying past seemed remotely awed by the spectacle. Silverdun, who had seen such things before, was less affected by them, and led the way, pulling Sela by the shoulder. A glance back at Ironfoot showed that he was also doing his best not to show his amazement.

As they walked, boys approached them offering to carry their bags, arrange them cheap passage on private vessels, or sell them sweetmeats and hot buns. Voices of shipmasters and cargomen cut through the buzz of talk that surrounded them.

Silverdun led them through the crowd, waving away the boys as though none of this was in any way new to him. As they approached the outer platform across a wide bridge, a warm breeze blew up from below, lifting up Sela's skirts, and she realized why she'd been instructed by Paet to wear the form-fitting underskirt.

From behind her, she felt Ironfoot's momentary titillation at seeing her calf and smiled. The thread that connected her to Ironfoot was a pleasant thing. He found her pretty and liked her, but that was all. His roving eye found most every other young woman at Blackstone House, but he respected her role as a colleague. At least that's how she interpreted the sensations she took from him. She tried her hardest not to invade his privacy with her talents.

Silverdun, of course, she could not read at all.

Mab's Contempt lay moored directly ahead. It was a long, narrow craft, with a single mast. Sela knew little about ships, but it appeared to have been built for speed: all clean lines, streamlined. It looked fast, anyway.

They showed their tickets to a man standing in front of the ship. He glanced at the tickets and waved them up the ramp that led to the ship's main deck without even looking at their faces.

"Enjoy your journey," he muttered as they passed.

On board they wound their way through a tangle of deckhands and dockworkers busy stowing the ship's cargo. A few soldiers, in uniform but on leave, lingered abovedecks, smoking at the ship's prow. A family with a quartet of young children were making their way belowdecks. Silverdun waved Sela down the narrow stairs behind them, taking her handbag from her.

"After you, my darling," he said. Their cover story was that she and Silverdun were newlyweds; he was a bookkeeper and she was the daughter of an innkeeper. Ironfoot was Silverdun's brother. They were returning from a holiday in Mag Mell. Sela had found the whole thing terribly romantic when Silverdun had first come up with the idea, but the reality of it left her feeling a bit pathetic, her awkward fantasy coming to life as a mere illusion.

At the bottom of the steps, Silverdun put his arm around her. It felt good, but Sela couldn't decide whether she was enjoying herself or not.

The main cabin consisted of a few dozen rows of plush leather seats. Wide windows were set into the hull, admitting bright shafts of morning sunlight. Silverdun led them to the rear of the cabin, where they sat facing the young family.

"Good day to you all," said the husband, a friendly fellow with smiling eyes. His wife nodded to them and went back to tending the children.

Sela eased into her seat and suddenly felt the weight of their travels come down on her. Before *Mab's Contempt* even slipped its moorings, she was asleep.

Sela knows from books that a Fae girl's sixteenth birthday is special. It is the day she becomes a woman. The crones have promised her a fantastic gift for her birthday, and Sela can't wait to see what it is. The only other gift she's ever received was the mechanical bird that Lord Tanen brought her, the one he crushed beneath his boot. She has asked the crones if this gift will be like that, but they scoffed at her and told her to stop being foolish. Girls like her don't have birthdays.

The day comes and Sela awakes early, with the sun. She dresses in one of the special gowns, the ones that the crones have shown her how to wear. For dances in the city. She has been taught how to match shoes and earrings, how to put her hair up in glamoured combs, and how to apply the paint to her lips and eyelids. She knows quadrille and farandole and tarantella, and how to hold a fan. All of these things will someday be useful, but she doesn't know why.

She hears Lord Tanen's carriage before she sees it. She is sitting on the steps of the manor, making a daisy chain, making holes in one stem with a stolen sewing needle and threading the next stem through, flower upon flower. The crones will not approve of this, but she thinks that because it is her birthday they won't punish her for it. She has nearly completed a necklace when she hears hoofbeats echoing through the trees.

Lord Tanen steps out of his carriage, and she can see that someone is with him. He holds out his hand to the stranger and she descends. It is a girl, Sela's age, dressed in a gown of whitest linen. Her hair is gold and put up in shining plaits, her face scrubbed clean. Sela gets up and runs toward the carriage, but halfway there she stops, her breath caught in her chest.

What if this girl has been brought to replace her? What if she is going to be taken away in that carriage and left in the forest? In stories sometimes this happens. A girl is taken away by a cruel parent, usually a stepmother, and left in the forest to die. These children usually end up as princesses, but Sela has been told by the crones that her parents are dead now, and that she is worthless on her own; her only value is what Lord Tanen gives to her.

But her thoughts of being replaced vanish when the girl looks at her and smiles, showing a row of crooked teeth under bright blue eyes.

"Happy birthday, Sela," she says.

"Who are you?" asks Sela, mystified.

"I'm Milla," the girl says.

Sela looks at Lord Tanen, confused.

"This is your birthday present, Sela," says Tanen. "A most special gift for a most important birthday."

Sela still doesn't understand.

"I've brought you a friend, Sela. I've brought you someone to love."

Someone nudged Sela awake. She sat up, startled, not sure where she was for a moment. Sunlight, sky, soft chair. She was still on board *Mab's Contempt.*

Silverdun leaned into her. "Camellia blossoms," he said.

"Hm?" she mumbled.

"Laurel blossoms. Whatever. There may be trouble," he whispered.

"How long was I asleep?" she whispered.

"About an hour. You drooled a little, by the way."

Irritated, she wiped her chin with the back of her hand.

"What's going on?" she asked.

"A few minutes ago, I saw a message sprite flit past the window toward the main deck."

"And?"

The young husband across from them was giving her a questioning look. She smiled at him and kissed Silverdun on the cheek. She reached out for a thread with the young husband and found it: He was tired and hungry, and a bit suspicious as well. *Everything's fine*, she pushed into the thread. He seemed to relax.

"There was a bit of a commotion on deck, and then *they* showed up down here." He nodded toward the front of the cabin, where the Unseelie soldiers they'd seen earlier were walking slowly toward them, examining the passengers.

She looked over at Ironfoot, whose face was buried behind a newspaper.

"Do you think they're after us?" asked Sela.

"Who knows?" said Silverdun. "Either way, we'd just as soon not be noticed."

Sela strained her feelings toward the soldiers, but it was no use. She needed some kind of emotional connection to sense a thread, and the soldiers didn't know she existed. Yet.

They continued down the aisle, engaging each row of passengers in turn. When they came a bit closer, she could hear snippets of conversation.

". . . two men and a woman . . ."

". . . persons of interest . . ."

Sela noticed the young husband across from her looking at them, an odd, curious expression on his face.

Silverdun leaned in again. "I'm going to try something. Follow where it goes."

He leaned forward to speak to the young husband.

"Do you have any water?" he asked the husband. "I'm parched."

The young man's eyes widened. "What sort of water?" he asked, his voice quivering a bit.

Silverdun looked the man directly in the eye. "Water from the freshest stream."

What was Silverdun talking about? Whatever it was, the young man seemed to understand, because he nodded and leaned forward himself, putting his hand on Silverdun's shoulder.

"There is water in abundance," he whispered.

Silverdun nodded.

"Where are you coming from?" asked the husband quietly.

"Mag Mell."

The husband smiled.

The soldiers came closer. When they reached Sela, Silverdun, and Ironfoot's row, they stopped, eyeing them with suspicion.

"Would you three be traveling together?" asked one, looking at Silverdun. "Just the three of you?"

"No," said the young husband. "We're all together. Just returning from a holiday in Mag Mell."

"Ah," said the soldier, his eyes brightening. "May we see your passports, then?"

The soldier took each passport in turn. The family, as it happened, had indeed just returned from Mag Mell themselves, according to their passports.

"Is there a problem?" asked Ironfoot, casually.

"We've received word that there might be some persons of interest aboard ship. Two men and a woman traveling together."

The young man's wife blanched. "Goodness, are they dangerous?"

"I don't think so," said the soldier. "Heretics. Aba-lovers."

"Ah," said the husband. "I've found that you can always tell an Arcadian by the glassy-eyed stare of blind obedience." He raised his eyebrows.

The soldier chuckled. "You may be right, sir."

He nodded to the group. "Sorry to have bothered you."

His eyes rested on Sela for a moment, and the thinnest of threads leapt into place. He thought her pretty, nothing more. But it was enough. *Believe me*, she nudged.

"I saw two women and a man on the platform before we came on board," she said. "They looked very suspicious. I remember them because they were about to hand over their tickets, but then all of a sudden changed their minds and headed back to the terminal. Isn't that odd?"

The soldier nodded. "Indeed! You've got a keen eye, ma'am."

He turned to his fellows. "Looks like they slipped away before getting on board," he said quietly. "I'll send the sprite back and tell them to stop wasting our time." The soldiers shared a quiet laugh and retreated toward the front of the cabin.

Once they were gone, Silverdun took the hand of the young husband. "Thank you," he said.

"I'm your brother," said the young man. "There is nothing to thank me for."

Sela gave Silverdun a questioning look. "I'll explain later," he whispered.

chapter twenty-six

Alpaurle: Let us speak, then, of the good man. How do we
determine which is the good man?

The High Priest: That is easy. He is the one who thinks
and acts virtuously, and avoids sin.

Alpaurle: And how do we know which thoughts and
actions are virtuous, and which are sinful?

The High Priest: Is the distinction not obvious?

Alpaurle: It is not obvious to me, but then, very little is.
Perhaps you can explain it to me?

—Alpaurle, from *Conversations with the High Priest of Ulet*,
conversation VI, edited by Feven IV of the City Emerald

The rest of the trip passed without incident. They all slept through most of the day.

Sela's dreams were fleeting and strange, incorporating the dream imagery of those sleeping around her. She saw Silverdun lying in a field of wheat, kissing a woman in white. The woman had long golden hair, and wore a band around her arm, an Accursed Object. Sela felt warm, drew in closer, felt the wheat tickling her ankles. Silverdun bent down to kiss the woman's neck and Sela saw her face; it wasn't Sela. She was younger, her features sharp and her eyes bright with pleasure. She looked at Sela and laughed with joy, bent her head back, arched her back, pressed against her lover. The dream faded and was replaced in turn by others, but its sensations lingered.

She came awake with a start. "Just in time," said Silverdun. "I think you'll want to see this." He pointed out the window.

At first Sela couldn't understand what she was seeing. A thousand stars spread out beneath *Mab's Contempt*, a night sky inverted. Then her eyes adjusted and she saw that they were not stars, but the lights of a city. A city unlike any she had ever seen before.

Preyia spread out below them, huge, an island rising up from a black sea. It was difficult to gauge distances, but it seemed almost as big as the walled portion of the City Emerald. It rose in seven massive tiers, each smaller than the one below it, in pleasantly irregular curves.

Massive sails rose from each tier, glowing in red and blue and gold witch-light. Ships large and small came and went from it, like moths circling slowly around a lamp. The entire scene was softly bathed in moonlight.

It was impossibly large, but as *Mab's Contempt* continued to approach it grew even larger, until it blocked out the sky and it almost seemed as though they were approaching solid ground.

A few minutes passed and then there was a soft shudder as the transport ship docked with Preyia.

Around her, weary travelers rose, collecting their belongings.

The young husband across from them stood and stretched. "Come out with us, brother. Let us be seen leaving the ship together."

Silverdun smiled. "That's kind of you. Thanks."

They came out on deck, and the lights and sounds of Preyia exploded in Sela's senses. Music, shouting, the buzz of conversation. Great lights on rotating bases searched the sky. Avenues radiated out from the docks, bathed in multicolored witchlight.

"Welcome to Preyia," said the young wife, taking Sela's arm.

Cooking smells assaulted Sela as they stepped onto the dock, roasting meats and cooking onions and exotic spices. Her stomach growled.

Once they were away from the crowd, the group stopped. The children were cranky; two of them were crying and whining to go home. Silverdun and the young husband took each other's arms.

"I cannot thank you enough," said Silverdun. "That was a lucky thing, us ending up opposite one another."

"For shame!" said the young man. "Luck had nothing to do with it."

"Of course, you're right."

"We must do what we can. And live to serve Aba another day."

"Aba be praised," said the wife.

"I think we're safe now," said Silverdun. "Go in peace."

"You as well," said the husband. He scooped up one of the children, and the family disappeared into the night.

"All right," said Ironfoot. "What was that all about?"

"Arcadians," said Silverdun.

"So I gathered," said Ironfoot. "Why did they go out of their way to help us?"

"Because I asked them to."

"All that business with the water," said Sela.

"Yes. It's a code. It's the Arcadians' way of asking for help in unfriendly circumstances."

"Are you an Arcadian?" asked Sela, confused.

"I used to be," said Silverdun.

"He was a monk," said Ironfoot.

"A very bad one," scowled Silverdun. "Anyhow, all of that I learned from my mother. She was an Arcadian at a time when it was dangerous even in the Seelie Lands."

"Why haven't you ever told me this?" asked Sela.

"Some things, I've found, are best left in the past."

"We'd best get going," said Ironfoot, pointing to a clock tower that rose above the docks. "Our rendezvous is in an hour."

"Just a moment," said Sela. "I'd like to look over the edge. May I?"

"Be my guest," said Silverdun.

They walked past the docks, to a railing that stretched out of sight to the north. The docks were on the lowest tier of the city, so there was nothing beneath to obstruct the view.

Sela leaned over the edge of the city and looked down. The ground seemed so very far below. There was a slender sparkling line of silver that she realized was a river. Boulders like pebbles. And the tiny circles were the tops of trees, colored green-gray by the moonlight. There was also a large oval spot, pitch black.

"What's that?" she asked. "A lake?"

Silverdun looked. "It's called the umbra. It's the shadow of the city," he said. "Supposed to be extremely unlucky to walk through it."

For some reason, the thought of a shadow that large made Sela deeply uncomfortable.

"Perhaps we could save the sightseeing for another time?" said Ironfoot. Sela could feel his anxiety.

"Of course," she said. "I'm sorry. I just wanted to see."

"It's fine," he said. And he meant it. "But we must be going.

They made their way through the city, up grand stairways, along wide avenues, always upward, from tier to tier. It was a festival night, and the streets were filled with revelers celebrating the beginning of summer. Both spring and autumn were bitterly cold in the Unseelie Lands, and Sela had heard that in some northern cities, there was even snow from time to time at the height of autumn.

They moved slowly through the packed streets, where drummers sat in circles beating the rhythms of the season. The Fae of Preyia danced in time, smiling and laughing, shouting verse after verse of summer song.

"Look at them all," Sela said.

"What about them?" asked Silverdun.

"They're all so happy. So joyous."

"What of it?" asked Ironfoot, who had been whistling along.

"These are the enemy, aren't they? How can that be? They seem so kind."

"Tell them you're a Seelie spy and see how kind they are to you then," said Silverdun, winking at her.

It was at moments like these that Empathy was not a gift at all. A chaotic rapture of threads pulsed around Sela, at the edge of her vision, wanting to draw her in. She wanted to be drawn in. How many of them could she kill, right now, if she chose to, before they could strike her down? How much of the joy could she drown out?

When surrounded by happiness, she thought automatically of pain. Lord Tanen had taught her that. The precipice loomed, always waiting to claim her. If she gave in to the joy, if she let the rapture wash over her, she would be annihilated. At Copperine House, they'd told her that this simply wasn't true, that she'd been taught to believe that in order to fulfill Tanen's cruel desires for her. But she knew that he'd been right all along. If she let herself get lost in the festival, she would never return from it. The thought terrified her to her bones.

As they ascended, the crowds grew smaller, the lights fewer. The higher tiers were reserved for the homes of the wealthy and the palaces of government. When they ascended the final broad swath of steps to the Opal Tier, the second highest, Sela was out of breath, but Ironfoot and Silverdun weren't even breathing hard.

Silverdun consulted a map, as inconspicuously as possible. "It's this way," he said, pointing down a narrow street. This was one of the more dangerous parts of the expedition. If they were stopped by the City Guard, it would be difficult to explain their presence on the Opal Tier, which was populated exclusively by the homes of the wealthy.

A few carriages passed them, but none stopped. Here and there, revelers in bright costume piled out of cabs and carriages, happy and tired after the night's festivities.

They reached their destination without incident. It was a two-story brick home built on a semicircular bluff that extended over the lower tiers of the city to give an unobstructed view of Preyia. These, Silverdun told them, were called Bow Villas, because they occupied the foremost position in the city as it moved forward through the air. Thus it was always above and, more important, upwind of, the rest of the city—which, Silverdun said, was reputed to smell vile during the summer months.

The door was opened by a slender woman in an expensive silk dress. Sela would have loved to own such a dress. Starlight, the actress back at Copperine House, had owned one very like it.

"May I help you?" asked the woman.

"We've come to retrieve a package from Hy Diret," said Silverdun. It was the agreed-upon sign.

"Of course," said the woman. "I believe I've got it here somewhere. Do come in." Her response meant that all was well. If she'd said to come back another time, it would have meant that the mission had been compromised somehow.

Sela was beginning to think that this *would* be easy.

"Welcome," said the woman. "My name is Elspet. I'm so glad to see you." She ushered them inside. The home's interior was elegant, but sparsely decorated.

"We do what we can to maintain appearances," said Elspet, noticing Sela's look. "My husband manages the central bank, and we're expected to live in a certain manner."

"How so?" asked Ironfoot.

"Aba counsels us to live beneath our means," said Elspet. "All of this finery on display could be used to feed the poor. But as I said, we can do more with the wealth we save than if we were to earn nothing at all."

Silverdun looked wistful as the woman spoke, but it was hard for Sela to understand why.

"But you're not here for me," said Elspet. "Come, I'll take you to Timha. He's desperate to meet you, as you can imagine."

She led them through the house and out back, where a large balcony, itself nearly the size of Copperine House, overlooked the city's leading edge. There was a small garden with a patch of grass, and flower boxes affixed to the incongruous-looking spar that rose out from beneath the balcony.

At the far end of the balcony was a small flier dock, with a sleek yacht tied there. Close to the house was a carriage house, from which a wooden driveway extended toward a gate at the main home's side.

Elspet took them up a flight of stairs on the side of the carriage house to its second floor. "He's been staying in here," said Elspet. Sela looked out from the top of the stairs and was awash in wonder all over again. From here she could look out and see the moon and the stars and ground beneath her, with nothing whatever to obstruct her view. It felt as though she were flying. Of course, she realized, she *was* flying.

They went inside. Dim witchlamps illuminated a small guest apartment with a bed, a table, and a small cookstove. Sitting on the bed was the most nervous-looking man Sela had ever seen. Timha was pale and gaunt; his maroon robes looked several sizes too large for his frame. His hair was dirty and unkempt, and his eyes were furtive.

He licked his lips when they entered. "Are you them?" he answered. "Are you the ones who've come to take me to Seelie?"

"We are," said Silverdun.

"Oh, thank you," said Timha. He collapsed on the bed, relief spreading over his face.

Silverdun, Elspet, and Sela sat at the table, but Ironfoot remained standing. Timha sat up and looked at him.

"Well?" he said, excitedly. "When do we leave? Let's go!"

"Not so fast," said Ironfoot. "Before we can leave, I need to have a look at these plans of yours."

Timha blanched. "Plans? Why? We don't have time for that. You wouldn't understand them anyway." He licked his lips again. "They're highly advanced thaumatics; not like the plans for a tree house or something."

"I should introduce myself," said Ironfoot. "I'm Master Styg Falores, the Alpaurle Fellow at Queensbridge, in the City Emerald. I have a feeling I might be able to make heads or tails of them."

Timha goggled at him. "But . . . what are you doing here?"

"Examining your plans," he said. "Hand them over."

Timha nodded and reached under the bed. He drew out something that Sela couldn't see and placed it on the bed. But there was nothing there.

Timha made a motion with his hand and suddenly there *was* something there: a leather satchel stuffed with documents and slender volumes.

"It's all here, I swear," said Timha, looking nervously at Ironfoot. "Why would I lie about something like this?"

"I can't imagine," said Ironfoot. "But I still need to examine them."

Sela examined the thin, wavering thread that connected her to Timha. "He's telling the truth," said Sela. "Quite desperately, in fact."

Timha gave her a sidelong glance. He seemed to sense that she was connected to him, and didn't like it.

"I still need to look," said Ironfoot.

"All right," said Silverdun. "But can you hurry it up? I tend to agree with Timha here that the quicker we get this over with, the better."

"Go ahead, go ahead," said Timha. He looked at Elspet for support, but she merely shrugged.

"This is between you and them now, Journeyer Timha," she said kindly. "The Church wishes you well, but we have brought you as far as we will."

She stood. "I'll go prepare the yacht," she said. She nodded to them and stepped outside.

"Stand up," said Ironfoot. Timha stood, and Ironfoot began spreading out the documents on the bed, peering at them one at a time, deep in concentration.

After several minutes, Silverdun sighed. "I have to say, Ironfoot," he said, "that I'm beginning to side with Timha on this one. Can't we speed this up a bit?"

Ironfoot gave him a withering glance. "As Journeyer Timha here so elegantly put it, this isn't a tree house we're talking about here. Give me a moment."

As the minutes passed, Timha seemed to become more and more anxious. He hadn't paid much attention to Sela, which was fine because she didn't really care to experience firsthand what he was feeling.

Finally Ironfoot put the documents down. "If this is a ploy, it's an incredibly intricate and convincing one. Without studying this at length, I'd say there's a very good chance it's the real thing."

"Then can we *finally* be on our way?" asked Silverdun.

There was a scream from outside. Silverdun was at the door, knife in hand, in a heartbeat. Looking out, he said, "Damn! We've been discovered!"

Ironfoot folded up the documents and shoved them haphazardly into the satchel. "Come on," he said to Timha. "Stay behind me."

"Oh, no," said Timha. "This isn't happening."

"Oh, but it is," said Ironfoot. "Move."

Sela took the small dagger from her bodice and weighed it in her hand. It wasn't a throwing knife, and she couldn't have thrown it even if it were. The training Lord Tanen had given her was geared toward up-close work. Still, the knife was something. She followed Silverdun out the door.

"Stay behind me!" he hissed. She looked over his shoulder and gasped. Easily a dozen of the City Guard were arrayed across the large balcony, all of them with crossbows. Elspet was kneeling on the ground with a crossbow at her neck, her head bowed.

The man in front had a different insignia on his uniform than the others; Sela racked her brain to remember the ranks of Unseelie guardsmen. This one was a sergeant, she believed, and the others were deputies.

"Drop the knives and come down the stairs slowly," said the sergeant. "You are under arrest."

"What do we do?" Sela asked breathlessly.

Ironfoot and Timha were directly behind her. "Surrender!" said Timha. "They'll kill you if you don't!"

"Avert your eyes," said Silverdun. "I'm going to dazzle them with a bit of witchlight."

"That's not going to give us enough time to get to the yacht," said Ironfoot.

"Do you have any better ideas?" asked Silverdun. "My old friend Mauritane can snatch crossbow bolts out of the air, but I, alas, cannot."

"Let's pray, then, that we can grow back internal organs as well as hands," said Ironfoot.

"Come down now," said the sergeant, "or we *will* fire."

"Now," said Silverdun. He raised his hand as if to surrender, but then flicked his wrist. Sela looked away.

The air around her exploded with light. She shut her eyes, but even so the light shone through her eyelids, splashing smears of blue and red across her vision.

Men below started screaming. Sela couldn't help herself; she looked.

The entire balcony shone as if Silverdun were a sun. The guards were stumbling, clutching at their faces. They cast perfect black shadows on the wall of the house behind them. The sergeant was feeling out in front of him; his face was bright red.

"What did you do?" asked Ironfoot. He was also staring now, as the light began to die away.

"That was a *bit* of witchlight?" said Timha. "I've never seen anything like it!"

Silverdun looked down at the scene below him. "Ah," he said.

"We need to go now," said Ironfoot. "Before anyone else shows up."

Below, the guards were still scrambling, looking for shelter, terrified.

"You've blinded them," said Sela.

"He did more than blind them," said Ironfoot. "Look at their faces."

Sela looked and saw the face of one of the guards close up. His skin looked as though it had been pushed into a fire.

"Fall back!" shouted the sergeant. The men attempted to flee.

Silverdun led the way down the stairs. He picked up one of the guards' crossbows and hurried toward the yacht, with Ironfoot close behind. Timha followed, his head down.

Sela ran to Elspet and helped her up. With her head hung, she'd escaped the worst of it and still had her sight, though it was clear she wasn't seeing particularly well.

"Come with us," whispered Sela.

"I can't," said Elspet. "I'll tell them you broke in. My husband is a powerful man. They'll believe me, and I have important work here."

She grabbed Sela's arm. "Get him out of here or all this will have been for nothing."

Sela turned and ran to catch up with Ironfoot, Silverdun, and Timha, who were already climbing on the yacht.

"Come on!" shouted Ironfoot.

One of the guards fired his crossbow at the sound of Ironfoot's voice, and the quarrel lodged in the mast next to him. Silverdun held up his stolen bow and fired back, dropping the guard where he stood.

Sela fled toward the dock. She'd almost made it when she felt a hand on her wrist and she sprawled down onto the wooden floor, the wind knocked out of her. The sergeant had grabbed her, even blind.

"You're not going anywhere!" he shouted.

"Help!" she shouted at Silverdun.

On the yacht, Ironfoot flicked his wrist. Something flashed in the air, and the sergeant made a choking noise. The hand around her ankle went limp.

She turned to see Ironfoot's dagger lodged in the sergeant's throat. She picked herself up and stumbled toward the yacht. Silverdun yanked her on board, Ironfoot cut the mooring line with another knife, and the yacht lurched into the air, sending Sela sprawling onto the deck.

Ironfoot did something to the yacht's mainsail and the yacht turned. Suddenly there was wind where there had been no wind before, and the city seemed to jump away from them. The yacht veered sharply in the city's wake, nearly toppling.

Ironfoot took the wheel and turned it sharply. There was a grinding sound below, and the ship righted itself. The city began to recede quickly now.

"I can't believe we got away!" said Timha. He was laughing nervously. "I don't know how you did it but . . . that was amazing!"

"I wouldn't start celebrating just yet, friend," said Silverdun, pointing.

A trio of fliers was headed in their direction.

"I think somebody noticed Silverdun's light show," said Ironfoot.

"Can't you go any faster?" asked Sela.

"Not unless you know how to make the wind blow harder," said Ironfoot.

Timha grabbed a crank and used it to tighten one of the ropes that held the sail in place. The yacht accelerated, but not by much.

"They've got the wind behind them," said Timha. "And by the time we turn to run, they'll have us. We should surrender!"

"Shut up!" shouted Silverdun. Ironfoot turned the wheel hard, and the yacht dipped to the left.

"Come about and put your craft in irons!" came a spell-amplified voice from one of the approaching guard fliers.

"Irons?" said Sela, confused.

"It means to turn the bow into the wind," said Ironfoot. "He wants us to stop."

Silverdun took a bolt from the small quiver attached to the front of his crossbow and put it in place, cranking the crannequin as he spoke. "No more bright lights?" asked Ironfoot.

"I haven't got a drop of *re* in me. You?"

"If they all came on board and sat patiently with us, I could probably throw some Leadership at them."

"Fine," said Silverdun. "Then we run and take our chances."

It was soon clear, however, that running wasn't going to work. The guard ships were faster; they had engines of Motion that added to the speed of their sails, whereas the yacht's power only allowed it to stay in the air.

"Stop and prepare to be boarded!" came the amplified voice again.

"What do we do?" shouted Sela. Silverdun gripped the crossbow tightly, his knuckles white.

The guard fliers were gaining, nearly alongside now.

"Stop now or we will fire upon your craft!"

"Damn!" shouted Ironfoot. He turned the wheel hard to the right, veering the yacht directly toward one of the guard fliers.

"What are you doing?" shouted Timha.

"Let's see how sturdy this yacht is!" shouted Ironfoot.

The guard flier dipped in the air to avoid them, but it was too late. The yacht's prow collided with the flier's mainmast. There was a horrible scraping sound, and the cracking of wood. Crossbow shots came from below—the guards in the flier were firing on them.

Silverdun leaned over the prow of the yacht with his own crossbow and fired. There was a loud crack, and the flier came loose beneath them, drifting off astern.

Sela heard a loud snap and turned to see something bright arcing toward the yacht from one of the fliers. It was like a miniature sun. It went high and wide, just missing the smaller sail in the front of the craft. Sela could feel the heat of it as it passed.

Another snap, and another sun flew toward them. This one ripped through the mainsail and smashed into the deck just in front of Ironfoot, who let go of the wheel and jumped backward, tripping over Timha.

The deck erupted in flame. Timha crawled out from beneath Ironfoot and drew a sigil in the air with his hands. The tiny ball of flame rose straight up, then turned at a right angle and struck the stern of the flier that had fired it. The guards aboard the flier hurried to put out the flames.

Sela looked back and realized that Timha had been too late. The fire was spreading across their deck; the wheel was aflame. Ironfoot and Timha were backed into a corner. Timha continued to make his sigils, but whatever he was attempting didn't appear to be working. Silverdun was struggling to reload his crossbow, but the crazy movement of the vessel made it nearly impossible.

The yacht stalled, then lurched. A gust of wind caught the loose mainsail, and the world began to spin around Sela. Flames licked the sail, and it caught fire as well, smoke spiraling up from the top of the mast.

Then came a percussive sound that made Sela's bones shake. The deck dipped and swayed. Sela lost her balance and fell onto the deck, and then somehow the deck was above her, and she was spinning, spinning, falling.

She turned over in the wind, and now she could see below her. Wind ruffled endless wheat fields like waves in the ocean, growing gray in the moonlight. In the center of the wheat, however, was a great, irregular oval of blackness, a space of utter darkness. Strangely, it did not look as if she was falling. Had Silverdun or Ironfoot done something to arrest their descent? All around her was smoke and flame. She couldn't see anything other than the ground below her.

Wind blew up at her, forcing her skirts up and her hair back from her head. Her skirts and sleeves were whipped by the air, flapping frantically against her skin.

Now she saw that she was falling, but from such a great height that it hadn't seemed like it at first. The black oval was like a mouth; it reached out toward her. The farther she fell, the larger it grew, and she realized that she was falling directly into the center of the umbra, the shadow of Preyia. Where it was bad luck to stand.

Now the ground was rushing toward her, the blackness expanding around her on all sides. The umbra was pure, velvety blackness; no moonlight illuminated its depths.

She fell and fell, her breath caught in her throat. The blackness grew and grew until it was everywhere and there was nothing but the black below and the smoke and the fire above and they came together and Sela gasped and the flame met the blackness with Sela in the middle. Dark and light. A loud rush and a silence.

chapter twenty-seven

The only Fae surface dwellers in the Unseelie are the Arami, that strange breed who maintain the ways of the wild Fae clans from before the time of Uvenchaud. They scrupulously avoid their airborne counterparts, or anyone else, for that matter. Thus, very little is known about them.

It is speculated that the odd, guttural language that has so confounded linguists (on the rare occasions the Arami have consented to be interviewed) is actually a variation of the original Elvish tongue. If they are to be believed, they are the last remaining vestige of the aboriginal Fae.

The Unseelie take no heed of the Arami. The Unseelie only leave their flying cities to take water from the wells that dot the landscape during periods of little rain, which are common in that northern clime. The Arami scrupulously avoid them when they come to ground.

—Stil-Eret, "The Arami: The Unknown Fae of the North," from *Travels at Home and Abroad*

Patterns. Ironfoot was lost in patterns. Two of them, one superimposed on the other. They were similar, but not the same. Almost identical, in fact. But at the heart of them was a discrepancy, an error, like an elegant equation that hid an undefined term somewhere within it. Everything looked right on the surface; it was only by traversing the threads of the patterns that the impossibility was visible.

But where was this error? What caused it? He traced the pattern in his mind, but it was so large and elusive that he couldn't hold it. As he envisioned one portion of it, the others slid away from him; it was impossible to connect it all. He needed paper, and his map.

He reached for paper, but his arm wouldn't move. He tried to sit up, but something heavy was on top of him. He began to panic. He opened his eyes. It was dark, black within black. His throat made a strangling noise, halfway between a whimper and a scream. Where was he?

"Over here!" came a voice. "I heard something!"

Ironfoot reached into his body and tried to calm it, as Paet had tried to teach him during one of their regular trainings a few weeks earlier. He'd never quite understood what Paet had meant; but his mind was attuned to patterns at the moment, and suddenly he could read the patterns within his own body, the energies that coursed through him and the objects that the energies connected. There was his heart, thudding. He willed it to slow and it slowed. There was another tiny thing, spitting out panic into his blood. He willed it to stop, and it stopped.

He willed strength into his arms and pushed. He and Silverdun had lately developed what they referred to as Shadow strength, far beyond what they'd once been used to. The thing above him moved, but not by much. But here was a bit of useful information; there was only so much Shadow strength in this body of his. He'd pushed too hard, and now his arms fell weakly to his sides in the enclosed space.

It wasn't good enough. But then again, it never was.

When Ironfoot was a child, his father had always goaded him. "Don't end up like me, boy," he'd said as the two of them sheared sheep. The price of wool had dropped for three years straight, and his father had already sold off three of his best ewes. "You're smart," he'd said. "You have to make something of yourself."

So when Ironfoot enlisted in the army, it was with the determination to do everything he could to get ahead. He knew he was smart, and that he had several of the Gifts, but there was no place for a shepherd's son at a school like

Queensbridge. Most of the students at such schools were the sons and daughters of lords or wealthy guildsmen, and they'd all been sent to expensive academies as children. Ironfoot, on the other hand, had gone to the village school until the age of ten and then had gone to work for his father. He'd stayed up late, long after his father had gone to bed, reading, studying basic thaumatics, teaching himself to make the witchlight that he read by.

He'd moved up quickly in the ranks as an enlisted man, but as a commoner, there was a point beyond which there was no advancement.

Then came the Gnomic War. He'd been a sergeant in the Third Battalion of the Dragon Regiment, responsible for Ram Company. In the army, Ironfoot had made a reputation as a perfectionist. He demanded nothing but the best from himself and from his soldiers. Some hated him for it, most complained, but they all respected him. And it soon became clear as the Gnomic campaign progressed, and Ironfoot's company led in kills without losing a single soldier, that he was a fine commander as well.

His own commander, however, Colonel Samel-La, was far less fine. Put simply, Samel-La was a fool, and was totally unsuited for combat. He had no knowledge of tactics, believing that the solution to every problem was to throw battle mages and soldiers at it until it went away. As a commander, he was lax and allowed his junior officers to curry favor with him, listening to those who agreed with him and ignoring those who did not. Even after Ironfoot earned four Laurels serving beneath him, Samel-La refused to take his advice. It didn't take long for Samel-La and Ironfoot to find a way to butt heads.

When they entered the Gnokka River Valley, just south of Cmir, everything went wrong all at once. The Gnomics were waiting for them, having taken up positions along the slope on either side. Ironfoot saw the trap immediately, and warned Samel-La to retreat, but Samel-La claimed that Seelie never retreated, especially against savages like the Gnomics. Ironfoot attempted to explain that retreat was one of the fundamental tactics of war, but Samel-La refused to listen.

The battle very quickly turned ugly. Casualties began mounting by the dozens. More and more Gnomics appeared over the rim of the valley, and still Samel-La refused to retreat.

It was not until they'd been flanked in the rear, when retreat was no longer possible, that Samel-La decided he'd had enough. He took a single company and bolted to the rear, his intent apparently to break through the Gnomic line and flee, stranding his own battalion. He and his entire company were slaughtered moments after they left the main Seelie force.

Confusion reigned for a few desperate minutes, in which none of the Seelie soldiers knew what to do and the lines were folding in. It appeared as though they were doomed to a slaughter.

But Ironfoot stood up in his saddle and shouted orders to his company, taking command of the battalion. He drew in and stitched up the lines, reuniting the soldiers into a unified force. Together they not only repelled the Gnomic attack, but took the valley, forcing the Gnomics into a retreat.

When it was over, the regiment commander, General Jeric, explained to Ironfoot that it was not possible to award him a fifth Laurel for his valor in this particular battle. Samel-La had been the son of an influential lord who had his fingers on the army's purse strings. And thus Samel-La would be said to have died of wounds sustained leading the Third Battalion to victory in the battle of Gnokka Valley.

General Jeric, however, understood what Ironfoot had done, and what was taken from him. He asked Ironfoot whether there was anything he could do to cushion the blow.

"I want to go to Queensbridge," he'd said, without a moment's pause.

Three days later, Ironfoot was honorably discharged from the Seelie Army, just hours after being commissioned a lieutenant. As an officer in the Seelie Army, he was eligible to attend Queensbridge, and with the warm personal recommendation of the Third Battalion's commander, he was happily accepted.

At Queensbridge he'd become more of a perfectionist than ever. He wasn't satisfied unless he got not just top marks, but *the* top marks. At any task of thaumatics, he demanded success from himself. He never quit. He worked harder and did more and he succeeded.

And he hadn't ever been able to stop.

Here he sat now with the greatest challenge of his life in front of him. It wasn't just that success was important. It was everything. Nothing less than perfection mattered.

Nothing.

There was a crunching noise above him. "Right here," came the voice again. Silverdun. "Well, don't just stand there. Help me!"

The object above him moved a little; then it began to rise slowly. There came the sound of voices grunting in labor. The object lifted a bit more, and then was shoved sideways.

A silhouette looked down at him, surrounded by witchlight. "Still alive, I take it?"

"Silverdun!" he gasped.

"I know you're always eager to display your manliness," said Silverdun, "but pinning yourself under a yacht seems excessive, even for you."

Ironfoot stood, shakily, and stumbled. Beneath him was not solid ground, but something soft and springy, like a feather mattress, only infinitely more pliable. Silverdun reached down and pulled him up onto . . . something.

In the dark it was difficult to comprehend what he was seeing. There was very little light other than witchlight, which illuminated Silverdun's relieved expression. There were a number of robed figures standing nearby. Next to him, a black hulk, was the fore half of the yacht. It registered that he had briefly lifted the entire thing on his own. They were surrounded on all sides by strange shapes, and the place smelled faintly of garbage.

Something slapped against Ironfoot's hip as he took a step toward Silverdun. It was Timha's satchel. Somehow he'd managed to hold on to it.

Sela was behind Silverdun. She had a huge gash on the side of her head, and blood streaming down her dress, but she seemed not much the worse for wear. Silverdun was a bit rumpled, but otherwise seemed fine. Timha was stumbling toward them as well, his breathing ragged and hitching with what might have been sobs.

All else was darkness. No, not quite; on the horizon he could see silver wheat swaying in the moonlight.

"What happened?" he said.

"More to the point, what did *not* happen?" said Silverdun. "What didn't happen was that we didn't get crushed to bits after falling a thousand feet in a burning yacht."

"And how did that not happen, exactly?" asked Ironfoot, baffled. The last thing he remembered was being on board the yacht, flames hissing through the air. After that it was all a little fuzzy.

"Because of them," said Silverdun. He gestured toward the robed figures standing nearby. Ironfoot noticed that most of them were carrying bulging sacks; two of them were carrying a large item between them. A table?

One of them stepped forward. All that Ironfoot could see of him was that he was lean and tall and his head was shaved clean. "Hello," he said. "I am Je Wen. Welcome to the ground." He spoke Common haltingly, in a thick, strange accent.

"You saved us?" said Ironfoot. "How?"

"We did not save you," said Je Wen. "You fell into our net."

A chaotic groaning sound issued from all around, and the ground swayed beneath their feet, as though they were on a ship on the sea. Ironfoot, Sela, and Silverdun toppled over, but the robed figures remained on their feet.

"We're standing on a sheet of Motion," said Silverdun, shakily rising to his feet. "A massive one. Incredibly soft and flexible; like a great fluffy pillow."

Je Wen looked back at his fellow. "Let us take what we need and be gone," he said. He turned to Silverdun. "We would like for you to come with us."

"Who are you people?" said Ironfoot.

"They're Arami," said Timha. "And if they saved us, they'll want something for it."

"I thought you didn't interact with the Fae of the cities," said Ironfoot.

"Only that one," said Je Wen, pointing at Timha, "is of the cities. You are not."

"How——?" Ironfoot began, but the sea of objects around them groaned again, and the swaying grew in fierceness.

"We must go," said Je Wen. "It would be wise for the four of you to accompany us."

Ironfoot looked at Silverdun, and Silverdun shrugged. "Unless you have something better to do?"

"You can't trust these people," said Timha. "I'm telling you."

"You've been overruled," said Silverdun. "Let's go."

Sela nodded as well. Ironfoot followed Je Wen and his fellows toward the silver light on the horizon. In the back of his mind were two similar patterns, twirling in his thoughts, but they were indistinct now, and he put them out of his mind.

Ironfoot tried to keep up with Je Wen, but it was difficult. The ground continued to sway beneath him, and the terrain was uneven and sometimes slippery. "What am I walking on?" he asked.

Je Wen smiled. "Our net collects what those above discard. All that they do not want they simply throw onto the ground."

"So we're walking on their refuse," said Ironfoot.

"Indeed. Castoff furniture, uneaten food, animal scraps, feces. If they do not want it, we catch it in our net."

Feces.

"Why?"

"Because the Arami are scavengers, who make nothing of their own," said Timha, straggling along behind.

Je Wen smiled. "Because they are wasteful, and we are not."

After a few minutes of slow travel across the strange sea of refuse, they began to near the edge, and the debris began to thin until Ironfoot found himself standing on a flat surface that gave beneath his feet, cushioning his steps.

"This is soft," said Ironfoot. "But I don't see how it kept us all from being smashed to bits."

"It is a very clever net."

They reached the edge, which was a perfectly straight line, and Je Wen hopped off onto the ground, a few feet below, which seemed to be moving beneath them. It was lighter here, and now Ironfoot could see Je Wen's face. It was strong and lined, there was a bit of light stubble on his head, and he had a neatly trimmed beard that glowed white in the moonlight. His eyes were clear and light, though it was difficult to tell whether they were blue or gray in the monochrome world of night.

Ironfoot looked back into a sea of darkness.

"Come along," said Je Wen. Ironfoot noticed that Silverdun and Sela had already jumped from the edge of the blackness, and that the other Arami were handing their collected loot off to their comrades. They were moving slowly away from him. A little way away, wide carts pulled by long lines of the tiniest horses Ironfoot had ever seen were stopping nearby.

He jumped off and stumbled again on the moving ground. He turned and realized that, of course, it was not the ground that was moving, but the "net," which followed along beneath the city.

"Does it track the city wherever it goes?" asked Silverdun.

Je Wen shook his head. "Only at night, and only when they pass nearby. We know their paths and follow them as need requires."

Ironfoot watched the umbra recede. He looked up at the underbelly of the city. From beneath, Preyia was an eyesore. Its hull was discolored and uneven, dark. A fine mist fell from it.

"All that," said Ironfoot, pointing, "is one night's worth of garbage?"

"As I said," said Je Wen, "they are a wasteful people."

Timha was the last one off the net. He scowled at Je Wen, but came anyway.

They walked to the carts as a group. Sela pointed out that it would be polite to offer to help carry what the Arami had collected. Ironfoot took a sack from one of the robed figures, who nodded in thanks, but did not speak. As Ironfoot carried it to the carts, he peeked inside: a half-eaten loaf of bread, a cabbage, a belt, a bolt of cloth, a cheese, and other items that he couldn't identify in the darkness.

They reached the carts, and Ironfoot realized with surprise that the creatures pulling the wagons were not horses, but goats. Tall, short-horned goats that made quiet guttural sounds as they stood impatiently in their harness. The carts were low and wide, and their wheels huge.

"Come along," said Je Wen, motioning for Ironfoot, Silverdun, and Sela to climb aboard the carts. "A large quake will come to this place in a few minutes."

Presently the carts were all loaded with both goods and passengers. The loot was carefully tied down in the backs of the carts. Ironfoot, Silverdun, Timha, and Sela sat in the front cart with Je Wen. The goats hopped along, pulling the cart faster than Ironfoot would have suspected, their heads popping up comically out of the tall wild grain that the carts now passed through.

The ground suddenly shook, and the cart jerked to the left. Ironfoot realized why it was built so wide; the wheels on the right side of the cart leapt off the ground for a moment, but there was no danger of the thing tipping. The goats barely seemed to notice. Their hopping gait continued as if nothing had happened.

"Look," said Je Wen, pointing. The city and its shadow were receding across the uneven plain. The Arami net, seen from the side, was a large irregular black disk that floated a few feet off the ground. A loud crack like thunder pealed in the night, and the earth beneath the city cracked open in a shower of dust. The net crumpled and fell in on itself, and its contents spilled haphazardly. Much of it fell into the new ravine that had been created by the quake.

"Lovely, isn't it?" said Je Wen. "Everything returns eventually to its source."

"Lovely" wasn't the first word that sprang to Ironfoot's mind, but it was certainly impressive. He watched Preyia drift like a cloud across the sky, and was glad to see it go.

The carts reached the end of the tall grain stalks, jostling along through aftershocks of the quake that lessened over time and distance. They came to an uneven, rocky plain peppered with tiny thornbushes and joined a rutted track that cut across it toward a tiny valley. In places the track vanished only to reappear a few yards on, and in other places the ruts zigzagged haphazardly, as if the ground beneath them had been torn apart and inexpertly replaced. In the distance they heard the cries of wolves, which spooked the goats, but they never saw them.

The track descended into the valley, where tents and cooking fires were arranged in a circle with a large bonfire in the center. More goats were penned nearby. Children came out of the tents and ran toward the carts as they approached. They were dressed in a chaotic assortment of Unseelie clothing, wilted finery and rough-hewn commoners' tunics. They shouted out in a strange, staccato language that Ironfoot didn't recognize. When they saw Ironfoot, Timha, Sela, and Silverdun, however, the children stopped and looked to Je Wen.

Je Wen spoke to the children in the same rapid tongue, and they continued onto the carts, taking the bags of loot and the larger items. The children remained wary of the newcomers, however, and gave them a wide berth.

A very tall, very slender woman came out of one of the tents and looked at the carts. She was dressed in a gentleman's silk blouse and a housemaid's dress. A necklace of wooden beads was around her neck. All of the Arami stopped what they were doing and watched as she approached. Clearly, she was someone to be reckoned with. She stopped in front of Je Wen's cart and looked at Silverdun, then Sela, then Ironfoot, and finally Timha without speaking. The entire camp had gone silent. Up close, Ironfoot saw that she was in early middle age, perhaps forty, with a few streaks of gray in her long, wavy black hair.

Finally she scratched her head and said in unaccented Common, "I was wondering when you four were going to show up."

The woman's name was Lin Vo, and she was the clan's leader. She ushered them into her tent, which was no different from any of the others. A bit smaller than most, in fact. The interior of her tent was decorated simply, in the same random assortment of styles as her clothing. Nothing matched, and some of the furniture seemed ludicrously unsuited to a nomadic lifestyle. There was an expensive oil lamp atop an antique side table. The bed was a wide mahogany four-poster complete with a gauze hanging atop it; the frame had been broken, but had been efficiently nailed back together. The sheets were silk, but stained with wine.

"Can I get you tea?" said Lin Vo, once they'd all been seated on comfortable cushions that were strewn on the mat-covered ground.

"Tea would be lovely, thank you," said Sela. Sela had a strange knack for understanding what it was that people wanted to hear, so Ironfoot went along with her and accepted as well.

Lin Vo went outside to her cooking fire and came back inside with a battered kettle filled with hot water. She measured some tea into an earthenware teapot and emptied the kettle into it. Then she placed the pot and five chipped porcelain cups on a silver tray and set it down in the midst of her guests. She did all of this without speaking.

"You pour," she said to Sela. She watched carefully as Sela lifted the kettle.

"Might I ask—?" began Silverdun, but Lin Vo cut him off with a harsh look.

"Don't talk while someone's pouring tea," she said.

Once the tea was poured, Lin Vo took a cup and raised it to them. "The Arami welcome you," she said.

"Now," she said, cutting off Silverdun, who was about to speak again. "We can skip the formal introductions and back and forth. I know who all of you are, and I know why you're here, and how you ended up here."

"You have the Gift of Premonition," said Silverdun.

Lin Vo scoffed. "You people and your Gifts. You always have to have everything in nice neat rows. Twelve Gifts, twelve months in a year, twelve constellations looking down over you. Have you ever seen a Chthonic cynosure? Big dodecahedron. They'll go on for hours about all the lines and facets and vertices on it and what they mean."

"What do you want from us?" asked Timha. He'd been silent since they'd arrived at the Arami camp, and was clearly scared out of his wits.

Lin Vo laughed. "Oh, Journeyer Timha. You're frightened, and I can see why. But that's no excuse to be rude. Besides, it's not about what I want from you, which is nothing, and all about what you need from me."

"And what is it that we need from you?" asked Silverdun.

"Well, it seems to me that you need a couple of things. You need to get back to where you came from with our friend Timha in tow, and in order for that to happen, you're going to need Je Wen to lead you down to the border. Because if you try to make it on your own, you'll be dead in two days."

"A premonition?" asked Ironfoot.

"Merely stating the obvious," said Lin Vo. "Folks from up in the sky who find their way down here have a tendency to wander into quakes or get eaten by wolves."

"This is nonsense," said Timha. "Premonitive or not, this woman is lying. We're most likely going to be held for ransom, and this tale is simply to keep us docile in the meantime."

"I can see you're not going to let me get any work done," said Lin Vo to

Timha. "So let's get this over with now. Here's what you think is going to happen. You think you're going to waggle your fingers under your robe and do something nasty and I'm going to fall over dead and you and your friends are going to fight your way out of here."

Timha glared at her but said nothing.

"What's really going to happen is that you're going to try that and fail, and then you're going to sit there and listen, and then when we're done you're all going to say 'Thank you very much, Lin Vo,' and then I'm going to send you off with Je Wen at first light."

Timha still said nothing. Lin Vo looked at Ironfoot and said, "Watch closely, Ironfoot. You're going to like this."

While her head was turned, Timha lifted his hands and drew a sigil of unbinding in the air. This was the call to some spell that he'd memorized previously and kept fully formed in his mind with a binding around it to keep it contained. The sigil was meaningless to Ironfoot, but when the *re* started condensing around him, he recognized immediately what Timha was doing. He was creating a space of Motion around Lin Vo, stopping the vibration of all matter in a sphere around her. This sphere would not only immobilize her, but it would also render her body and the air around her solid and freezing to the touch, killing her. Lin Vo sat looking at Timha, doing nothing, looking disappointed.

Ironfoot watched closely, his *re* sense having become heightened along with his strength and his other senses. What had Jedron done to him back on Whitemount? He could almost see the flow of essence from Timha, channeled as Motion, enveloping Lin Vo. She was going to die.

"Timha!" shouted Silverdun, who was probably seeing this as well as Ironfoot was. "Stop!"

Ironfoot moved to rush Timha, but before he could get up, something strange happened. Lin Vo didn't move, but a warm pulse of *re* shot from her, filling the room. But it was like no *re* Ironfoot had ever seen. Somehow Lin Vo had used *re* without channeling it through one of the Gifts. It made no sense. It was like a colorless color, or an animal that wasn't of any species, or a sung note with no pitch. It was the reitic equivalent of division by zero. It was simply not possible.

But there it was. Ironfoot watched, enthralled, as Lin Vo's *re* encompassed Timha's Motion. It wasn't like a duel between battle mages; there was no confrontation, no conflict. The two essences combined, and where Timha's Motion had been, suddenly there was Elements, and the Elements swirled back toward Timha, and the air around him turned to water.

Suddenly soaking wet, Timha flinched backward, staring at Lin Vo in astonishment.

Lin Vo looked at Ironfoot. Only a second or two had passed since she'd last spoken. "See what I mean? You liked it, didn't you?"

Ironfoot nodded, stymied. What he had just seen wasn't just impossible, it was . . . paradoxical.

Lin Vo took a deep breath and settled herself on her cushion. "There's a towel behind you," she told Timha. "I had a feeling something like this might happen."

There was indeed a towel. It was monogrammed. Timha rubbed his hair with it, looking haunted. Lin Vo's display had not been lost on him, either.

"What did you just do?" asked Ironfoot.

"Me?" said Lin Vo. "That was nothing. I just changed things around a bit."

"You have the Thirteenth Gift," said Silverdun. "Change Magic."

"There you go with your Gifts again," said Lin Vo. "Everything's a Gift with you people."

She sighed. "Now if we're done with the histrionics, I'd like to get the conversation going, because it's going to be light in a few hours, and that's when you need to leave."

Silverdun rolled his eyes and said, "Please tell me you're not going to launch into a rambling, vague prophecy of some kind, telling us our fate."

"No," said Lin Vo. "And I don't like that word 'fate.' There's no such thing as fate. There's only the river."

"What river is that?" asked Sela.

"Time is the river, Sela, and we're all floating down it. It's a strong current and it carries us. We can paddle this way and that and we can try to swim upstream for a while or make ourselves go faster, but we're headed down that river one way or another.

"What you call Premonition is just the ability to sit up a little bit and look downstream. Sometimes you can see rocks ahead; sometimes you can see that we're all about to go over a waterfall."

"Why are you telling us all this?" asked Silverdun. Ironfoot could see that he was growing impatient. Silverdun claimed to have a philosophical bent, but Ironfoot had noticed that he was always far happier when he was in action.

"Because there's a waterfall just up ahead."

"If we're all going over it anyway," said Silverdun, "then why bother telling us?"

"So you can go down it feet first, with your eyes open, silly." She sipped her tea. "So I sent Je Wen out there to wait for you to come falling out of the sky, and here you are."

"Surely you didn't do this out of the goodness of your heart," said Silverdun. "What do you want in return?"

"Oh, my! How cynical you are," said Lin Vo. "Sometimes people do the right thing because it's the right thing to do."

She touched his knee. "There's a war coming, Silverdun. War is the greatest waste there is, and we Arami are particularly indisposed to waste, as you may have noticed. And this isn't just any war. This is a war that has the power to end Faerie. The power to turn this world to dust."

"The Einswrath," said Ironfoot.

"There you go," said Lin Vo. "That little device changes everything, as the four of you know all too well. In fact, none of you would be here if it weren't for the Einswrath."

"There aren't any Einswrath," said Timha.

"What?" said Silverdun, glaring at him.

"We couldn't figure out how to do it," said Timha, his eyes downcast. "We tried. We did everything we could. They said they would kill us all if we didn't."

"And that's why you ran," said Sela.

"But you've got the plans with you," said Silverdun. "Are you saying they're not real?"

"No!" shouted Timha. "They're real. They're extremely detailed, and they were drawn by Hy Pezho himself. But he's gone and he can't explain how it all works."

"*Now* he tells us," said Silverdun.

"I didn't want to die," said Timha. "I'm giving you the plans; that's how badly I don't want to die. If you can figure out how to make the thing work, then you'll have the Einswrath and Mab won't. Don't you get it? Don't you understand what I've done?"

"Funny name, 'Einswrath,'" said Lin Vo. "The wrath of Ein. Strange thing to name a weapon. You wouldn't think they'd name it after a made-up god who's supposedly been buried in the ground for thousands of years."

"So you don't believe that any gods are real?" asked Silverdun. "I'd always heard that the Arami worshipped the Chthonic gods."

"Oh, the gods are real," said Lin Vo. "Just not the way you think. And you're all going to have to learn how to think things anew if you're going to survive."

"A premonition?" asked Silverdun.

"A fact of life," said Lin Vo. She looked at Timha. "Not you, though. You just keep doing what you're doing."

Silverdun stood, clearly irritated. "I don't know about my companions, but I've had enough clever presentiment for one night. I appreciate your hospitality, but I think I'd prefer a bed."

"I don't blame you, Silverdun. This *is* all very tiresome and vague. Premonitives have a reputation for that. But true vision isn't something that can be expressed in words. To put it into words is to render it false. I can only point you in a direction; I can't tell you what you'll find when you get there. Maddening, I know. Not too different from the gods, really."

"Ah," said Silverdun. Ironfoot could tell that Silverdun was tired. The pressure of leading this assignment was wearing him down.

"You go rest, Silverdun. I don't have anything more to tell you; in fact, the less I tell you, the better. Take Timha and Ironfoot here with you. Je Wen will find a place for you to lie down."

"Thank you," said Silverdun, visibly relieved.

"What about me?" asked Sela.

"Let's talk about you, Sela. Let me pour you a cup of tea, because this is going to take a while." She looked up at the men. "Go on, you three. Ladies only."

Ironfoot, Silverdun, and Timha left the tent, and found Je Wen waiting for them outside.

"Was your conversation profitable?" he asked.

"I have no idea," said Ironfoot.

Je Wen gave him a knowing smile. "Come with me."

The tent next to Lin Vo's held four mattresses piled with blankets and pillows, and not much else. Silverdun sprawled on one, his eyes wide open, and Timha was fast asleep on the other by the time Ironfoot got his boots off.

"I thought you were tired," said Ironfoot, looking at Silverdun.

"I am. More exhausted than I can remember being in a long, long time."

"That was an . . . unusual conversation."

Silverdun sat up, rubbing his temples. "People like her drive me utterly mad," he said.

"Did you see what she did to Timha?" Ironfoot asked. "The way she used *re*?"

Silverdun shook his head. "I haven't the slightest idea what happened there. I saw Timha channeling Motion, and the next thing I knew, he looked like he'd been dunked in a pond. Strangest thing I ever saw." He lay back down and closed his eyes.

"Get some sleep," he said. "I have a feeling we've got a couple of long days ahead of us."

Ironfoot lay down as well, but couldn't sleep either. When he closed his eyes he saw the patterns in his mind again, and the colorless color of Lin Vo's magic.

An undefined term. Division by zero.

Some time later, just as he was drifting off, Sela slipped into the tent. He caught a glimpse of her in the firelight from outside. Tears glistened on her face, but she didn't look sad. Quite the opposite: For the first time he could remember, she looked at peace.

Ironfoot awoke what felt like a moment later, although it must have been at least four hours, because gray dawn was already filtering in through the tent flaps. Though he'd slept little, and fitfully, when he stood up he felt fully awake and rested. Another perk of the change wrought upon him and Silverdun at Whitemount, whatever it had been. He needed little sleep these days, and what little he got worked wonders.

Hell, it even grew back a hand if necessary.

"About time you woke up," said Silverdun. He was already up and pulling on his boots. He looked as refreshed as Ironfoot felt.

"How do you feel right now, Silverdun?" he asked.

"Just fine," said Silverdun.

"After just four hours of sleep."

"I'm not questioning it today," said Silverdun. "Just grateful for it. I woke up in fine fettle and don't intend to let anything bring me down today."

"That's uncharacteristically optimistic of you," said Ironfoot.

"Apparently my previous character wasn't doing me much good," said Silverdun drily.

"Is it morning already?" said Sela. She sat up on her mattress and looked around, groggy. "I feel as though I just fell asleep."

Outside, the Arami tribe was already up and active. The central fire pit had been covered over with sand, and the tents were being struck. Timha walked through the camp, his eyes half-closed and suspicious, but took coffee and a pipe when they were offered. Je Wen was rolling up a portion of tent canvas when they found him.

"Good morning," Je Wen said. "I trust you all slept well?"

"Your trust is misplaced," said Silverdun. "We all slept poorly. But we're ready to go when you are."

They made their preparations for travel as the camp was dismantled around them.

"Is the whole group coming?" asked Ironfoot.

"No," said Je Wen. "It's time to move camp. There will be a quake today. This valley will split open like a wound."

The tents were loaded up into the goat carts, but all of the furniture, and most of the bric-a-brac that had been inside the tents, was left on the ground.

"To feed the bound gods," said Je Wen with a knowing smile.

They were ready to go, but Lin Vo's tent was still standing, and she had yet to appear.

"Won't we see her again?" asked Sela, distraught.

"She has said all she has to say," said Je Wen, shrugging. "Let's go."

A pregnant woman approached Je Wen and handed him a shoulder bag stuffed with what appeared to be provisions.

"My wife," said Je Wen. He patted her stomach gently. "And my son," he said, smiling.

Je Wen kissed his wife gently on the cheek. She said something in Arami, clearly an admonition, and he put his hand on her cheek. She turned and went back to her tent, unsmiling.

"I imagine she's not thrilled with your leaving," said Silverdun.

"I'll be back in plenty of time to see the child born," said Je Wen.

He led them through the emptying camp, opposite the direction of the carts.

"We won't be taking one of those?" said Timha, despondent, pointing at the carts.

"Not where we're going," said Je Wen. "I hope you all know how to climb."

They set off. When they reached the far rim of the valley, Ironfoot looked back. Lin Vo was standing in front of the line of fully packed carts, facing them. She seemed to be looking directly at Ironfoot. Then she turned around and walked past the carts, until Ironfoot could no longer see her.

chapter twenty-eight

Then the goat and the bear were married and lived together all their days. And whether it was that the goat became mad or the bear became sane, no one will ever know.

—from "The Goat and the Bear," Seelie fable

The first day they did little but walk through endless fields of wild grain and across windswept rocks. They stopped a few times to eat the food that Je Wen had packed, but spoke little.

Silverdun and Ironfoot had boundless energy and were able to keep up with Je Wen easily, but Sela was still exhausted, and had refused to be spell-rested. Timha had spellrested himself but was still miserable. He was clearly unused to exercising any part of him other than his mind, and his boots were unsuited for hiking. He spent most of the morning gasping for breath and asking constantly to stop for rest.

Silverdun was growing sick of Timha. When Timha wasn't complaining about his feet or his exhaustion or the meager nourishment, he was feeling sorry for himself. A small but growing part of Silverdun felt like slitting Timha's throat and putting them all out of their misery. As he pondered this, it occurred to him that a year ago the thought would never have come to mind. His experience as a Shadow was changing him, had already changed him.

They continued south, following the course of a river for a time.

"How far to Elenth?" Silverdun asked Je Wen when they crested a small rise only to see endless mountains before them.

"Two days," said Je Wen, pointing southwest. He looked back at Timha, who was straggling up the hill. "Three with him along."

Silverdun sighed. "And from there two days' ride to the border," he said. "Three days lost without our speedy yacht. I suppose it could be worse."

"It can always be worse," said Je Wen.

"Well said."

"We could shave off a few hours if you were willing to cut through the Contested Lands," said Je Wen. "I've traversed them before."

Silverdun had crossed the Contested Lands with Mauritane a year previously, and had no intention of ever returning. He told Je Wen so in no uncertain terms.

They continued in silence for the rest of the first day. Aside from the occasional rumble of a quake and the wind hissing through the stalks of grain, there was little sound. The few animals they saw fled quietly on sight. As they progressed, the ground grew ever steeper, and Timha's complaints increased in frequency and volume.

Night fell, and Silverdun and Ironfoot helped Je Wen gather wood for a fire while the others rested. Sela and Ironfoot had both been lost in thought for most of the day. Sela, particularly, was more withdrawn than Ironfoot had ever seen her.

When the fire was lit, and the rations passed around, a torpor settled around the camp. Je Wen stared into the fire, singing softly to himself in the Arami tongue. Ironfoot sat with Timha's satchel, poring through one of the books that Timha had packed. Timha passed out as soon as he'd finished eating.

"Would you like to go for a walk?" Silverdun asked Sela.

She looked up at him and smiled weakly. "Only if it's a very brief one," she said.

They walked slowly from the camp up to a ridge that overlooked a wide plain and the mountains beyond. The mountains were black in the moonlight.

Silverdun's feelings for Sela were as complicated as they'd ever been. His attraction to her had only grown over time as he'd gotten to know her. She was thoughtful, insightful, and she was strong in a way that he'd never experienced. But there was that deep darkness in her that lingered behind her eyes. The night they'd met, she'd looked into him with Empathy, and he'd pushed her out again. There had been something desperate in the connection and it had, frankly, frightened him.

"You seem strange tonight," Silverdun said softly.

"It's been a strange couple of days," she sighed.

"Agreed."

Silence.

"You spent a while alone with that Lin Vo woman," he finally said. "What did she tell you that's got you so pensive?"

"I'm not sure how to explain it," she said after a moment. "I could tell you the words, but I'm not sure it would make any sense to you. The words were the least of it. And some of what she said—well, I'm not sure I'd want you to know. She was very wise, Silverdun."

"She's a Premonitive," said Silverdun. "They always seem wise, but rarely does anything they say actually help anyone."

"No," said Sela. "She knew things. And she spoke to me in a way that no one has ever done. In a way that I believed only I knew how to speak."

There it was. The darkness. Whatever it was that had happened in Sela's childhood, which she never discussed, whatever it was that had landed her in Copperine House, it was there in her eyes.

"Who are you?" said Silverdun.

Sela leaned over and kissed his lips. She closed her eyes. Silverdun stiffened at first, then relaxed into her, kissing back. She opened her mouth, her lips going soft. But there was something hesitant in her kiss, something confused.

"Open yourself up to me, Perrin Alt," she said. "Let me feel you."

Silverdun felt uneasy and strangely guilty. But she was so close and felt so good. He relaxed the binding that protected him from her Gift of Empathy, and felt himself flowing into her and her into him. There was lust, and love, and a desperate longing. But whose emotions were whose very quickly became inseparable. She pressed against him and he held her tightly. She moaned quietly and drew her fingernails across his back as if trying to pull him into her.

He ran his fingers down her arm and touched the filigreed silver band around her arm. It was hot to the touch.

"Why do you still wear that thing?" he whispered. "I thought it was only for the guests at places like Copperine House."

"Shh," she said, moving his hand to her breast.

They sank to the ground, falling into one another. It felt so very good.

He reached to unlace her gown and she put up her hands to stop him.

"No," she said, pulling away. "I can't."

"It's easy," he said. "People do it every day."

"Not me," she whispered. "I've never kissed a man. I've never been touched like this."

The Empathy wavered between them and Silverdun put his arms around her, kissing her neck, trying to restore it. But it was too late.

"I can never be that way with you," she said.

"Why not?" asked Silverdun, his insides constricting.

"Because I love you," she said. "And you don't love me."

She stood up and hurried off, back to camp, leaving Silverdun on the ground, stunned.

Perrin Alt, now Lord Silverdun, is engaged to be married. Gleia isn't clever. Or interesting. But she's gorgeous, and popular at court. And everyone approves of the union. Silverdun isn't in love with Gleia, nor she with him. But such unions have little to do with love, and everything to do with status and propriety.

Truth be told, Silverdun would prefer not to get married at all. But his friends at court have pressured him into it; an unmarried lord above a certain age raises questions. Better to get it over with and settle into a life of torrid and illicit affairs—which, his married friends assure him, are more exciting than the unmarried sort anyway.

Gleia insists on a massive, extravagant wedding. Silverdun has no objections; any excuse for a party, after all. He sends a message to Uncle Bresun asking for a rather large sum of money, and to be prepared for Gleia's assault on Oarsbridge Manor, with her lavish plans for decorations and accommodations and musicians and all that.

Instead of a lump sum and well-wishes, however, Silverdun receives a terse note demanding his presence at Oarsbridge. Alone.

Silverdun notices upon his arrival that his uncle has redecorated the manor house in a style more lavish by half than any his mother would approve of. Bresun himself, however, is nowhere to be found. He's in the village on business.

"Where is my mother?" Silverdun asks a maid, deciding that the time has come to see her. He's surprised by the maid's answer.

The servants' quarters are unadorned, but spotless. He finds his mother in a room at the end of the hall on the first floor. The room contains only the barest essentials, along with a few small portraits and likenesses of Silverdun and his father.

"Perrin," says Mother, putting aside a book of Arcadian poetry and embracing him. "It's so lovely to see you."

Silverdun hasn't seen his mother in over a year. Has, in fact, been scrupulously avoiding her since the debacle following his father's death. Clearly she's gone mad in the interim.

"Mother, you do realize that these are the *servants'* quarters, don't you?"

"I don't care for what your uncle has done in the manor house," says Mother, shrugging. "And I have everything I need here."

Silverdun sighs and sits on the bed. "You're really intent on carrying this Arcadian business as far as possible, aren't you?"

"Tell me about yourself," she says, sitting next to him, ignoring his remark. "I haven't seen you in so long."

"I know I should write more often," he says weakly.

"How are you?" she asks, waving away his half-apology. "Are you in love?"

"It's funny you ask," he says. "I'm getting married. I thought I should tell you in person."

"But are you in love?"

"Her name is Gleia. She's all the rage at court."

"Oh, Perrin."

"Now, Mother, don't be so sentimental. Were you in love with Father when you married him?"

"No," she admits. "But I wanted better for you. I tried so hard to . . ." she trails off, starting to cry.

"Mother," says Silverdun, touching her arm. "You don't have to weep over me."

"I tried so hard to show you another way of living. A better way. I knew early on that you might not accept Aba, but I hoped that you would see that there is more to life than drinking and carrying on at court."

"Don't fret, Mother," says Silverdun, smiling. "I can assure you that I'm perfectly happy."

"And the fact that you are, or think you are, is the saddest thing of all. You were such a bright boy, Perrin. So sweet and so innocent. So *good*. How did I lose you? What did I do wrong?" She is openly crying now. Silverdun has never wanted to leave a room more.

"You didn't do anything. I'm prodigal by nature. If I was more decent as a child it was only from the nearness of you."

"There's still time for you," she says. "There's still time for you to decide what kind of man you want to be. You're very young yet."

"I'm old enough to be married," he says, a bit petulantly.

"Don't do it, Perrin. Don't marry that woman."

Silverdun is annoyed now. "You don't even know her," he says.

Mother laughs bitterly. "You don't think so? You don't think that I knew a hundred women just like her when I was at court myself? You think me naive, Perrin, but I can assure you that I've seen everything you have and more."

"I'm going to marry her, Mother. It's the smart choice."

"No," she says. "It's the easy choice. There's a difference."

"I shouldn't have come," he says.

"I'm sorry," she says, sitting up straight, wiping her eyes. "I'm so sorry, Perrin. I didn't want it to be like this. I'm just an old widow, sorting through my regrets and praying for forgiveness here in my tiny room."

"Will you come to the wedding?"

Mother sighs. "There isn't going to be any wedding, Perrin. You don't get that?"

"What's that supposed to mean?"

"Talk to your uncle," says Mother. "And you think *me* naive."

"Well, this is all very mysterious," says Silverdun. "I'm going to go wait in the house—you know, where the family is supposed to live—and straighten this all out."

"I'm sorry, Perrin," she says.

"For what?"

She only smiles sadly and waits for him to go.

He finds Bresun waiting in his father's study, which Bresun clearly now thinks of as his own, from the framed Nyelcu degree to the hideous stuffed boar's head mounted on the wall.

"We have a problem," says Bresun.

"What's that?" asked Silverdun.

"I was under the impression that you had no intention of ever marrying, Perrin. 'A bachelor unto death,' isn't that what you told me?"

"Things change," says Silverdun. "It seems the thing to do."

"I'm afraid I can't allow it," says Bresun.

"I wasn't aware that you were in any position to allow or disallow me anything. I'm the lord here; you merely manage my estate."

Bresun strokes his mustache and sighs. "You are an immature fool. Did you really think that? Here all this time I was under the impression that you'd figured out what was going on here and had meekly accepted your lot in life."

"And what lot would that be?" asks Silverdun, thinking back to Mother's comment about naiveté.

"*I* am Lord Silverdun, in all but name," says Bresun. "That you carry the title is but a formality. Over the past several years I've transferred all of the leases, all of the deeds, and all of the tax documents into my name. You have nothing except what I give you.

"But if you marry, then an awkward situation is created. Your lady love will no doubt wish to take up residence here at Oarsbridge, which I cannot allow. She will want to squeeze out little baby Silverduns, which does not conform to my plans at all."

"You cannot divest me of my title," says Silverdun. "I want you out of here."

Bresun laughs. "Did you hear what I said? All of those boring documents you've signed for me over the years assigned the ownership of everything you see around you to me. Your *title* is all you have left. And whatever monies I choose to send you. Which I will continue to send, so long as you call off this wedding."

"I can petition to have the lordship nullified," says Silverdun. "Yield everything to the Crown. You'd end up with nothing."

"And you'd be a commoner, with no money, no skills, and no friends. Do you think your companions at court will so much as look your way if you do such a thing?"

Bresun leans forward at his desk, looks Silverdun in the eye. "Don't try to bluff me, brat. I will destroy you."

"This isn't over," says Silverdun.

Back in the City Emerald, Silverdun sits in his sumptuous townhouse and weighs his options. Is everything Bresun told him true? He imagines it was. Bresun is a clever, careful man.

Is he truly willing to yield his title? One look around the townhouse answers that question.

He sends a message sprite to Gleia canceling the wedding, and avoids her usual haunts, and in a few months the whole thing is all but forgotten.

Honestly? He's relieved. He never wanted to get married in the first place.

The next day dawned foggy and wet. The mountains were no longer visible. It was chilly and breezy, and the fire had gone out during the night. Everything was damp, and Silverdun was forced to conjure up witchfire because there was no dry wood. Witchfire was hot and gave off light, but food cooked on it always had a strange taste, and spending too much time in its warmth became unpleasant.

There was no good humor in camp that morning. Je Wen, who seemed unflappable, gave them all a wide berth, packing up camp on his own while the others stamped around in their boots trying to fend off the chill.

"It will grow warmer during the day," he said.

Silverdun tried to catch Sela's eye, but she studiously avoided him, making idle conversation with Ironfoot whenever he came near her. Timha said nothing at all. Only pulled on his elegant, impractical boots with a grimace and stood waiting.

The second day was slow going. In places it became necessary to climb, and neither Timha nor Sela was an expert climber. Silverdun thanked whatever gods had provided him and Ironfoot with their newfound strength. He'd never felt better. At least, not physically.

As Je Wen had promised, the day grew warm, and the fog was entirely gone by midday. They walked and climbed, falling into a rhythm that lulled Silverdun into the mirage that this was the whole world. That life was just this. Everything else seemed far, far away.

After the sun went down, they found a comfortable, dry cave to sleep in. It turned out that Ironfoot and Je Wen knew some of the same tunes, though with vastly different words. They sang anyway, Je Wen in Arami and Ironfoot in Common. The bawdy words of the Seelie versions made Je Wen laugh, and his laughter was contagious. Even Timha was persuaded to join the chorus of one that he knew as well. Silverdun had no aptitude for singing, but listened contentedly, happy to have something to take his mind off of things. When they reached Elenth tomorrow, they would be rejoining the world, and all the troubles that came along with it. The call to war would still be resounding in Corpus. The Einswrath would still be a threat.

And there was the matter of their near capture in Preyia. It was too reminiscent of what had happened in Annwn. They'd been expected; in both circumstances, someone had alerted the local constabulary of the Shadows' presence.

The singing continued into the night. He watched Sela watch Ironfoot and Je Wen, studiously avoiding his gaze. She smiled, but he could still feel an echo of their connection, and he knew that there was no mirth behind that smile. Whatever contentment he'd felt earlier in the evening had been drowned out by worry, and when Silverdun finally slept, it was against the protestations of a troubled mind.

The next morning was cold again, and the fog had become a light rain. A few minutes after they stepped out of the cave they were drenched, and all of the previous evening's bonhomie was washed away. They continued to climb.

Just when Silverdun was certain that Timha was about to give out entirely, Je Wen stopped at the top of a steep embankment. It was midday, and the light rain had given way to a flat, glaring sunlight that warmed them somewhat but didn't entirely remove the chill.

"There," said Je Wen. "Elenth."

Silverdun looked down and saw a wide valley. At the base of the mountain upon which they stood, tilled fields reached out toward a small city nestled against the hills on the other side of the valley. The valley glowed in the sunlight. In the distance Silverdun could see farmers dotting the fields, tiny wagons and horses coming in and out of Elenth. He realized that they hadn't seen anyone other than the Arami in three days.

"Civilization at last," said Silverdun. Part of him wished there were another three days still to go.

"Quiet!" snapped Je Wen. It was the first time Silverdun had ever seen him not looking placid. He had his head cocked to the side, listening intently.

"What's happening—?" started Timha.

"I said quiet!" snapped Je Wen.

Everyone stood still. Silverdun looked at Ironfoot, who shrugged.

"We must move," said Je Wen. "Quickly. We must get down from here."

"What's going on?" asked Ironfoot.

"A quake is coming," said Je Wen. "A big one."

Silverdun looked around him. They were in a narrow pass between two thick boulders on a wide, uneven ridge. Loose rocks were everywhere. The slope downward in front of them was steep and rocky. It would require them to pick their way with care.

"Come!" shouted Je Wen. He started down the slope without looking back.

For a minute it seemed as if Je Wen had been wrong. They picked their way down the mountainside with no hint of anything awry.

Then Silverdun pitched into the air as if he'd been thrown. He heard shouting. There was dust all around him. Sela screamed.

Something roared beneath him, bellowed, rattled the air. Silverdun landed hard, smashing his hip and shoulder against solid rock. The pain was numbing, vibrating through him, matching the vibration of the earth below.

Another ear-splitting bellow, and now the ground fell away beneath him only to let him crash onto it a second time.

"Silverdun!" came a voice through the roar. He felt a hand on his shoulder, saw a face. Je Wen was reaching across to him. "Jump to me!"

Silverdun looked down and saw the dirt at his feet shake and disintegrate, pouring downward into darkness. He leapt toward Je Wen and landed on a narrow ledge that swayed but didn't topple.

"Where are we?" shouted Silverdun. "We have to find the others!"

"This way!" Je Wen called back.

It was nearly impossible for Silverdun to find his footing; every time he found a place to step, it jumped away from him. Je Wen didn't seem to have this problem; he stepped where the ground was heading, not where it was.

Sela screamed again, and Silverdun lurched forward. He saw her hair before he saw the rest of her, a gold swirl in a maelstrom of dust. She was hunched beneath an overhanging boulder as rock and dirt poured down around her.

"Come with me!" shouted Je Wen. He reached for Sela and pulled her toward them. He thrust her into Silverdun's arms and pointed. "Go that way!"

Je Wen stepped forward. The ground lurched beneath his feet, and he dropped to his knees. A thick slab of a boulder slid down on top of him with an ugly thud. Sela screamed; Silverdun wanted to.

Je Wen was dead, his chest crushed.

"Run!" shouted Silverdun.

They carefully crawled past Je Wen's body onto a solid, level place. With a final crash, the ridge rumbled and then fell still. Dirt and rocks cascaded around them from higher up the peak, but the ground had stopped moving. The quake was over.

Silverdun and Sela sat down hard on solid rock, both gasping for air. Dust had settled in Sela's face and hair, and tears streamed down her cheeks. They sat that way, staring at each other, for a long moment.

"Help!" came Ironfoot's voice, cutting through the dust. "Silverdun! Sela! Je Wen!"

Silverdun was up and running, leaping across the new landscape of the ridge toward the sound of Ironfoot's voice. Dust was still thick in the air. "Slow down!" shouted Sela, but Silverdun kept running, the panic that had only just begun to settle now rising up in him again. He tried Ironfoot's trick of reaching in, found his panic and quelled it, but not by much.

"Ironfoot!" he shouted, now unsure where to go. The ridgeline here broke in two, split by a steep cleft.

"Over here!" came Ironfoot's voice, strained. "Hurry, dammit!"

Silverdun ran toward Ironfoot's voice. The dust parted, and he stopped just before falling over a ragged cliff. A thick stream of rocks and dust was spilling down over the edge. Silverdun looked down and saw Ironfoot clinging to the barest of handholds on the cliff face with four fingers, the open air beneath him. The ground was at least a hundred feet below. Ironfoot held Timha slumped in his other arm, and the leather satchel hung on his wrist.

"Get me the hell out of here!" shouted Ironfoot.

"Is Timha alive?" Silverdun asked, getting down on his stomach.

"He's breathing," said Ironfoot. "But neither of us will be if you don't get us up!"

Silverdun reached down. His fingertips went down just far enough to graze Ironfoot's handhold.

"Careful!" shouted Ironfoot.

"What now?" asked Silverdun, the panic again rising. He reached in and damped it down again; this time it was easier. In a few seconds, he was calm again.

"You could let Timha drop," said Silverdun soberly. "Better him than both of you."

"I didn't go to all this trouble to collect him only to let him go now," Ironfoot grunted. It was taking all of his Shadow strength to hold on. He put his mouth to Timha's ear. "Wake up, you son of a whore!"

Timha lifted his head and opened his eyes. "Do not move," hissed Ironfoot. "What I want you to do is—"

Timha screamed and jerked, kicking out with his feet. Ironfoot swayed out from the cliff face, digging in with his fingers. Blood began to ooze out from beneath his fingertips where the sharp edge of the handhold cut them.

"Dammit, I said don't move!"

Timha froze. He shut his eyes.

"Now listen," said Silverdun. "Timha, I want you to reach up, ever so delicately, with your left hand, and take mine. And when I say delicately, I mean as delicately as the wooing of a swordsmith's daughter."

Shaking, Timha slowly, slowly reached his arm up. Ironfoot growled in pain, his face red with exertion.

Silverdun reached out and grasped Timha's wrist, and pulled as hard as he could. He grunted and dug in—Timha was heavier than he was. For a few harrowing seconds he believed that Timha was actually going to pull him over the edge. Then Timha's arms were both up on the cliff top and Timha was scrambling up and away.

Silverdun reached down once more. Ironfoot's fingers were slipping, the blood making the handhold impossible to maintain.

"Take my hand!" shouted Silverdun.

"I don't think I can," Ironfoot whispered. "I'm almost empty, Silverdun." His free arm dangled at his side.

"Reach in and strengthen your muscles," said Silverdun. "You know how; you taught me."

"I don't have any *re* left."

"Then take mine," said Silverdun.

"How?"

"When we were at Whitemount, Jedron did it to me," said Silverdun. "It must be possible." Silverdun pushed out toward Ironfoot, not really knowing what he was doing, just pushing raw essence. Something grabbed at him, began to suck at him, just as Ilian/Jedron had. Without the cold iron bars repelling the *re*, it was slower, but just as certain.

"I can feel it," Ironfoot muttered. He lifted his free arm, wincing at the pain, and raised it, inch by inch, over his head. Silverdun grabbed him and pulled, and that was when Silverdun realized his mistake. He'd given all of his strength to Ironfoot and had none left for himself. Ironfoot was far heavier than Timha was.

"Pull!" said Ironfoot, his eyes wide.

"I'm working on that," said Silverdun. "Just a moment."

"Silverdun, you bastard!" shouted Ironfoot. His hold began to slip.

Silverdun felt something moving over him. A hand reached down and clasped over his. Sela's hand.

"Together now," she said.

A minute later, the four of them—Silverdun, Ironfoot, Sela, and Timha—lay on their backs on the flattest part of the ridge they could find, all breathing heavily.

"Where's Je Wen?" asked Ironfoot.

Silverdun allowed his silence to answer the question.

"He had a pregnant wife," said Ironfoot.

"That he did."

Ironfoot let out his breath and closed his eyes. Blood dripped from his fingertips onto the dusty rock.

chapter twenty-nine

You can't change what is, but you can always make it look like something it isn't.

—Master Jedron

Just before sunset they shuffled off of the lowest hill into a row of wheat. They were bloodied, covered and caked with dust, their clothes torn.

They headed toward a farmhouse at the end of the field, next to a stout green barn. A few cows raised their heads to watch them approach.

A farmer was out in the yard behind the house, throwing out grain to the chickens. He looked up at them and froze.

"What now?" said Ironfoot.

"I'll handle him," said Sela, stepping forward.

The farmer stood and watched them approach.

"What can I do for you?" he said. Silverdun couldn't imagine what he must be thinking. Three bloody, disheveled men and a beautiful woman, all covered in dust, appearing in his barnyard.

"We were out for a walk in the mountains," said Sela, her eyes all apology. "It was foolish, I know. One of those impetuous ideas a girl has from time to time. We were caught in the quake."

"Yes, we felt it down here, for sure."

"We'd be extremely appreciative if you'd avail us of your pump, and perhaps some fresh clothing," said Silverdun. "We'd be happy to pay you."

"Out for a walk?" said the farmer, contemptuously. "I know what you were doing up there. I've seen it before."

Silverdun looked at him, confused. He started to kneel down as if to tie his bootlace, going for the dagger in his boot.

"You think you boys are the first three that ever tried to escape a draft?"

"What draft?" said Sela. She gave the farmer an odd look, and the man's expression grew thoughtful.

"You don't know about the draft," he said.

"Of course not," said Sela. "We've been out all day."

"It's all over the city," said the farmer. "A flier came in yesterday from the City of Mab. All able-bodied men in the city are being called up."

"What?" said Silverdun, his voice sharp.

"There's going to be war," said the farmer.

Silverdun looked at Ironfoot, and they shared a look of despair.

"If that's the case," said Silverdun. "Then we need to get back to the city immediately. As I said, I'm happy to pay for some clean clothes." He reached into the pocket of his waistcoat for a few silver coins.

"Keep your money," said the farmer. "You boys are going off to fight the Seelie. A few pairs of trousers is the least I can do."

He looked sadly at Sela. "You might fit in some of my wife's old things. She was a bit bigger than you, but with a little bit of tucking and tying, I imagine it'll do until you get home."

"Thank you," said Sela. She gave him the same odd look as before, and he actually smiled.

"It's my pleasure," he said. "We're all in this together, after all."

The farmer took them into the house and handed out towels and fresh clothes. They took turns at the pump next to the barn, washing the dust from themselves, but regardless of how long he dunked his head under the pump, the grit never left Silverdun's hair.

The farmer's clothes were a bit tight, and far from fashionable, but Silverdun didn't care. The news of the draft had sent a chill down Silverdun's spine, and every part of him wanted to race away from the farm, but the last thing they needed was to make the farmer suspicious.

Eventually they were as clean as they were going to get, and all dressed. The farmer—whose name, they discovered, was Tiro—gave them cold chicken to eat. Silverdun wasn't hungry until the plate was set in front of him, but as soon as he took the first bite, he found he was ravenous.

It was night when they finally bade Tiro good-bye.

"Are you sure I can't drive you back to town in my cart?" he asked. "It's two miles to the gate from here."

"No," said Sela, taking his hand in hers. "You've done too much already."

"Whatever suits you," said Tiro.

"Thank you so much," said Sela.

Timha, who had said little up to this point, offered, "You are a great friend in Mab."

"We all do what we can in her service," said Tiro.

Tiro looked at Silverdun, very serious, and motioned him aside. "Let me give you some advice, son," he said. "I know a little of the ways of the world, and if you've got any sense, you'll marry that young lady before you go off to fighting." He nodded toward Sela.

Silverdun thought of correcting Tiro, but stopped himself. "That's wise advice," he said.

They took the road to the city, but veered away before they reached Elenth proper. Instead, they headed up a side road up the far slope of the valley, to the south of the city, to a villa where the Arcadian priest Virum was waiting for them. Virum would provide them with mounts and escort them to a closely guarded secret spot along the border where they would be able to cross unobserved.

The villa was dark when they arrived. Odd, since the evening wasn't that far gone, but not worrisome; they were three days late, after all.

The villa was a great pile of moss-covered stone set amid a stand of willow trees. An old rope swing hung from a willow branch in the wide, walled-in front garden. In the stable next to the house, horses quietly whickered at their approach.

Silverdun led the way through the gate and up to the house. He knocked. Receiving no answer, he knocked again, louder.

"What do we do?" asked Sela.

"Perhaps Virum doesn't want to take any chance of being seen with us that he doesn't have to."

Silverdun tried the door and found it unlocked. They went inside. There was no one to be seen.

The house was elegantly decorated; thick damask curtains hung over the windows, and the furniture was plush and well crafted. Timha spied a soft divan in a parlor off the entryway and slouched toward it. Silverdun raised a bit of blue witchlight, looking for a lamp.

"Hello, Journeyer Timha," came an oily voice from the parlor. "So lovely to see you again." A tall, thin figure dressed entirely in black stepped out of the shadows and swiped at Timha's throat. Blood spattered purple in the witchlight, and Timha fell to the floor, gasping.

The slim figure stepped into Silverdun's light. It was Bel Zheret. Another appeared on the stairwell, and another materialized out of the darkness of the hallway. Each of them held a long, serrated knife.

"You are the Shadows, yes?" said the one in the parlor. His knife was smeared with Timha's blood. Before Silverdun could react, he said, "Hold a moment, won't you? We have no wish for further violence."

Silverdun stopped, knife in hand. No one moved. From everything Paet had told them about the Bel Zheret, a fight in close quarters could well be suicide.

"What do you want?" said Silverdun. "Other than murdering poor Timha."

"I am called Asp," said the Bel Zheret in the parlor. "My colleague on the stairs is Dog, and in the hallway is my dear old friend, my boon companion, Cat."

"Lovely meeting you," said Silverdun. "Again, what do you want?"

"We Bel Zheret take our promises very seriously," said Asp. "It's in our nature, you see. We were lovingly crafted by Mab to be loyal, honest, and most of all, reliable. I made a promise that I would kill Timha if he failed his queen, and I am unable—constitutionally unable, mind you—to ignore that oath. Surely you can understand."

"Of course," said Silverdun. "A promise is a promise, after all."

"Now," said Asp. "As I'm sure my old acquaintance Paet has informed you, you Shadows are woefully inadequate to the task of defeating us in combat. He probably told you to flee us on sight, as he did us, back in Annwn."

"Tell me," said Cat. "Does he still walk with a cane?"

Silverdun felt an odd sensation. He turned to face Sela and saw her glancing at him. She was pressing against him with her Empathy. He dropped his guard and let her in, much as it pained him to do so. He allowed her access to him, and immediately regretted it. The remorse and sense of loss was palpable; it washed over him, draining what little hope he had of escaping this confrontation alive.

"He does, in fact," said Silverdun. "It's a jaunty thing, too. Head in the shape of a duck."

He felt a thought forming in his mind. *I can stop them.* It was less a statement than a collection of emotions: aggression, confidence, concentration. But the intent was clear. Then came worry, concern. *You and Ironfoot must be out of the way.* She looked down at the band around her arm. Frustration, impotence. *Make this go away.*

And fear: *Run.*

"Well, here's a proposition for you," said Asp. "We've been here waiting for you for a few days, and it's given us a chance to talk and think about things, reminisce over old acquaintances.

"It also gave us time to nibble on that priest Virum. And my, was he tasty."

Both Paet and Sela had been cagey about exactly what purpose Sela's armband served. It was a restraining band—that much was obvious. They were generally used to bind prisoners with Gifts, to render them reitically harmless. Sela was already a powerful Empath. What would happen if she removed the band? He wasn't sure he wanted to find out, and he certainly didn't want to be connected to her when it happened.

"So we decided on a fun compromise," Asp continued. "You came all this way for poor Timha, and you didn't get him, so I don't see that letting you go could do much harm. So we'll just take *one* of you, and let the other two go free. On the assumption that if we were to fight, there's some chance that you might kill at least *one* of us. I think that's a very good bargain."

Silverdun glanced quickly over at Ironfoot, who nodded. He was connected with Sela as well.

Asp frowned. "Please tell me you're not planning some kind of secretive maneuver," he said. "It's just going to get you all killed."

"Fine," said Silverdun. "You can have the woman."

"What?" said Sela, looking at him in horror. Had he misunderstood her? Or was she simply playing the part? Her connection to him vanished before he could sense the answer.

"Oh," said Asp. "Well, that's lovely! I honestly didn't think you were going to agree. All that Fae propriety and so forth."

"We Shadows have no use for propriety," said Ironfoot. "They leached it out of us, just as your masters did to you."

"Not quite," said Asp. "We never had any to begin with."

"So, we give you the woman, and you let us leave?" said Silverdun.

"Why, I suppose so!" said Asp, seemingly delighted.

"Then come along, Ironfoot," said Silverdun.

"But the next time we see each other," said Asp. "I wouldn't expect any such bargain."

"Understood," said Silverdun. He and Ironfoot backed slowly toward the door. Sela looked at him, forlorn, empty.

At the doorway, Silverdun stopped and said, "I'm so sorry, Sela." He stepped toward the door, raised his hand as if to bind the witchlight in the room to keep it lit, but instead channeled Elements, and dissolved the silver lining around the iron band on Sela's arm. He heard it clatter to the floor, heard Sela shriek.

The world exploded with light. Not actual light, like the witchlight that Silverdun had conjured in Preyia. Something else: an illumination of reality that separated and defined everything in Silverdun's vision: each blade of grass, each willow, each stone on the garden path. He and Ironfoot ran, and when he looked at Ironfoot, he saw a being of light, a superimposition of bone and blood and flesh and something else, a column of white entangled in a web of blackness. That web, he knew, was in him as well. It was what made him a Shadow, he realized with total certainty. The pit that Jedron had thrown them in, the pool of blackness. It was in them and around them and it had somehow become them.

A sound came from the house that Silverdun had never heard before. A howl—no, a *pair* of howls—rising shrilly into the night sky, a sound of infinite pain, infinite horror.

Reality shifted back to its normal state. The front door to the house slammed open, and one of the Bel Zheret, Asp, lurched out of the front door, lunging at Ironfoot.

"Monsters!" he screamed, tackling Ironfoot. The two of them went down in a tangle. "She killed them! She took them! You are all monsters!"

The Bel Zheret was stronger by far than Ironfoot, who was still recovering from his close call with Timha on the ledge. All for nothing, Silverdun realized. He ran and kicked Asp in the stomach as hard as he could.

Which, it turned out, was harder than he imagined. The Shadow strength flowed through him. The Bel Zheret flew off of Ironfoot and slammed into a nearby willow trunk, his knife clattering from his hand. Silverdun pursued him.

With astonishing speed, Asp righted himself and met Silverdun's approach. He grasped Silverdun by the throat and hammered him with his fist, in the solar plexus, driving Silverdun's breath out of his chest and knocking him backward. The force of the impact twisted Silverdun's neck in Asp's iron grip, and it felt as though his throat was about to split open with the strain.

He hit back, his dagger still in hand, slashing across the Bel Zheret's belly, drawing blood that came out black in the dim moonlight. Asp barely seemed to notice. He shoved Silverdun to the ground and stomped on Silverdun's ribs. Silverdun tried to catch his breath, and couldn't. Spots appeared and wavered in his eyes. He felt Asp snap his wrist, prying the dagger out of it. Felt teeth on his throat. Felt the percussive damage of fists on his face, in his groin. He swam toward consciousness but felt himself slipping deeper and deeper into the darkness.

He looked up and saw Ironfoot standing over Asp, holding Asp's own knife, reaching it around to slit the Bel Zheret's throat, just as Jedron had taught them: the certain kill.

But it was too late. Asp already had Silverdun's knife and was digging it upward through Silverdun's belly, twisting it, angling it, plunging it into his heart.

Ironfoot slit the Bel Zheret's throat, and it fell over Silverdun.

"Silverdun!" Ironfoot shouted. He yanked the Bel Zheret's body off of Silverdun and hurled it at a tree. It was dead, its eyes blank, its black blood running out onto the lawn.

Ironfoot looked back at Silverdun. He wasn't moving. His eyes were closed. There was no breath.

Silverdun was dead.

Ironfoot heard sobs coming from the door of the villa. Sela!

He ran into the house and saw Sela, alone, on the floor of the entryway, weeping. The other two Bel Zheret were nowhere to be seen. Sela was holding the iron band up on her arm; he could see that the bare iron was burning her skin, and that it was a severe effort for her to hold it on.

Ironfoot was no Master of Elements by any stretch of the imagination, but he could manage a simple shaping.

"Give me the band," he said. "I can resilver it."

"No!" she shrieked. "You can't remove it. Can't! Can't! Not ever again!"

"Okay, okay," said Ironfoot. She was hysterical, her eyes crazy and wandering.

Ironfoot held up the Bel Zheret's long knife; its blade was of hardened silver. He touched the knife's edge to the iron band. The band repelled it with a force like magnetism. He had to push the blade onto the band. It dug into Sela's arm and she shrieked, pulling away.

"Hold still, dammit!" he shouted.

"It hurts!"

"I know it hurts; if you'll hold still, I can stop it."

He channeled Elements into the silver of the dagger and pushed hard against it, flowing it off the blade and onto the iron band. He'd never worked with iron, and realized that he didn't know the binding that compelled it to bond with the silver coating. He channeled Insight into the binding on the knife and saw that it was not particularly complicated. So he simply copied the binding from the dagger and placed something similar on the band, wrapping it around the silver coating. The binding took hold, thankfully, and the silver coating stuck onto the band. It was by no means pretty, but it worked. He tossed the dagger aside, and Sela collapsed in his arms.

"Sela, what did you do to them?" he asked, bewildered.

"I showed them things as they truly are," she answered, her voice thick. "It's okay. They're not real." She closed her eyes and slumped against him.

Ironfoot had never felt so alone in all his life.

Ironfoot didn't sleep that night; he sat watching Sela sleep, wondering whether more Bel Zheret were on their way. He was too tired to care.

When Sela awoke it was morning. Ironfoot told her about Silverdun, and she broke down all over again. She knelt next to his body, weeping, which was exactly what Ironfoot felt like doing.

"We have to go," he told her after a while.

"I know," she said, gathering herself. "We have to bury Silverdun first, though."

"No," said Ironfoot. "We're taking him with us."

"I don't think that's a good idea," she said. "He's dead; he doesn't care where he's buried."

"That's not it," said Ironfoot. "Paet insisted that if one of us died, we were to return the body. If the Unseelie find him"—he nodded toward the dead Bel Zheret—"they can use the Black Art to find out everything he knows."

"Oh," said Sela.

She stood. "I'm going to look inside the villa for some proper clothes," she said. "Clearly a lady lives here, or lived here." She disappeared into the house.

Ironfoot looked down at Silverdun. "Sorry, friend," he said.

They wrapped Silverdun's body in a rug. Ironfoot fed and bridled the two strongest-looking horses in the stable, and tied Silverdun to the back of the saddle. He placed an inexpert glamour on the awkward bundle to make it look like a saddle roll, but it would only pass the most cursory of inspections.

They found hard bread in the pantry of the villa and ate a sullen breakfast. On the way out of the house, Ironfoot stopped and looked down at Timha's corpse, at his dead eyes staring blankly.

"Some help you were," he said. He patted the leather satchel that he still wore. "But at least I got your plans, you bastard."

Something glinted in a corner. It was one of the Bel Zheret's long serrated knives. Its owner wouldn't miss it, so Ironfoot took it and put it in his belt.

They mounted without speaking and rode away, to the south, toward the Seelie Lands.

Elenth was one of only three Unseelie cities on the ground. There were few places in Mab's territory that would support permanent structures, and even those in Elenth were squat and sturdily built against the quakes in the nearby mountains. To the south of the city they rode up the side of the valley and found themselves in a thick forest.

"If we keep heading this direction, we'll hit the border tomorrow evening," Ironfoot said. "Of course, I have no idea what we'll run into along the way, since that was Virum's job."

Sela said nothing, only nodded glumly. She would be worse than useless if there was more fighting.

The wood stretched on for miles and miles, relatively flat and not particularly thick. The going wasn't easy, but they were able to maintain a steady walk throughout.

Near the end of the first day, Ironfoot looked ahead and saw a break in the trees ahead. A road? Something was moving past, something huge. He waved for Sela to stop her horse and listened. A regular rhythm. Soldiers on the march.

Ironfoot dismounted and waved for Sela to remain where she was. She didn't respond. He looped his reins over a nearby branch and crept toward the road, using all the skills of silence that Jedron had taught him, which were enhanced by his changed body. He reached the edge of the road and crouched carefully, watching.

Company upon company of soldiers, grizzled veterans and fresh recruits alike, were moving toward the southwest. Toward Wamarnest, the city closest to the Seelie border, where cavalry had been drilling for months.

War was coming, and soon.

But there was a more immediate problem. The few border crossings would now be more closely guarded than ever. The Border Wall stretched across most of the length of the border; it had been created during a long-ago treaty, and maintained by both sides ever since. It was composed of interlocking bindings, one Seelie, one Unseelie, and was impossible to cross from either side. Presumably Virum had known of a secret crossing, one of the spots where the resonance from Shifting Places of the nearby Contested Lands created soft spots in the Border Wall. These were all guarded, but from time to time new ones cropped up. The problem was that Ironfoot had no idea where Virum's soft spot was located.

Once the column of soldiers had passed, he returned to Sela and they continued, hurrying across the road and back into the forest. That night they camped without a fire, eating berries and nuts and the last of the stale bread they'd taken from the villa.

The next morning they continued their ride. They must have made good time, because the sun was still well above the western horizon when they ran into the Border Wall. Ironfoot dismounted and examined it. It was merely a low stone wall, nothing particularly imposing, though runes were scattered across its surface. He put his hand out to reach across, and met with resistance. He pushed his hand farther and the resistance grew stronger. A little farther and the resistance became physically painful. He quickly withdrew. There would be no crossing here.

They followed the Border Wall to the southwest, where hopefully he could find a border crossing that wasn't too crowded. He had no idea what he'd do when he found one, but there wasn't much of a choice. Every step they took to the southwest, though, took them closer to the remains of Selafae, and Sylvan beyond.

Near sunset, they came upon a group of soldiers stationed along a length of the wall. Not particularly attentive soldiers, since they had yet to notice the two riders approaching them, and not a true crossing, simply a soft place. That was a lucky break. Ironfoot counted ten soldiers, however, and that was less lucky.

Nothing to do but try to talk their way through.

"Sela," he said in a low voice. "I need your Empathy here. We're going to have to talk our way through these men."

"I don't know," said Sela. "It hurts so badly." She clutched her arm, where red welts from the touch of the uncovered band had burned her skin.

"You're going to have to try, dammit!" said Ironfoot. "You're a Shadow, Sela. You have a job to do."

"I know."

"Then wake up and do what needs to be done."

She looked at him, angrily at first; then her expression hardened. "You're right," she said. "I will be what I was made to be."

Ironfoot wasn't sure what she meant by that, but if it brought her back to her senses, he was glad. They rode toward the soldiers.

"Who goes there!" one of them shouted.

"We have orders to cross the border," said Ironfoot. "A mission from the City of Mab itself."

"Dismount," said the foremost soldier, who was a lieutenant, and a young one.

"I don't have time, Lieutenant. Now get out of my way or I'll move you."

The officer stood his ground. "No one crosses the border," he said. "I have my own orders, and I don't care what yours are."

Ironfoot looked at Sela, who was concentrating on the lieutenant. "Who are you?" he said, looking at her.

"We're on a critical mission," she said, her voice clear and distinct. "Surely you understand that." Ironfoot could see the tension in her gaze. The struggle.

"I don't know," said the lieutenant, faltering.

Another of the soldiers approached. "You heard the lieutenant," he said. "Dismount now, or we'll dismount you."

Just Ironfoot's luck; the officer didn't have his men at all well in hand. In Ironfoot's army days he'd had a few such commanders. Smart infantrymen knew how to manipulate them to keep themselves from getting killed. Apparently the soldier now eyeing Ironfoot was one of these.

"We can't do that," said Sela. She was trying, but she'd been through too much in too brief a time, and these were strong-willed, suspicious men.

"All right," said Ironfoot. He dismounted and, with deep regret, drew the Bel Zheret's knife.

It was amazing, even to Ironfoot, how quickly he managed to kill them all. He whirled and struck, all of his anger and frustration flowing into his actions. All philosophy and higher thought evaporated. There was only motion and balance and cut. Blood and bone. Shriek and hiss.

There were ten of them, and the last barely had time to draw his sword before Ironfoot pierced his neck with the point of the Bel Zheret blade. If Ironfoot hadn't been a complete Shadow before, he was now.

He remounted, slowly, after wiping the Bel Zheret knife on the uniform of one of the fallen soldiers. They circled back and then took the wall at a run, the horses' hooves clearing it easily.

They must have spoken at some point during the long night ride to the Sylvan road, but Ironfoot couldn't remember saying anything. They stumbled on the road out of the forest at the break of dawn, and in less than two hours they were at Sylvan, having passed column after column of Seelie soldiers heading north.

When they returned to the City Emerald, in a fast carriage loaned by the Seelie Army, Paet was waiting for them at Blackstone House. He received the report of their mission—of the flight from Preyia, the Arami, the deaths of Timha and Silverdun—in silence, asking no questions. When Ironfoot was done speaking, Paet thanked him in a quiet voice.

"When will Silverdun's body be delivered to his family?" said Ironfoot.

"It won't. There will be no funeral."

"Excuse me?" said Sela. It was the first thing she'd said since they'd arrived.

"Shadows don't get funerals," said Paet. "We're never so lucky."

Ironfoot fumed, but Paet wasn't someone who could be argued with.

"I'll be gone for several days," said Paet, standing. "I expect you both to spend that time recovering. When I get back, there will be much to do."

"Paet," said Ironfoot. "They knew we were coming. At every step along the way."

"I know," said Paet. "And I have no idea who's responsible."

"I want to get back to work," said Sela. "Now. I don't want to rest."

"I agree," said Ironfoot.

"Some things cannot wait," said Paet. "And some can. If you insist on working, Ironfoot, go over Timha's notes with a fine-toothed comb. The Unseelie couldn't figure them out, but perhaps you can."

"In time for them to be useful?" said Ironfoot.

"You never know when something will be useful," said Paet.

"I'd like to go through intelligence reports," said Sela. "From everywhere. Look for anything that might tell us who our traitor is. There are some leads I discovered before we left for the Unseelie."

"Any ideas?" asked Paet.

"I'll let you know," she said.

Paet left soon after, leaving Sela and Ironfoot alone in the Shadows' Den. Ironfoot took Timha's notes and plans and books and spread them out in the mission room. The Unseelie had some very bright minds, but Ironfoot had one thing they didn't have. He had the map of Selafae.

He pored over these things for hours, carefully juxtaposing the plans for the Einswrath. Just as he had on his return to Queensbridge from Selafae, he became lost in his work, the rising sense of fear growing with every hour.

But Ironfoot's relationship to fear had changed in the intervening months. Fear was a driving force now, and it was something he could control. Whenever it got to be too much, he simply reached in and damped it down.

From time to time, Sela poked her head out of the den to see how he was doing, or to go collect another stack of briefs and dispatches from the analysts upstairs. Neither of them took a break, even for a moment. To stop would be to think about what had happened, and neither of them had any interest in that.

The two patterns from Ironfoot's dream upon the Arami net reappeared on paper in front of him, and he saw what these patterns had been all along. Not too surprisingly, one was the map, which he'd stared at so many times that he had the thing damn near memorized. The other was the overview from Timha's plans, which he'd examined just minutes before falling out of the sky in the burning yacht. The two were clearly connected, but something was very, very wrong.

It was morning before he realized what it was. He'd gone over everything a dozen times before he spotted it.

"Sela," he said, coming into the Shadows' Den and falling into his desk chair. "I believe I've worked it out." He was smiling.

Sela had dozed off at her own desk, and now looked up.

"What? What have you worked out?"

"I've discovered exactly why the Unseelie thaumaturges were unable to construct an Einswrath weapon from the plans that Timha gave us."

"Really?" said Sela.

"Yes," said Ironfoot. His smile widened. "Because they're fake."

"What?"

"Oh, it's a very clever hoax, but that's all it is. Whoever dreamed it up, presumably the estimable Hy Pezho himself, spent a great deal of time composing plans for a massive feat of thaumaturgy that is brilliantly, extravagantly, and quite subtly, a total fraud."

"What are you saying?" said Sela.

"There's no way these are the plans for the Einswrath," said Ironfoot, standing. He stood and kicked his chair violently, where it struck the wall with a loud crash and shattered.

"You get it?" said Ironfoot, laughing. "They're totally worthless! It was all for nothing! Silverdun died for nothing!"

Ironfoot continued to laugh, and at some point his laughter turned into tears. He sat down on the floor, crying. After a moment, Sela came and sat beside him, and they wept together.

chapter thirty

An Easterner calls a lightsmith to his home to charge the witchlamps. "What color would you like them?" asks the lightsmith.

"Oh, it don't make a lick o' difference," says the Easterner. "I'm blind, you see."

"Then why do you need your lamps charged?" asks the lightsmith.

"Well, I hates to admit it," says the Easterner, "but I'm afraid o' the dark."

—Seelie joke

Black.

But not black. Black implied sight, seeing nothing. This was the lack of sight, lack of the *knowledge* of sight.

Things had been going well. Very well. He'd been as close as one could get to the fulfillment of his every dream. Everything had fallen into place just as he'd planned. And then at the moment of his ultimate victory, his triumphant revenge, like a beard-flicking villain in a mestina he was defeated utterly. The *fel-ala*, his own personal wraith of vengeance, had turned on him and devoured him, at the moment it ought to have devoured his nemesis. Yes, *nemesis*. After what he'd gone through as a result, he had a right to absolutes. He had a right to thoughts of revenge that passed understanding, that left logic and justice and morality far, far behind.

Where the *fel-ala*'s tentacles had touched him, there was pain. A deep burning sensation that went beyond the skin and traveled through channels up his arms and legs, through his spine and into his brain. A fierce, unbearable sting, infinite, breathtaking, unfathomable. Then the wraith enveloped him and swallowed him whole. Inside the creature was darkness, a darkness he'd thought complete.

He'd known nothing about darkness then.

Inside the beast was the pain of dissolution. The knowledge that he was being devoured. Eaten alive. The thing had something like teeth, but they were hooked; they dug into the flesh and tore, slurping away skin and blood. They reached around bone and snapped and sucked. Time slowed for him, a reitic property of the *fel-ala* that he himself had designed. The purpose of this was so that each cut could be experienced fully, individually. His consciousness was forced into the depths of the pain, each slice, each bite, one after another after another.

This was the pain he'd devised for *her*. The nemesis. Using only himself as a measure, he'd constructed the most nightmarish end he himself could imagine. And now it was his to experience.

As he twisted and thrashed in the belly of the *fel-ala*, it occurred to him that the pain was only the prologue. Only the appetizer to the true meal. Knowing it was coming made it all much, much worse.

If he ever escaped from this—and he wouldn't, he knew—he'd have to remember that knowing made it worse. A bit of useless knowledge to ponder forever.

Because that was the meal; that was the meat. After the pain, came the eternity. Even as he thought it, he felt the pain begin to recede, not because the *fel-ala* had finished with him, but because there was less and less of him to sense it. His body had been consumed almost thoroughly. His eyes had been ripped from their sockets, his manhood shredded, his entrails drawn from him, tied in knots with nimble hooks and yanked piecemeal from within. He'd felt internal organs puncture, rupture. By the time his lungs collapsed and he stopped breathing, it was almost a relief. The death of the body was imminent.

There was the rising panic and wholly other pain of suffocation. His chest, what was left of it, bucked and heaved. He would not have guessed that he'd have the energy for that by now. The pressure grew in his chest and head. The pressure soon pushed out all of the other pain. He felt his heart stop with a sickening, straining leap. Then it all faded away. The sound of flesh tearing and his own gurgling (and from somewhere, tinkling laughter). The visceral, seething agony. The smell and taste of the *fel-ala's* digestive liquids and his own blood mingled. And last, the blackness that was not yet complete. The blackness that was a painting of night compared to night itself.

True darkness. Infinite darkness, eternal. It embraced him. A silence beyond silence.

If he'd had a body he would have shuddered. The lack of sensation of any kind enveloped his mind, and at first he was relieved; the pain was over, finally over. For a time he was calm. Had he any lungs he would have breathed deeply, sighed.

Then he noticed the darkness. The *lack*, the total lack of light, of sound. The lack of being. Nothing with which to reach out, nothing with which to see or hear. Nothing.

For a time there was only the darkness and the horror of the darkness.

Then the itching started.

In his quest for power he had seen enough horror—caused it, experienced it—that he had lost the ability to go insane. It was a requirement of the Black Art, one of the first things his father had taught him. And if he was unable to lose his mind, then his nemesis was doubly so. She had been committing atrocities when the gods themselves were young. This was only an expression applied to anyone else, but with her it might have been a reality.

It was cliché, he knew, to think that it was thoughts of revenge that sustained him. He'd been avenging his father's death for as long as he could remember. But now it was his own death that demanded satisfaction, his own torment. This was new.

No, he would never lose his mind. And in that knowledge there was a slim hope. The slimmest. Even though he'd been certain of his victory, some paranoid part of him had compelled him to devise an insurance policy. Even if it never did him any good, the thought of those idiots bumbling around trying to follow in his footsteps, using useless plans for his masterpiece, gave him a touch of satisfaction. And a touch of hope.

They would never guess. How could they? Only Hy Pezho could be so audacious. Never in the wildest dreams of any of Mab's great thaumaturges would Hy Pezho's solution occur.

That was what put him above all others: He dared what no other would.

Thoughts of revenge sustained him for a very, very long time.

In an instant, nothing then something. Everything. Pain, blood, sound. Harsh smell, rank spellcraft odor. Darkness, but only the mundane kind. Only a lack of light. If he had eyes, they'd be blinded by the brilliance of this blackness.

But he did have eyes. They rolled in their sockets.

His chest hurt. A chest! Why? Something familiar digging at him.

Breathe. In. Out. Yes.

Fingers, legs, arms, a neck. Movement, restricted. Restrained? Injured? Where was he?

Sounds, musical. Lilting familiarly. Tinkling. Tinkling laughter. Laughter.

Mab. Queen. Lover. Empress.

Nemesis.

Her voice. The sounds were her voice, and in the voice were words. Words to hear with ears.

"Awake, Hy Pezho," she said. He thought that was what she said. "Awake now and serve your empress as you once feigned to."

He was tied to a table. Helpless.

A shiver, joyfully afraid.

He pissed himself.

Bliss.

Hy Pezho sat up, testing his new body. It felt different from his old one. Leaner, stronger. He was in a small room, a thaumaturge's workshop. Mab's workshop. What horrors had been wrought here in this very room?

Mab was smiling at him. She wore no glamour, and the sight of her true face chilled even him.

"Clever," she said. "You're a clever, clever boy, Hy Pezho."

"That's what made us such good friends," he said, trying his voice. His speech was slurred a bit, but only because he hadn't attempted it in so long.

"I should have known that the great Hy Pezho would have found a way to cheat death," she said.

"So your coterie of thaumaturges have admitted that they can't duplicate my masterpiece?" He chuckled. "Even with the carefully crafted blueprints I left them? Or are they still plugging away at it?"

"I've killed them all," she said.

"Ah."

"And this new body of yours, Hy Pezho, has been built with some protections, so I pray I will not have to kill you as well. Kill you in the true death."

"I live to serve," said Hy Pezho. And with horror, he realized that he meant it. He wanted nothing more than to serve her. Would die to serve her.

"What have you done to me?" he said.

"You've been given a great, great honor," she said. "I've brought you back not in a frail Fae body, but in the body of my most loyal and faithful and mighty servants."

Hy Pezho looked down at his arms. Long, thin, strong. No.

No.

"You're Bel Zheret now, Hy Pezho," said Mab, her tinkling laughter falling on him like sparks. "Congratulations on your promotion."

She leaned over him and took his face in her hands.

"Now let's get started building some more of those Einswraths, shall we?"

"Einswrath?" he said, fighting the urge to comply with her every whim.

"That's what they've dubbed your masterpiece," she said. "A lovely name, if a bit religious for my tastes."

Hy Pezho laughed out loud. "And so much more appropriate than you can possibly know."

"Do tell."

Desiring nothing more than to please her, nemesis no longer, Hy Pezho explained exactly how the Einswrath worked. He wasn't sure, but he thought that she—Mab, who had seen everything—grew pale as he spoke.

"You're a madman," she said.

"I am bold," he said. "There is a difference."

Part Three

Each city in Faerie has its own variation on the Procession of the Magi during the solstice festival, but my favorite is in the small city of Hawthorne-by-the-Sea. Rather than the solemn function seen most places, the procession in Hawthorne is a bawdy, ribald affair, replete with laughter and inebriation, in which the townspeople dressed as the magi are insulted and openly mocked by the citizenry as they make their way around the square.

The first in line is a "general," representing Leadership. This is a plum assignment and is given to the fattest man in Hawthorne. He barks orders that no one heeds, and does his best to run the parade into walls and blind alleys.

Next comes a "Master of the Gates," representing Folding. He complains that walking does not suit him, for he can fold where he wishes.

A "Master Toucher" follows, representing Awareness, riding a touched donkey, which is in reality two boys in a costume. The donkey wanders back and forth, ignoring the Master Toucher's commands, and insulting him in the foulest language imaginable.

Each magus comes in turn and is ridiculed. The spell-hardener representing Binding, carrying a floppy sword made of reeds. The blind Glamourist. The bargemaster representing Motion, who bears a heavy log on his back.

A fearful, accident-prone thaumaturge for Resistance. A faux hunchback for Poise, an idiot for Insight, an always-wrong seer for Premonition, a mean-spirited brute for Empathy.

The final mage is always an Elementalist who pretends to eat horse dung, claiming that he transforms it into roast beef in his mouth. He typically gets the biggest laugh.

The last in the procession is a hooded figure who represents no Gift; the meaning of this figure is lost to the ages. Some say that he represents Death; others believe him to be an avatar of the fabled Thirteenth Gift. No one I spoke to in Hawthorne could tell me what that Gift might be. The crowd does not acknowledge his presence, and when the parade ends, he slips off into the night without revealing his identity.

—Stil-Eret, "The Unruly Eastern Provinces,"
from *Travels at Home and Abroad*

chapter thirty-one

Fate is fond of her little reversals. All the better to stab you in the back.

—Master Jedron

Silverdun awoke in his tattered bed at Whitemount, feeling unbearably hung over. He sat up, his mouth dry, his ears ringing, his stomach twisting in his belly. He leaned over and retched, but nothing came out.

On the table next to the bed were a pitcher of water and a small loaf of fresh bread. He drained the pitcher without bothering to pour it into the nearby glass and wolfed down the bread. A fresh change of clothes awaited him on the floor.

He had been plagued by dreams. Sela. Ironfoot. Preyia. Falling in flames. Bel Zheret.

He stood up long enough to dress, but then his head started to spin again, and he sat back on the bed. How had he gotten here? He couldn't remember. Everything since his last visit here was a blur, a mélange of disconnected images swirling in his mind.

The door opened and Ilian entered. No—not Ilian. Jedron.

"It's about time you woke up," he barked. "This isn't an inn, you know."

"What happened?"

"My guess is that you had one too many whiskeys last night and now you've come to learn the evils of drink firsthand."

"I don't remember how I got here. How did I get here from Elenth?"

"Elenth?" said Jedron, his brow furrowed. "What are you talking about?"

"The last thing I remember I was in the Unseelie city of Elenth. We were to meet a priest named Virum, but then the Bel Zheret appeared and . . . I don't remember the rest."

"You're talking nonsense, boy. You've been here at Whitemount for the past six weeks. And if you're done hallucinating, it's time to get back to your training."

"What?"

"Training. It's what you were sent here for, remember?"

Silverdun's mind reeled. "Are you saying . . . ?"

Jedron snickered, then laughed out loud. "You gullible fool," he said through chuckles. "I had you going there for a second, didn't I?"

"Damn you, Jedron!" shouted Silverdun. He picked up the water pitcher and flung it at his old teacher. Jedron caught it handily and threw it back at him, hitting him square in the forehead.

"Get up," he said. "You've got to get back to work."

"I don't understand," said Silverdun. "What happened to me, you old bastard?"

Jedron was already at the door. "Oh, that. You died. Come on."

Silverdun followed Jedron down the stairs of the castle. Nothing had changed since his first visit there months earlier.

"Jedron?" Silverdun shouted. "What the hell are you talking about?"

"Just shut up and follow me. I have something to show you."

Silverdun sighed and followed. His weeks at Whitemount were jogged back fully into memory by his presence here. He'd forgotten just how much he disliked this man.

"Wait," said Silverdun. A flash of images came to him, and the memory of pain, and fear. "I remember. The Bel Zheret stabbed me. I felt him pierce my heart!"

"I know," said Jedron. "I heard all about it."

They left the castle, and the sunlight hurt Silverdun's eyes. The sea around them was a deep blue, and as he looked to the east, he could just make out the spires of the City Emerald.

"You can gather wool later," said Jedron, glaring. "I have things to do." He went to the steps leading to the pit and started down them. Silverdun followed, muttering a string of obscenities under his breath.

"I can hear you," Jedron said, not turning around.

"I know," said Silverdun.

They stood together at the pit, looking down into it. It was dull gray in the sunlight, dank and deeply unpleasant. The temperature here seemed easily ten degrees colder.

Jedron said nothing at first, then sighed.

"Here's the truth," he said. "Perrin Alt, Lord Silverdun, is dead."

"I know that," said Silverdun. "I felt the knife go in."

"That's not what I mean. Silverdun died here, in this pit. On the last night of your training. Ironfoot and I hurled him in here, and what was inside the pit ate him. He is no more." Jedron reached inside his robe and withdrew a small white object.

"Here's all that's left of him. A tooth. Maybe a molar."

Silverdun took the tooth and looked at it, remembering the bone he'd found in the pit after watching Ironfoot go into it.

"The problem with your theory," said Silverdun, "is that I'm standing right next to you."

"Yes, you are. But you're not Silverdun."

"No? Then who am I?"

"A shadow. A shadow of him. You're a thing that's taken his form, taken his mind and memories. A sylph, to be precise."

"A sylph."

"Never heard of them?" said Jedron. "I'm not surprised. They're very rare, and we don't advertise their existence.

"Elusive little creatures. We get them from an island across the sea. The way they hunt is to eat animals—deer mainly—and assume their shape. Then they join the herd and kill the animal's friends and relatives at their leisure. Nasty things."

"I don't feel like eating my friends or my relatives," said Silverdun.

"Well, we alter the sylphs a bit first," said Jedron. "It's a complicated and expensive process, I can assure you. And an extremely classified one. That's why we never told you. The less any of our people knows, the better."

"In case I was captured."

"Yes."

"So I'm not who I think I am," said Silverdun.

"Who *is?*" Jedron shrugged. "People make such a fuss of identity and the concept of self. But it's only because they're mortal and afraid to die.

"Listen, you have all of Silverdun's memories, all of his feelings, all of his emotional detritus. You have all of his Gifts. You're him, more or less. More, really, since you're stronger, faster, more powerful, and you can be brought back from the dead. I'd like to see the *old* you try that."

"But . . . what about the soul?" said Silverdun.

"How the hell should I know? Have I ever given you any indication that I might be a philosopher?"

"So," said Silverdun, understanding everything Jedron had told him, but not accepting it. "Ironfoot?"

"The same."

"And Paet?"

"Yes. And I as well. And scores of others down through the centuries. I'll admit, I found it a bit troubling at first, but once I realized it didn't make a rat's shit worth of difference, I got over it. So will you."

"What about Sela?" asked Silverdun. "She was never brought here."

"No."

"Why not?"

Jedron thought about it. "We were afraid to," he said. "The man who made her what she is did a far better job than I ever could. To do to her what we did to you could have been . . . disastrous."

"What do you mean by that?"

"None of your damn business."

Jedron spat into the pit and turned away. "Let's go," he said.

"How long have you been here, Jedron?" Silverdun asked.

"Four hundred years or thereabouts. I stopped counting a long time ago. But I think I might retire soon. Get a little cottage somewhere, with some trees. I miss the trees." He stopped and stared into the distance. "Honestly, the caliber of trainee they've been sending me the past few decades has made me fear for the future of Faerie."

"Shocking."

"Who knows?" said Jedron. "Maybe I'll teach you all my secrets one day, and you can take my place." He stroked his beard. "On second thought, I'd probably pick Ironfoot over you. He's a bit brighter."

"Wait," said Silverdun. "What happened to Paet? If we're so indestructible, why isn't he still active? Why does he have a limp?"

"Bel Zheret got to him five years ago. Ripped out most of his spine, ate part of his brain. You can regenerate most things, as I believe you've noticed, but you're *not* invincible. So don't go thinking you are. If you die out there and aren't brought back, well . . . Paet didn't bring you here because I missed you. And don't even ask what I had to do in order to bring you back. To say it's a Black Art doesn't even begin to describe it."

He clapped Silverdun on the shoulder, the only mildly friendly thing Silverdun had ever seen him do. "Now let's get going. Paet's waiting down at the dock."

Silverdun looked down into the pit, thinking. "You'll never have that cottage, will you? You can't ever leave Whitemount, not with the things you know."

Jedron looked at him, serious. "No," he said. "When I get too sick of it to stand it another day, I imagine I'll walk into the ocean and drown myself. And if Paet tries to revive *me*, I'll slit his throat."

"Thank you, Jedron," said Silverdun.

Jedron punched him in the face.

Silverdun is having an excellent time at the café until he looks up and spies his mother. She is moving toward him very slowly, glaring at him the way she once did when she caught him doing things he oughtn't. He rises from the table and staggers toward her, nearly falling. He's had quite a bit to drink.

He meets her at an empty table halfway, and they sit together.

"Who's your new lady?" comes the drunkenly stupid voice of one of his friends. He waves it away.

"Mother, what in the name of Auberon's pale ass are you doing here?"

"Language, Perrin," she says primly.

Silverdun sighs. "What in the name of Auberon's pale *hindquarters* are you doing here, then?"

"I can see that I should have sent a sprite ahead of me."

"That might have been wise."

Mother places her hands gently on the table before her. "There wasn't any time. I had to see you right away."

"Oh, but you never come to the city, and it's so lovely this time of year, Mother," says Silverdun, his mind wandering. "Tomorrow night there's a mestina you simply must see, and—"

"I'm dying, Perrin. I came to say good-bye."

Silverdun stops, words colliding on his tongue.

"Whatever does that mean?"

"It means that I am dying, and I intend to do so not at our family home, but at a convent in the South."

"You. What?" Silverdun can't compose a proper question. "You aren't dying," he says stupidly.

"I can assure you that I am. Several well-paid physicians have confirmed it."

"How long—?"

"A few months, possibly. Impossible to know."

"But . . ." Silverdun doesn't quite know. But what?

"So I came to say good-bye to you, Perrin."

"No, no," says Silverdun. "You'll come stay with me. I know the queen's personal physician. She'll take care of this. We'll go to the mestina together."

Tears are beginning to insinuate themselves across Silverdun's vision. "You're going about this all wrong."

"This would be much easier if you were sober," says Mother.

Silverdun concentrates. Working Elements while drunk isn't wise, but Silverdun has no great reputation for wisdom. He hums a sobering cantrip that's come in handy more than once and is rewarded with a powerful headache for his efforts.

"Oh, hell!" he says. "I'm sober now."

He realizes now how pathetic he must look to his Arcadian mother. The wastrel Lord Silverdun at a café in the wrong part of the city, drinking with his wastrel friends. Sons and daughters of the gentry, all. One of them once joked to Silverdun that they should start a musical group and name it "The Grave Disappointments."

"I'm sorry," he says.

Mother takes a deep breath, and Silverdun can now see that it is an effort for her to do so. He cringes.

She reaches up and touches his cheek. "You have nothing to be sorry for, my sweet boy."

"This isn't who I wanted to be," he says.

"I know."

"Why aren't you angry at me?" he asks.

"You're angry at yourself enough for both of us, I think. I'm finding that I'm too grateful for what *is* to worry about what might have been."

"That does it," says Silverdun. It's as though a dam has burst in him, but he doesn't know what the dam is or what it's been holding back. "Tomorrow I'm going to call my solicitor and I'm going to take back Oarsbridge, and I'm going to give it all away to those bloody farmers once and for all."

"I don't want you to do that anymore," says Mother.

"Why not?"

"Because if you try, your uncle will have you killed. I'm certain of it."

"I'm not frightened of Bresun," says Silverdun, straightening his back.

"Whether you are or you aren't," says Mother, "he will not part with Oarsbridge. He believes he *is* Oarsbridge, and Lord Silverdun in all but name only. He'd rather die than give that up."

"And what about those poor noblemen? The villagers and the farmers?"

"I'm a dying old woman, Perrin. If I want to prefer my son over all of them, then Aba can grouse to me about it himself when I see him."

Silverdun sighs. "What do you want from me?" he asks.

"To be happy, Perrin. What else?"

The next morning, he watches her carriage drive off through the city, feeling certain that he will never see her again. He's reassured her that he will let the matter between him and Bresun drop.

As soon as the carriage has disappeared, however, Silverdun goes directly to the family solicitor's office. He knows the way well, as this is where he goes every month to draw upon his trust.

"You're a week early," says the solicitor, when Silverdun barges into his office.

"I'm here about something else entirely," says Silverdun. "I'm here to take back my lordship."

The solicitor looks at him through squinted eyes, tapping a long white quill pen against an inkwell as he considers Silverdun's words.

"I was wondering when I'd finally hear you say that," says the solicitor, smiling.

Silverdun explains his plan, and the solicitor listens patiently, asking questions, making suggestions. When Silverdun returns home, he feels alive for the first time in as long as he can remember. It is time. Time to become a man. He goes to bed thinking about his childhood, about the day when he showed his mother how far he could walk around the wall. He feels as if something important has been given back to him.

The next morning, Silverdun awakes to find a quartet of burly Royal Guardsmen standing in his bedroom.

"Perrin Alt, Lord Silverdun," says one, reading from an official document, "you are hereby detained for the crime of treason."

"Excuse me?" says Silverdun. "I'm fairly certain I've never done *that* one."

Silverdun's next meeting with his solicitor is far less friendly, and takes place in jail.

"I can't believe you'd betray me like this," says Silverdun. "You worked for my father." He eyes the solicitor across the small table with genuine fury. He can't remember the last time he felt something so white-hot.

"I did work for your father," says the solicitor. "But I work for your uncle now." As if this justifies his betrayal.

"How can I possibly be charged with treason?" says Silverdun. "Isn't that a bit excessive?"

"You signed documents in my office yesterday signaling your intent to take an estate from its rightful owner and provide it to an organization that does not respect Seelie sovereignty. That is a traitorous act."

"*I* am its rightful owner!"

"That's not relevant, legally speaking."

Silverdun fumes. "And what makes you think you're going to get a judge who'll play along with this 'organization that does not respect Seelie sovereignty' nonsense? Times have changed."

"Perhaps," says the solicitor. "But not all judges have changed along with them. And it so happens that the court official who does judicial assignments is a very good friend of your uncle's."

Silverdun is offered a choice. He can stand trial, and almost certainly be hanged, or he can plead guilty and spend the rest of his life in prison.

Silverdun is sitting in his holding cell pondering these options when he receives a note from his mother.

Perrin,

I would have come in person, but I am now too weak to travel, so this letter must suffice. I've received word from your uncle apprising me of your situation and asking me to implore you not to take your case to trial. I will so implore you, but not for him. Bresun wants to avoid the spectacle and would much prefer that you disappear quietly. I, however, simply want you to outlive me. Please respect a dying woman's last wish in this regard.

You will not believe me, but I know that Aba is not finished with you. This is a great detour, but it is not the end of the road. Know that.

You made a headstrong, stupid decision by choosing to go against your uncle as you've done. And I must say that I have never been more proud of you.

Perrin, I predict that your life is just beginning.

Love,
Mother

When Silverdun arrives by coach at the prison of Crere Sulace, a testy message sprite is waiting to inform him that his mother has died.

Silverdun's arrival is the talk of the prison for a few weeks, but his notoriety is short-lived. A few months later, Mauritane, the captain of the Royal Guard, is convicted of treason and sent to Crere Sulace as well.

For a long time, nothing happens. Then Midwinter descends, and Mother's prediction comes true most spectacularly.

When Silverdun and Paet stepped into the Shadows' Den the next day, Iron-foot and Sela leapt to their feet.

"Silverdun!" shouted Sela. She ran to him and embraced him, and he was more than happy to let her.

"You're alive," said Ironfoot.

"That's a matter of some philosophical debate," said Silverdun. "I'm here, anyway."

"What happened?" asked Ironfoot. "How is this possible?"

"Pray you never find out," said Silverdun. He looked at Paet, who shook his head. "Apparently it's a bit of a trade secret."

"We can celebrate later," said Paet. "Right now there's work to do."

"But—" began Sela.

"Another time," said Paet. "Silverdun's untimely death has stolen away valuable time. So catch us up. Any progress on the Einswrath?"

Ironfoot's face fell. "Unfortunately, yes." Ironfoot filled them in on his discovery about the plans Timha had brought them.

"I'm sorry," he said. "I wish I could give you better news."

"What are you talking about, man?" said Paet. "That's excellent news!"

"How so?" asked Ironfoot.

"Because if they don't have the real plans," said Silverdun, "that means they don't have any Einswrath, either."

Ironfoot's eyes widened. "So we may have a chance after all."

"We need to tell Everess immediately," said Paet. "If this is true, then we may be able to avoid a war entirely. Mab was clearly counting on having the Ein-swrath in order to bolster her attack. She may be having second thoughts now."

"What makes you think that?" asked Silverdun.

"Remember what Timha told us," said Ironfoot. "Mab's thaumaturges were under heavy pressure to complete the thing. They were on a strict timetable. She committed to a war footing in the hope that it would be fin-ished on time."

"We hope," said Silverdun.

"If nothing else," said Paet, "if we let Mab know through diplomatic means that we're aware of this, she may stand down, and we won't have to engage in a war that we can't possibly win."

"Even without the Einswrath?" said Sela.

"The last time I spoke to Mauritane," said Silverdun, "he admitted that we're hopelessly outmatched. We now know that Mab's been drafting soldiers from all over the Unseelie Lands, and with the Annwni Army at her disposal, we're outnumbered nearly two to one. The Einswrath was merely the shot of whiskey in the beer."

"I'm off to talk to Everess," said Paet.

Paet sat in Everess's office at the Foreign Ministry, with Everess and Baron Glennet, and told them what Ironfoot had discovered.

"Wonderful news," said Everess.

"I believe that if we pass this information to Ambassador Jem-Aleth and he spreads it around the City of Mab, then she may think twice about her invasion. We could avert this whole nasty business."

"Perhaps," said Everess, thinking.

"No," said Glennet. "Those in Corpus will disagree. They'll argue that the only information we should send to Jem-Aleth is instructions to abandon the embassy and return to the City Emerald. What you've just told us is the best argument I've heard yet to proceed with Corpus's plans."

"Which plans are these?" asked Paet.

"Corpus has asked General Mauritane to prepare for a preemptive strike against the Unseelie," said Everess.

"Where does the queen stand on this?" said Paet.

"Titania keeps her own counsel," said Glennet. "She has informed Corpus that she will consent to whatever they decide."

"This is Regina Titania we're talking about, right?" said Paet. "The Stone Queen, the Fist of Cold Iron?"

"The queen is not as she once was," said Glennet. "It is sad, but true. She's become far less involved in affairs of state since midwinter."

"But Baron Glennet," said Paet. "General Mauritane has said that—"

"Mauritane is more concerned about the safety of his troops than the safety of his kingdom," said Glennet. "I'm sorry if that sounds harsh, but we must consider the larger issues here. If we strike now, then there will be no invasion of the Seelie Kingdom. We will take them by surprise."

"And you agree with this assessment?" asked Paet.

Glennet shrugged. "My role in this, as always, is to try to reach consensus. There are factions in the House of Lords who feel as you do, but most of the guilds feel otherwise, and they've brought a number of the lords over to their way of thinking. Elvish memory is long, Chief Paet, and Selafae is far from forgotten. Some of these members were furious when Mauritane didn't continue north after the Battle of Sylvan and finish Mab off entirely."

"That would have been suicide," said Paet.

"I didn't say I agree with them," said Glennet.

"Well, what's done is done," said Everess. "If we're going to war, then we need to prepare for it. Paet, you'll need to shift your focus onto developing intelligence on Mab's tactics and strategy."

"I feel deeply uncomfortable with this," said Paet.

"You feel deeply uncomfortable about everything," said Everess. "Now go and do as you're told."

Paet stormed into Blackstone House, hurling his cloak at Brei, the receptionist, and glowering at the copyists and analysts on his way downstairs, all of whom knew better than to disturb him in this mood.

He came downstairs, went into his office, and slammed the door, fuming. Would Everess ever stand up for what was right? Or would he spend his entire career doing only what brought him more influence? And Glennet, so well known as a peacemaker, hadn't done anything that Paet could see to remove the fire from the boiling pot the Seelie government had become.

And where was the queen in all this?

There was a knock at the door. "What is it?" he shouted.

A timid analyst hurried into his office and handed him a slip of paper, a summary of a sprite's message. The analysts all knew better than to provide transcripts from such conversations. Paet's hatred for message sprites was legendary.

He read the paper once, then again. "Shadows!" he shouted. "Get in here now!"

Silverdun, Ironfoot, and Sela filtered into the office, as always slower than he preferred.

"What are you bellowing about now?" said Silverdun.

"We've just received word from your man Estiane, Silverdun. He received a horrified note from an Arcadian housemaid in Mab's palace."

"What was in the note?" asked Ironfoot.

"Hy Pezho is alive. Hy Pezho. The Black Artist. The man who created the Einswrath is *alive*."

"But we'd heard from numerous sources that he'd been executed by Mab herself," said Ironfoot.

"Well, Silverdun died," said Paet. "And there *he* is."

"What do we do now?" said Sela.

"We panic," said Paet. "And I go back to Glennet and Everess. Maybe now they'll reconsider their preemptive strike."

"What should we do?" asked Silverdun.

"Silverdun, you go get your old friend Mauritane and have him meet us at the foreign minister's office. I don't care what he's doing. If he's making love to his wife, tell her she can finish on her own."

"Done," said Silverdun. "Though, having spent some time with Mauritane's wife, I pray it doesn't come to that."

"Ironfoot," said Paet, standing and stuffing the slip of paper in his pocket, "you get back to your map and your books and you figure out how that weapon works. I don't care what it takes. I don't care how much you have to spend or who you have to kill to do it. Am I understood?"

"No one is more eager to make that happen than I am," said Ironfoot. "I'll do my best."

"Your life literally depends on it, Ironfoot. If you can't figure it out, I believe we are all dead."

He strode out of his office. "And now I'm off to see if I can at least put our deaths off for a little while."

Sela called out to him. "Paet," she said. "I really would like you to look at the dispatches I've found."

"Later!" snapped Paet. He stormed back up the stairs, leaving Sela and Ironfoot glaring after him.

chapter thirty-two

Lord Valen once asked me how I defined true friendship. I told him that a true friend is one who forgives any indiscretion. I thought it a particularly fine thing to say, as I was having an affair with his wife at the time.

—Lord Gray, *Recollections*

A meeting was swiftly arranged at the Barrack, where Mauritane was knee-deep in planning for the imminent invasion. When Silverdun entered his office, he was surrounded by a horde of junior officers and amanuenses, all clamoring for his attention.

"We're on, Mauritane," said Silverdun. "They're waiting down the hall."

"Later," Mauritane said brusquely to the group around him.

"What's this all about?" whispered Mauritane as he and Silverdun made their way down a long hallway toward the meeting room. "As you may have noticed, I'm rather busy at the moment."

"Attempting to clear your schedule is what this is all about," said Silverdun.

Already in the meeting room were Everess, Paet, and Glennet. Everess and Paet were in the midst of an argument, but cut it off when Mauritane entered the room.

"So good to see you, General Mauritane. How goes the war?"

"War only goes one way," said Mauritane.

"It's only an expression, General," said Everess. "Have a seat and let's discuss. Chief Paet here has information that he believes is of enormous significance."

"It *is* of enormous significance," said Paet.

"It most certainly is," said Glennet, his hands raised. "No one's arguing that. The question is what to do about it."

"Is anyone going to tell me what it is?" asked Mauritane, taking his seat, glowering. "Or am I supposed to guess?"

"The Black Artist Hy Pezho has been spotted alive and well in the City of Mab."

"I understood he was dead," said Mauritane.

"There's a lot of that going around," said Silverdun.

"What this means to you, General," said Paet, "is that if Hy Pezho is indeed alive, then there's every chance that Mab is busily developing the Einswrath as we speak."

"I received a memorandum earlier this morning," said Mauritane, "from *you*, telling me that there were no Einswrath. I've spent the entire day furiously rewriting my battle plans as a result. And now you're telling me you were wrong?"

"We received new information," said Paet.

Mauritane breathed deeply. "If I am to wage a war, it would be extremely helpful if the capabilities of the enemy did not change from hour to hour."

"The question to you, then, General, is this," said Everess. "Knowing what you now know, do you still support the invasion?"

Mauritane growled. "I've already committed the troops! They're marching now! I can't just call everyone back and tell them to forget the whole thing!"

"Perhaps not," said Paet, "but we could merely fortify the border, rather than launch an invasion that will force a conflict. Who knows how long it will be before Mab crosses the border?"

"In five days' time all of my troops will be fully deployed," said Mauritane. "How long do you expect them to stand around?"

"If we attack Mab now, all of your men will die," said Paet.

Mauritane sat silently, thinking. Everess began to speak, but Mauritane cut him off with a sharp wave of his hand, and Everess faltered into silence. Silverdun had to admit that he genuinely loved his old companion at times.

"I agree with Paet," he finally said. "We should postpone the invasion until we're certain. If Mab's got the Einswrath, then all of my men and women are dead. If not, we may be able to stop a war with diplomacy. As far as I know, there has been no threat from Mab, no declaration of war."

"But she's massing troops along the border," said Glennet. "Any fool can see—"

"A fool can see many things," said Mauritane. "But we don't know what Mab is doing. These troop movements could simply be to keep us in check, to test our response. They could be a feint in order to draw out another enemy: the Four Kingdoms, or a foe in another world entirely. Mab is famous for such tricks."

"It's too late for this," said Glennet. "We must invade, and we must do it now before we find Mab standing at the gates of the Great Seelie Keep while we're still sitting here arguing."

"I was against this invasion from the beginning," said Mauritane. "I was against it when we only suspected that Mab still had the Einswrath, and now I'm tempted to be certain of it.

"The only good war, Baron Glennet," he continued, "is the one that's never fought. Everess told me so himself, when he was going about justifying the creation of his Shadows to me. The nature of war has changed. And now you want to go running off into the same old war?"

"It is not me you must convince," said Glennet. "Corpus has decided."

"Then make them change their minds," said Mauritane. "If we move now, we'll be going to our deaths. Even without the Einswrath, Mab's Army outnumbers us. And with the Annwni legions, we'll be totally overpowered. My soldiers are the best there are, but they're still only Fae."

"I'm sorry," said Glennet. "It's too late. The decision has been made."

Paet started to raise an objection, but Everess cut him off. "You heard the man, *Chief* Paet. Your job is to provide intelligence. You've done that. Now go back to work and let General Mauritane do his job."

"All right," said Paet. "What is it you've been dying to tell me?"

They were in the mission room at Blackstone House. Sela had laid out several documents in front of Paet, while Ironfoot and Silverdun watched.

"I'm curious to know myself," said Silverdun. He'd asked Sela to tell him what was on her mind, but she seemed to be actively pained in his presence since his return. After their night in the Unseelie lands together and her declaration of love, coupled with his recent demise, he didn't suppose he could blame her. Ironfoot, for his part, could barely be torn away from his studies on the Einswrath. Both Sela and Silverdun sensed that he was onto something and didn't want to bother him.

"When we returned from our last mission," Sela began, "you asked me to go through everything I could find to determine who it was that had given away our plans; first in Annwn, and then in the Unseelie. I've come up with something, but I'm not sure how definitive it is."

"Let's have it," said Paet. He was clearly having a hard time concentrating, but Silverdun knew that Paet was not a man who'd ignore important information despite his other worries.

"I began concentrating on dispatches from Annwn, around the time that Silverdun and Ironfoot first went there, and didn't come up with much. But then I decided to check on anything at all that even mentioned Annwn. And I found something peculiar."

She pushed one of the documents in front of Paet. "This is a report from one of your informants in Mag Mell, a barmaid at a tavern on Isle Siolain. She reported in passing a meeting between Baron Glennet and the Annwni ambassador, the same day you arrived."

"Hm," said Paet. "That's not strikingly unusual."

"Not in itself, no," said Sela. "But at this point, I must admit that I was desperate to find out anything at all. So I went back and checked the itinerary Glennet filed with the Foreign Office."

"And?" said Paet.

"And there was no scheduled meeting," she said. "Glennet was supposedly there for a meeting with a mining concern."

"That's what he told us," said Silverdun. "Remember, Ironfoot? We saw him at the locks."

"That's right," said Ironfoot. "There was no mention of a meeting with the Annwni ambassador."

"Indeed," said Silverdun. "And the fact that he didn't mention the meeting is strange, since—"

"Since he was well aware that you two were on your way to Annwn," said Paet. "Glennet receives briefings on every mission on foreign soil. He always knows where we're going, and when. It seems more than a little suspicious."

"The queen's tits," said Silverdun. "Could it have been him all this time?"

"Ah," said Sela. "But there's more. I started going through Glennet's records at the Hall of Records."

"How in hell did you get access to a *baron's* records?" asked Paet. "I've never been able to get that kind of access."

Sela smiled. "You don't have the powers of persuasion that I have, I suppose," she said. "Either the magical kind or . . . the more mundane kind."

Silverdun felt a sudden blossom of affection for her. She looked up at him and gave him an odd look. Had she felt him?

She seemed to lose her train of thought for a moment, but quickly regained it.

"Not long after the Battle of Sylvan, Glennet began investing heavily in the industries of war," said Sela. "He sank enormous sums of money into the Armorers' Guild, the Smiths' Guild. The Textile Guild, too, though I wasn't sure why."

"Uniforms," said Ironfoot. "An army needs lots of uniforms."

"So the baron wanted to get rich off of a war," said Silverdun. "That doesn't necessarily make him our traitor."

"No," said Sela. "That doesn't. But there's more."

She pushed another stack of papers in front of Paet. "These are loan documents, filed with banks in the City Emerald, Estacana, and Mag Mell. Every penny Glennet invested in the guilds was borrowed."

"I seem to recall rumors even when I was at court that Glennet had financial troubles," said Silverdun. "He loves his card games."

"So he found a way to get rich off of the war effort," said Ironfoot.

"But then a year went by and there was no war," said Sela. "The interest on those loans began to mount."

"Glennet needs a war," said Silverdun. "The guilds can't pay him until the government requisitions their supplies."

"And the government doesn't requisition supplies until there's a war."

"There's more," said Sela. "And this is fairly damning, I'm afraid. I checked with the analysts upstairs and found that Glennet has been regularly sending spell-encrypted messages in the weekly packets to Jem-Aleth for the past year."

"That's not uncommon, though," said Paet. "Glennet's involved in all sorts of Foreign Ministry business. He's got plenty of legitimate reasons to send such messages, and anything sent classified is required to go encrypted."

"Well," said Sela, "we're required to retain copies of those documents. I decrypted one of them. One sent two days before we left for the Unseelie."

Paet looked at her, wide-eyed.

"Well, I didn't decrypt it myself," she said. "One of the analysts may have helped a bit."

"What did the message say?" asked Paet.

"It gave explicit details of our travel plans, including our physical descriptions, and our itinerary."

"Dammit!" said Silverdun. "Those soldiers on the transport to Preyia. They knew exactly who they were looking for."

"The message also contained the location of our rendezvous in Preyia."

Paet leaned back. "Well. That is fairly conclusive, I think."

"But why would he come after us?" asked Ironfoot. "That's the part I still don't understand."

Paet looked at him. "Because Everess went all over the city selling the Shadows as the best deterrent to war that Elfkind had ever devised.

"And," added Paet, "if you were killed, then it not only stops us from doing that very thing, but also adds yet another reason to go to war, once your deaths are pinned on our enemies."

"And I thought *Everess* was a bastard," said Silverdun.

"I believe Glennet was Everess's mentor," said Paet.

Paet looked at Sela, who looked pleased with herself. "Sela, I must say that I'm amazed at this bit of detective work," he said.

"No more than I was," she said. "I was amazed at how much I enjoyed it. And how good I was at it."

"Simply astonishing," said Paet, looking over the documents.

"I'm glad you think so," said Sela, suddenly becoming serious. "Because I've decided I don't want to be a Shadow anymore. I want to be an analyst."

"What?" said Paet. "Are you serious?"

"I am," said Sela, looking down. "I was raised to be something. A killer. A monster. But I was also trained very well to use my Empathy. I understand people, and what drives them and what they want. So I've made my decision. I'm not going on any more missions."

"But you're a Shadow, Sela. You'll always be a Shadow."

"Call me a Shadow, then. I can work just as easily in the Den. But don't send me out on any more missions."

She touched the band on her arm, the crude thing that Ironfoot had fashioned. "I'm never taking this off again."

She stared hard at Paet. "Never."

Paet and the Shadows went to Everess, and Sela went through the documents with him as she'd done with Paet.

"Very good work, Sela. Very good," said Everess once the story was done. He leaned back in his chair.

"Do we recommend him to the high prosecutor?" asked Paet.

"Heavens no," said Everess. "We can't let him know we suspect anything."

"You can't think to let him get away with this!" said Paet.

"Oh, he won't," said Everess. "But Glennet is a very powerful man, one who's owed many, many favors. Who do you think recommended the high prosecutor to his post? No, we can't take the direct route with someone like him."

"Are you proposing that one of my Shadows eliminate him?" asked Paet dourly. "I thought I made myself clear on that point."

"No, Glennet is more useful to us alive and well at the moment," said Everess.

"At the moment," said Silverdun.

"At the moment," repeated Everess. "And trust me, I know precisely how to take care of him after that."

Everess fell silent, lighting his pipe. "We've a more pressing problem, though," he said. "Our troops are outnumbered by a great margin, and if war is indeed inevitable, we need to find ways to even the odds. Any suggestions?"

Silverdun sat up. "I've got a few ideas," he said.

Estiane's office was as warm and cozy as Silverdun remembered it. When he barged in, Estiane was sitting at his desk with a huge slice of peach pie in front of him. Estiane made to hide it, then saw it was Silverdun and decided not to bother.

"Perrin! It's good to see you, though I'm told that things are not progressing as one might hope with our neighbors to the north."

Silverdun sat. "It's worse than you know," he said. He told Estiane what he could, leaving out the more classified details.

When he was done, Estiane said, "What can I do to help?"

"I'm glad you asked," said Silverdun. "Because I'm about to ask something very large of you."

"What's that?"

"We are going to war with the Unseelie," said Silverdun. "That seems inevitable now. All we can do is try to make it as unpleasant for the Unseelie as possible."

"I'm not sure how I can help, other than by praying."

"How many devout Arcadians are there in the Unseelie?"

Estiane frowned. "It's hard to say for certain. Perhaps five thousand? Ten thousand at the most? As I told you before, the less we know about them, the safer they are."

"I want you to contact them, as many as you can, in secret."

"And what shall I tell them?" Estiane now looked deeply worried.

"You're going to tell them to do everything they can to sabotage the Unseelie war effort. Disrupt supply lines, disrupt communications, destroy spellcraft depots, steal weapons, horses. Stab commanders in the back. Whatever they're able to do."

"I can't ask that of my people!" said Estiane. "These are Arcadians! They're committed to love and peace. That is what brought them to Aba in the first place." He pushed the pie around on his plate and dropped the fork in frustration. "I won't do that. I'm sorry."

"You *will* do that," said Silverdun. "You put yourself on a pedestal, making a martyr of yourself, believing that if you do a little evil in the name of good, then you're protecting your people. You claim that this is a sin you take upon yourself to save others. But now it's time to give all of your followers in the Unseelie the same opportunity. If they're as principled as you, they should be happy to make the same choice."

"You don't know what you're asking, Perrin," said Estiane. "Joining Everess and his Shadows has changed you. You've forgotten what it means to be an Arcadian."

"I haven't forgotten," said Silverdun. "I've just learned a few things since then."

"I'm sorry, Perrin. I won't do it."

"If you don't, then Paet is prepared to testify in the High Court that you conspired with the foreign minister to have the husband of the secretary of states murdered in a brothel."

Paet had promised no such thing, but Estiane didn't know that.

"That's preposterous!" said Estiane. "I had no idea what Everess was planning!"

"Maybe not," said Silverdun. "But you know there are elements in Corpus who would be more than happy to see the Church fall on its face. It's not that long since Arcadianism was considered a dangerous cult by most Fae."

"You'd bring down the Church to get your way," said Estiane.

"No, but I would bring it down to save the Seelie Kingdom."

"I could excommunicate you for this," said Estiane.

"It wouldn't matter," said Silverdun. "I don't think you can excommunicate a dead man."

"Are you serious about this?" asked Estiane.

"I've never been more serious about anything."

"Aba will turn his back on you for this."

"I believe that the ends will justify the means, Abbot." He stood. "You taught me that."

chapter thirty-three

The basis of the Chthonic faith is the mistrust of divinity. How fortunate we would be if all religions had the decency to lock up their gods!

—Beozho, *Autobiography*

Ironfoot was desperate.

He'd stared at these documents a hundred times in the past two days. He'd read every single one of the books that Timha had brought with him, examined every bit of Hy Pezho's fake plans on the off chance that some bit of the actual mechanism might be concealed somewhere within them. The best lies, he knew, were based in truth.

It wasn't just that the Einswrath threatened the Seelie Kingdom. He understood that, of course. But that still seemed remote, a possible contingency. This was personal.

It was at times like this that he could not control his anger, when he was in the thick of a problem. At any moment the dark thoughts would creep in: *You are not smart enough, or good enough. You are a shepherd's son. You don't deserve to be here. You will fail and then everyone will know who you really are.*

He was fighting those dark thoughts when Sela came downstairs into the mission room carrying a stack of briefs. She'd begun sorting through intelligence from the Unseelie, trying to get some idea of where Hy Pezho had come from, and when.

"How is it going?" she asked.

Ironfoot looked up at her. "How does it look like it's going?" he said blandly.

"I don't suppose there's anything I can do to help."

"Not unless you know how to circumvent the exponential decrease of reitic force in unbindings."

"Sorry," Sela said.

"If only I could remember," said Ironfoot. "Something that's bothered me ever since I first came to Selafae."

"What's that?" asked Sela.

"All around the crater, there was a smell. Sort of like roast meat, but acrid, like tar. I don't know how to explain it."

"Do you remember the smell?" she said.

"I'll never forget it."

"May I smell it?"

"It's a long way from here to Selafae, and I doubt the smell is still there anyway, after last spring's rains."

"That's not what I mean," she said. "Open yourself up to me. Open your mind and think about the smell."

"You can smell my memory with Empathy? That's new."

"I have skills other Empaths don't," she said.

He shrugged. "Why not?" He closed his eyes and opened his mind. He felt something—not a presence, more like the sense of being watched by someone unseen. It made him wary.

"Relax," she said. "Think of that smell." He did.

"Got it," she said.

Ironfoot opened his eyes and looked at her. She was smiling.

"You know what that is?" he said.

"I do. When I was very small, before . . . well, when I was very small, my parents used to take me to the Chthonic temple in the city on holidays. That's the smell of the prayer bowls just after they've been lit."

"You're kidding," said Ironfoot.

"Have you ever been to a Chthonic holiday service?" she asked.

"Just once," he said. There aren't many Chthonics down south, where I was raised. But I went to a wedding once in Sylvan. . . ."

Ironfoot sat up. "Auberon's hairy balls, Sela! That's it!"

"What's it?" Sela looked excited, though she clearly had no idea why.

"Auberon's big, sweaty, hairy balls!" he said, digging through the stack of papers on the table. He couldn't find what he was looking for.

"Prae Benesile," said Ironfoot. "Where's Prae Benesile?"

"*Who's* Prae Benesile?" asked Sela.

Ironfoot ran past her into the den and attacked the piles of books on his desk.

"Prae Benesile was an Annwni scholar who was murdered in Blood of Arawn five years ago," he said, digging. "Before he died, he'd received a few visits from one Hy Pezho. Looking at Hy Pezho's plans, Prae Benesile is referenced more than once, but we had no idea why. I started to assume that Hy Pezho included the references to him just to confuse those who came after him."

"But you don't think that anymore."

"No. It didn't make sense. Why did Hy Pezho go so far out of his way to meet with this doddering old lunatic? Why did the Bel Zheret kill him during the Fall of Annwn?"

"And now you think you know?"

"I'm beginning to, yes." Ironfoot found the book he was looking for. It was Prae Benesile's *Thaumatical History of the Chthonic Religion*.

"I believe that the answer we're looking for is right here," he said.

"Do tell," said Sela.

Ironfoot opened the book and began paging through it. He was instantly reminded why he'd only glanced at it before now; it was a collection of incoherent ramblings, observations about history, religious maunderings. Though it claimed to be a "thaumatical" history, there was no formal thaumatics anywhere in it.

"Hm," said Ironfoot. "This may take a while."

The Temple of Bound Althoin was a towering, imposing heap of gray stone located in a once-fashionable part of the City Emerald. It was one of twelve Metropolitan Chthonic temples scattered throughout the known worlds. These were the focal points for the faith, each overseeing a large collection of smaller temples.

The Chthonics were a respectable old faith, but hardly relevant in modern Fae society. Even those who professed the faith tended to downplay it; many of its adherents acknowledged their gods with a wink, insinuating that theirs was more of an ancient tradition than a true belief. Weddings and funerals were often held in Chthonic temples because of their grandiose beauty. But attendance at holiday services, especially in the cities, had been in a slow decline for hundreds of years.

When Ironfoot entered the temple, its sanctuary was empty. Smoke from incense drifted lazily into the still, cool air. Light from pentagonal windows set high up in the circular space sent shafts of light through the smoke, intersecting in strange geometries.

The smoke from the incense burned Ironfoot's nostrils. It was part of the smell from Selafae, a distinct part of it, but not all of it.

Ironfoot stood at a railing looking down at the center altar, also five-sided, which was encircled by rows of pews. Above the altar hovered a glowing, multicolored object, suspended in space, about three feet in diameter. The cynosure. Directly beneath it was a wide brass bowl, a stylized alchemist's thurible.

Ironfoot made his way down a nearby aisle toward the altar. As he approached, he saw that the cynosure was a polyhedron, multifaceted, each face a pentagon. It spun slowly, its various facets casting moving smears of light in the dim room.

He stopped at the altar and examined the cynosure. It looked solid enough, not a glamour. A simple binding held it aloft; he didn't need Insight to tell him that. He channeled Insight into it anyway and found that the object was made of ceramic, hollow, but what was inside he couldn't determine because of the reitic resonances on it. Whatever the thing was, it had channeled plenty of *re* in its time. He couldn't remember having seen one like it at the wedding he'd attended, but that had been a long time ago.

"Are you Master Falores?" came a voice from the far side of the sanctuary. A priest about Ironfoot's age was coming down one of the aisles opposite him.

"That's right," said Ironfoot. "I appreciate your taking the time to speak with me."

"I am Guide Throen," the priest said, bowing. "I am properly addressed as Guide, if you wish to do me that honor."

"A pleasure," said Ironfoot. "Now, this is going to sound a bit odd, but I'm in a hurry, and I'm hoping we can skip courtesy and just get down to business."

"Any way I can help, although your sprite left me a bit confused. Are you here on behalf of the university, or on behalf of the Foreign Ministry?"

"Which will make you more forthcoming?"

Throen smiled. He had a serious look about him, though, that the smile didn't temper much. "Either way, I am at your service."

"Thank you," said Ironfoot. "I have some fairly in-depth questions about your cynosure here; I can't give you much of an explanation for that, but I can tell you that this is a matter of vital importance to the Crown."

Throen was nonplussed by this. "I'm not sure I understand."

"Just tell me about it, if you'd be so kind."

"The cynosure," he said slowly. "It is the central symbol of the Chthonic faith."

"Yes. But what is it for?"

Throen looked confused. "It is the mystical dodecahedron. Twelve faces, one for each of the bound gods. Five sides per face, one for each of earth, air, fire, water, and *re*. Twenty vertices to represent the twenty stations of repentance. Thirty vertices to represent the thirty virtues.

"It is placed on the altar during holiday services; one just ended about an hour ago. I was about to return it to its cabinet just before you arrived."

"It has some rather interesting reitic properties," said Ironfoot. "Can you tell me what it does?"

Throen faltered. "Its thaumatic aspect is designed to . . . heighten the awareness of the faithful. Some herbs are burnt, a simple mnemonic recited. That is all."

He was holding something back. "Are you sure?" said Ironfoot. "Because I'm channeling Insight through it, and it seems a bit more complex than that."

"Why are you asking these questions?" said Throen, stiffening. "I'm glad to help the Crown, of course, but this is highly irregular."

Ironfoot wasn't sure how to proceed. It would have been a good idea, in retrospect, to have brought Sela along with him. "I don't mean any disrespect to you, Guide Throen, but I think there's more to your dodecahedron than you're telling me, and believe it or not, it may be the most important information you've ever dispensed, so please tell me the truth."

"Are you threatening me?" said Throen.

"No. But I very much need you to tell me the truth."

"These are the deepest mysteries of our faith," said Throen. "It's not the sort of thing one simply discusses with anyone who walks through the door."

"I'm not just anyone," said Ironfoot. "That's what I'm trying to tell you."

Throen thought briefly, uncertain. "Fine," he said. He reached into his robe and took out a small prayer book and a packet of herbs. "When the service begins, these herbs are burned in the thurible, along with a few drops of blood. The Guide's blood, that is. Mine. The herbs are a combination of things: some fairly common, others decidedly more rare. We read the incantations here." He opened the book to a well-thumbed page and indicated an incantation spelled out in angular runic High Fae script. "That activates the focusing charm."

"This incantation is just a call to a stored binding," said Ironfoot. "What does it actually do?"

Throen looked confused. "I've already told you; it focuses the reverence of the faithful."

Ironfoot held up the herbs and sniffed them. The smell, like that at Selafae. Missing only the added texture of burning blood. What did this mean?

"Do you even know what the stored bind does?" said Ironfoot.

"I'm not a thaumaturge," said Throen, beginning to lose his temper. "I'm a Guide. This is a sacred object, not a spellbox."

"I don't think you're going to like this," said Ironfoot. "But I've got to take your cynosure with me."

"That's impossible!" said Throen. "You can't simply come into this temple and walk off with our most sacred instruments! This is outrageous!"

Ironfoot reached for the cynosure, removing its Motion enclosure with a flick of his wrist. The thing fell into his hands; it was much heavier than it looked.

"I'm sorry," he said. "I truly am, but—"

Throen flung himself at Ironfoot. "Get your hands off of it!" he shouted. "You are desecrating it!"

Throen grabbed at the cynosure and pulled; he was stronger than he had any right to be. Ironfoot pulled back. Throen's face was red; he was grunting.

Suddenly Ironfoot was struck by the absurdity of what was happening. Here he was, in a church, fighting with a priest over a holy relic as if it were a game ball. He almost laughed, but before he did, Throen shoved him hard, knocking him off the altar dais and slamming him into the first row of pews. The sound of the impact echoed like a cannon shot in the huge sanctuary. Throen was still on him, still pulling at the cynosure as if his life depended on it.

"Let go!" he shouted.

Ironfoot winced and pulled as hard as he could, throwing all of his Shadow strength into the motion. The cynosure came free of Throen's grasp, and Throen fell to the floor.

Ironfoot took the thing and ran.

"You will pay for this obscenity!" Throen shouted. "The Church will sue the Foreign Ministry for this!"

"Tell them to go after a Lord Everess," said Ironfoot over his shoulder. "He's the one they want."

A little later, Ironfoot and Silverdun were in the mission room, huddled over the cynosure. Sela sat on a nearby table, watching.

"Right here," said Ironfoot. "Separate it along this edge." Ironfoot was getting impatient. He was onto something and he knew it. He watched Silverdun channel Elements carefully into the ceramic enclosure of the object, splitting it open.

"Careful," he said.

"You mentioned," said Silverdun. "I'm being as careful as I can. If you think you can do better, by all means be my guest."

Ironfoot looked up to see Paet coming down the steps.

"What are you two doing?" said Paet. "We've got work to do."

"Ironfoot's decided to set off a holy war," said Silverdun. "So we're boldly desecrating a holy artifact. You might want to let Everess know that if we all survive the next week, he's going to get a very unpleasant visit from the Synod of Chthonic Bishops."

"Careful, Silverdun!" snapped Ironfoot.

"Wonderful," said Paet. "And where did we get this artifact?"

"Ironfoot beat up a priest in a Chthonic temple and stole it," said Silverdun.

"May I ask why?"

"Remember our report from our first visit to Annwn?" asked Ironfoot, looking up. "When we spoke to Prae Benesile's son, he told us that Hy Pezho stole something from Prae Benesile. A box. The son didn't know what was in it, but I'm almost certain that it was one of these—a Chthonic cynosure."

"What good would it have done him?" asked Paet.

"If this relic does what I think it does, it may be the very secret to the Einswrath," said Ironfoot. "Under better circumstances, this would be the discovery of a career."

"Well, get on with it then," said Paet. "And Ironfoot, I don't need a thesis. I just need a way to stop the damn thing."

"I'll write the monograph later," said Ironfoot.

Paet went into his office and shut the door.

Silverdun finished the cut, and Ironfoot removed the ceramic casing. Inside was one of the most complex thaumatic mechanisms he'd ever seen. Tiny plates of solid gold and silver sandwiched together, inscribed with minuscule runes and lines of force. Diamonds were set into these lines. They were probably reitic capacitors of some kind.

"This is unbelievable," said Ironfoot. "I've never seen anything like it."

"What is it?" said Silverdun.

"I'm not entirely sure," said Ironfoot. He pointed to one of the leaves of gold. "Look at this. It's a force binding. And this is . . . no, that's not possible."

"What's not possible?"

"This bit here," said Ironfoot. "What does that look like to you?"

Silverdun looked closer.

Silverdun shrugged. "It looks like ancient High Fae that I was never particularly good at deciphering."

"It's the binding for a fold," said Ironfoot. "This thing channels Folding."

"That's ridiculous," said Silverdun. "Only Masters of the Gates can fold, and it takes years of training. No priest could channel anything useful into something that small."

"What are you two talking about?" asked Sela.

"The Gift of Folding," said Silverdun. "It's what powers the locks to travel between worlds. It allows objects and energy to pass through the folded spaces."

"But the Gift is extraordinarily rare," said Ironfoot. "Almost no one has it, and those that do are immediately snapped up by the Masters of the Gates."

"And look here," said Ironfoot, pointing again. "These figures specify the target for a translation." He paused. "I think."

Ironfoot separated a few more of the thin leaves from the device. At the center was a tiny mesh of silver, of threads so narrow that they were barely visible.

"And what is that?" asked Silverdun.

Ironfoot channeled Insight into the mesh. He couldn't believe what he saw there. It was the same sensation he'd gotten when Lin Vo had responded to Timha's attack. The same impossible, unchanneled essence. The music without pitch. Division by zero.

"Well?" said Silverdun.

"It's undifferentiated essence," said Ironfoot.

"The Thirteenth Gift," said Silverdun.

"It's not a Gift," said Ironfoot. "It's beyond Gifts. It makes the Gifts obsolete."

"So?" said Sela. "What does it mean?"

"I have an idea," said Ironfoot. He'd never been more excited in his life. What Lin Vo had said to him in the Arami camp was beginning to make sense. *You're all going to have to learn how to think things anew.*

"Give me a little time," he said. "I think I understand. Everything."

A little time turned out to be almost a full day. Ironfoot worked without stopping, writing notes and equations, muttering to himself, shouting, sometimes hurling things. He was so close! Everything was coming together: the map, Hy Pezho's falsified plans, the cynosure. He now understood how Hy Pezho had sent the Unseelie thaumaturges in circles. He'd simply removed all reference to the Thirteenth Gift, knowing that none of them would ever suspect its use. How could they? Almost nobody had ever heard of it, and those who had didn't believe that it existed.

A few times, Silverdun or Sela or Paet would approach, questioning looks in their eyes, and Ironfoot would wave them away, sometimes gruffly, sometimes angrily. He needed to be alone. It would take as long as it took.

Finally he had it. He checked and rechecked his figures. Translated the etchings on the gold and silver plates twice, three times. Reread every word of Prae Benesile's Chthonic history. Now that he knew what the hell Benesile was talking about, the book was practically a reference guide. Benesile's problem had not been that he was a lunatic; quite the contrary. He'd been so brilliant that he'd assumed too much from his readership, hadn't bothered explaining what to him had seemed obvious. There were no equations in the book because Benesile had believed them to be implied.

It was as though a great weight had been removed from his shoulders. The tension of this one problem had been pressing down on him for the better part of a year, coloring everything he'd done and thought and said ever since he'd returned to Queensbridge from Selafae. It had hung like a vulture over his head the entire time he'd been a Shadow, watching him, waiting for him, until he thought he might go insane.

And now it was over.

He called Silverdun, Sela, and Paet into the mission room.

"Do you have some news for us?" asked Silverdun. "Or have you called us in to let us know that you have indeed gone stark, raving mad?"

"I know where Hy Pezho is getting the power for the Einswrath," he said. "The problem I could never understand is how he was able to condense so much *re* into such a small space. There's no way of doing it, and no way of binding it once it's done. And Hy Pezho must have sent the Unseelie thaumaturges who came after him into even worse fits than mine because he included every bit of instruction on how to create the Einswrath except for the one small bit of information that is the entire secret of his creation."

Ironfoot held up the ceramic casing of the cynosure. "This relic is old. How old, I don't know. A thousand years? Two thousand? Ten? There's no way of knowing, and I'm not a history buff, but I think it's safe to say that this thing I'm holding in my hand has been in constant use for millennia."

"Doing what?" asked Silverdun.

"Taking in the *re* of Chthonic worshippers. Their spiritual devotion is focused onto this during their most private holiday services, those for believers only. In Benesile's book he describes the intensity of these rituals. On the outside, the Chthonics may seem like a fairly lackluster bunch, but these ceremonies are grueling affairs, lasting hours. There's a set of incantations that's said, some herbs that are burned, and it has the effect of drawing out the essence from everyone in the room and focusing it on the cynosure."

"And then what?" asked Silverdun.

"And then it takes that essence, undifferentiates it, and sends it through a fold."

"To where?" asked Paet. "And why?"

"I can tell you where," said Ironfoot. "The directional mapping is there, though it'll take me a little while longer to pinpoint it.

"As to why? I haven't a clue. Perhaps the ancient Chthonics simply wanted a way to store up massive amounts of *re* to do the very thing with it that Hy Pezho did. I can't imagine what you might do with that much energy."

"What did Hy Pezho do with it?" asked Sela.

"Well, it turns out that the Einswrath, for all of its apparent complexity, is really quite simple. All it does is reverse the process. It creates a fold, draws that very same undifferentiated *re* out, and releases it. The difference is that this stored *re* is highly concentrated, and as soon as it's unfolded . . ."

"Boom," said Sela.

"Exactly."

"So, knowing this," said Paet, "can you build one of your own? Can you create a means of defending against them?"

"Not in the next four days," said Ironfoot. "I don't know exactly how Hy Pezho pulled it off. But it doesn't matter. I think I may be able to do something just as good, if not better."

"What's that?" asked Paet.

"I can take us to wherever all that *re* is stored," said Ironfoot, "and channel it all off into the ether." He paused. "There's just one problem."

"Which is?" asked Silverdun.

"In order to get there, we need someone who is able to work this undifferentiated *re*. Someone who has the Thirteenth Gift. And the only Fae I've ever met that can do it is an old Arami woman out somewhere in the Unseelie, on the other side of a massive army."

"Actually," said Silverdun. "I may know of one other. A girl I once met." Silverdun looked at Sela, who blanched and turned away.

"Where is this girl?" asked Paet.

"In Estacana, last time I checked."

Paet sighed. "Go get her. Now."

He looked at Ironfoot. "And while we're waiting for him to return, I've got a job for you."

chapter thirty-four

The renewal of an old acquaintance is a gift both given and received.

—Fae proverb

The suite of the chief high councilor of Blood of Arawn was quite a step up from the magyster's office that Wenathn had held the first time Ironfoot had met him.

"Brenin Molmutius!" said Wenathn warmly, when Ironfoot was admitted into the office. Ironfoot was known in Annwn as Brenin Dunwallo Molmutius, the chieftain of one of the Mag Mell Isles. It required an elaborate glamour to pass as a Mag Mellian, but so far the disguise had worked just fine.

"Thank you for seeing me on such short notice," said Ironfoot.

"Please, sit," said Wenathn. "What can I do for you?"

"That's an excellent question," said Ironfoot. "Quite a lot, really."

Ironfoot took an envelope from the hidden compartment in his satchel, closed with the seal of Lord Everess. "Read this," he said.

Wenathn broke the seal and read the letter inside.

"I don't know about this," he said.

"You knew there would be a price for our assistance," said Ironfoot. "That someday the bill would come due."

"But what you're asking," said Wenathn. "The repercussions."

"You've read the letter," said Ironfoot. "It's signed by Everess and carries his impress."

Wenathn smoothed the letter on his desk and reread it. "From what I'm told, Lord Everess's stamp may not be worth much in a few days."

"That's a chance you'll just have to take," said Ironfoot. "Though I imagine that if word got out about the means of your rise to power, your own stamp might not press paper soon either."

Wenathn nodded. He was no fool.

"You and I both know that there are many on your council who would back this in an instant, especially with the full, written support of the Seelie government."

"How long do I have to decide?" said Wenathn.

"I can stay at least until lunchtime," said Ironfoot, putting his feet up on the chief high councilor's desk.

Faella was on stage, alone, performing the final movement of "Twine" to a mostly empty house. The troupe had rebelled against her desire to present it earlier in the show, and it had been relegated to the dregs of the performance, the closing act performed after midnight, when most of the patrons had already left for the taverns or their beds.

It was a subtle piece, to be sure, and not what the Bittersweet Wayward Mestina was known for. Their audience wanted grand spectacles: ferocious battles, the machinations of kings, bawdy farces. These were what paid for the theater and the salaries of her employees and the outrageous Glamourists' Guild dues.

But "Twine" was dear to her heart, and she was determined to perform it. For the most part she'd taken herself out of the other pieces, much to the chagrin of the audience. The clashes of swords and noblemen and half-dressed bodies were fine as far as they went, but as time went on, Faella couldn't help but see them as any more than what they were: mirages, fantasies to pass the time. "Twine" was more than that, though she couldn't say what, exactly.

The dozens of red, gold, and orange strands whirled and spun in a ferocious ballet of longing and emotion until Faella, spent, wove them together into a bright braid of emotion and wound it around herself, where it exploded in a shower of sparks.

She bowed to scattered applause and left the stage, sweating. It was time for her to go.

Backstage, the mestines were removing makeup and costumes, lingering over bottles of cheap wine, laughing. She'd never felt more remote from them. It wasn't enough anymore. Nothing was ever enough.

She went to the theater office and went over the documents she'd prepared: assignment of title, bank slips, instructions. She was leaving the Bittersweet Wayward Mestina to the company as a whole. They would now be a self-owned collective. It could be a disaster, but she wouldn't be here to see it. She was moving on.

Over the past few months, her powers had only grown. She now found herself able to maneuver Elements and Motion, to work glamours of astonishing complexity, to do things that didn't seem to match any kind of Gift at all. To be honest, she wasn't sure what others meant by the Gifts. She'd only ever known Glamour, and had never thought of it as "channeling" some raw element through a thing. There was only the thought, the desire, and the deed. She'd always assumed she didn't understand because she had no formal training.

But as her abilities increased she'd begun reading more, sneaking into the university libraries and working her way painfully through textbooks. She was no scholar, and little of what she read made any sense. But there was nothing in her reading that shed any light on her strange new talents. In fact, everything that she'd read seemed to indicate that much of what she was doing was impossible.

She'd even gone so far as to seduce a professor of natural philosophy in order to pick his brain on the subject, but he'd been far more interested in her more mundane talents, and hadn't been any help at all.

And with each passing day, the certainty that she was wasting her life in Estacana grew. That feeling that she was meant for greatness never left her. In her most fanciful moments, she dreamed that she was destined to heal the whole world of Faerie, just as she'd healed Rieger's knife wound.

Whatever it was she was meant to be, it wasn't the owner of a middling mestina in Estacana. She'd already booked passage on the mail coach for the City Emerald in the morning. The City Emerald was the center of the Seelie Kingdom, where every decision of importance was made, and she would find a way to insinuate herself into its movements, just as she'd found a way to do everything else she'd ever done.

And yes, Silverdun was there. But that wasn't why.

There was a knock at the door of her office, and she quickly hid the papers under a blotter. She had no intention of saying good-bye. She intended to simply leave the packet of documents on the stage, with a bound glamour of herself, waving good-bye.

"Someone waiting to see you in the lobby," said Rieger.

Since the incident in his room, when she'd healed him, Rieger hadn't been able to look her in the eye. Something inexplicable had happened to him that night. He was both grateful and at the same time clearly frightened of her now. They hadn't touched each other since that night.

Faella stood and adjusted her hair in the mirror. She'd deal with whoever was waiting in the lobby and then retire back to her office with a bottle of that cheap wine and finish signing the papers, wait for everyone to go home, and then stage her exit.

The lobby was nearly empty; a few stragglers stood at the door: couples prolonging their dates, lonely men and women with no place better to go. She couldn't see anyone who might be looking for her.

"'Twine' was most remarkable," said a voice behind her.

She turned, and there was Perrin Alt, Lord Silverdun, new face and all. He was dressed not as a nobleman but as a merchant from the City Emerald, a hat pulled low over his forehead. He looked her in the eye and smiled wide.

"Lord Silverdun," she said evenly. "What a surprise." Her heart was bolting in her chest, threatening to break out of her and go running off down the avenue.

"It's good to see you again," he said. His voice was plain, honest, not at all vengeful or contemptuous. Either he'd forgiven her, or he was doing an excellent job of faking it.

"You as well," she said. Was her voice shaking? She prayed it wasn't.

"I need to speak with you," he said. He looked around the lobby. "In private, if we might. It's a matter of some importance."

A matter of some importance.

"Of course," she said. "Come with me." She led him through the lobby, behind the ticket counter, backstage, and into her office. He shut the door behind them.

"What is it that I can do for you?" she asked.

He reached out and took her by the shoulders, pulled her to him. He pressed himself up roughly against her, kissing her.

Oh.

All of her fantasies suddenly realized in a moment, Faella's head swam. She wasn't sure at first how her body was responding, her thoughts spinning so wildly that she almost forgot where she was.

But then she felt his hand on the small of her back, and it was clear that her body was responding just fine without her.

She leaned back on the desk, pushing the blotter out of the way, drawing him on top of her. As her carefully prepared documents fluttered to the floor, she considered simply leaving them there and letting the Bittersweet Wayward Mestina work it out on their own.

"I was wondering how long it would take you to find your way back to me," she breathed.

He stopped kissing her neck long enough to whisper, "I was wondering how long I could resist."

chapter thirty-five

It is the rare man who is both foolish enough to make a stupid decision and at the same time wise enough to profit from it.

—Master Jedron

"This had better work," said Everess. "By my reckoning, the invasion of the Unseelie begins any minute now, and we're making these Chthonics angrier by the minute, mucking around in their temple like this."

Four days had passed since Ironfoot's revelation. In that time, war preparations had been completed and troops massed at the border. Jem-Aleth, the Seelie ambassador, had been expelled from the City of Mab yesterday without comment. War had come.

Ironfoot stood on the altar of the Temple of Bound Althoin, carefully composing a set of bindings. The deconstructed cynosure was back in place, floating above the altar, but now it had been rebuilt with some crude additions: a few hard runes, a channeling glass. Several of the paper-thin leaves that had once resided within the cynosure were now connected to it by lengths of silver thread, their surfaces etched by Silverdun's Elements with additional markings of Ironfoot's design. "I told you," said Ironfoot, not looking down. "The device is calibrated to work from this location only. If we try to use it somewhere else, we'll end up in the wrong place."

Royal Guardsmen had been posted at all the exits. Guide Throen had been furious when Ironfoot had walked out with his cynosure; now he was livid, having been ejected by the Royal Guard from his own temple. The

Church elders were gathering nearby for a protest, and Everess had spent a good part of the morning trying to placate them, to no effect.

Sela and Paet sat in a pew, watching Ironfoot. Sela was nervous; she could feel the tension in the room, and could also sense with Empathy the resonances of old emotions in this space. Strong emotions. Fervent ones.

"I wish Silverdun would get here soon," said Paet. "We've been going out of our way to offend every religious order in Faerie this week, and I'd like to get this operation settled before we're damned to any number of various hells."

"He'll be here," said Sela. "I can feel him."

"He'd better be." Paet stood up. "How much longer?" he said to Ironfoot. His voice rang out in the wide space of the sanctuary.

"Not much longer," said Ironfoot. "But as long as it takes. I assume you'd prefer that we survive this experiment?"

Paet harrumphed, but sat back down without speaking.

Sela watched Ironfoot. He was handsome enough, clever, intelligent. Why couldn't she have fallen in love with him instead? He had his own complications, certainly, but she could happily have overlooked them.

Then again, there was a reason she'd been taken with Silverdun. As much as she hated to admit it, she could never have fallen for Ironfoot. He wasn't hard enough. At Silverdun's core was something dark and bitterly tough, and that was what drew her.

As if her thoughts of him had summoned him, Silverdun appeared at the entrance to the sanctuary, a young woman on his arm. Faella.

She was pretty, but not as pretty as Sela. She was young, too, barely out of her teens. She took in the sanctuary with a glance, her face haughty, her eyes fierce. She was used to having all eyes on her. Sela despised her instantly. She could have happily murdered her right there and then. She knew plenty of ways to do it.

For an instant Faella's eyes met hers, and she sensed that Faella knew exactly who she was, and exactly how she felt about Silverdun. Sela consciously avoided creating a thread with her. She had no desire to feel what this girl was feeling.

Faella smiled at her. Oh, how Sela wanted her dead.

"You must be Faella," said Ironfoot, bowing slightly in her direction. "Silverdun believes that you can help us with this. Is he right?"

Faella strode almost regally down the aisle, her gold-embroidered skirt brushing the carpet. "I'm certain that Lord Silverdun has overestimated my capacities," she said. "But I have a great power and I will do my best."

What horse dung. Great power, indeed. Insecure little girl. Sela couldn't help it; she reached out and let the thread form. It sprung up, perfectly white. Sela was baffled. She'd never seen a white thread before. She didn't know what it meant. Examining it more closely in her perceptions, though, she realized that this thread was actually many threads, of all colors intertwined. Only when she examined it from a distance did it appear white.

Who was this woman?

Her emotions, as she strode toward Silverdun, eased into Sela, and Sela saw something she couldn't believe. This haughty woman, this young ingenue, believed every word she said. Faella really did believe herself to be great, but believed it with a purity that astonished Sela. Not insecurity; quite the opposite. Utter confidence.

Faella stopped halfway down the aisle and looked at Sela. A small smile spread across her face. "Not what you expected?" she said. Embarrassed, Sela looked away.

Silverdun looked to Faella, then to Sela, and cringed visibly. Clearly a fear of his was being realized. So much the better.

Sela needed to stop being petty. There was work to do here.

"Lord Silverdun explained some of what needs to be done," said Faella, "but he left the technical details to you, Master Falores."

"Ironfoot will be fine, miss."

"As you wish."

Ironfoot began to explain the workings of his plan to Faella. She asked a number of questions, urging Ironfoot to put the more esoteric details into terms she could grasp.

"I must say," she finally said, frowning, "I'm not sure I quite understand."

Sela bit her lip. "Perhaps I can help," she said.

Faella looked at her and smiled that same seductive smile. "Can you?"

Sela walked to the altar and let the threads spring up between her and Ironfoot and Faella. It would be tricky to connect the two of them to one another, but not impossible.

But before she even began to channel Empathy in order to relate the two of them, Faella picked up on what she was doing and handily did it herself. Sela did her best to hide her feelings of resentment, but knew that they were spinning out from her on the thread and that Faella was receiving them.

Images, thoughts, words, incantations flowed freely between Faella and Ironfoot. It was tiring to channel actual thoughts as opposed to emotions, but each new channeling that Sela opened, Faella expanded. Within a few minutes, Ironfoot had shared everything that needed sharing, and they were ready.

"Thank you, Sela," said Faella. And she meant it. Sela snapped the thread away, feeling stupid and inferior. She wanted to hate Faella, but couldn't. Faella was better than she was. Silverdun's love for her was justified.

"Then let's begin," said Ironfoot. "Just to be clear, I have no idea what we'll find on the other side of this fold. As far as I know, we could all be killed instantly. But if all of this *re* is being folded there, it must be there for a reason, and there must be something there to contain it. Which means that others have gone before us."

Silverdun looked at her. "Sela, I know you don't want any more missions, but we don't know what we're about to face. We need you."

Sela's heart jumped. If anyone other than Silverdun had asked her, she would have said no.

"Of course I'll go," she said.

"Then let's begin," said Silverdun.

"Yes, please," said Ironfoot. "I have a feeling that any minute now a judge in the Aeropagus is going to send an order for us to clear out of here, war or no war. So by all means, let us begin."

"You know what to do?" said Ironfoot.

"I do," said Faella.

Without warning, the world disappeared.

Sela is finally happy. She has Milla.

They sleep in the same bed. They eat their meals together. They play together on the lawns, weaving the daisy chains that Sela has taught Milla how to make. They put on plays for one another, read aloud (mostly Sela reads and Milla listens), sing each other to sleep. They make rude jokes about the crones and even sometimes about Oca. Sela learns a new word from Milla— "eunuch"—about Oca. They are inseparable. Except for Sela's "special studies" each morning.

After bringing Milla, Lord Tanen went away, and so things at the manor have been breezy and light. The crones watch her and Milla playing together, but say nothing. Their constant ministrations have ceased, replaced only by a curious *watching*.

Before he left, Lord Tanen took Sela and explained that there are some things Milla can never know. And that if Milla discovers them, that she will have to be taken away. Sela didn't have to be told what he meant: the killing.

Sela enjoys killing, and looks forward to her training in the basement of the manor house each day. She has known for as long as she can remember that the killing is a special secret. The unreal enemies that Lord Tanen has been training her to protect against are ever watchful. Milla has been told that Sela's killing time is her time for "special studies." Milla has no interest in studies, though.

"What is it you do down there all morning?" Milla asked her once.

"I train to use my Gift. I have Empathy."

Milla shrugged. She has no use for the Gifts, possessing none of her own. She smiled. "You're so lucky."

Sela knows that Milla is not very bright. She is sweet and kind and trusting, but she has a very hard time understanding things that are simple to Sela. At first this bothered Sela, but now she's used to it.

Sela makes her very first thread, with Milla, one evening after supper. They are in their bedroom, laughing about the wart on Begina's face. Begina is one of the crones, the coldest one, the one most likely to slap Sela with a ruler.

They are laughing, laughing, and Sela takes Milla in her arms and holds her as tight as she can. Milla tickles her and they fall over laughing; then Milla falls backward and hits her head on the floor.

"Ouch!" says Sela, holding her head.

"Why are you ouching?" says Milla, sitting up, laughing, holding her own head. "I'm the one that fell."

"I don't know," says Sela. She looks at Milla, and there it is: a fat, fluffy, pink-and-gold thread, made of light, extending from her to Milla. It's not a real thread, like in the sewing box. And it's not actually made of light, either. It's a connection of some kind, and Milla's thoughts and feelings mingle with her own along it. Sela has never felt so close to anyone before, believes that it isn't possible to feel so close to anyone.

"What's happening?" says Milla. "I feel very strange."

"I feel like I could just let go and disappear forever," says Sela, her voice soft and airy. She's starting to forget who's who. Is she Sela, or Milla? Is she anyone at all?

She gets a glimpse of something, something that is powerful and true. As Sela slips into Milla and Milla and Sela slip away together, something deeper and more real than either of them begins to appear in its place. Sela is filled with a rush of emotion she can't explain.

"I don't like this," says Milla. Sela looks at her and sees the thread that isn't a thread convulse, thick runnels of purple and green and brown now coursing through, spoiling the pinkness, pulling it taut, making it ugly.

Revulsion. Milla's or hers? Milla is afraid of her: has *always* been afraid of her. Has always found Sela unsettling.

No, Sela's revulsion. Disgust at Milla's betrayal.

Who is feeling this?

The door slams open and Lord Tanen bolts into the room. He is not supposed to be here!

"Sela!" he shouts. "She is one of their spies! Milla is an assassin of the unreal!"

"No!" screams Sela, jerking back, away from Milla.

Milla and Sela are terrified. Milla and Sela want to be away.

Lord Tanen is carrying something, something that shines. Milla and Sela are afraid of it.

No, Milla is afraid of it. Sela wants it. Sela reaches out for it.

Lord Tanen puts the knife in Sela's hand, and the thread between her and Milla goes black, black, black.

"You know what must be done," says Tanen.

Milla skitters backward. Sela can feel her confusion and terror. Terror of Sela. She knows who is who now.

Sela advances on Milla and, with trembling fingers, kills her. It's so easy; the ones that Lord Tanen provides for her lessons have far more fight in them. The thread vanishes not in an instant, not as the knife slices the flesh, but slowly, sluggishly.

"Congratulations," says Lord Tanen. "Today you have completed your training."

Sela turns on Lord Tanen, the knife wet in her grasp. A girl's blood looks just like anyone else's. A real girl? An unreal girl? Sela draws the blade of the knife across her wrist, severing the vein there. The blood is just the same. No difference.

"It's too much for her," comes a voice behind Lord Tanen. One of the crones. She's not sure which one. "You went too far with this one, just like we told you."

"Hush!" shouts Lord Tanen, wheeling on the crone. "She's just fine. She's stronger than any of the others."

Too far. Sela lets go of the knife. It's a meaningless object, a protrusion into space of lines and angles. A weight, nothing more. A minute ago she'd almost seen something, something beyond all of this meaninglessness. She has it in her grasp, but knows that if she looks there again, she will cease to be.

"Come along now," says Lord Tanen. "It's time you and I had a long conversation."

Sela's body is, she realizes, unreal. It too is simply space and lines and angles. Machines moving and humming, insensate, collaborating in the illusion of being. It is coming at her again, the thing she saw, from a different angle. The thing that will consume her.

"What is it?" asks Lord Tanen, looking into her eyes. A thread forms. Very unlike the first. Sela sees him and knows him. Knows who and what he is and what he wants and why, but it's much too much, and the thing that wants to eat her is reaching up to swallow her into everything, and so she shows it to Lord Tanen instead.

Lord Tanen makes a funny sound. Not just odd, but humorous. Sela almost giggles. Everything is too big and horrid, and this thing that wants to eat her is consuming Lord Tanen and his only response is to make such a silly little noise.

Someone screams. One of the crones, she assumes. She shows the thing to the crone, too. Why not? It will eat everything sooner or later, she knows. Only a matter of time. Might as well save Sela for last.

More screaming, and now running, slamming. Sela has closed her eyes; she doesn't want to see any of this, no thank you.

It goes on like this for quite some time. Hours. Sela is waiting for the thing to return and show itself to her, but instead something hits her from behind, hard, and she bites her tongue.

"Get that accursed thing on her *now*," comes a frightened voice.

Someone is sliding something up over her wrist. A bracelet? A gift for me? Up over her elbow, and then snug against her arm. The thing she's been showing to everyone loses its teeth, yawns, goes to sleep.

What was that thing? Sela is certain that it was big and dangerous, but can't quite picture it anymore.

That voice again. "We've got her, Lord Everess," it says. "She's secure."

Secure.

Sela saw light. Light, energy, heat, all around her. She was being burned alive. But she wasn't really seeing it; she was experiencing it on some level other than sight. There were no eyes, no body.

A thread erupted out of her. A thick, ropy thread connecting her to a presence larger and more terrifying than any she had ever known. An ancient intelligence, a wisdom beyond eons, beyond stars. It saw her and knew her.

She was being incinerated in flame. She was vanishing. Then her body was jerked to the side—but there was no body, of course—and she dropped, hard, onto stone.

"Sorry about that," came a girl's voice. Faella.

Sela opened her eyes. She was on her knees on a platform of stone. Silverdun, Ironfoot, and Faella were here as well. Faella had landed on her feet, but both Silverdun and Ironfoot were picking themselves off the hard floor of the platform.

The platform was circular, with a stone railing. Beyond the railing was nothingness. Not darkness, not light. Just . . . nothing. Sela had no words for it. Emptiness without form or substance, or even absence. It was deeply unsettling.

"I apologize for almost killing all of us," said Faella. "But I'm afraid we didn't take into account that the fold would feed us directly into the receptacle, not into a happy landing spot. So I made an adjustment in midfold. Harder than it sounds, I can assure you."

"Where are we?" asked Sela, her voice shaking.

"Look behind you," said Silverdun.

Sela stood, turning. Behind her was a wide road that ended at a great stair leading up to a massive, black edifice, a squat castle without tower or battlement, streaked reddish orange. It was blocky, unadorned, huge. Larger than the Great Seelie Keep and twice as high.

Before them, at the start of the road, was a tall stone arch, and on the arch was inscribed a line of script in a language that Sela didn't recognize.

"What is that?" she asked.

Ironfoot looked up at the arch, puzzling out the characters.

"This is Thule Fae," he said. "I studied it at Queensbridge. But it's an odd dialect. Give me a moment."

"What does it say?" asked Silverdun.

"It says 'Beyond This Arch Lies Death.'"

"Not very welcoming," said Silverdun.

"Great. So what's the plan, boss?" asked Ironfoot.

Silverdun scowled. "We go inside and look around," he said.

"And that sign?"

"Pray it's a bit of hyperbole."

"I hate to bring this up," said Faella. "Because you may find it a bit dispiriting, but there's something I need to tell you."

"What now?" asked Silverdun.

"While we were in the fold, I'm afraid some time may have passed. Rather longer than you might have expected."

"How long?" asked Ironfoot.

"I think it was about four days," said Faella.

Silverdun swore. "Then the war's already begun!"

chapter thirty-six

Morale is worth its weight in gold. Given the choice
between a hopeful soldier with a club and a disheartened
soldier with a sword, I will take the one with the club
every time. After the Battle of Coldwood, General
Ameus was asked how he prevailed despite being heavily
outnumbered. He famously answered, "We were less
interested in dying than they were."

—Cmdr. Tae Filarete, *Observations on Battle*

auritane didn't agree with the invasion, but that didn't mean he wasn't
going to do it properly.

He stood outside his tent facing north, reviewing his Seelie Army troops
as they marched west along the Border Road toward the ruins of Selafae,
where they would amass and cross into the Unseelie at dawn. The Border
Wall itself was a hundred yards farther north, separated from the road by a
swath of swampy ground.

A seemingly unending line of soldiers, wagons, and horses flowed past,
kicking up dust along the road. The air smelled of dirt, horse dung, sweat,
and the spiced preparations of the battle mages.

The battle plans for this invasion had been drawn up a week earlier and
had been distributed to all of his generals, as well as to the Foreign Ministry
and the office of the secretary of states. A copy had also been sent, encrypted,
to Jem-Aleth, the Unseelie ambassador, signed by Baron Glennet. That plan
was probably even now circulating among Mab's commanders on the opposite side of the border. At least, he hoped it was.

The plan was a fiction, of course. They would not be attacking from Selafae. They would be going over the Border Wall. The soldiers weren't marching; they were taking their positions. At his signal, they would turn to the north and march directly to Elenth.

Six months ago, Mauritane and a pair of trusted battle mages had traveled to this very spot, miles from any village or city on either side of the border, carrying a unique spellbomb. No Einswrath this; it was specifically crafted to disrupt the bindings that kept the Border Wall impassable. It had performed its task perfectly, flattening down the barrier of Motion, allowing Mauritane and his mages to hop easily over the border. Two days ago, under cover of night, Mauritane's mages had strung identical bombs along a three-mile section of the wall.

Mauritane looked at the sun. It was time. He called his head support mage, Captain Eland, to his side.

"It's time," he said.

Eland nodded and gathered up his mages. Across the border, a company of Unseelie cavalry stood, watching but doing nothing. The Seelie men hurled good-natured insults at them as they went, though the cavalrymen certainly couldn't hear them from this distance. They were in for quite a surprise.

One of Eland's men raised his hand, and a flare of witchlight shot up, flashing bright red in the sky. It made a small pop as it exploded. Across the border, one of the Unseelie cavalry pointed to it, talking to the man next to him.

A series of closely timed explosions ripped across the Border Wall. Even at a hundred yards, they were loud enough to hurt Mauritane's ears.

Mauritane's troops required no other signal, but he gave one anyway.

"The Seelie Heart!" he called, his voice magically amplified.

"The Seelie Heart!" answered the voices of a thousand men. The battle cry echoed up and down the lines.

The army turned as one and began marching north toward the curtain of black smoke that was now rising where the Border Wall had been. About a mile farther north, they would meet a very unprepared column of Unseelie troops, and the battle would begin in earnest.

The Unseelie cavalry turned and fled, but they were too late. Percussives fired from the lead battle mages blew them to bits within seconds.

Thus began the Third Unseelie War.

It took a few hours, but to their credit, the Unseelie realized quickly what had happened and altered their own plans in response. There were a number of small skirmishes—during which Unseelie forces, caught utterly off guard, were slaughtered handily—but those were few.

The first battle was just south of the Unseelie village of Claret. Mab's forces were waiting for them in the village and struck as Mauritane was advancing up the hill toward it.

The first spells began to clash overhead as the battle mages unleashed their opening salvos. Streamers of smoke intertwined in a riot of color, percussives and incendiaries canceling each other out in the sky. Those percussives that struck among Mauritane's troops, however, were devastating in their capacity.

Still no Einswrath.

The cavalry and infantry met on the outskirts of the village. Bowmen attempted to clear a path through the Unseelie line, but the force was too large. Mounted soldiers clashed, their swords glinting in the sunlight. Men on the ground fought with sword and pike. There were screams, shouted orders, the thunder of hooves, the endless scrape of metal on metal. And Mauritane was at the center of it all, urging his commanders onward, calling out his own orders.

He, of course, could not fight. He wore a blade, the one he'd taken from the prison at Crere Sulace, but hadn't swung it in months. Command was fine, but watching his men advance, he dearly wished to be in the middle of it, a cavalry officer on a clever touched mount, leading the charge.

They took Claret after two hours, but there were casualties. Scouts reported Unseelie reinforcements approaching by the hundreds.

Mauritane's strategy depended on the taking of Elenth on the fourth day of the campaign. If the city could be taken and supply lines fortified, they might stand a chance of repelling the direct onslaught of the main Unseelie force, which was even now coming at a forced march from the border crossing at Selafae, where a half-regiment of Mauritane's Fifth Battalion waited, both as a lure and as a hedge, in case Mab decided to try for Sylvan anyway.

Soon there would be Mab's battle fliers, hurling balls of flame and arrows down from above. There would be a flag city bearing down on them, its civilian population offloaded to other cities. The ground war was only the beginning.

The problem with the flying cities, the reason Mab was cautious with them, was that it was not impossible to bring them down, as Mauritane and his friends had proven prior to the Battle of Sylvan. He'd done it by infiltrating the city and slaughtering the strange hybrid creatures that manned the Chambers of Elements and Motion, which provided the force that kept the cities aloft. But Mauritane had developed missiles of Elements that could be fired at the underbellies of these cities. He knew the location of the Chambers of Elements and Motion in most of the flag cities now, thanks to Paet and the Shadows. If a city appeared, he might be able to down it with a single shot.

They pushed forward. They fought. Men and women fell. Too many of them. At this rate it wasn't certain they would even reach Elenth, let alone take it.

The second day they mostly marched, meeting only a few lost companies of Unseelie who'd gotten separated from their battalions in the confusion. These were taken down with relative ease, but even in these skirmishes Mauritane lost soldiers.

There was another battle at Downvalley, a day's march south of Elenth. Again Mauritane took the day, but at a substantial cost. Reports from his generals across the front reported similar losses.

Had he stretched his force too wide? Had he underestimated the flexibility of the Unseelie?

And there was still no word from Silverdun. According to Paet's latest report, they'd vanished in a flash of Folding three days earlier and hadn't been heard from since. No one wanted to say it, but it seemed certain that they wouldn't be coming back. If Hy Pezho had new Einswrath weapons, there would be no stopping him. And nothing Mauritane was doing would matter at all.

On the fourth day they reached Elenth, only to find it guarded by the entire Eagle Regiment of the Unseelie Army, with five battalions. And three battalions of Annwni.

Mauritane had only six battalions, and had already taken heavy casualties.

This was going to be difficult. This was going to be a serious battle. Time to invoke a bit of Fae propriety.

Mauritane rode out under a flag of parley and met with the Unseelie commanding general. They bowed deeply and made all the appropriate noises to one another, and agreed that they would join battle at dawn. All very civilized.

When Mauritane rode back, his troops were already setting up camp on the southern slope of the valley. Mauritane's aide, Colonel Nyet, found him and took him aside, scowling.

"Someone to see you," said Nyet, pointing.

Baron Glennet had arrived with a delegation from Corpus, including Lord Everess. But Glennet was the ranking nobleman here, and it was clearly his show. This was a time-honored ritual on the eve of a great battle; a ranking member of the nobility could secure the right from the queen to lead the charge. It was a pure formality, of course. Glennet would review the troops, make a grandiose speech, and offer homilies and platitudes. The troops would love it, and Glennet would have his ego boosted. On the morning of the actual battle, he would graciously yield command of the army back to Mauritane, and then go home to his cozy bed and be saluted by the court for his bravery. In the official history, Baron Glennet would be reported as the commander of the assault on Elenth, not Mauritane. This was nothing new, and most commanders accepted it as a matter of course.

Mauritane greeted Glennet and Everess with full propriety. His propriety with Glennet was exactly as sincere as it had been with the Unseelie general minutes earlier. The difference was that Mauritane had actually respected the general. Their meeting was done in full view of Glennet's staff and Mauritane's officers. As a commoner and a military man, Mauritane was required to take the lower bow, which probably pleased Glennet to no end.

Mauritane knelt and presented Glennet with his sword. "I offer you command of my troops, and defer to Your Lordship in all things."

Glennet raised the blade high above his head and the men cheered.

Once the formal greetings were concluded, Mauritane, Everess, and Glennet spoke privately in front of Mauritane's tent.

"I must say we were all surprised by your sudden change of stratagem," said Glennet.

"That was the idea," said Mauritane.

"You could have informed *us* what you were doing," said Everess, clearly annoyed.

"The best way to keep a secret is not to tell anyone," said Mauritane. "That's what my mother taught me."

"Just so, just so," said Everess. "But still."

After mess, Glennet made his inspirational speech to the troops. The parts of it Mauritane paid attention to were genuinely stirring, and it did the frightened troops some good. These were Seelie soldiers, brave and true, but it had been a difficult campaign so far.

Once the speech was over, Mauritane shook Glennet's hand and thanked him profusely and sincerely. Before he could get back to work, Lord Everess corralled him. Everess was holding a valise.

"I've got a few things to show you, General," said Everess, patting the valise.

"I don't need any military advice," said Mauritane.

"Oh, these aren't military documents. And I think you'll be *very* interested in the story that goes along with them."

Dawn came, and Mauritane was ready. He'd slept briefly during the evening, and had been up making preparations since midnight. He'd done his best. He was probably riding to his death this morning, but there was no turning back now. If he retreated, the Unseelie forces to the southwest would simply divert from their present course and cut them off at the rear. They'd be caught between two massive bodies of Unseelie troops. The only way to survive was to take Elenth.

When the sun appeared over the plains to the east, Mauritane stood mounted before his troops, with Glennet on a great white stallion on one side, and Everess on a slightly less impressive mount on the other. Glennet still held Mauritane's sword, ready to yield it back to him.

"On this day, we have a special honor," said Mauritane. "We are gratified indeed."

Glennet raised the sword, and the troops cheered again.

"A lesser nobleman would have accepted command of you in name only, and then yielded it back to me. A lesser nobleman would have taken the credit for the battle without actually fighting."

Glennet looked at Mauritane, confused.

"But not our illustrious Baron Glennet! No, this great man has boldly chosen to retain command, and to lead you all into battle against the Unseelie at Elenth!"

The troops roared their approval. This was unheard-of in the modern day, a historic event.

Glennet shifted in his saddle but said nothing. What could he say? If he contradicted Mauritane, he would be reviled as a coward who had changed his mind at the last moment. He'd be laughed out of Corpus. He looked at Everess for assistance, but Everess only smiled.

Glennet was trapped, and knew it. "I could not stand by," he said, "and watch you ride out today knowing that I had not done everything I could to bring a victory!"

The troops went wild with approval.

Mauritane smiled. "Then take your position at the front of the line, as is your ancient right," said Mauritane. "And call the charge!"

The infantry and cavalrymen took their positions along the wide line. The drums sounded. At the bottom of the hill, the Unseelie were in formation, awaiting the charge. This was going to be a bloody, terrible battle.

As Mauritane and Glennet rode out to the front of the line, Glennet dropped his facade. "What is the meaning of this?" he growled.

"You wanted a war," said Everess. "Here you have it."

Mauritane turned his horse and cried out to his troops. "I give you your battle cry!" he called. "For Glennet!"

"For Glennet!" the troops answered.

Mauritane and Everess rode back behind the lines, leaving Glennet alone before the army.

Glennet paused, and then raised Mauritane's sword. If anyone saw Glennet's hands shake, they never mentioned it afterward.

Glennet dropped the sword and kicked his stallion. With a crash of drums and incendiaries and hooves, the charge was begun.

Mauritane watched as the mages streaked the sky, the archers filled it with arrows. Watched the cavalry cloud the valley with dust and the infantry charge. He would have given anything to have been in Glennet's place.

Everess rode toward him. "I believe this is our cue to be leaving," he said. "We fancy folk don't want to get in your way any more than we've already done."

"Good," said Mauritane. "Go."

"I appreciate your help with Glennet," said Everess.

"Don't thank me. I didn't do it to help you. I did it because he was a filthy traitor who tried to have my best friend killed."

"Such loyalty!"

"And don't forget," said Mauritane, "now I've got something to blackmail you with if I ever need to." He kicked his horse and rode off toward his tent.

The two lines met outside the city walls and things swiftly turned ugly. Whatever grim satisfaction Mauritane might have had at sending Glennet to his doom swiftly vanished into the frenzy of command. The Unseelie regiment was engaging Mauritane directly, and the Annwni battalions were positioning themselves for a flanking maneuver. Mauritane knew his soldiers were the best in Faerie, but these were unbeatable odds and he knew it. Even if his troops killed two for every one lost, they'd still be behind in sheer numbers, and the Unseelie had a strong position to fall back to, behind the walls of Elenth. Everess should be grateful that he and his friends were already on their way back to the City Emerald.

But this was a day that every commander knew he might someday face. Leading his men into death, praying for a miracle. Knowing that he had done everything he could do, Mauritane nearly resigned himself to loss. If the tide did not turn soon, he might actually consider surrender. The war would end then, and there would be nothing to stop the Unseelie incursion across the border. But his troops would survive the day. And an Unseelie occupation would meet with strong resistance. Even in the darkest hour the Seelie would find a way to hope. They would bend, but they would not crack.

As the morning progressed, things grew worse. The Annwni were nearly in position now, and once they joined, the Seelie would be finished. Mauritane was determined to announce his surrender before that happened, before any more lives could be lost. He mounted his horse, feeling lower than he had ever felt, even worse than the day he'd arrived at Crere Sulace after being branded a traitor. He'd thought that there could be no worse feeling than that. He'd been wrong.

An aide approached, somber. "Shall I fetch the flag, sir?"

Mauritane took a last look down the hill. The Annwni battalions had taken formation, but not where they ought to have. They were in no position to flank the Seelie. In fact, they were far better suited to—

A horn sounded and the Annwni charged. But not at Mauritane's troops. Instead, they rushed the Unseelie at its exposed right flank. Caught utterly off guard, the Unseelie force crumbled; chaos rippled through the army from right to left as the Annwni plowed into them.

Mauritane reached down from the saddle and grabbed his aide by the neck. "Get word to the commanders in the field," he shouted. "Move left and block the Unseelie retreat!" The aide looked at him, wide-eyed.

"Move!" shouted Mauritane, kicking the man in his shoulder.

"Wait!" he cried. "Come back!" The harried aide circled back around. "Give me your sword," said Mauritane, holding out his hand.

"But sir!" the aide said.

"If you don't give me that sword this second, I will take it from you and remove your head with it, boy!"

The aide gave him the sword. Mauritane tested it in his hand and flicked it in the air. It wasn't *his* sword, but it would do.

"Sir, you can't just—"

"My officers know what to do," said Mauritane. "Give them the order and tell them to get to work!"

Mauritane dug in his heels and sprinted out of camp, nearly knocking over the aide. He waved his sword and felt the air rushing past him. This was good.

When the first soldiers spied him approaching, they raised up Mauritane's famous battle cry. "The Seelie Heart!" they shouted. The cry was taken up across the front. Mauritane rode up through the lines, toward the battle.

There was a chance.

A flier came in low from the north, its sails luffing in a crosswind. It had traveled at speed all the way from the City of Mab without stopping and had nearly used up its entire supply of Motion. The pilot fought the tiller, trimmed the sails as much as he could, trying to catch as much air as possible.

It was a near thing, but the flier managed a safe landing just outside the north gate of Elenth. The pilot leapt out of the flier, carrying a wooden box. He was met by a lieutenant at the gate, who took the box from him and lashed it to his saddle, then mounted and raced into the city, knocking down a frightened fruit seller as he passed.

The lieutenant whipped around a corner and rode directly up the outside stairs to the rooftop garden of a townhouse in the middle of the city. When he reached the top, his comrades were still setting up the catapult.

"What's wrong with you?" shouted the lieutenant. "This should have been set up last night!"

"It only just arrived," grumbled the sergeant in charge of the assembly. "We've been having trouble with the supply lanes. Saboteurs everywhere."

"What saboteurs?" said the lieutenant, dismounting and untying the box.

"Arcadians, if you can believe it," said the sergeant, pulling hard on a rope threaded through the catapult. "Damndest thing," he said. "Suddenly seem to be everywhere."

"Well, that doesn't matter. Once we've annihilated the Seelie, there'll be plenty of time to deal with them."

The lieutenant placed the box carefully on the ground and unlatched it. Inside were two dark objects, not much bigger than oranges. They were rough globules, and they pulsed to the touch.

"That's it, then?" said the sergeant, breathing heavily, afraid to touch them.

"That's the Einswrath," said the lieutenant. "You may fire when ready."

The sergeant gingerly reached out and picked one up. It was heavy.

"Hurry!" he shouted to his men.

"This should be quite a show," said the lieutenant.

chapter thirty-seven

We await and fear your release.

—Chthonic prayer

Silverdun led the way along the road. To either side there was only the unsettling emptiness. Before them was the great black castle, imposing and—frankly—terrifying. Silverdun kept his eyes on the road.

Ironfoot caught up to him and they walked in step, with Sela and Faella just behind. Silverdun looked down at Ironfoot's boots; they kicked up small clouds of dust from the road.

"Why do they call you Ironfoot, anyway?" Silverdun asked.

Ironfoot looked at him. "When I was a boy I used to trip a lot."

"Ah," said Silverdun. "I was hoping it was something more menacing than that."

"I take it back then," said Ironfoot. "I once kicked a man in the head so hard that he forgot his name."

"Much better."

"Does anyone feel something strange?" asked Sela.

Silverdun looked back at her. "That implies that there's some part of this that *isn't* strange."

"I've got the oddest sensation," said Sela. "As though I'm being pushed backward, but I can't feel a wind."

Now that she said it, Silverdun could feel it as well. It was slight, but noticeable. As though a light breeze he couldn't feel was blowing into his face. Or perhaps more like the heat from a distant fire radiating toward him. But it was not fire or air that was pushing against them. It was their own *re.*

"The queen's alabaster ass," said Silverdun. "Do you know what I think?"

"What?" said Faella.

"I think that castle is made of iron."

"What?" said Ironfoot. "That's impossible."

"I've had a few run-ins with iron, friend. Trust me. That's what you're feeling."

By the time they reached the bottom of the stairs, the sensation of being pushed backward was unmistakable. It was becoming difficult to walk. And as if that weren't enough, the steps themselves presented a problem. They were each waist high, and there were easily a hundred of them.

"Stairs for giants," said Silverdun.

"Or gods," said Ironfoot.

"Don't get superstitious, Ironfoot," said Silverdun. "I admire you for your powers of reason."

"There's nothing reasonable about any of this."

"That inscription is just to scare off visitors," said Silverdun. "Whatever awaits us up there may be ominous, but it's not divine."

"If you say so," said Ironfoot.

"Well, boys," said Faella. "Are we going to stand here nattering all day, or are we going to storm yonder castle?" She was smiling. Faella was many things, but apparently she was no coward.

The steps were just high enough to be an enormous bother without being an impassable obstacle. Silverdun and Ironfoot hauled themselves up each one, reaching back to help Faella and Sela up, neither of whom was quite tall enough to manage it themselves. After twenty steps his back was aching, and they weren't quite a quarter of the way to the top.

The closer they came, the stronger the repulsion grew. It was painful now. Not excruciating yet, as it had been when "Ilian" had yanked him into the bars of his cell, but bad enough.

Halfway up, Silverdun was out of breath, and Sela and Faella were both struggling. Silverdun and Ironfoot had the benefit of Shadow strength and resistance, but neither of the women did. Thinking of his Shadow nature recalled his conversation with Jedron at the pit. Silverdun was dead. But that was insane. *He* was Silverdun. In every way that mattered, anyway.

But if Silverdun was truly dead, where was he? Was his true self in Arcadia with Mother and Father now? Were Je Wen and Timha there, waiting to blame him for their deaths? And the others he'd seen fall: Honeywell, Gray Mave, all the men he'd killed at the Battle of Sylvan?

Was this Silverdun merely a ghost? Was that what he'd become?

After what seemed like ages, they reached the top of the steps. The castle loomed before them, giving off waves of reitic repulsion; it was like standing in front of a bonfire. It burned the skin and stung the eyes. Before them was a wide door, easily forty feet high. It was opened just a crack.

"Not to be defeatist," said Ironfoot. "But what in hell are we supposed to do now?"

Silverdun paused. He'd been so intent on reaching the castle that he hadn't given much thought to what they'd do when they got there. One thing at a time.

"What, indeed?" he said.

"You forget, Lord Silverdun," said Faella, "that I am a talented girl."

He looked at her. Still smiling, eager even. He realized that he was in love with her, and always had been.

"What are you going to do?" asked Ironfoot. "Make us all impervious to iron?"

"No, Master Falores," said Faella. "I'm going to remove the iron."

"There's no way to do that with the Gifts," said Silverdun.

"There is with the Thirteenth Gift," said Faella. "Change Magic reaches into the very nature of things. I'm not really sure how it works. I'm no Ironfoot. But I believe I can manage it."

"I'll believe it when I see it," said Ironfoot.

"There's just one thing," said Faella. "In order to change something, I have to touch it."

"No," said Silverdun. "That much iron—it'll kill you."

"Not just that," said Faella. "I'm afraid I don't have quite enough *re* of my own to get the job done."

"Meaning what?" asked Sela.

"Meaning I'll need Sela to join us all in Empathy, so I can draw from you all."

"I can do that," said Sela. Silverdun looked at her. She was looking at Faella, her head high. She clearly wasn't going to let Faella take the award for bravery without a fight.

"Ironfoot, can you think of any alternative?" said Silverdun.

"No," said Ironfoot. "But I have a hard time believing this will work either."

"Allow me to surprise you," said Faella.

They linked hands. Silverdun stood between Sela and Faella, with Ironfoot at Faella's other hand. Silverdun opened up and felt Sela flow into him. He felt the same swirl of beauty and darkness and pain and hope that he'd always felt from her. But now it was tinged with a keening sense of loss. Silverdun knew that he had caused this feeling, and he cringed. Then Faella flowed into him as well, and Sela faded into the background. Faella. There were no words for her. She was simply Faella. That was all she cared to be, and no matter how much he had tried to deny it, it was all Silverdun wanted.

Faella stepped forward all at once and placed her palm against the door. Silverdun felt what she felt. It was torture, agony. For an instant they were all blinded by the pain, by the magnitude of the hurt, the relentless force of the iron's push.

But then, something changed. Dimly, Silverdun sensed a fleeting thought coming from Ironfoot: *Just like Lin Vo.* Silverdun had a little touch of Insight, and channeled a bit of it to try to figure out what Faella was doing, but he only caught a brief glimpse, and as soon as Sela noticed him channeling, she threw her own thought at him: *Stop that!*

There was a crackling sound and a burst of heat: real heat. It burned Silverdun's skin, but then was whisked away. With it went the force of the iron. The repulsion was still there, but much reduced. Tolerable. Silverdun looked at Faella's hand against the door. The hand was red and blistering. Her pain, which Silverdun could still sense, was more than he could have borne on his own.

Beneath Faella's hand, the door began to change. From the deep black of iron, it became lustrous and gray. The change spread out in veins from Faella's fingers, growing like the branches of a tree, each branch sprouting others. The branches grew and overlapped, and after a few moments the door was all gray, and Silverdun felt no repulsion from it at all.

Faella dropped her hand from the door and clasped it in her other. Silverdun looked at her face and saw that she was crying.

"I've started the change. I made it into a little binding—it's funny, once I started it, it sort of took off on its own; there was energy in the change itself, as the iron became something else."

"What kind of energy?" said Ironfoot. He let go of her hand and touched the door, rapping against it.

"Oh, I'm sure I don't know," said Faella. "But I sort of nudged it a little and it turned into *re*. There's *re* here, lots of it. Everything here wants to become it. I don't know how to explain."

A bit of the door chipped away in Ironfoot's hands. "What is this?" he asked.

Silverdun took the chip and channeled Elements into it. "Cobalt," he said.

Ironfoot frowned at him. "Geology was a required subject in Elements," said Silverdun. "Boring as all hell."

It took all four of them, but with some effort they managed to pry the door open on its hinges. Silverdun looked at Faella.

"Your hand," he said, pointing. "It's healed."

"Oh, that," she said. "That's not so hard."

The door opened onto an entry hall with a pair of great doors just opposite the ones they'd entered. It was dark inside, but there were witchlamps on the walls, and Silverdun lit them. Once lit, they revealed the continuation of Faella's work; the iron around them turning slowly into cobalt, branches of gray flowing out in all directions.

"I suppose what we're looking for is through there," Silverdun said.

After a moment, the second doors were changed enough to touch. They were even more difficult to open than the first, but they eventually gave as well. Beyond them was a great chamber, also dark, but there was a gray light flitting in the distant darkness. The slightest footstep echoed in the space beyond. From within came a quiet droning sound.

"I believe there's someone in there," said Silverdun.

"How is that possible?" asked Sela. "How could any Fae survive in there?"

"Let's find out," said Silverdun.

He started through the doors and was immediately struck with vertigo. Waves of *re* reverberated through the chamber, condensed by the surrounding iron. It was like walking into water. It was a curious, warm sensation. Not unpleasant. Like being bathed in warm light. It took a moment for Silverdun to regain his bearings.

"I can't see a damn thing," said Ironfoot. "Should we chance some light?"

"Let's hold off for the moment," said Silverdun. "It might be best if we catch whoever's in there by surprise."

They pressed forward. Silverdun could hear his companions' breath strangely muffled in the cavernous room. They were all breathing quickly.

The gray light beyond was still now, and as they approached it, the droning grew more intense. Not knowing what else to do, Silverdun led the way toward it. Whatever the source of the light was, it was hidden behind something massive in the room, something he could sense more than see from the way that sounds and *re* echoed from it.

They reached a wall that cut across part of the chamber, and stopped behind it.

"Wait here," Silverdun whispered to Sela and Faella. "Ironfoot, you're with me."

"I want to come with you," hissed Faella. "We both do."

"Ironfoot and I can move in total silence," said Silverdun. "Neither of you can. Wait here."

Silverdun and Ironfoot continued, making no sound whatsoever. They came closer to the source of the light, and Silverdun now began to notice that there were a number of other massive objects in the room. The wall they'd left Sela and Faella behind was actually the base of one of them. The droning noise grew as they approached, the light remaining constant.

They reached the edge of the tall obstruction that hid the light. Just as they were about to peer around it, the droning whine stopped, and the room grew impossibly silent. There was a slight rushing sound, and Silverdun felt a breeze on his face. The light began to approach them, its reflection moving along the wall behind it. Silverdun and Ironfoot both drew knives and slid around the corner.

Approaching them was a glowing silver moth, huge and hovering ten feet in the air, flying directly at them. It was the source of the illumination; its body and wings emanated witchlight.

The creature noticed them and flapped its wings, stopping in the air. Now that it was no longer in motion, Silverdun could see it better. It was not a giant moth, but a Fae man, dressed head to toe in bright silver armor, a helmet covering his head entirely. A pair of great wings, composed of silver so thin it was nearly transparent, emerged from the shoulder plates of the armor, easily thirty feet from tip to tip.

The flying man reached up and raised the visor of the helmet. He looked astonished.

His face was that of a Bel Zheret, but his eyes were those of a true Fae.

"Who the hell are you?" he said.

chapter thirty-eight

The only perfect battle plan would be the one that acknowledges that no such plan exists.

—Cmdr. Tae Filarete, *Observations on Battle*

The catapult was finally finished, no thanks to the lieutenant who wouldn't stop breathing down Sergeant Hy-Asher's neck.

"Where do we aim?" he said. "Into the main force?"

"No, you idiot," said the lieutenant. "You'd be killing our forces as well. Aim for the camp on the hill. Take out General Mauritane and the war's as good as won."

Hy-Asher's men tested the wind and maneuvered the catapult into place. A private wound the roller handle, and the beam came down slowly and was hooked into place. With shaking hands, he placed the Einswrath into the bowl and nodded.

Mauritane was at the front of the line, leading Bear Company toward the gate of Elenth. Once the gate was breached, they could fight their way into the city, and he and the Annwni commanders could rendezvous. The battle, he felt in his bones, was as good as over. All around him men shouted, swinging blades in strong arcs. Clatter and shriek. Hoofbeat and shout.

A new sun erupted behind him, and a moment later a force like the hand of a god threw him from his horse, landing him facedown on the trampled ground. Surprised shouts and screams of pain came from all around him.

Mauritane sat up and looked back toward his camp. A column of flame rose up from the top of the rise at the edge of the valley. Trees hundreds of feet away were on fire. Smoke rose from the flattened grass on the slope. The Seelie camp was gone. If he hadn't rushed into battle, he'd be dead now.

The Einswrath had come. The Shadows had failed. After so much effort, so many turns, it seemed there was no escaping the inevitability of loss.

But at this point, Mauritane didn't care. He stood up, waved his sword in the air, and screamed. "The Seelie Heart!" he rasped. "Onward to Elenth!"

Many of his soldiers rose along with him, rallying to the sound of his voice. Not all of them, but perhaps enough.

Across the Unseelie, things began going wrong for Mab. In her rooms atop the new City of Mab, reports went from bad to worse. The Annwni High Council had rebelled against her, slaughtering her governor and proconsul. They'd sent word to their troops to ally with the Seelie, and now they were wreaking havoc across the entire front.

At the same time, every Arcadian in the Empire seemed to have risen up as one. They were stealing horses, dismantling supply wagons, intercepting orders. An entire company of the Fifth Battalion had defected to the Seelie: Every one of them had been infected with Arcadianism.

Mab paced in her rooms. Hy Pezho would be back soon. He would swiftly build more Einswrath, the lunatic. If only he didn't somehow manage to wake Ein in the process.

Mab and Ein had a history together. Their relationship had ended on a sour note.

Soon Hy Pezho would return. And Titania would finally kneel before her. All the rest was just a momentary hiccup.

chapter thirty-nine

"Why?" only matters over the long term. In the moment,
"How?" will suffice.

—Master Jedron

"We're Shadows," said Silverdun, stepping toward the flying man,
dagger in hand. "Who the hell are you?"

"The infamous Shadows! I should have known!" said the man. He bowed in
the air. "And I am Hy Pezho. The Black Artist. I'd be hurt that you didn't recognize me, but I'm a bit changed of late. I suppose now *you* are my nemeses."

"We're here to stop you building the Einswrath," said Silverdun. "We're
here to end it."

"Hm," said Hy Pezho. "That's interesting."

"Is it?" said Silverdun.

He cocked his head to the side. "No, I was just wondering: How are you
standing on the floor? It's solid iron."

"Not anymore," said Silverdun. "We've changed it. If that's why you're
in the air, you can come down."

Hy Pezho's face took on an expression of pure horror. "What do you
mean, you *changed* it? That's impossible!"

"We have our little secrets," said Silverdun. "Now come down from
there. You're outnumbered."

"Stop it!" shouted Hy Pezho. "Whatever you're doing, stop it at once!
Do you have any idea what you're doing?"

Silverdun looked at Ironfoot. This wasn't quite the reaction he'd have
expected from the Black Artist Hy Pezho.

Hy Pezho threw up his arms and illuminated the entire room with bright white witchlight. "Look around you, you fools! Don't you know where you are?"

Silverdun looked. It took a moment for him to take in what he was seeing. The space took up the entire interior of the castle save for the small entryway through which they'd passed. It was empty except for a number of massive platforms, made of iron, but already changing to cobalt under the influence of Faella's spell. Each platform was the height of a man, and at least forty feet long and twenty feet wide.

But it was what rested on the platforms that gave Silverdun pause. Wrapped in bindings of iron were twelve giant bodies. They had the features of the old Thule Fae, the true elves, their ears long and swept to elegant points, their eyes large, their bodies tall and slender. They were all dressed the same, only in different colors and with different insignia on their long gowns. Six were male, six female.

Twelve figures in all.

"What is this place?" said Silverdun.

"You don't know?" shouted Hy Pezho. "You're meddling around in here and you don't know where you *are?*"

"Well, we will if you tell us," said Silverdun.

"I should think it was obvious," said Hy Pezho. "You got here the same way I did, I assume. Using a cynosure to direct a fold?"

"That's right," said Silverdun.

"A Chthonic artifact," said Hy Pezho. "Look around you; *these* are the Chthonic gods. The bound gods."

"You're kidding," said Ironfoot.

"You're in Prythme," said Hy Pezho. "The place where the gods were locked up millennia ago. And if you don't stop whatever it is you're doing," he said, pointing at the branches of gray that were even now spreading across the bindings that held the figures down, "you're going to let them out."

Hy Pezho glared at them. "And trust me when I say that you don't want that to happen."

"This is ludicrous," said Ironfoot. "Bound gods, Prythme. And I suppose that you're actually Uvenchaud and you just came from slaying the last of the dragons."

Hy Pezho gingerly landed on the ground. The silver armor flowed off of him, its individual pieces retracting to allow him to simply step out of it. He was dressed in a simple robe and was unarmed. The silver suit flitted up into the air and disappeared in the shadows among the arches on the ceiling, where Hy Pezho's witchlight did not penetrate.

"Trust me, this is all very real."

Faella and Sela stepped around the platform beyond which Silverdun and Ironfoot were standing. Hy Pezho looked curiously at Faella. "You're doing this, aren't you?" he asked. "The *re* coming from you. It's like that of the . . . hell, you're *her*."

"Who am I?" said Faella.

"You're the one with the Thirteenth Gift. Faella. You think that Mab hasn't noticed you? You burn in Faerie like a bonfire in the night."

"I'm flattered," said Faella.

"Mab launched her invasion for two reasons," said Hy Pezho. "One was to grind Titania under her heel. The other was to kill *you*."

"And why do I merit such undue favor from your empress?" said Faella.

"Because you're capable of doing incredibly stupid things like what you're doing right now," said Hy Pezho. "If you don't stop and turn those bonds back into iron, we're all dead. Maybe worse than dead."

"Explain to me what this place is, and perhaps I shall."

Hy Pezho looked up at the platform next to them, which was growing more and more gray by the second, and sighed. For some reason the branches seemed to have a harder time crawling up the platforms. Were they somehow reinforced?

"It was during the *Rauane Envedun-e*," said Hy Pezho, "the era during which the vast majority of the most ridiculous and dangerous things in Fae history took place." He looked up again, licking his lips. "The Chthonic faithful had been around already for a thousand years, happily worshipping their twelve gods. Worshipping them with an astonishing fervency, in fact.

"Now, at the time, these gods didn't actually exist. They were the prehistoric Thule beliefs, inventions of superstitious natives to explain the rising of the sun and the fortunes of war. One sees such things in many worlds.

"But Faerie, of course, is not like other worlds. And during the *Rauane*, there was more free *re* than at any time before or since. Magic was everywhere, capable of just about anything. So the worshippers of the Thule gods inadvertently performed a staggering feat of thaumaturgy, perhaps the greatest ever accomplished.

"They channeled all of their vast essence into their faith, into their devout worship. They prayed for so hard and so long that they actually *worshipped their gods into existence*."

"You're saying they created *gods* on the spot," said Silverdun.

Hy Pezho looked up at the ever-graying bonds and glared at Silverdun.

"Not just that. They did such an incredible job of manifesting them that the gods actually became what the faithful believed them to be. They truly *were* responsible for the rising sun, and the fortunes of war, and for who fell in love with whom. The believers wished their gods into existence from the beginning of time, so that they not only existed, but *always had*. They created immortal gods out of whole cloth."

"That seems a bit far-fetched," said Ironfoot.

"This was the generation of Fae who turned the rain to wine when they were too drunk to stand up for another bottle," said Hy Pezho. "They turned the sky orange for fun, drafted sea monsters from their imagination on a whim. One of them taught an entire forest of trees to talk as a practical joke. There was nothing they couldn't do."

"How did the gods end up here?" asked Sela, looking strangely sad.

"Well," said Hy Pezho, and now he was talking through clenched teeth, his anxiety growing by the moment. "It turned out that having their gods among them was far less fun than the original Chthonics had imagined it would be. The gods were created to be in charge, so they took charge. They were created to judge, and they judged. They had been set above the Fae, and they took to their assigned parts with relish.

"Unfortunately for them, however, not all of the Fae were believers. They did not care to be judged by gods that they, themselves, did not believe in. So a very large and powerful coterie of wizards crafted a very large and powerful binding, and went to war against them. There was a great battle, the gods lost, and the wizards locked them up down here for eternity."

"And that was that," said Silverdun.

"Not exactly," said Hy Pezho. "The Chthonics continued to worship their gods. They worshipped them even though they were powerless, trapped in this otherworldly prison. At the end of the *Rauane* one of their cleverest thaumaturges constructed the cynosures, whose sole purpose is to direct the faith of the Chthonic worshippers here, into Prythme."

"To keep them alive," said Sela.

"To keep them alive and to one day free them," said Hy Pezho. "These bodies are massive storehouses of pure undifferentiated *re*. Growing more full with every passing Chthonic service. Someday they would have been strong enough to break their bonds, I suppose, though it would have been long after we were dead. Of course, you've moved up their timetable quite a bit."

"So the power source for the Einswrath," said Ironfoot. "It comes from them."

"Each bomb contains a single drop of Ein's blood," said Hy Pezho. "That's him up there, by the way. Ein, I mean." Hy Pezho pointed up at the platform where he had minutes before been floating. "I was drilling out a few drops when you showed up."

Hy Pezho stepped toward Silverdun and looked him in the eye. "And now that I've explained to you in explicit detail exactly what you've stumbled into, would you please tell your pretty friend here to stop what she's doing before these gods wake up and decide to take back Faerie, drunk on *five thousand years* of stored vengeance?"

Faella frowned. "I don't know how," she said.

"What?" said Hy Pezho.

"It wasn't so hard to turn the iron into cobalt," she said, "if that's indeed what I did. But I wouldn't have the slightest idea how to make it go the other way. I was just pulling the iron apart, like shattering a glass. I can't put it back together."

"Then, my dear," said Hy Pezho, "the five of us are all dead, and Faerie is doomed." He smiled at Faella in cynical resignation. "And it's all your fault."

Hy Pezho sighed. "All *I* did was make a bomb."

"He's telling the truth," said Sela. "He knows all this to be true. He's studied ancient texts, peered into the past with dark powers. Everything he's saying is right."

"Indeed," said Hy Pezho. "And as much as I'd like to stay here and be the first to be devoured once these gods awaken and so spare myself from their rule, I am now Bel Zheret, and I have been ordered by Mab to create more Einswrath. I've got enough blood to build a sufficient amount to bomb the Seelie Kingdom into oblivion. Really, I'll be doing them a favor, assuming I get to them first."

The silver armor fluttered down from the ceiling, and Hy Pezho stepped toward it. "Within a day the Great Seelie Keep will be a smoldering ruin," he said. "And then the Chthonic gods will rule us all. Ironically, Titania might have been the only one powerful enough to stand a chance against them."

"You're not going anywhere," said Silverdun. "You're going to stay here and help us stop this."

"That wasn't in my orders," said Hy Pezho. "I belong to Mab heart and soul, and I must do as I'm bidden."

Hy Pezho reached out his hand and waved. A blast of Motion struck Silverdun and slammed him backward. Sela, Ironfoot, and Faella were all flung in different directions.

Hy Pezho climbed into his armor. "Good-bye, Shadows," he called. "Fare thee well." The wings began to flap, and he rose off of the floor, beginning to chant an incantation of Folding.

Silverdun channeled Elements and pried open the front of the armor. Hy Pezho fell to the floor, his concentration broken. The silver armor listed to the side, its wings flapping crazily. Silverdun ran at him and tackled him, knife in hand.

"Ironfoot!" he shouted. "Get with Faella and find a way to stop this!" He slashed with the knife, but Hy Pezho slipped from his grasp and kicked out, catching Silverdun in the face. He was as strong as the other Bel Zheret had been. The one that had killed him.

The floor shook. Silverdun cast a brief glance upward and saw Ein's hand open and close. The god's bonds rattled.

A voice boomed into the wide space, speaking in a very, very old dialect of High Fae. "Who pricks my skin and wakes me from my slumber?"

In the rooftop garden in Elenth, Sergeant Hy-Asher supervised the reloading of the catapult with the second Einswrath. The lieutenant was looking over the edge of the rooftop toward the battle.

"Hurry!" he shouted. "They're almost to the gate!"

"You understand," said Hy-Asher, "that if we lob it this close, we'll kill our own troops, and probably half the city as well."

"Who cares?" said the lieutenant. "If they get through the gate, we're all dead anyway!"

Hy-Asher continued winding back the beam, a feeling of dread that he could not control stealing over him.

chapter forty

The High Priest: I fear that we will never agree, then, on what constitutes a good man.

Alpaurle: Is it wise to fear disagreement? Should we not, rather, embrace it?

The High Priest: Surely it is better to agree on such matters.

Alpaurle: You must be correct, of course, as you are very wise. But that is not what I asked. Should we not embrace a state of disagreement, on the grounds that from debate comes knowledge?

The High Priest: In matters of morals, I believe that unanimity is key. I find the idea of ambiguity in such matters disquieting.

Alpaurle: Why?

The High Priest: Because I desire to know the truth, of course!

Alpaurle: But what if truth is to be found in ambiguity?

—Alpaurle, from *Conversations with the High Priest of Ulet*, conversation VI, edited by Feven IV of the City Emerald

Ironfoot ran toward Silverdun to help him, but Silverdun waved him away. "No! Stay with Faella!" he shouted. "You can tell her how to change all this back into iron!"

Ironfoot turned back to Faella and Sela, while Silverdun wrestled with Hy Pezho a dozen yards away.

"Sela," he said. "Join me and Faella together, like you did back in the temple. Let's see if we can stop this."

"Take my hands," said Sela. "I'll do what I can."

Ironfoot closed his eyes and felt Faella and Sela flow into him. Now was the time to be perfect. Now was the time not to fail. Now was the time to be the best.

Ironfoot tried to sift through Faella's understanding, but it was difficult; she had no thaumatic training, no understanding of what it was she was doing, or how she did it. She was raw power, a creature of pure intuition.

And what she did, what Lin Vo had done back at the Arami Camp, was beyond anything Ironfoot even understood. All of his equations, all of his understanding about the workings of the Gifts—none of these applied here. This was an entirely new approach to magic. And he was going to have to work it out right here, right now, while his partner fought a demon to the death and gods rose up all around him.

What was iron? What was cobalt? What lay beneath Elements and Insight? What was at the heart of things, beyond reason and understanding? What was the quotient of division by zero?

Silverdun struggled against Hy Pezho, trying to work the knife up into his ribs. Hy Pezho had all of the strength and quickness of Silverdun's previous opponent, but what he lacked was Asp's skill, his experience. Asp had enjoyed a lifetime of killing before Silverdun had met him. Hy Pezho probably knew a thing or two about killing as well, but not the Bel Zheret kind. Not the punching, kicking, biting kind.

They rolled on top of each other, slammed up against the base of Ein's column. Above them, Ein bellowed and strained.

Ironfoot and Faella walked together through the substance of things. He asked questions without words; she provided answers without thoughts.

Slowly he began to understand. The ground shook around them and Sela cried out, but Ironfoot couldn't worry about that right now.

As he watched Faella flail against her lack of understanding, trying to reach out with her Giftless *re*, Ironfoot began to see something. It wasn't music without pitch, not colorless color, but something that lay behind pitch, beyond color. It wasn't a Giftless Gift, but that which lay beyond Gifts, gave rise to them. Beyond iron and cobalt lay something else, a deeper reality. Both were expressions of a deeper whole.

There was no division by zero. That was a function of numbers that applied to the Gifts. The Gifts were not the reality, though. They were a special case of reality. The thaumatics that applied to them, applied to them only in their special cases. In the depth beneath that spawned them, those equations simply did not apply. That depth was the genesis of the equations and was not bound by them.

He and Faella saw it at the same time. Cobalt and iron were simply variations on a theme, as were the Gifts. Thaumaturges had believed in the Gifts for so long that they had made them the reality, just as the Chthonics had made a reality of their own gods. Believing made it so.

Believe in iron, Ironfoot told Faella. Something reached out of Faella, colorless color beyond sight, and twisted.

chapter forty-one

The truth is sharper than any blade.

—Fae proverb

Sela watched Faella and Ironfoot think back and forth at each other, marveling at the speed and clarity of their thought. Sela understood almost none of it. It was all beyond her. Color without color? Belief in iron? It made no sense.

She looked away from them to catch a glimpse of Silverdun and Hy Pezho. Hy Pezho had Silverdun on the ground, kneeling over him, wrestling the knife from Silverdun's grasp.

She screamed "Silverdun!" Oh, how she loved him. Despite all that was going on around her, all she wanted was for him to be safe. She knew he could never love her. It hurt, but it didn't change how she felt.

After all that Lord Tanen had done to her, after all that she had seen in her time with the Shadows, she wondered whether she could ever be whole. Lin Vo, in the time they'd spent alone together in the Arami's tent, had told her that she was like a bird who'd lived all her life with clipped wings. She was capable of flying higher and farther than other birds. She was capable of seeing so deeply into the heart that if Lord Tanen had nourished her rather than hobbled her, she might have ascended beyond what she was.

Sela had no idea what Lin Vo meant by "ascended," but it brought back memories of childhood. Memories of a feeling of wholeness, of a knowledge of things that now baffled her. It was something akin to what Ironfoot and Faella were now discussing. Seeing beyond. Seeing through. When she was a child she had known bliss.

And then Lord Tanen had come and taken that bliss away from her and turned her into a monster. That word "ascended" also reminded her of the thing in her that she'd showed to Lord Tanen and the crones, to the doctor at Lord Everess's apartment, and to the Bel Zheret in Elenth.

She'd asked Lin Vo whether she could ever be whole again.

"No," Lin Vo had said sadly. "Not in this life. You will never know bliss. But you may find a way to live."

She heard Silverdun grunt and Hy Pezho swear. She looked but couldn't see them anymore.

Ironfoot and Faella had reached some sort of understanding. Something flowed out of Faella, something that Sela could neither see nor comprehend, and everything began to change. Pain leapt up at her from the floor, a hot wind of *re* blowing up from beneath her.

Caught off guard, she lost the threads with Ironfoot and Faella, but it didn't matter. Faella already had what she needed. She was in rapt concentration. All around her, the floor was turning dark, becoming iron.

Unfortunately, Faella and Ironfoot appeared to have forgotten that they were now standing on it.

There was a violent crash, then a series of smaller concussions that reverberated in the chamber. Sela swayed and fell, scorching her palms on the now-iron floor. A chunk of cobalt landed on the floor next to her and she leapt onto it. Ironfoot was with her.

"Faella!" he shouted. "A little help for the rest of us!"

"Sorry!" said Faella. She waved backward toward them, and a disc of pure silver flew from her palm and slipped beneath their feet. It rose up into the air and the pain withdrew.

Sela looked up and gasped. One of the bound gods, Ein, was bound no more. He was sitting up, stretching. He was impossibly large. Sitting up on the platform, his fiery red hair nearly brushed the ceiling. He looked around at the scene below him.

"What is this?" his voice boomed. So loud that Sela covered her ears. "Awake, brothers and sisters!" he shouted, even louder. "Awake! Our bonds are broken at last!"

"No!" shouted Faella. Sela could feel the *re* in the room swirl, faster and faster. Whatever Faella was doing, it was stirring the essence into a frenzy.

Sela looked around. "Where's Silverdun?" she said.

"I don't know," said Ironfoot, holding on to her. "As soon as Faella's finished I'll go find him."

"It's working!" shouted Faella. I got to the bonds before the other gods could move. They're still trapped!"

Ein looked over at her, his eyes glowing. "They might be, little Fae," he shouted. "But I am not." Ein lifted his finger and gestured, and Faella flew backward, halfway across the chamber, slamming into a wall that was now made of pure iron. She screamed.

Silverdun was fading fast. A chunk of Ein's bindings, if that was what it had been, had struck him in the forehead, hard enough to make his head spin. It had given Hy Pezho the advantage he'd needed to pry Silverdun's knife out of his hand. Now Hy Pezho had the knife and was trying to bring it down across Silverdun's neck. Silverdun gripped Hy Pezho's wrist with all his strength, but it wasn't enough.

Silverdun heard Ein's voice rattling in his ears, so loud he couldn't make out the words. He heard Faella shriek in the distance. "Faella!" he shouted. "I'm coming for you!" But there was nothing he could do for her. There was little he could do for himself.

"You have no idea what I went through to survive," hissed Hy Pezho. "You have no idea what I've sacrificed. Only to become Mab's errand boy. I was to have been an emperor. Now I'm a lackey. And a *happy* lackey at that. She has turned all of my ambition to love."

"I really couldn't care less about your problems," Silverdun managed. "To be honest, I don't really know who you are. To me, you're just some evil bastard who likes to blow things up."

Hy Pezho made no response, but pushed the knife down farther.

Oh, well.

"You!"

Ein's voice was so loud that Silverdun thought his eardrums would burst. He looked straight up into Ein's bearded face, his enormous eyes glaring down at him. But Ein wasn't speaking to him. He was speaking to Hy Pezho.

"You are the one who pricked me while I lay helpless! You are the one who taunted me, thinking me asleep!"

Ein leaned down farther, and Silverdun could feel his terrible breath, the heat of a thousand ovens, the stink of death. "I have not slept! I lay in wait, gathering strength bit by bit over eons, waiting for my time. And you, flittering insect, dare to steal from me! From *Ein?*"

Ein's fist came down hard toward them. Silverdun rolled, flipping Hy Pezho off of him, and the knife clattered to the floor.

But now the floor was of iron, and it burned Silverdun's hands. The pain was white-hot, intense. He lurched for the knife, snatched it from the ground, burning his knuckles anew as he wrapped his fingers around the hilt.

Ein was slow, very slow, but made up for it in strength. His fist connected with the floor in a shattering blow, spilling Silverdun down again. He could barely feel his hands now.

Hy Pezho was next to him. He'd fallen as well, and was now scrabbling to his feet.

Silverdun thought of calling out to him, speaking his name to resume their fight face-to-face, as propriety dictated.

"To hell with that," he muttered. He stabbed Hy Pezho in the back, and the Black Artist fell to the floor, quivering on the iron as it burned his skin.

"Well done," said Silverdun. "But *now what?*"

Sela had never felt so helpless. She and Ironfoot were standing on the floating silver disc, twenty feet in the air. Ein had stood and was stomping his foot, howling in rage. On the other side of the room, Faella lay writhing, trying to get to her feet, but the iron burned her all over, stealing her ability to use *re*.

"What do we do, Ironfoot?" she cried.

"I don't know!" he said.

Something glittered in the corner of her eye. A moth fluttered toward her, swaying and dipping crazily. Hy Pezho?

No, not Hy Pezho. *Silverdun.*

She smiled in spite of herself and cried out.

"Amazing little creation!" Silverdun shouted. "I haven't a clue how to fly it, though!"

He flew toward them, almost collided with the ground, then righted himself and glided toward them. He hit the disc a little too hard, with his midsection, and glanced off of it. The disc shuddered but remained erect. Again Silverdun righted himself and fluttered back, grabbing hold of the disc's edge.

"Where's Faella?" he asked.

Sela pointed.

"Let's go," he said. He squinted in concentration and the wings of the armor flapped violently, pushing them forward, toward where Faella lay.

Ein continued stomping, his footsteps like percussive spellbombs. The literal wrath of Ein was dreadful to behold.

"Apparently, Hy Pezho made himself an enemy," said Silverdun.

They reached Faella, and Silverdun let go of the disc and drifted down to her. He gathered her carefully in his arms and rose, placing her gently on the disc next to Sela.

"Faella, darling," he said, fluttering next to her. "Wake up. You need to get us the hell out of here."

She opened her eyes, groggy but conscious. "Silverdun, love," she whispered. "You came for me. You didn't leave me again."

Silverdun looked at Faella. "Never again, love," he said. "Never again."

Sela's feelings were contorted into an unrecognizable shape that dug inside her like a many-pointed knife.

"Ein," said Faella. "He's loose."

"We need to go," said Silverdun.

"No," said Ironfoot. "Look."

Ein had finished with Hy Pezho, and now turned to regard his bound siblings.

"Althoin!" he cried. "The wise! I must know your counsel!"

Ein stepped toward the platform next to his own. He grabbed the iron bonds on his brother Althoin and pulled at them. They creaked but did not break.

"Althoin!" he shrieked. The bonds began to give way.

"Get us out of here!" said Silverdun.

"Yes," said Faella. "Let me think of how to reverse the fold. Give me a moment."

Sela looked at Ein and felt his pain. He was alone, bound for so long, a bird with clipped wings.

"Here we go," said Faella. "We'll work it out, won't we?"

"Let's just get clear," said Silverdun. "One thing at a time."

The air began to shimmer.

Sela leaned over, off the edge of the disc, and kissed Silverdun lightly on the lips. "Good-bye," she said.

She leapt.

"Sela!" shouted Silverdun. But his voice was faint, distant. Silverdun, Faella, and Ironfoot vanished into the fold.

Sela was on the floor. The pain of the fall mingled with the fire of iron on her skin. She stumbled, staggered toward a chunk of cobalt, one of the few remaining. She pulled herself up on it and stood.

"Ein!" she called.

Ein continued to tug at his brother's bindings.

"*Ein!*" she shrieked. "*Look at me!*"

She grabbed the Accursed Object and tore at it. For a horrible instant it clung to her, but it slipped on the sweat that covered her and fell away for the last time.

Ein turned.

He looked.

A thread formed.

She knew a god.

He flowed into her and she flowed into him. She showed him all that she was and all that she could have been. He let out his grief in waves that nearly consumed her. She showed him her childhood, her sweetest memories of devotion in the Chthonic temple of her youth, showed him Lord Tanen's cruelty and Milla's dead body. She showed Ein what he was. The full extent of her power, without the Accursed Object. To show what truly was. What was beyond what was.

She let it all flow out of her, into her, though her. Without the Accursed Object to restrain her, she drew in all of the *re* around her, channeled it into Empathy, hurled it all at Ein. All of her love and her loss and what remained of her purity.

All of her.

The thing that had risen up in her, that had destroyed Lord Tanen, the doctor, the Bel Zheret. It wasn't inside her. It *was* her.

Her last thoughts were of love.

Mauritane's company reached the gate and dispatched the terrified guards— those who remained, anyway. Many of them fled back into the city.

Outside, the Unseelie troops, now cut off from their escape route into Elenth, began to retreat to the east, away from the city and away from the reinforcements that were hurrying to join them from the southwest. The battle had turned, and with it, the war. It all depended on the Einswrath now. It all hung on that.

An odd silence came over the battlefield. One of the odd lulls that sometimes occurred, when every combatant was silent: falling, or gathering breath, or swinging.

Something small and dark flew up into the sky. Mauritane watched it arc and begin to fall. It was headed straight for him.

He closed his eyes and said a prayer to Aba. Why not?

A horse whinnied in the distance. Mauritane opened his eyes. A black blob the size of an orange had landed on the ground twenty feet away from him.

The fighting had ceased. Everyone knew what it was; they had all heard the stories. Einswrath. They all waited to die.

But the thing just lay there. After a moment it began to sizzle, then shudder, then it melted into a black puddle and soaked into the ground.

Mauritane offered the remaining Unseelie soldiers the opportunity to surrender and they happily obliged.

An hour later, the Seelie flag hung over Elenth.

Just before sunset, while the dead were being cleared away, Mauritane walked through the field, deep in thought, looking.

It took him almost an hour to find Baron Glennet. He would have found the body sooner, but a horse had fallen on top of it. Mauritane's sword was on the ground next to him, bloody but unbroken.

Mauritane called out to a nearby private. "Have someone send a message sprite to the City Emerald." Mauritane wiped the blood from his sword in the grass. He wondered whose life Glennet had managed to take, and whether the Unseelie soldier he'd killed knew how lucky he'd been.

"Tell them that Baron Glennet led the charge at the battle of Elenth, and that he died a hero of the Seelie Kingdom."

chapter forty-two

Immortality is a predicate only in the abstract.

—Prae Benesile,
Thaumatical History of the Chthonic Religion

Once Elenth was taken, the other landed Unseelie cities soon fell against the combined forces of the Seelie and the Annwni. Now unable to land troops, the Unseelie had attempted to bring one of their cities to bear above Mauritane, but Mauritane had dispatched it with one of the missiles he'd brought for that purpose. After that, the Unseelie had been forced to concede defeat. General Ma-Hora of the Unseelie Army and Mauritane signed the Treaty of Elenth two days later. The treaty ceded all three landed Unseelie cities to Queen Titania, extending the border roughly eighty miles north to the base of the Tyl mountains.

Silverdun learned all this en route to Elenth, with Ironfoot and Faella. The knowledge that the Einswrath had failed, that Sela had succeeded at whatever she'd done, was heartening, but none of them felt much like celebrating. They were exhausted and in pain, both physically and emotionally. The act of folding them back to the Chthonic temple had shattered the cynosure, meaning that they now had no way to return for Sela. Not that any of them were physically up to the task, or that any of them truly believed that Sela had survived.

Still, Silverdun had no intention of giving up on her. It was fortunate for many reasons that the war had gone as it did. To their immediate purpose, it was critical; the nearest Metropolitan Chthonic temple was located in Elenth. According to Prae Benesile, each Metropolitan maintained its own cynosure.

When they arrived in Elenth, they went directly to Mauritane's temporary headquarters in the Elenth City Building. Mauritane must have been surprised to see Faella, whom he knew only as the ingenue daughter of a mestine he'd met two years earlier, but he was as impossible to read as ever, and greeted her without comment. When their brief congratulations had ended, and they told him what had happened at Prythme, however, he did in fact raise an eyebrow. And when they explained why they were in Elenth, he grew visibly chagrined.

"That won't be easy," he said. "The Chthonics have been extremely accommodating to us since our arrival, and have done much to smooth relations between us and the Unseelie populace. I'm loath to ask them to allow you to go mucking around in their temple."

"Understandable," said Silverdun. "Consider, however, that we have no idea what happened after we folded away. For all we know, these bound gods are dusting off their lightning bolts and preparing to annihilate all of Faerie."

"No course in the academy on how to handle a situation like this, is there, General?" said Ironfoot.

"I'm willing to give you the benefit of the doubt," said Mauritane. "In fact, it would be best if the cynosure were destroyed entirely, if it does what you say it does."

"We won't make any friends doing that," said Ironfoot.

"I didn't come to Elenth to make friends," said Mauritane, sighing.

By nightfall, Ironfoot was ready. His modifications to the cynosure proceeded more quickly than the first time, and he'd been able to use what he'd learned from the first journey in order to ensure a smoother trip.

The Chthonic priestess had, of course, been furious at the idea. But she also realized that at the moment she needed Mauritane far more than he needed her, and ultimately acquiesced.

"Are you sure you're up for this?" Silverdun asked Faella.

"She loved you, you know," said Faella, as if this answered her question.

"I know," said Silverdun. "I think we owe her this much."

Faella folded them, not only directly into the chamber of the gods this time, but directly onto the silver disc she'd created to protect Ironfoot and Sela.

It was dark. And silent.

Silverdun flared witchlight, and the room erupted in white light. Ein was gone, his platform empty. The other gods were silent, unmoving.

"Sela!" called Ironfoot.

Ironfoot channeled Motion and they floated throughout the chamber looking, but Sela was gone. The only sign of her they discovered was the silver-coated iron band that she'd always worn. The Accursed Object, she'd called it. Ironfoot plucked it gently from the ground, his hand wrapped in his cloak.

They returned to the temple in Elenth without incident. As soon as they arrived, Silverdun snatched the cynosure off of its pedestal, hurled it to the ground, and smashed it to pieces.

chapter forty-three

So carry me down, carry me down,
Lay my bones upon the ground.
Curse the gods that I so vexed,
Then pray to 'em that you're not next.

—Seelie Army drinking song

Baron Glennet's memorial service was a lavish affair, held at a special session of Corpus. His bier was laid before the speaker's podium, adorned with garlands of blue and yellow flowers. Silverdun watched with mostly hidden disgust as lords and guildsmen ascended the podium and delivered long-winded paeans to the man who had attempted to start a war for his own personal profit.

Lord Everess delivered one of the most touching eulogies, praising Glennet's years of service to the Seelie Kingdom, restating his many contributions to Corpus and to his peers, and calling him one of the great heroes of the realm and an exemplar of the Seelie Heart.

Very few in Corpus were fooled by the official explanation for Glennet's demise. Most assumed that he'd ridden into battle in an attempt to end his life in dignity after falling into financial ruin. If any of his coconspirators in the House of Guilds—either his creditors or those with whom he'd invested —suspected the truth, they were wisely keeping it to themselves.

To add to the insult, when Silverdun had arrived in Corpus he'd discovered that Lord Ames had been using his chair as an impromptu liquor cabinet for years. Granted, Silverdun had only sat in it once in his entire life prior to today, but it was the principle of the thing. He made a show of polishing off one of Ames's finer bottles of whiskey during the proceedings.

Well, Ames could have the damn chair. Silverdun would never sit in it again after today.

Afterward, Silverdun met Ironfoot, Paet, and Everess at a café on the Promenade. They raised an ironic toast to Baron Glennet and then sat in silence for a while.

"You laid it on rather thick in there," Silverdun told Everess, after draining his glass.

"Never pass up an opportunity to praise a fallen colleague in open session, boy," said Everess. "It's just good politics."

"I suppose there won't be much resistance to the Office of Shadow now," said Ironfoot.

"Oh, we still have our enemies," said Everess. "But they now know the price of going up against me."

"Us," said Silverdun. "They know the price of going up against *us*."

"Just so," said Everess. "Just so."

That evening, in the tangle of brush behind Blackstone House, Paet, Silverdun, and Ironfoot buried Sela's iron band in a small hole near the wall. They passed around a bottle of very expensive brandywine (purloined from Lord Ames) and spoke little.

"I'm surprised you agreed to this, Paet," said Silverdun. "Didn't you tell me once that Shadows don't get funerals?"

Paet looked at him and opened his mouth as if to speak. Instead, he simply shrugged and walked away.

Once he was gone, Silverdun and Ironfoot sat on the ground next to the tiny mound of dirt and finished the bottle.

It was late afternoon when the hired carriage stopped before Oarsbridge Manor, and Silverdun and Faella stepped out of it. Autumn leaves blew across the front walk, skittered across the lawn. Spring was approaching, but autumn still had work to do.

A servant admitted them into the house; Silverdun didn't recognize her, but then he'd been gone a very long time. She gave no indication that she had any idea who he was. Tea was offered and accepted.

They were sipping it in the parlor when Bresun appeared. "Why, if it isn't Perrin Alt, Lord Silverdun," he said calmly, as if he'd been expecting their arrival. "And the lady . . ."

"Just Faella," Silverdun said, as Faella rose and curtsied. "Not 'Lady' anything."

"I see," said Bresun, though he clearly did not. "How may I be of service?"

Silverdun paused, wanting to keep Bresun in the dark for as long as possible. What must the man be thinking? He'd probably been dreading this moment every day for the past two years, since "Lord Silverdun the Traitor" became "Lord Silverdun the War Hero." Silverdun had been happy to let him swing on the hook.

"Small point of propriety," said Silverdun. "There is no Lord Silverdun any longer, I'm afraid." He shrugged. "You'll just have to call me Perrin from now on."

"Excuse me?" said Bresun. Silverdun could see that his uncle's feigned politeness was about to be shed.

"It's true," said Silverdun. "I petitioned the queen to have the lordship annulled, and she has graciously agreed to my petition. Both Oarsbridge and Connaugh are now estates of the Crown."

Bresun simply stared at him. It was impossible to tell what he was thinking.

"I should add that the dissolution of the lordship means that all of your titles to the lands and properties are, sadly, revoked."

"You can't do this," said Bresun, shaking his head. "You can't. You'll lose your title! You'll be penniless! We've been through all this before!"

"Oh," said Silverdun. "It's not so bad. I have a job, you see."

"And I don't care about money; I love him for his looks," said Faella, touching Silverdun's knee.

"By the way," said Silverdun. "The overseer for the Crown is going to be here tomorrow, and he'd appreciate it if you'd be out by then. Short notice, I know, but some things can't be helped."

"You're mad," said Bresun. "I told you one day that I'd destroy you, and I still can."

Silverdun glared at him. "I think you'll find me a rather more able adversary than when last we met."

He smiled. "And anyway, it's not me you're up against. This is between you and Regina Titania, I'm afraid. You can take it up with the overseer, of course. You'll like him. Arcadian fellow, very peaceful and forgiving, as those sorts tend to be."

Bresun sputtered, but said nothing.

Just before sunset, Silverdun and Faella walked hand in hand down the lawn to the family burial plot. Generations of Silverduns had been interred here, and were now simply names on stones.

His children, Silverdun realized, would not be noblemen. But he could live with that. As he had once pointed out to his mother, if they were all descendants of Uvenchaud, they were *all* lords.

And honestly, most noblemen were asses, anyway.

Silverdun looked down at his mother's headstone for the first time. He searched for some kind of sentiment to match the occasion, but came up with nothing.

Finally, he sighed and said, "Well, Mother, I finally decided what kind of man I wanted to be. I'm not sure that you would have approved of my choice, though."

"Come, love," said Faella, kissing his cheek. "If we leave now we can be home by dawn."

about the author

MATTHEW **STURGES** has written a number of comic books for DC Comics, including *House of Mystery*, *Jack of Fables*, and *The Justice Society of America*. This book is a sequel to his first novel, *Midwinter*.

He lives in Austin, Texas, with his wife, Stacy, and their two daughters. Visit him online at http://www.matthewsturges.com.